Mar[illegible]st. A louder scream [illegible]ed her steps. At the entrance to the alley, she [illegible]ld she return to the carriage? Nay, she answered herself. It was she who had forced the issue. She must not be a coward.

"You will leave the girl alone!" Jason's abrupt, commanding voice came to Margaret. "Stand back, or you will be sorry!"

There was light ahead, and Margaret hastened forward. She stopped again, profoundly shocked at the scene before her. In the circle of light cast by a torch, she saw a naked, screaming girl. The girl was sprawled on her back on the dirty cobbles, and kneeling before her, his breeches about his ankles, was a heavyset man with a scarred face and a shock of wiry dark hair.

"If you're thinkin' o' savin' this slut," William Mitford said, looking up at Jason, "you'd bes' think again. There's more'n one o' us, my fine gen'leman." Calmly, Mitford rose to his feet.

Drawing up his breeches, he fastened them with a piece of rope that served him as a belt. His smile was insolent as his eyes traveled slowly over Jason's immaculate gray-clad person, lingering on the high stock at his throat, the lace edging his cuff, and the long, ringed fingers. "A real dandy, ain't you? What you think you c'n do agains' all o' us, eh?"

The expression in Jason's eyes was cold and dangerous. "You would be foolish indeed, my man, were you to allow yourself to be deceived by appearances," he said in a level, colorless voice. "If need be, I am quite capable of rendering you ineffectual. I think I can promise you that, at the very least, you will be nursing a split skull."

CONSTANCE GLUYAS

The House on Twyford Street

MAGNUM BOOKS
Methuen Paperbacks Ltd

A Magnum Book

THE HOUSE ON TWYFORD STREET
ISBN 0 417 02680 3

First published 1976
by David McKay Company, Inc., New York
Magnum edition published 1978

Words of the song on pages 71/2
by Donald Gluyas

Magnum Books are published
by Methuen Paperbacks Ltd
11 New Fetter Lane, London EC4P 4EE

Made and printed in Great Britain
by Richard Clay (The Chaucer Press) Ltd,
Bungay, Suffolk

Chapter One

(London 1662)

London sweltered beneath a June heat wave. St. Paul's Cathedral, outlined majestically against the harsh blue of the sky, and standing in proud dominance above the surrounding buildings, was bathed in a dazzling glare of golden light. The sun gilded the opulent houses of the wealthy along exclusive Whitehall and managed to lend a transient beauty to the shacks and houses jumbled near the waterfront, and the decaying tenement houses of the poor. Swarms of flies hovered over the open gutters running along the centers of the cobblestoned streets, and the heaped laystalls, placed in various parts of the city, crawled with fat white maggots, sending forth a noxious stench of filth and decay. In most of the streets, however, where the tall, narrow houses leaned drunkenly toward each other, shutting out most of the daylight, the sun was subdued to thin golden fingers that sought in vain to brighten the shadows.

The girl seated in the doorway of Thomas Grant's apothecary shop was oblivious to the weather and to the choking reek that hung over the city. Huddled with misery, her thin arms clasped about drawn-up knees, her eyes tightly closed, Sarah Barry had temporarily detached herself from the sights, sounds, and the smells of bustling Carey Street.

To the people who passed by, or those who stepped over her to gain entrance to the apothecary's shop, she was of no more interest than if she had been a dog or a cat. Their glances skimmed her without a vestige of curiosity. In this part of London, and especially in Carey Street, where families crowded in miserable crumbling garrets, where thieves and prostitutes roved the area, the people were used to human misery, and they held life cheaply. They assumed that she was probably a prostitute deep in a drunken sleep, or she might be dead. If the former, she would eventually awaken and go on her way. If the latter, then the city authorities would eventually take a hand. Then, if she was found to be without means, she would be taken away for burial in the paupers' graveyard. It was just another incident among many.

One woman, perhaps less calloused by poverty, or, judging from the healthy country color in her cheeks, new to the neighborhood, stopped to stare at the huddled figure with pitying eyes. The girl's face, she saw, was colorless and gaunt, her body thin to the point of emaciation. Red hair straggled in untidy wisps from beneath a battered black bonnet adorned with a once proudly curling green feather, her green bodice was torn at the shoulder, and her black skirt, rent in numerous places, revealed glimpses of her pale legs. With a swift glance at the man standing beside her, the woman stooped over the girl. "Poor little wench," she said. "She looks ill, Tom."

"Maybe she is, and then again, maybe she ain't," the man answered her in a harsh voice. "If you was to ask me, I'd say she was drunk. If you're thinkin' about tendin' to that whore, you'd better think again."

"Don't be so unkind," the woman rebuked him. "She's naught but a bit o' a lass. How can she be drunk?"

The man gave an unpleasant laugh. "How? It's easy enough for the wench ter be drunk, ain't it? Or maybe you've forgot that our own lass took ter drinkin' when she was younger'n this one?"

"No, Tom, I've not forgot. You won't let me."

"Never mind. This wench is a whore. I knows one when I sees one, believe me."

"Aye," the woman answered him in a dry voice, "you should. You've bedded aplenty of 'em."

"Don't you talk ter me like that!" the man said in a low, furious voice. "One more word out o' you an' I'll bash your bleedin' nose in! Get along wi' you. Leave that drab be!"

The woman sighed. "I'm coming," she said in a resigned voice. "Don't keep pullin' on me arm."

Sarah Barry was neither asleep nor drunk, but she was deeply resentful to find that their voices had sundered the veil of her detachment. Against her will, she recalled the ugly word with which the man had branded her. "Whore," he had called her. Faint anger stirred. If she was a whore, then Jemmie Taylor, with his lies and his deceit, had made her into one. Whore and thief, that was what Jemmie had made of her. He had turned her life upside down, and he had tried to strip it of all those values that once she had held so dear. But Jemmie was dead now, she thought, with a leap of savage joy. He would never trouble her again. Perhaps, had she been stronger, less desperate to belong to somebody, to be important, to be loved, he could never have gained such a hold upon her. So, in all justice, the blame was not entirely his. Aye, Jemmie's death had left her free. But free to go where, to do what?

A strident voice calling, "Pies! 'Ot savory pies!" reminded the girl of her gnawing hunger. Sarah put her hand in her pocket and nervously fingered her few remaining coins. Should she buy herself a pie, or should she wait and see what fortune might bring her? She held both hands out before her. Staring at them, she was conscious of a sick dismay. Those trembling blue-veined hands, the hands of Sarah Barry, pick-pocket, were all that stood between her and certain starvation. What could she do? What would happen to her if they would no longer obey her will?

The pieman, passing the doorway, broke in on her unhappy thoughts. From the tray slung about his neck by a leather strap, there drifted the savory smell of mutton pies. Sarah's mouth watered with longing, and she clenched her hands together to keep herself from calling out to him. She must think of the cost, she argued with herself. A penny for a pie! Nay, she could not afford it. The money she had left would buy her a bed somewhere. Perhaps, if good fortune attended her, she would eat tomorrow.

Trying to forget her hunger, Sarah deliberately turned her thoughts back to happier times, to those times before she had known Jemmie Taylor, her nemesis. She had been just six years old when her father, James Barry, had realized a long-cherished dream. They were to leave the cottage where she and her sister and her two brothers had been so happy. The schoolhouse, where James Barry had taught for more than ten years, was to know him no more. They were leaving quiet, green, peaceful Worcestershire behind them. They were going to London. Her mother had wept to leave the dear and familiar life behind. But her father, his blue eyes burning with enthusiasm, had been adamant. His dream had been to educate and enrich the lives of the children in the London slums, and that dream was about to come true, Joshua Randall, a local squire, who believed in education for every child, be they rich or poor, had donated money for this purpose. And so, with a building readied in London's dock area, and sufficient money, thanks to Joshua Randall, with which to run the school, her father was ready to put country life behind him. All his time and energy were now to be devoted to those underprivileged children.

Across the years, Sarah could still hear her father's deep, earnest voice trying to explain to her reluctant mother. "Mary please! You must try to understand. I was lucky to find someone like Randall to back me. He is as enthusiastic about this cause as I am. Think what it will mean to those children. They have so little, Mary. Think of the circumstances in which they live. They are without education, without hope. Is it any wonder that many of them, in sheer desperation, turn to a life of crime? I tell you, if they were educated, the prisons would not be so full."

Sarah remembered that, for a time, her mother had continued to weep and protest. But in the end, she could not bring herself to spoil her much-loved husband's dream. So to London they came. They had lived near the dock area. Their home had been on the second floor of a shabby, narrow house on Bliss Street.

Sarah shuddered. She had been only a child, and her horror and disgust at her first sight of London had been the strongest emotion she had experienced in her short life. It was a great, teeming place, and it smelled like a long-neglected privy. From the very beginning she had hated this frightening and alien London. The dark cramped rooms in which they lived were the haunt of cockroaches, smelling perpetually of soot and smoke, mice and bugs, and other unpleasant odors that she could not then put a name to.

The houses lining either side of Bliss Street, all of them dark and shabby and crumbling from want of repair, leaned so far forward that their eaves all but touched. They shut out the sunlight so effectively that she had the thought that, with this move, God had withdrawn the sunlight from them forever. She did not always heed her mother's command to "Play outside, Sarah." The truth was that she was afraid. For whenever she ventured out, she had the terrible feeling that those crazily leaning timbered and plastered monstrosities of houses were only waiting their chance to snatch up her small body and crush it between them.

Bliss Street, surrounded by a bewildering maze of aimlessly rambling streets, alleys, and narrow footpaths, was, in Sarah's opinion, the worst street in that squalid neighborhood. The rakers and the scavengers, whose duty it was to clean out the refuse choked gutter running along the center, rarely put in an appearance. Consequently, the evil stench of putrefaction was sometimes more than she could bear. Her brothers laughed at her when, forced to walk along the street, she kept her kerchief tightly pressed to her nose. Her fastidious withdrawal, her horror, as more and more of the city's ugliness was revealed, was a source of constant amusement to the two boys. Unlike Sarah, or her sister, Felicity, they were delighted with London. They played happily in the mean streets. They did not shrink, as she did, from walking over the loose cobbles of the street that were made slippery and stinking by the urine and excrement that was daily thrown from the upper windows of the houses. They wandered ceaselessly, sometimes losing their way in the streets that seemed to follow no set pattern. But they always found their way home, laughing, ready for more adventure. Waiting until they were sure that they had Sarah's full attention, they would jump daringly over the festering gutter, at times, to her horror, only narrowly avoiding a disastrous tumble. They gazed with awe at the fearful traffic jam on London Bridge, and they listened to and memorized the vile curses that came both from the frustrated drivers of the vehicles and from the occupants of the sagging houses lining the bridge.

Once, believing their parents to be out, they had swaggeringly, if a trifle self-consciously, used this language in front of Sarah. Their consternation when their father entered the room was great. Both of them were soundly thrashed for indecency of speech. Having learned their lesson the painful way, they apologized profusely and were instantly forgiven by their tender-hearted father. Both of them giving their word of honor that they would never again profane their lips, or the ears of their sisters.

They kept their word. They also continued to wander. Of all the sights they had seen, they were most impressed by the

Tower of London. They spent much time gazing at the great gray sentinel, with its huge and menacing bulk overlooking the river. The Tower of London, their father had told them, had been the scene of much tragedy. It was doubtless this, and the blood-chilling stories he told them, that gave the ancient building much of its fascination.

Sarah had often wondered how they had failed to see the change in their father. But with the selfishness and the thoughtlessness of children, they had not noticed that he was growing paler and thinner and, surprisingly for him, uncertain of temper. He seldom smiled. The small jokes with which he had been wont to enliven the conversation at mealtimes were conspicuous by their absence.

Gradually, Sarah came to realize that her father's "great experiment," as he called it, had failed. Lying in her bed at night, it frightened her to hear her mother's pleading voice, the rustle of her gown as she paced up and down the room, a sound which somehow conveyed her agitation. "Jim!" her voice came clearly to Sarah through the thin wall. "Have you not learned by now that the children are uninterested in education, or that their parents do not want it for them?"

Her father obviously did not believe this, for Sarah heard him say angrily. "Both children and parents are wary of something new, that is all it is, Mary. They are unused to someone caring about them."

"But, Jim, everywhere you turn you are baulked. Please sweetheart, come away! Do not break your heart over these children. Let us go back to Worcestershire, where your genius for teaching is appreciated."

The bitterness in her father's answering voice sent a shiver of pain through Sarah. "A genius for teaching! Then tell me, Mary, if I have this genius, why have I failed?"

"You have not failed. The children do not want to learn."

"I believe that they do. It will, however, take a little time before they realize it. In the meantime, somebody must care for their welfare."

"But not you, Jim! Not you!" Her mother's raised voice caused Sarah to stiffen in fear. "The parents and the children regard you as their enemy, not their friend."

Although she hated London, Sarah had not known how much she herself longed to return to Worcestershire. Not until, her heart sinking, she heard her father remove all hope. "We will stay here, Mary," he said in that voice that meant he could not be moved. "I have no intention of giving up. In time, they will understand what education can mean to them. When that happens, they will come willingly to school."

But the children had never reached the understanding for which her father had hoped. Yet still he would not acknowledge final failure. Grimly determined, suffering inside for them, he continued to wage his battle against poverty and ignorance.

So the years passed. Years that were dotted here and there with small bright patches of happiness, but more often with the gloom of frustration and despair. They lived through the dark period of the civil war, and the tragic and senseless vindictiveness of the execution of King Charles the First, an event that shook England to its very foundations. And then, a bright torch of hope lighting the darkness, they heard of the coming of the martyred King's son. Charles the Second was coming to reign over their sundered country. And with his coming, the yoke of sober Puritanism was thrown aside. England became merry again. Oliver Cromwell, Protector of England, that grim man, could now be forgotten.

Sarah put a hand to her shaking mouth. Two years ago, in 1660, the glorious year of the Restoration, when she was eighteen years old, the final tragedy had struck the Barry family. The sweating fever, that scourge that periodically struck at London, had struck this time at her parents, killing them both. They had died within an hour of each other. A day later, her two brothers and her sister had succumbed. And yet, miraculously, she had not been infected. She had felt no gratitude for the miracle. How could she? She was alone in this alien London, for it was still alien to her. Alone, and terribly afraid.

Living once more in the memory of the heartbreak and horror of that time, tears welled into her eyes and fell down her gaunt cheeks. London had been gay with bunting and flags. From every part of the city the bells were ringing to herald the coming of King Charles the Second. Their joyous clamor filled the room, emphasizing her grief and despair. Her father had been a poor man. The little money he had left went frighteningly fast. She learned a new lesson. When you are penniless, you have few friends. Before long, she found herself homeless. It was at this hopeless period in time that Jeremy Taylor walked into her life. Jemmie, so tender at first, and then so brutal. The man who, gradually, had molded her into a thief like himself.

Sarah sat up straight. She did not want to think of Jemmie now. She did not want to remember that she was once more alone in the world. She looked about her. The scene before her looked strangely unreal, wavering, as though she were seeing it through water. Concentrating, trying to keep thoughts of Jemmie at bay, she craned her head and stared at the small shops that lined both sides of Carey Street. The shops were interspersed here and there with houses that leaned perilously toward each other, so that some parts of the street were in sunshine, some in shadow. Over everything there hung a pall of smoke. The smoke had drifted from the factories of the soap makers in the adjacent alley. It hung in the air, a thick yellow fog that blurred the passing people, making them seem to her to be more than ever unreal. The hawkers, as ever undaunted by smoke, or changing seasons, ran past her, bawling their wares, their voices first raucous, then wheedling, as they exhorted the passers-by to sample their wares, to touch them and feel the quality, to smell their fresh meats. "Come on, guv. Take a swaller o' this, an' you'll think you're in bleedin' Paradise."

The street, though always busy, seemed unusually thronged today, the people intent on purchasing goods from the shops, or from the clutter of stalls farther along. Suddenly, a great wooden-wheeled carriage turned the corner of Rosemary Lane and came clattering down Carey Street, its huge wheels spraying out fans of mud. The clumsy, swaying body of the carriage knocked over one of the stalls, sending a stream of vegetables and fruits rolling in the mud that still remained from last week's heavy rainfall. Carey Street, though wider than most, had one thing in common with the other streets in that area—it had no sidewalks to guarantee the safety of the pedestrians. There was, therefore, only one choice. The people, to avoid being trampled beneath the hooves of the team of horses, were forced to fling themselves to one side. One man, clinging tensely to a wooden post, his face a mask of mud, his clothes spattered, spat on the ground, and shouted a curse. "Bleedin' swells! Don't care if you runs us all down, eh? A bloody pox on you, then!"

Sarah saw a hand draw aside a leather curtain, and a woman looked out of the window of the carriage. Before it turned the next corner, it slowed, and she had a fleeting glimpse of elaborately curled golden hair beneath a plumed bonnet of ruby-red velvet. From the expression on the woman's face, she appeared to be amused at the turmoil the vehicle had created.

Sarah watched the cursing hawker heave his stall upright. Several of the shoppers hastened to help him pick up his spilled merchandise, some of them surreptitiously helping themselves in the process. One small boy, clad in tattered breeches and an equally tattered shirt, was blissfully engaged in biting into a stolen fruit. The hawker gave a bereaved bellow. "Thievin' little sod!" he shouted, dealing the boy a stinging slap round the head. Enraged, he turned on his helpers, his wizened face sharp with suspicion. "'Ow many o' you bleeders 'as been apinchin' o' me choice goods? 'Ow many, I asks?"

Listening to the protestations of innocence that arose, Sarah suddenly felt very tired. She sank back into her former slumped position. Immediately, Jemmie Taylor's swarthy pockmarked face and piercing light-gray eyes obtruded itself on the screen of memory, taking her back to the time when he found her aimlessly wandering the streets. When he had approached her, she had been too dazed and worn out with grief to repulse him. He was someone to talk to, someone who genuinely seemed to mind that she was unhappy. Before long, words began to pour out of her, and she had told him everything. She was to find that there were many sides to Jeremy Taylor's nature, but on that night, he had chosen to be kind. He had spoken to her with such friendly warmth, and there had been such concern on his lightly pocked, not unattractive face, that the hard core of her grief began to melt. Jemmie was sympathetic and so persuasive, and she was hungry and cold. So, at his invitation, just like a stray cat looking for a home, she had followed him to his lodgings. He lived on Cole Street, in the overcrowded quarter that lay not far from London Bridge, on the top floor of a tenement house, whose filthy and decrepit condition far exceeded that of the neighboring houses.

The grief that had thus far shielded her against any thought of what he might do when they found themselves alone, now gave way to apprehension on the moment that she stepped into the room that doubled as living quarters and bedchamber. Her relief was great when she found that she had no need to fear Jeremy Taylor. His kindness continued, and he treated her with respect, like a sister. He even gave up his bed and slept uncomfortably on a sagging couch.

A week later, on a chill evening, with the rain spattering the grimy curtainless windows, and the little room cosy with flickering firelight, Jemmie began to talk at great length. He told her of everything that had happened in his life, and ended by telling her how he made his living. He was a thief, a pickpocket!

Sarah's lips curled into a mirthless smile as she recalled her utter and unbelieving shock. In a few words, Jemmie convinced her that it was true. And then he told her something else. He wished to train her in the delicate art of picking pockets. "You're small, see," he said in an eager voice. "And I've noticed how quick and light on your feet you are." He took her hands in his "Look at them fingers," he went on in the same eager voice. "Supple, that's what they are. Perfect, you'll be. Them coves won't never rumble a little un' like you."

For a long time she had resisted him. But when Jemmie began to complain of pains in his joints, giving it as his opinion that it would be a long time before he would be able to fork a pocket, she had felt the trap closing about her. When the last of the coal burned low in the squat grate, and the only food left had been consumed, she knew that she had no choice. She had tried to find honest work, but there was none available. The trap snapped shut. She could not expect Jemmie to continue keeping her, and so, reluctantly, she gave in.

Jemmie seemed to come to life then. He taught her all the little tricks, and drilled her for so many hours on end that she found herself drooping with fatigue. How they had managed to live in that time of training, she never did find out. Doubtless, she thought, when food appeared in the cupboard, Jemmie's friends, of which he seemed to have plenty, had provided. It was not long before she was delighting Jemmie with her dexterity. Very soon she had become more expert at picking pockets than Jemmie had ever been. Her first time on the streets had terrified her, but as she grew bolder she even managed to find a small thrill in the act when she lifted a particularly heavy purse. And an even greater thrill in supplying the supposedly ailing Jemmie with comforts and even some small luxuries. For by this time, she had convinced herself that she was in love with him. Much later, she knew that she had needed to believe this. It was the only way she could reconcile her conscience to the life she was leading.

Jemmy's condition improved to the point where he finally admitted that he was now quite well. But he made no move to relieve her of the burden she was carrying. And then he changed in another way. He no longer treated her like a sister. At every opportunity, no matter how tired she might be from the strain and her hours of trudging, his hands would greedily explore her body. With his eyes glittering, his mouth loose and ugly with desire, he had become a different man.

Clinging still to the belief that she was in love with him, she was nonetheless adamant. "I will steal for you," she told him, "but I will not become any man's whore."

She grew weary of fighting him off, and she made up her mind to leave him. It was then that Jemmie, his voice unusually abrupt, offered to marry her.

The offer of marriage had not been prompted by love, but rather by a fear of losing his easy life. For it became increasingly plain that the pupil was now much more adept than the master. But, happily accepting his offer, she had not known or even guessed at that. And so Jemmy had arranged the false marriage. It seemed strange to her now that no suspicion of the truth had entered her head. Believing herself to be a wife, she had thrilled to the coarse but exciting violence of his lovemaking and her own ardently responding body. She was happy, she told herself. Very happy!

A month of marriage saw yet another change take place in Jemmie. Now he abandoned all pretense. Having gained a husband's ascendancy over her, he treated her with a cruelty that fast became a scandal, even in that neighborhood where wife beating was commonplace.

Life became a nightmare. And then Jemmie was killed in a street brawl. His unexpected death brought her release. She tried to feel grief, but she could feel only the most profound relief. Jemmie had scarcely been placed in the ground when she found out that she had never been his wife. She had owed him no loyalty, and she could have left him at any time she chose. Bitter and resentful, she listened as Jemmie's so-called friends, barely troubling to hide their laughter, informed her exactly what she had been to Jemmie. His whore! His meal ticket!

Without a backward glance or a regret, she left the tenement house on Cole Street. At that time, as she walked steadily away, it had been easy to tell herself that she would steal no more. But, moving from one bug-infested room to another, her money fast dwindling, her erstwhile firm determination had wavered. Again she tried to find work. And when she could not, it became a case of steal or starve. So she went back to picking pockets. But that vital something that had motivated her before had left her. She was tired of struggling, of her sordid life, and so she made only half-hearted attempts. As a result, she had indifferent success. Several times she had almost been caught. And, for the last three days, fear had stayed her hand. But she must do something today, she told herself desperately. She must find her courage again. She could not go on like this!

Sarah started out of her unhappy thoughts as the door behind her opened with a sharp click. "You there, lass," a brusque voice said, "be off wi' you. I've been patient wi' you, but now I think you've sat in me doorway long enough."

Panic touched her. She could not get to her feet yet. She was too weak! She looked appealingly at the thin, gray-haired man standing over her. "Just a few m—more moments," she begged. "Please! I would be s—so grateful."

The man looked at her closely, his shrewd blue eyes narrowing in surprise at her unexpectedly cultured tone. He noted that, for all her sick, half-starved look, she was extremely pretty. If she were fed and cared for, she might even be beautiful. Her hair was of that particular shade of red-gold that he had always admired. Her eyes, fringed by thickly curling black lashes, were wide and soft and very blue. He had thought her to be one of the whores who frequently used his shop doorway for a resting place after their night's labor. But this one, despite her tawdry clothes, looked and sounded like a lady. He knew all the jessies on the whoring lay, and he knew that she was not one of that particular sisterhood. Then what was she doing here in this district of thieves and vagabonds? What had brought her to this sorry pass? "Come," he said in a softer voice, "this ain't no place for you. Whyn't you go home?"

Sarah thought of her few remaining coins. She had scarcely enough money to buy her a bed for the night. "I have no home," she answered him in a flat voice.

Something about her moved him, and for a moment he was tempted to invite her in. There was a little room at the back of the shop where she could rest undisturbed. It might even be, if his old woman was in a good mood, that she would give the lass something to eat. He thought it over, but then firmly decided against it. It would never do. To do a good turn was all very well, but if the word got round, he'd have all the trollops trying to impose on his good nature. Hardening himself, he said curtly, "Your troubles ain't no concern of mine. The Duke's comin'. I don't want you hangin' around the shop no more."

"Did you say the Duke?"

The man laughed, clearly enjoying her startled surprise. "Aye," he answered, "that's what I said. He ain't really a Duke, though. That's jus' what we calls him roun' here. Still, he is one o' the swells. So he might be a Duke, for all I know." Seeing her upward glance, he added defensively, "I don't like the swells, never did, but this un's different." He chuckled. "Cold as ice, he can be sometimes. Aye, look right through you wi' them eyes o' his, if so be he's inclined. But he's a good man."

"But who is he? Does he come here often?"

"Ah, that's got you puzzled, ain't it? I don't know his name. An' I can't rightly say as I knows why he keeps acomin'. It ain't many swells as'd choose to roam aroun' here."

"No, indeed."

" 'Twas about two months ago when we first laid eyes on the Duke," the man went on, responding to her interest. "His coach broke down right outside this very shop." He laughed again. "Bill Dailey, him what keeps the pie shop, he tried to fork the Duke. But Bill never was any good at forkin' pockets, an' he got himself caught. The Duke laid him out flat, then he hands him over to the Watch. Won't take no nonsense, not the Duke. Anyway, seems he got talkin' to some o' the folks. He's been comin' a visitin' ever since."

"Has he? Why?"

The man heard the suspicion in her voice. "As to that," he said, thoughtfully scratching his stubbled chin, "I did hear as he's helped a lot o' the folks. Maybe that's it. He likes to help." He shrugged. "Anyway, whatever the way o' it is, the Duke's all right. There's no one here as'd tell you different. We all respects him, sce? An' what's more, he's as safe roun' here as in his own home." He looked at Sarah sternly. "Now then, that's enough jabberin'. You be on your way, lass. The Duke'll be here soon. Someone tol' me they seen him."

Further pleading would be useless. With something of an effort, Sarah rose to her feet. Walking slowly away, she was aware of the man's eyes following her. She did not go far. She felt light-headed, and she had the feeling that her legs were about to collapse beneath her. It was curiosity as much as weakness that kept her standing there. She wanted to see this man whom the people called "the Duke". It was strange that these normally wary and suspicious people should hold him in such esteem. She had learned well the code of the slums. How often had she heard Jemmie's voice reciting it. "Listen to me, Sarah, girl," he had warned her, "don't you never trust a swell. Poor people is dirt to 'em, jus' somethin' what they uses to wipe their feet on. Turn your back on a swell an' he'll yell 'thief!' An' when he's done yellin', he'll have you nobbled by the Watch."

This was the code that Jemmie and most of them lived by. They all had a deeply ingrained mistrust of the members of the upper and ruling classes. She herself, despite her more gentle upbringing, had come to believe that their suspicions were justified. What then was so different about this man? What magic did he possess that enabled him to break down the barrier of mistrust and prejudice?

Her thoughts broke and scattered as somebody raised an excited cry. "'Ere he comes! 'Ere's the Duke!"

Sarah was swept forward by a surge of people. Then she saw the man who was the cause of their excitement. A tall man, with an indolent walk, accompanied by a group of wildly yelling children.

He drew nearer, the crowd parting to give him right of way. He must be at least six feet two inches, maybe more, Sarah thought. He was handsome. His shoulders were broad and powerful-looking, his figure elegant and erectly held. He had boldly cut somewhat arrogant features, and his lean face was lightly bronzed. Against the bronze of his skin, his teeth appeared almost startlingly white, and his eyes a deep and vivid blue. He was not wearing a wig, and he did not appear to possess a hat. His dark-blond hair was clubbed back with a brown ribbon, but curling tendrils of hair, escaping the restraint, fell over a broad, intelligent forehead. Sarah felt a slight surprise at the plainness of his dress. She found herself recalling the time when she had persuaded a surly and unwilling Jemmy to take her to see the King, on his daily promenade through the public park. She had found the King's attire, and that of the nobles attending him, to be fantastically lavish. For some reason, she had expected this man's costume to be equally so. Instead, he was wearing a severely cut light-brown jacket with matching breeches. A brown cloak lined with crimson fell in elegant folds from his shoulders to the top of his soft leather boots. The plainness of the jacket, however, was relieved by the double tier of white lace ruffles that edged his wide cuffs and a white satin stock, held in place by a wide gold pin set with a large sapphire.

A little man, standing next to Sarah, drew a deep, awed breath. "Look at the bleedin' great blinker," he said in a raised voice, pointing to the sapphire. "It don't 'ave much 'o a sparkle, but I bet it's worth a 'eap o' money."

The Duke stopped before him. "So it is, friend," he said, giving him a quizzical look. He touched the sapphire with his finger. "Are you, by any chance, making plans to steal this jewel from me?"

"What, me?" the little man said on a note of deep offense. "I could've forked you any time I'd a mind ter. You know that."

"I do indeed, Ned. You are very skilled in your—er—your profession."

"Well, then?" the man answered, still fiercely belligerent. "If that don' go ter show you, I dunno what will. Could've done it, but I ain't. The day ever comes when Ned Leadbetter steals from you, guv, may 'e be struck down bleedin' dead!"

The Duke's tawny brows rose. "A little drastic, perhaps," the deep, pleasant, lazily drawling voice said, "but you have made your point. Let us hope, should your resolve falter, that the Almighty has turned a deaf ear on you this day." He touched the man's shoulder lightly with the silver-headed swagger stick he carried in his right hand. "Does your wife do better with the new physic, Ned?"

"Aye, guv, that she do. Thank you kin'ly for askin'."

"I am glad to hear it. Give her my good wishes. Tell her that I am in hopes that she may speedily be restored to full health."

The little man nodded, his mouth grim. "She'd better be soon recovered, guv. I can' keep on adoin' all the work in the shop on me own."

The Duke's mouth twitched at the corners. "You must tell her how you feel upon the matter. I feel sure that your unselfish concern will do much to aid her recovery."

The little man grinned. "Laughin' at me, ain't you? Aye, I knows you now. Still, you're all right, you are."

"I am glad I meet with your approval, Ned, else would my —er—bleedin' great blinker be lost to me." The Duke's smiling blue eyes rested for a brief, incurious moment on Sarah. Then, nodding to the man, he turned away.

Sarah's eyes followed him as he strolled on, still attended by his retinue of children. She saw him put a hand into his pocket. When the hand came out again, holding a bag, which, she guessed, contained sweetmeats, it was seized by the children with shrill yells of delight.

Sarah heard his laughter as the children scrambled for their share, and she felt a sudden surge of resentment and antagonism. It was so easy for him to play the great and benevolent my lord in this squalid district. The only cost to him was a few kindly words, a smile here and there, and a supply of sweetmeats for the children. No doubt, she thought bitterly, he walked these streets to alleviate the boredom of his rich and useless life. Perhaps it amused him to win the regard of these humble people. It might well be, when he returned to his own surroundings, that he laughed to himself at their gullibility. Her mouth tightened. Perhaps, today, he might find that his little stroll would cost him a great deal more than he had anticipated.

The belief that her skill had died with Jemmie was with her still, but hunger fostered determination. She must remember that Jemmie had thought her fingers to be the most skilled in the business. Surely, if that were so, she could relieve the swell of his purse? Fine beads of perspiration stood out on her forehead as she moved after him. As she drew nearer to her quarry, she was dismayed to find that she was trembling. Had she not been so desperate, she would have turned back, for she had the sudden urgent premonition that this man was different. There was something about him, a force, a power. She had felt it in that brief moment when his eyes had rested upon her. The apothecary's words came back to her—"The Duke laid him out flat, then he hands him over to the Watch. Won't take no nonsense, not the Duke."

An agony of doubt seized her. Should she leave this man alone? Might it not be better to find herself an easier prey? Even as she hesitated, her empty stomach growled protestingly. She did not want to steal, God knows she did not! But what was left to her? It must be now or never, for if she did not soon have a meal, weakness would lessen future opportunities.

As she drew abreast of the tall figure, she heard the drawling voice say, "Young ladies, good gentlemen, I am plundered of all my treasure. I regret that I must disappoint you, but my pockets can produce no more. Might I suggest that you apply to me on the next time that I come this way?"

The children broke into laughter. And it was at that

moment, when she believed his attention to be suitably distracted, that Sarah's hand slid swiftly into his pocket. Even as her fingers closed about a leather pouch, she knew that she had failed. Her weakness had made her clumsy and amateurish. She withdrew her hand, trying a sideways stumble to cover her action.

"Thief!" a small boy shrieked, jumping up and down in his excitement. "'Ware, guv! The bleedin' drab's atryin' ter fork you of your purse!"

The boy's warning was unnecessary, for the Duke's fingers had already closed about her wrist. Through the roaring in her head, she heard him say, "Ah! And what have we here?"

"Please!" Was that her voice, that faint thread of sound? Swallowing hard, she looked at him with panic-blurred eyes. "Let me go, please! You are quite mistaken in believing me to be a thief."

"I am mistaken?" His voice stung her with its icy contempt. "Nay, wench, I think not." He pulled her round to face him. "A strange combination," he went on. "The voice of a lady, but a thief for all that."

Sarah quailed before the cold glitter in his eyes. "I stumbled against you," she said, trying to hold her head high. "Does that, sir, in your opinion, make me a thief?"

"Nay, wench, not that in itself. But when I felt your hand fitting so snugly into my pocket, it did rather tend to convince me."

"How dare you! Release me at once!"

His fingers tightened. "Shall we now have done with this little game of words? For you will admit, I trust, that you have just given a most remarkable imitation of a thief?"

"I will admit no such thing. I—" Her voice trailed away. It was useless. Why did she continue to protest? No matter what she said, he would not believe her. She had not really expected him to do so. She was fairly caught, but she would not show fear. "All right." She looked at him with bold defiance. "Aye, I did try to steal your purse. What are you going to do about it?" She glanced swiftly at the gathering crowd, hoping for their support. The people stared back at her, stonyfaced, condemning. She clamped her lips tightly together, suppressing a burst of hysterical laughter. They dared to condemn her, these people! Most of them were thieves, housebreakers, or worse! This man must indeed hold a very special place in their hearts! Glaring at her captor, she said in a loud voice, "If you go slumming, you must expect to be forked."

"Must I, wench?" The Duke turned his head and addressed a man standing in the forefront of the crowd: "Fetch the Watch, please."

The man hesitated, his eyelids flickering nervously. It was a very serious matter to give up one of their own kind to the Watch.

"Go on," a woman cried impatiently. "Do like what the Duke tol' you. The Duke's done us all a lot o' good, an' I don't 'old wi' this wench tryin' ter fork 'im. There ain't a one o' us 'ere what'd lay a finger on 'im. Go on, fetch the Watch. Ain't nobody goin' ter blame you."

The man's hesitation vanished. "She's right, guv. I'll go an' fetch 'em."

A silent scream welled up inside Sarah. The clamoring noise rang in her head. It echoed, until she trembled with the din, until she thought that the ugly sound of fear must surely burst from her lips. Oh, dear Christ! What was she to do? She must not let him know that she was afraid. At least she would rob him of that enjoyment. "Call the Watch," she cried. "Do whatever you please! Had I another opportunity, I would try forking you again."

He looked at her for a long, silent moment, and the expression in his eyes puzzled her. "The pity of it is," he said softly, "I believe you. You really would try again."

"Yes, yes!" she almost spat the words in his face. "Yes, I would!"

"In the first place, wench, my intention was merely to frighten you. But I see now that it would be wrong to allow you to go free. It may be that a spell in Newgate Prison will effect a change of heart. If it does not, it will at least soften your brazenness."

Newgate! Oh, God, dear God, no! She was drowning in fear, dying! She looked at his cold eyes, the implacable line of his mouth. He had merely intended to frighten her? Nay, she did not believe him for a moment. He was hard, cruel! What did this man know of hunger and desperation, what did he know of the misery that drove one to crime? Hatred rose in her, black, bitter hatred that swamped all reason. "Do as you please!" she shouted. "I care naught, do you hear me? I care naught!"

With an exclamation of disgust, he flung her from him. "When the Watch arrives, one of you will hand her over," he snapped. "Pray inform them that Lord Witherley will make formal charges on the morrow."

He strode away without a backward glance. For a moment she had a wild hope that this was his way of freeing her. Now that he had gone, surely these people would take pity on her? Her hope died as hands fastened upon her arms. No use, no use! She was trapped! What was his name? Witherley, that was it. Lord Witherley. Someday, in some way, she would pay him back for this!

Blackness descended upon her, and the babble of voices receded. She was still unconscious when she was lifted into the cart and borne away to Newgate Prison.

Chapter Two

(Newgate)

Sarah's dry, bruised lips moved as she tried to form words. "Water!" she wanted to say. "In the name of merciful Christ, give me water!" The words formed in her head, standing out jewel-bright against the muddled confusion there, but she found that she could not bring them forth. There was blood in her mouth, blood trickling down her throat, the brassy taste of it causing her to retch.

A voice said loudly in her ear, "Comin' out o' it, are yer dearie? Bes' try ter sit up if yer wants ter get fed. Ain't much ter eat, though. Jus' a 'unk o' bread an' some water ter wash it down with."

Sarah turned her head slowly and looked at the goblinlike woman squatting beside her. She was a creature out of a nightmare. A bush of snarled white hair hung over a wasted yellow face, and from this yellow mask, two small eyes glittered feverishly. Like the eyes of an animal, Sarah thought with an inward shudder. A savage animal! A tattered cloth was tied about her waist with a piece of frayed rope. Her breasts were bare. Pendulous breasts that sagged like empty water skins. In one filthy, broken-nailed hand, the woman was clutching a piece of bread. Grudgingly, she extended it to Sarah.

Sarah stared at the bread. There was the beginning of a green mold, and it looked soggy. Had the sogginess of the bread come from contact with the stone floor of the cell. The thought of the floor, foul with slime, vomit, urine, and the accumulated filth of years, brought a surge of nausea. She fought it down. "I am n—not hungry." She brought out the faint whisper with some difficulty. "You—you may have it, if you wish."

The woman grinned broadly, exposing brown stumps of teeth. "I was 'opin' as yer would say that. I never feels much like eatin' meself, a'ter I've 'ad a whoppin.' Not as yer was beat 'ard, gal." She poked Sarah's arm with a dirty finger. "Seein' as yer can lay on yer back, it proves as the skin ain't 'ardly broke."

Sarah touched her lips. "My—my mouth is swollen. It hurts."

The woman gave a cackle of laughter. "Should do an' all, a'ter that bash in the mouf what the turnkey landed on yer. Sam Fuller don' like yer, do 'e? Bes' watch out fer 'im. 'E'll pick on yer every time."

"But I have done nothing."

"Don't matter whether yer done nothin'. If 'e don' like yer, you're agoin' ter cop it. May'ap it's yer dainty ways what 'e don' like." Winking at Sarah, she crammed the bread into her mouth. "This is yer firs' time in Newgate, ain't it?" she said in a muffled voice. She leaned closer, and Sarah recoiled from the stench of her breath. " 'Ow'd yer like our 'appy 'ome, then?"

Ignoring the question, Sarah put out a shaking hand. "May I have the water, please?"

The woman scowled. "I was thinkin' as yer wouldn' wan' it." She groped on the floor and produced a battered cup. "Water ain't good for yer on an empty stomich," she added hopefully.

Sarah tried to sit up. Fiery pain stabbed through her lacerated back. "Will you help me to sit up, please?" She looked at the woman pleadingly.

" 'Elp yer, is it?" The woman glared at her indignantly. "Who do yer think yer are, then? Don' yer be thinkin' ter order Meg Barker about. I ain't yer perishin' la'ship's bleedin' servint!"

Sarah stared at her, wondering why such a simple request should rouse such a fury of indignation. "If you needed help," she said quietly, "I would give it to you."

The woman gave a scream of laughter. "I don' expect nothin', and I don' give nothin'."

"It is just that it is so painful for me to move."

"Ain't that a shame! Sorry for yer, that I am. Call that li'l ticklin' what you got a floggin'? You wait, gal, wait till 'e really lays it on yer." She whirled round and presented her back to Sarah. "Look at me back, gal. Tha's what yer call a real floggin'."

Sarah felt sick as she looked at half-healed scars, their edges puffy and purple. There were other wounds across the skinny back, red and angry, surrounded by shredded and suppurating flesh. "Well?" Meg said, turning to face her again. "What yer think o' that, eh?"

"I think, if—if I were ever flogged so brutally, I would die!"

"Nay," Meg said, scornful of this weakness. "Yer gets used ter it." She looked thoughtfully at the cup she still held. "Tell yer what. I'll 'elp yer la'ship ter sit up, if yer gi' me 'alf this water. Is it a barg'in?"

"Yes," Sarah answered. "Yes, it is a bargain."

"More fool you, then. You won' be so quick ter say it when yer been 'ere awhile."

Sarah winced as Meg's cold, rough hands jerked her upright. " 'Ere," Meg thrust the cup at Sarah. "Take a swig. But jus' yer remember that I gets 'alf."

Sarah nodded. She was about to raise the cup to her lips when, catching the wriggling movement in the cloudy water, her eyes dilated with horror. The water was dotted with black insects. "No!" she said through shaking lips. "No!" Her voice rose to an hysterical scream. Blindly, she thrust the cup at Meg. "Take it away!"

Meg snatched the cup from her. Tilting it, she avidly drained the contents. "Ah, tha's better," she grunted, wiping her hand across her mouth. Grinning, she threw the cup to the floor. "Stop your shiverin', do. You'll learn ter drink it, me fine la'ship. Aye, you'll come ter it jus' like the res' o' us, you see if yer don'."

"I would rather die!"

"Always talkin' 'bout dyin', ain't yer?" Meg scoffed. "Water's water, ain't it? You're jus' lucky yer ain't 'ad insec's in it afore this. Insec's gives yer meat, gal, as well as drink." With a last derisive look, she turned on her heel and shuffled away.

Shuddering, heedless now of pain, Sarah sank back on the wooden board that served her as a bed. Newgate! There was a rage of grief and anger in her. To be locked away like an animal in this terrible place! Hell must be like this, she thought wildly. But one did not need to die to experience hell. Hell was here, in this place! She stared about her with burning eyes, trying to shut her ears to the mumbling, the screaming, the shrill laughter, and the vile curses of the other prisoners. The room, overcrowded, foul with the odors of diseased and unwashed flesh, was narrow and dark and unbearably hot. Candles guttered in iron brackets set high upon the damp walls. Above the brackets, three small, barred windows let in dim fingers of light that did little to relieve the overall gloom. Over in a corner of the room, a woman sat on the filthy floor, absorbed in raking talonlike nails through her greasy hair. Sarah heard her exclamation of triumph as she caught and squashed a louse between her fingers. She turned her eyes away from the woman, her flesh crawling. Her own hair, uncombed for two months, was matted and had an evil odor. No doubt, she thought, it was full of lice. A sudden hacking cough drew her attention. It came from a woman lying near to her. Bessie Powers was very old, past eighty. Ten years ago, she had stolen a loaf of bread. She had been caught by the baker. She had spent more than ten years in Newgate. Now, because she was dying, her release was in sight. As Sarah watched, the old woman wearily raised herself, and hawked a great gob of bloody phlegm onto the floor. Catching Sarah's eyes, her mouth stretched into a faint, toothless grin. "It won't be long now, gal," she said in a husky voice. "Ol' Bess is agoin' to her Maker."

"Your Maker?" Sarah repeated. "You believe in God, then?"

Bess's dim eyes stared at her. "O' course I do, gal. Don't you?"

"But how can you?" Sarah burst out. She gestured wildly with her hand. "This place, this terrible place! If there is a God, how can He allow such suffering?"

"That's 'nough, gal!" Bess said sternly. "You don' wan' Him to hear you, eh? We all got to be tested, don' we? That's part o' His Divine plan, ain't it?"

Sarah shook her head, marveling that this woman, who had undergone such suffering, who was coughing her pitiful life away, could still believe. "I do not know," she said at last.

Bess sighed. "Jus' remember, gal, it ain't God who's evil. It's His creatures. He ain't responsible for what they does. You got to be good, see. You got to believe in Him." Her eyes drooped wearily. "I'm tired," she said, her voice changing to a fretful note. "I got to lie down." The breath rattling in her lungs, she sank back on the wooden board, her clawlike hand pulling a ragged piece of sheeting over her shivering body.

Vaguely, Sarah wondered how it was that Bess had been allowed to retain the tattered old sheet? In this place, every piece of material was fought over, the spoils going to the strong ones. So, perhaps, even in these bestial and degraded women there still lingered a spark of compassion. It was hard to believe, when one heard their howling blasphemy, the obscene language that seemed to be a part of their everyday speech. Some of them had been prisoners for a long time, and they no longer looked like women. Most of them were naked, their bodies stinking, marked by the lash, and grotesque with the running sores of disease, their hair wild and unkempt and alive with lice. Sarah frowned. It was true that they were bestial and degraded, but what did she know of the circumstances that had made them so? She knew nothing of their sufferings, or of the twist of fate that had brought about that final degradation: incarceration in Newgate. Perhaps some of them had been wrongfully accused. She thought of the quiet girl with the soft, pretty voice, who had died a week after her own entry into Newgate. It was hard to believe that that girl had been guilty of a crime. Hard to believe that, had she not died, she would have become like all the others. Sarah's heart jerked and raced with the fear that gripped her then. Would she become like these women? Please, God, no! Was it really only two months that she had spent in Newgate? It seemed like years and years!

Sarah started violently as a spiraling scream rose above the babble of voices. She raised herself on her elbows. Who had screamed like that? What was happening now in this hell-hole? Her questions were answered by an excited cry from the women. Simultaneously they began to stamp and shout, "Fight! Fight! Fight!"

A tall, naked woman, her round head almost hairless, strode into the space that had been hastily cleared by the women in anticipation of the fight. "Come on, you bitch!" the woman bellowed. "Don't you try to hide from me. Come on, bleedin' cow that you are! Let's see if you can fight as well as you call names."

A little woman, her bare breasts bobbing, her face twisted

and livid with rage, ran into the cleared space. "You'll see if I can fight, you bald-headed trollop, you bloody great mountain of flesh!"

Without further words, they flew at each other. With the snarling, spitting sounds they made, they were like enraged cats. The women circled the combatants, their eyes glittering with excitement, throats straining as they urged them on. The din was indescribable, a hideous cacophony that rose higher and higher.

The noise, penetrating through the thick door, brought almost immediate retribution. The door burst open, slamming against the wall with a resounding crash. Sarah shrank back as a man strode into the room. It was Sam Fuller. And of all the turnkeys, he was by far the most brutal.

"Shut your row!" Fuller bawled at the top of his lungs. "Fight will you, you scabby bitches! I'll give you fight!" He snatched his whip from his belt and began laying about him. The lash, with its heavily weighted tip, descended on heads, on shoulders, and on bare breasts. It tore a great furrow in the cheek of one woman, and bloodied the back of another. Fuller went on lashing at them until their terrified screaming had dwindled to moans and confused, babbling words that begged him for mercy. When at last he stopped, he was panting heavily, his hand trembling from the force with which he had wielded the whip. He stood triumphantly above the cowering women, his legs astride, his face flushed with angry blood, and his eyes narrowed into glittering slits. "Get back!" he shouted. "Get back, you mangy cows! If I hear another sound out of you, every one of you will be strung to the whipping post. I'll rip you clean open! You hear me?"

There was hatred in the eyes of some of the women, and in others there was fear, but they moved away obediently. Fuller stood there watching them. They were like dangerous animals, he thought, but, because they feared him, they would not attack. Over a long period of time, he had finally broken them to the lash. He found himself almost hoping they would make some rebellious move. He wasn't soft like some of his comrades. He enjoyed inflicting pain. It made his blood race faster through his veins, it gave a zest to living. His eyes roved the room, his gaze falling on Sarah. He smiled slowly. "So there you are, my dearie," he said, striding toward her. "I can't leave you out, can I? It would be downright selfish of me if I didn't give you a little taste of the whip, wouldn't it?"

Sarah stared up at him, her face drained of color, her eyes shadowed with fear.

Fuller looked at her tightly compressed lips. "Don't you want to say something, dearie?" he said softly.

Sarah shook her head. Fuller's smile was replaced with a scowl. "You're being rude to me, dearie," he said, fingering the whip. "I don't like people to be rude to me." He raised the whip.

Sarah's body tensed. The whip descended, touching her exposed stomach lightly, almost caressingly. Fuller began to laugh. "Thought you were going to get it, didn't you, dearie?" he said in a loud voice. "Nay, you'll find that I'm not greedy. I can wait until tomorrow."

"T-tomorrow?"

"So you've found your tongue, have you? Aye, lass, tomorrow. We're going to carry out the sentence that has been passed on you."

"What do you mean?" Her voice was shrill with terror. "What sentence?"

"Why, the sentence of the court, of course. You've been wanting to know about that, I'm sure?" His brown eyes were full of malicious amusement as he studied her face. "I'm not one to keep good news all to myself, you know that. I don't mind telling you what your punishment is to be." He paused, then he went on in that soft, taunting voice that she had grown to fear. "After you've been branded and flogged, you are to serve a nice, restful year in our cosy prison."

"What!"

"Aye, that's right," Fuller said, turning away. "You make sure you get a nice restful sleep, my dearie," he called to her as he strode over to the door. "You've to keep your strength up, you know. Don't you be worrying that I'll forget all about you. No, no, I'd never do that. I'll be coming for you in the morning, bright and early." With a last smile, he went out, banging the door behind him.

Sarah lay rigidly on the wooden board, her eyes tightly closed. Old Meg, drawn as always by impending tragedy, shuffled over to speak to her. "I 'eard 'im," she hissed, "the bleedin' sod!" She put her mouth close to Sarah's ear. "You ain't goin' ter be wantin' yer food for a while, are yer? Too painful ter eat it'll be. You say as I c'n 'ave yer share, then them other cows won' be agrabbin of it. You tell Fuller 'n' all. 'E'll put 'em right if they starts anythin'."

Sarah did not answer. Meg lingered for a while, then, with a disgusted sniff, she turned away.

Branded! Flogged! A year in Newgate! Sarah put a hand to her tight throat. God have mercy! Her mind went back to that mockery of a trial in the Sessions House. She saw herself, blinded by daylight after the darkness of the cell, her hair matted, clad in the few rags that were all she had been able to salvage after the savage onslaught of the rapacious women. Entering the Sessions House, she saw the judges seated in chairs, scarlet cushions beneath them. Behind them, the walls were draped in scarlet cloth. There was the canopy with the royal coat-of-arms above it, the sword of justice hanging beneath. My lord Witherley had been there, so calm, so poised, so elegantly garbed in deep-blue velvet with ruffles of lace at his throat and his wrists. To her, the time had passed in a daze. Faces were turned her way, mouths opened, spoke. Except when a rough voice called her to attention, she would not look at them. She kept her eyes fixed on the glittering sword of justice, and she prayed desperately that the verdict of the court would be lenient. She spoke when requested to do so. She answered questions. But later, when she thought about it, she found that she could not remember the questions, or what her answers to them had been. But some words she had heard and could clearly remember. A deep voice declaring her to be "Guilty!" After that, there had been a small bustle in the court. Wigged heads had been bent together in grave conference. Then another voice, lighter in tone, had spoken. "Sentence to be passed at a later date," the light voice said. "Take her away!"

Just before she had been led away, she had turned her head and looked straight at her accuser. My lord Witherley, his face impassive, had met her eyes calmly. Staring at him, she had had the feeling that no warm or human emotion would ever be allowed to ruffle that calm mask. Then his eyes had dropped lower to rest on the heavy manacles that circled her wrists and her ankles, and his expression had changed subtly. Was it pity she read there? Shock? She could not tell. For when he looked up again, his face was once more devoid of expression.

Sarah clenched her hands together. Pity? Shock? She had been a fool to wonder even for a moment. Safe in his rich and secure world, armed smugly in righteousness, he would not give one thought to her. She had attempted to rob him. She must be punished. Hatred such as she had never known before swept over her. She had hated Jemmie, but that hatred had been a colorless emotion when compared to the savage force of her hatred for my lord Witherley. For the crime of theft, or attempted theft, it was right that she be punished, but not like this! Branded! Flogged! A year to be spent in Newgate. It was too much! She had rather he had taken his sword and thrust it through her breast, it would have been kinder. Better, far better, to be dead than to be condemned to this hell!

A chill September wind, the harbinger of winter, touched her face as she was led into the courtyard. The whipping post loomed before her eyes, tall, built in the shape of a cross, its light wood showing the same dark patches as spattered the ground about it. A violent trembling seized her. Blood! Those patches were blood! Very soon now, it would be her blood that would pattern the post and spray the ground. She had been whipped before. Fuller had twice thrown her to the ground and beaten her savagely, but this was different. Somehow, to be bound to that post that had witnessed so much agony, to hang there helpless, unable to move, was doubly terrifying.

Her body gave a spasmodic jerk as a hand touched her shoulder. "Don't be standing there dreaming, Sarah, my dearie," Fuller's voice said. He pointed with his finger. "Get yourself over there, sweetheart. It's cold this morning, and we've built a nice little fire in your honor." His fingers squeezed her shoulder. "It's only right, we thought, only gentlemanly that we should do our best to keep a frail little thing like you all nice and snug and warm."

Sarah took two steps forward, then stopped short, unable to move. She stared at the great iron brazier piled with glowing coals. Even from this distance, she could feel the heat thrown off from its bulging sides. Red light touched the faces of the two guards standing over it. One of them held a long iron rod with a flattened head. The red glow stained his neck as he stooped and thrust the flattened end into the coals. He grunted as Fuller, propelling Sarah, approached. "It's been 'eating up a fair time," he said. "Jus' a few more minutes an' it'll be ready." He darted a quick look at Sarah's bloodless face. "The wench looks like she's about ter swoon. I don' like these kind o' jobs,

Fuller," he added gloomily. "Don' seem right ter do it to a wench."

Fuller smiled. "Don't take it to heart, Barcley. We'll be doing her a favor. Females like these little decorations. She'll have a nice, neat little T on her shoulder. Pretty, it will be. Why, I wouldn't be surprised if it didn't start a fashion."

Barcley looked at him uneasily. "I dunno 'ow you sleep at nights, Fuller. Nothin' don' seem ter touch you."

"Everything touches me, Barcley. I am a very tender-hearted fellow. The lass will tell you so." He took Sarah's cheek between his fingers and pinched it painfully. "Tell them, Sarah, dearie."

Sarah did not even hear him, nor did she flinch from the pain of his punishing fingers. With the fascination of complete horror, she was staring into the fire.

"You see, Barcley," Fuller went on, "she is too overcome with admiration to speak."

Barcley turned his eyes away from the smiling face. "You're the only one o' us tha's got education, Fuller. An' if tha's what education does ter you. I'm glad I'm ig'rant."

"Do you agree with Barcley, Webster?" Fuller said, addressing the other man.

Webster shuffled his feet uncomfortably. He was afraid of Fuller. "I don' agree with nothin'," he mumbled. "I don' think 'bout nothin'. I ain't paid ter think, only to obey orders."

"Very good, Webster. Now, if you and Barcley are of the same mind about obeying orders, you will strip that wench and hold her firmly." He hesitated. "No, on second thought, I will strip her. Stand by to hold her."

"Stan' by," Barcley grumbled, giving Fuller a sour look. "Any one'd think we was on a bleedin' ship, an' you the captain givin' of your orders."

"In this instance, Barcley," Fuller said smoothly, "you might say that I am the captain. I have been put in charge of this little party." He smiled at them. "I will put it more politely. Please stand by, gentlemen."

Sarah screamed as Fuller's hands tore the grimy tattered remnants of her gown away. Hands pressed hard on her shoulders, forcing her shivering naked body to the ground. Oh, God help me! Save me! The glowing coals swam in a red mist before her eyes. A cry came from her lips, but there was no strength behind it, it sounded like the feeble mewing of a kitten.

"Iron's ready. Hold her tight." Fuller's voice, a clap of thunder in her ears.

"I got 'er upper arms," Barcley grunted. He leaned closer to Sarah. "Don' look, gal. It'll soon be over. Webster, 'ere, 'e's goin' ter lie across your legs ter keep you steady."

"Stop that whispering!" Fuller rapped.

Sarah felt the heaviness of the man settle across her legs. Her heart was racing at a frantic speed, bursting! She did not want to look, yet she could not tear her eyes away. She saw Fuller's smile as he lifted the iron from the bed of white-hot coals. She felt the scorching blast of its heat against her face, and she heard the sharp crackling sound the iron made as he spat upon it to test it. Then he was turning toward her. One hand gripped her hair, lifting it away from her shoulders. The iron came down on her right shoulder, pressing hard, searing! And the world exploded in crimson fragments. From somewhere far off, she heard a demented howling. She was falling! Falling a long, long way down, plunging into merciful blackness.

Icy water splashed in her face, dispelling the cool blackness, forcing her to face once more the nightmare of pain. Someone was lifting her to her feet, gripping her arms hard. "Not again!" Her voice, raw with terror, but sounding strangely unlike her own. "Oh, please! Not again!"

"The branding is over, my dearie," came Fuller's soft

voice. "We'll just attend to that nice little flogging that you've been so looking forward to. After that, you can go back to your comfortable cell."

Her head fell forward, her long, tangled hair half obscuring her face. "Please!" she begged. "No more, no more!"

Barcley saw Fuller's eyes, and, at the expression in them, his face flushed a dull red. He himself was not a kindly man. He had flogged many a wench, but always, he felt, the floggings had been justified, and delivered by him in a spirit of healthy anger. But this was a different matter. Fuller was enjoying this. He did not understand the man, nor did he particularly want to. He only knew that there was something wrong with him. Something that was twisted and ugly. He was almost frightened to speak out, yet he felt that he must. "Look 'ere, Fuller. Whyn't you leave the wench be until 'er shoulder 'eals? It don' make no difference when you flogs 'er, do it?"

The deadly eyes were turned on him. "Now, Barcley, surely you would not have me deprive the lady of her pleasure?"

"Don' you gi' me all them fancy words. You ain't nothin' but a cold 'earted bleeder!"

Fuller smiled. "May I advise you to watch your tongue, my good Barcley? I have, you know, a certain influence in this prison."

It was true. The swine did have a great deal of influence. Barcley moistened his lips and tried a more conciliatory approach. "Tha's true what you said, Fuller. But what difference do it make ter you if you flogs the wench now or later? Seems ter me like a full-growd man'd break under this punishment."

"But I am not asking you to think, Barcley, only to obey. The female of the species, you will find, is remarkably resilient." Fuller's voice changed, hardening to command. "Lash her to the post. And while you are about it, remove her manacles. I want her wrapped round that post as though she were part of it."

Barcley shrugged. There was no help for it. Fuller, as he had said, was in command. Even so, he could not help wondering why he and Webster had been kept in ignorance of the verdict of the court against the prisoner, Sarah Barry? Usually, sentence was given immediately, Or, if deferred for some reason, the sentence, when received, was read out to the assembled guards, and the official date of punishment given. Again he felt that sense of uneasiness. He glanced at Webster. Webster looked back at him with dull eyes. What if Fuller had arranged this for his own private enjoyment? If that were so, Fuller would, when the verdict of the court finally came through, find some way of wriggling out of the blame. With his smooth tongue, it was far more likely that the blame would fall on Webster and himself. Full of misgiving, but unable to think of any way out, Barcley signaled to Webster to help him with the girl.

The manacles fell away. Sarah heard the clatter as they were flung to one side. Again hands were lifting her, pressing her body hard against the whipping post, bruising her breasts. Her wrists and her ankles were lashed tightly. Thin leather thongs bit into her naked body, holding her yet more securely. A voice welled up inside her, a voice that she was too weak to bring out. Let me faint! Let me die! it screamed in desperation. I cannot endure more!

"Ready!" Fuller shouted.

Sarah heard the high, vicious whine of the lash. It smashed against her back, a thousand red-hot talons tearing at her flesh. The whining sound, the blow. Again and again it came, bringing with it an almost unendurable agony. And rising high and shrill in macabre accompaniment, her agonized screaming.

"Ten!" Barcley shouted. "Tha's it, Fuller. You said as the sentence called for ten lashes."

"All right." Scowling, Fuller flung the whip from him. "Cut her down."

The leather thongs were loosening. She was sliding downward. She felt the chill of the ground against her raw body. "Gawd in heaven!" a voice exclaimed loudly. "Look at the wench! Ain't she a bloody mess?"

It seemed to her that she lay there for a long time. She tried to will herself into the darkness and peace of unconsciousness, but her will was not strong enough. She was to be spared nothing. Her head! It was so heavy, so muddled. She could not seem to remember who she was, or where she was. When she tried to recall her name, there was only that blankness. She could hear voices just beyond her. It was those voices, she thought resentfully, prodding at her, refusing to let her slip into unconsciousness, that were keeping her alive to every moment of this flaming agony. Her head turned slowly, seekingly. Through a wavering mist, her swollen, bloodshot eyes focused on three men. Two of the men began to move away. They went through a door, and she heard the heavy slam of it behind them. The remaining man was moving too. He was coming toward her. He was very near now, near enough for her to make out his features. Fuller! His name burst clearly into her pain-clouded brain. It was Fuller! Fuller! He was bending, kneeling beside her. She closed her eyes, afraid that he might read their expression. He had done this to her. He was the cause of her pain! Revenge, revenge! She would have it!

Fuller bent over her. The wench was, as Barcley had said, a bloody mess. Had he perhaps gone too far? He stared at her, his eyes faintly anxious. He thought of the busybodies who now and again, when they had nothing better to do, made it their business to inquire into conditions at Newgate Prison. If the wench were to die, it might arouse public indignation. His position then, would not be an enviable one. The sentence of the court had been five lashes and three months in the prison. It could very well come out that he had exceeded his authority. He could not allow her to die. He would have to see to it that she was taken care of until her wounds had healed. He frowned. If only there were another way of getting rid of her. A way that would not bring discredit upon himself.

Fuller's face was very near to hers. His warm breath, faintly redolent of onions, fanned her face. She would try to kill him! It would take only a little effort, surely she could force her remaining strength to the task? Now, in her mind, Fuller's face dissolved into that of Lord Witherley. Fuller! Lord Witherley! They were both to blame. Both of them evil men. She would kill them, if she could. Her eyes opened. Hatred, the madness born of excruciating pain, combined to make the effort less than nothing. Her blood-soaked arms flew up and wrapped themselves tightly about Fuller's neck. The grip, unexpectedly strong, forced his head down.

Fuller roared with surprise and pain as her teeth all but met in his flesh. Overwhelmed with panic and horror, he had to exert all his strength to free himself. Panting, blood streaking his cheek, he lifted his clenched fist and slammed it against her jaw. The eyes that had blazed hatred at him, rolled upward. Her head fell heavily to one side.

Shakily, Fuller rose to his feet. The savage bitch! She was insane! He was turning away when the idea came to him. He knew how he could be rid of her. He fingered his bleeding cheek. Damn the whore! She had tried to kill him! There was a place for the insane. Bedlam Asylum. The asylum would swallow up Sarah Barry as if she had never been. Very few inquiries were ever made into the plight of the insane. But if they were made, he would know how to deal with them. And if Barry should die in the asylum, who would know? Who would care?

Chapter Three

Except for the crackling of the log fire in the huge iron grate, complete silence reigned in the large, comfortably furnished room.

Doctor Joshua Sanders, displeased with the silence, moved impatiently in his chair and turned a choleric gray glare on the two young men seated on either side of the fire. He had the distinctly unwelcome suspicion that one, or perhaps both of them were asleep. He snorted loudly to show his displeasure. He had come out of his way to pay a friendly call on my lord Witherley, and here was my lord, apparently asleep, and his vacuous friend, Sir Peter Baxter, if not asleep, with nothing to say for himself, as usual.

The doctor crossed one plump leg over the other. Hitherto, when paying a friendly call at this house on Twyford Street, where he could be sure of a good meal and witty conversation to go with it, he had found it to be a welcome break in his daily round of visiting the sick. And today, what had occurred? He had been slighted! Lady Margaret, my lord Witherley's mother, was out. No doubt buying more useless fripperies for herself. My lord himself seemed disinclined for conversation. And as for that ninny-headed Sir Peter Baxter, it was quite useless to address an intelligent remark to him, not, that is, if one wished for an intelligent answer. Sir Peter's way of staring vacantly at one, his air of being backed into a corner, was distinctly annoying. No doubt, the doctor thought, his ire growing, and his glare concentrating on the unfortunate young man in question, the lad had been dropped on his head as a babe. There was no other way to account for it. Why in thunder my lord Witherley, who was scarcely the most patient of men, put up with the overdressed, dandyish nincompoop was more than he could comprehend. It was true that they had played together as lads, but there were limits. With another snort, the doctor banged his wine glass down on the table beside him and contemptuously dismissed Sir Peter from his thoughts. He had better things to do than to sit here sipping wine, twiddling his thumbs, and, as his wife was fond of remarking, listening to his hair grow. And so, in a little while he was determined to tell them.

My lord Witherley was not asleep. He was playing the game he had often played with the doctor when he was a boy. He had purposely fallen silent, counting to himself the moments before the peppery doctor would burst forth into indignant speech. With some amusement, he surveyed Doctor Sanders from the corner of his eye. The squat little man had uncrossed his legs, and he now sat stiffly upright in his chair. His white doctor's staff, which he had apparently neglected to put down, was clasped tightly in his right hand. By the side of his chair, within easy reach, was his large black bag. His round, rosy face, usually jovial with smiles, if things were going his way, wore a scowl, and his sharp little gray eyes were resentful. As usual, he had forgotten to remove his tricorn hat, and both hat and the long white wig beneath it were askew on his large, round head. There were snuff stains beneath his bulbous nose. His muslin cravat was pulled to one side, and his brown cloth coat and breeches looked as though he had slept in them. He scarcely looked like a respectable doctor. But, for all his bedraggled appearance, he was thought to be quite brilliant, and, in many of his ideas on the treatment of the sick, well ahead of his time. He had one other thing to recommend him. He was, for all his often irascible tongue, the most kindhearted of men.

The doctor's glare intensified. "Well, upon my soul!" His loud, hoarse voice shattered the silence and caused Sir Peter to start violently. "I must say, my lord, that this goes beyond everything! Damned if I'll sit here with the pair of you snoring fit to wake the dead!"

"No, I say!" Sir Peter mumbled in feeble protest. "Not snoring, old lad, would you say?"

My lord Witherley turned his head and looked at the doctor. "Just five minutes, Josh."

"Eh? What do you mean by five minutes? And don't call me Josh!"

My lord Witherley smiled. "Then do not call me that infernal my lord."

"What do you expect, when I have been treated so shabbily? And what do you mean about five minutes?"

"You have been silent for five minutes. A record!"

The doctor looked at him with sharp suspicion, then his face cleared. "So that's it. You've been up to your old tricks." He gave a fat chuckle. "A plague on you, you blasted young rogue."

Jason's brows rose. "Not so young. I have passed my twenty-eighth year, you know."

"And I've passed my seventieth. How far past I'll not be telling you. So we'll have no more of your sarcasm, young Jason."

Sir Peter, looking faintly alarmed, sat up straighter in his chair and ventured a remark. "Can't have this, old lads. Quarreling's bad for the digestion."

"Quarreling!" The doctor's snort was so indignant that he was forced to further loosen his muslin cravat. "Who's quarreling, you infernal young puppy? If you ain't got anything sensible to say, don't say anything at all!"

Sir Peter thought this over for a moment. "Right," he said at last. Lacing his fingers together, he settled more comfortably in his chair, his expression one of polite attention.

"You have hurt his feelings," my lord Witherley drawled. "For shame, Joshua."

"Nonsense!" The doctor sat forward in his chair. "Now then, Jason, what's this I've been hearing about you?"

"Many things, I imagine, and none of them to my credit. To what in particular do you refer?"

"You know very well," the doctor said impatiently. "Your mother was telling me that the King has commissioned you to investigate conditions in the poorer quarters of London."

"Very true. And I have done so. It was not exactly a commission, you know. It was more in the nature of an informal investigation."

"Well?"

Before answering, Jason rose to his feet and refilled the wine glasses. When he settled back in his chair, he did not speak at once.

"Well?" the doctor prompted him again.

"I found the conditions in which the poor live to be quite deplorable."

"Huh! I could have told you that. Have you given your report to the King?"

"I have."

"And what does he intend to do about it?"

"All that he can, I imagine. The decision to spend money to alleviate these conditions, is not, of course, entirely his. Parliament must be consulted."

The doctor grunted. "In that case, little or nothing will be done."

"We must wait and see."

"Wait, wait, always wait! How long did your investigation take?"

"I walked those streets for four months." Jason smiled. "In

that time, I became quite well known. The people called me the Duke."

Sir Peter gave a squeak of alarm. "Walked the streets, did you say, Jason? I wondered you dared."

"Well, we know you wouldn't have done it, young Peter," the doctor said. "Go on, Jason."

Jason nodded at Peter, including him in the conversation. "I was set upon once, and had my pockets forked twice, with—er, indifferent results for the pickpockets."

"Aye," the doctor chuckled. "You're a canny one, Jason. You know well how to take care of yourself. I pity the fellows who tried to fork you."

Jason frowned as he found himself recalling the girl with the red hair. What had her name been now? When she had come into the court, hobbling with the heavy irons that weighed her down, he had been stirred to pity. She had looked so young, so lost. He had wanted to stop the court proceedings, but it had gone too far. His frown deepened. They had not passed sentence upon her immediately. He found himself hoping that it had been a light one. He should have investigated, found out the sentence. He would have done so, had the King not sent him on another mission.

"They need places for the sick," the doctor went on. "Good clean places. Aye, and they need nourishing food in their bellies, warm clothes. And schools." He picked up his wine glass and sipped thoughtfully. "I did hear of a fellow who started a school. Near the dock area, it was. The fellow came from Worcestershire. Never met him, though I'd like to have done so. Name of Barry, I believe. Aye, that's it, James Barry."

Jason moved uneasily. Barry? The name struck a chord in his memory. Where had he heard the name before? In what connection? "I did not hear of this school, Joshua. Is it a success?"

"Might have been, given time. But I'm afraid that the

school is no more. The poor fellow up and died of the sweating fever. He, his wife, and three of his children. There was another child, I believe. A wench." The doctor frowned into his wine. "Heard she escaped the fever."

"What happened to her?"

"Just disappeared."

"How do you hear of these things, Joshua?"

"I've got patients among the poor, and I keep my ear to the ground. Not much escapes me. Wish I'd met the Barry fellow. I'd like to have shaken his hand." He glared at the luckless Sir Peter. "At least he was trying to do something. Not like some I could mention, who mince around in silks and satins and have never done an honest day's work."

"No I say!" Sir Peter waved a jeweled hand. "Jason works hard, you know. He is in constant attendance upon the King. To say nothing of that big estate in Gloucestershire. With all that to manage, the troubles of his tenants and various other things that need his attention, I would say that his time is well taken up." Sir Peter looked at the doctor triumphantly. "Besides, he would never mince around, as you put it, in silks and satins. Never saw such a fellow for plain clothes as Jason. His lack of ornamentation quite makes one wince!"

The doctor regarded Peter with satirical eyes. "Nincompoop!" he said at last. "For your information, I was not referring to Jason. Look closer to home, young Peter, my lad."

"Oh! Oh, yes, quite." Crushed, Peter subsided.

The doctor turned to Jason again. "You went through Newgate Prison, of course?"

Again Jason found himself thinking of the red-headed girl. He remembered the stench of the prison, the awful sights and sounds. He remembered, too, the shame he had felt that he had condemned the girl to such a fate. He had looked for her, but he had not seen her. Perhaps he would return to the prison, make some inquiries. He could not save all the poor unfortunates, but perhaps he could do something about this girl.

"Jason! Damned if you're not going deaf. I asked you if you went through Newgate Prison?"

"I did," Jason said curtly.

"All right, no need to snap my plagued nose off, is there? Upset you, did it? Good, good. If we can get a few more upset, mayhap something will be done about the place." The doctor took another sip of his wine. "And of course you visited Bedlam Asylum?"

"I did not."

"Not? 'Pon my soul, Jason, how come you to leave that place out?"

"I did not deem it necessary to inspect the place."

"Not necessary? If the King wants to know about human misery, the asylum is the very place to inspect. My God! If you think Newgate is bad, you should visit the asylum. I've seen cells that were less than seven feet in length, with fifteen or more unfortunates chained up like animals. No windows, black as the pit of hell. Nothing to lie upon but some filthy straw. Aye, covered in sores, most of 'em, sores, and their own filth. I've seen 'em unchained and taken out to one of those swinging cages, put up on show for the public. And when they were unchained, there were some of 'em that couldn't stand up straight. Crawled on all fours, they did, and had to be hoisted up to the cage. What do you think of that?"

"Please!" Sir Peter exclaimed, shuddering.

"Does it offend you, then?" the doctor snapped, turning on him in a fury. "Think of the offense to the poor patients, who, through no fault of their own, are mentally sick. Mental sickness is treated as a huge joke. But it is no joke, Peter, no joke at all!" He looked at Jason. "If you are at all sensitive, and despite your cold and haughty and touch-me-not manner,

Jason, I know you are sensitive, it takes courage to go through Bedlam Asylum."

"I believe, Joshua, that I am not without courage."

"Then you'll go through Bedlam Asylum?"

"I will."

"Today?"

Jason hesitated. "Aye," he said, shrugging, "today."

"Good." The doctor set down his wine glass. "No time like the present. Peter and I will go with you."

"No, no!" Peter protested. "Appointment to keep, you know."

"Bah!" The doctor rose to his feet. "Afraid you'll puke up your lunch, are you? You are going, so you might as well stop bleating."

"Look here. I resent your—"

"Resent it all you want. Get your cloak."

"Upon my word! Are you going to let this dashed fellow order us around, Jason?"

Smiling, Jason got to his feet. "Never argue with the man who brought you into the world, Peter. You know well that in the end he will have his way."

"That's all very well, Jason. But I have no wish to visit the dashed asylum."

The doctor chuckled. "Get your cloak, Peter. They won't keep you at the asylum. I'll speak up for you, lad."

Deeply offended, Peter went haughtily to the door. "I will go," he said coldly. "But I wish you to know that I do so under protest."

Now that the doctor had gained his way, he was in high good humor. "Popinjay!" he said. "We will have to toughen you up, lad. Can't have you drooping like a blasted lily at the thought of witnessing something unpleasant."

"I have a very weak stomach," Peter defended himself. He looked down his nose at the little man. "I cannot imagine why

Jason allows you to bully him."

"Oh, come Peter," Jason murmured. "Would you say that?"

"Yes, I would," Peter answered in an aggrieved voice. "I have been your friend for these many years, and never once have I managed to bend you to my will."

"If you would care to remind me of that at some other time, mayhap I will allow you one small bend."

"You see. Only sarcasm for me, your best friend!" With a last reproachful look, Peter went out of the door.

Grinning, the doctor rubbed the side of his nose. "Damned if that young scallywag don't remind me of a petulant wench at times. I don't see how you put up with him, Jason."

"Peter has his good points. As for you, Joshua, you are a fraud. You constantly fulminate against him, yet I am aware that he has his own place in that tough piece of leather you call a heart."

The doctor grunted. "Canny, ain't you? Aye, I like the lad well, for all his pernicketty ways. But if you tell him I said so, I'll deny it."

Chapter Four

From force of habit, William Mitford shrank back against the wall as the head keeper of A section passed him by. Then, remembering that today he would be leaving Bedlam Asylum, never to return, if he had his way, he squared his shoulders and looked insolently after the man. He was free, free! Thank God the old lady believed in his sanity. His old Aunt Liza had always believed that her husband had placed him in the asylum out of sheer spite. And so it had been from spite. But the swine was dead now. He couldn't interfere anymore. Old Liza had had some trouble, but she had secured his release. She would be coming for him soon.

As though conscious of Mitford's eyes upon him, the keeper stopped walking. Turning around, he came back. For a moment the keeper said nothing, he merely smiled unpleasantly as his hard eyes took in the tall, thickset man standing before him. In honor of the day, Mitford had been allowed a barber. His black, wiry hair stood up in untidy spikes over his large head, looking not unlike the quills of a porcupine. His coarse-featured face was flushed. his small blue eyes watering with the excitement that possessed him. The ugly scar that dragged down his right eye and traveled in a puckered line to end at the corner of his mouth, stood out in vivid scarlet relief. "What you doin' roamin' aroun' free?" the keeper demanded.

"I'm goin' 'ome terday, you know that," Mitford mumbled, deliberately leaving off the "sir". "I was told I could wait 'ere till me aunt comes fer me."

"Hmm!" The keeper rubbed his stubbled chin. "Told that, was you? All right, you c'n stay. But if you starts anythin', I'll 'ave you in chains quicker'n you c'n wink your eyes."

Mitford gave him a sullen look. "I ain't goin' ter start nothin'."

"See you don't, if you knows what's good for you." The keeper grinned, exposing broken and blackened teeth. "So you're goin' 'ome, eh? You shouldn' be let to go 'ome, you mad bastard."

Mitford longed to smash his fist in the sneering face, but his nightmare experience had taught him caution. Wait, he thought, just wait till I'm free. "I ain't no loonie," Mitford answered. "I never should'er been put in 'ere in the first place."

"Go on! You was ravin' somethin' shockin' when you was brought 'ere. We 'ad to smash you up a bit to quiet yer. You was still ravin' when we put yer chains on."

Mitford's eyes glittered dangerously. "You smashed me up all right, 'members that, I do. Aye, an' you chained me 'n' all. But I wasn't ravin'. I was sane, see? Sane!"

"Callin' me a liar, are yer?"

Again Mitford drew back from the edge of threatening danger. "O' course I ain't callin' yer a liar. It's me Uncle Ned what I'm callin' a liar. Lied about me, 'e did. But ol' Liza, tha's me aunt, she knows I'm sane. Tha's why, now the old swine's dead, she's acomin' for me. 'Cause she knows, she knows."

"Sorry for the ol' girl, I am. I jus' 'opes she won' regret what she's doin'." His eyes went to the scar again. "Ugly cuss, ain't yer? If I was a wench, I wouldn't like ter run across you in the dark."

Mitford touched the scar. "I got this 'ere scar in a street fight. Done wi' a broken bottle, it was. One o' me gang got the bleeder what done it, though. Got 'im good! 'E won' carve no one else up wi' a broken bottle."

"I 'eard about your gang. Call 'emselves The Scavengers, don't they?"

"Aye, tha's right."

"Bleedin' lot o' robbers an' murderers from what I 'ear. You goin' back ter that gang, are you?"

"Aye." Mitford drew himself up proudly. "Their leader, I am. Me aunt tol' me that they're waitin' fer me ter get out so's I c'n lead 'em again."

"In that case, Mitford, you'll soon be back 'ere."

"No! 'Cause I'm sane, see."

"Tha's what they all say. Well, I can' stay 'ere chattin' wi' you, sane man. I got me loonies to attend ter." He turned away.

Mitford's eyes were malevolent as he stared after him. He'd like to come across him in the streets just once. He'd cut out his heart! Shrugging, he dismissed the man. Jack Jennings, the keeper that looked after the red-headed loonie, would be coming by soon. He liked Jennings. Jennings was brutal, but not as brutal as some. He'd treated him decently enough. He had even, when it became known that his aunt was working for his release, allowed him to come along and watch, while he worked over the red-headed loonie. Mitford's eyes smouldered as he remembered her reaction when he bent over her. He'd just wanted to give her a kiss. Jennings had said that he could. But she had lifted her chained hands and torn at his face. He would like to come across her on the outside too. He would rape the bitch. And then he would show her what it meant to treat him the way she had. Perhaps Jennings would allow him to see her for the last time.

Chained and helpless, Sarah Barry crouched against the wall of her dark, airless cell. Jennings, the keeper, would be coming soon. Jennings, grossly fat, red-faced, always smelling of a combination of sweat, ale, and vomit. Perhaps he would have the scarred man with him. Sarah shivered. There was something about the scarred man that was evil. Jennings was brutal, but with a senseless brutality. He was not pure evil, as she sensed that the scarred man was. She looked down at the manacles that weighed down her wrists and her ankles. How long had she crouched here like an animal, an iron bar wedged between her legs, and held there by a chain wound first about her body, and then drawn up tightly about her neck. How long? Weeks? Months? Years? The chains had bitten deeply into her flesh, forming great open sores. Insane, they called her. But she knew well that she was not insane. If only she could remember her name, the last piece would fall into place. She had heard it said that mad people were unable to face the truth about themselves, but she knew beyond any doubt that she was sane.

Her head drooped as she remembered the terrible beating that Fuller had inflicted upon her. To her dying day, she would always bear the scars. But nothing—not the beating, not the branding—could compare with the nightmare of finding herself in Bedlam Asylum. She had regained consciousness just as the prison cart had passed through the gates of Bedlam Asylum. Tormented with pain, her body bound with stout leather straps, she had not realized what was happening to her. And so the grim building had swallowed her up. She had thought of Newgate Prison as hell, but Bedlam! Compared to Bedlam, Newgate Prison was a paradise! Weighted down with chains, she had been shut into fetid darkness with fourteen other women. The cell was cramped and the atmosphere stifling. She was in agony, her mouth gaping as she fought to draw in air. The filthy straw beneath her had obviously been in use for a long time, for it was soaked in urine. The stench coming from it was so overpowering that she had vomited. Her ears flinched from the incredible din all about her. The demented howling, the unintelligible gabbling. Hands groped over her person. Long jagged nails stabbed viciously at her face, her throat, her breasts. Crying aloud, she did her best to fight back. But her efforts were useless, she was too weak. Then, as suddenly as they had begun the onslaught, the women seemed to forget her. For a long time she had lain there, more dead than alive. She would never be able to forget those sudden bursts of insane laughter, the stench of foul breath and unwashed bodies. All the incredible horror that was Bedlam Asylum! There had been times when she had wished that she were really mad, anything that would help her to bear it. Other times, when her brain reeled, and she wondered if reason might be deserting her. How long she stayed with those women, how she had managed to survive, to ignore her reeling brain, to keep sane, she had no idea. Then, one day, Jennings came for her. Without explanation, he had brought her to this small cell, where she had been ever since. Sometimes she found herself talking aloud, anything to keep at bay the darkness, the loneliness, the feeling of suffocation. With an iron will that she had not known she possessed, she would clamp her lips shut against the foolishly babbling words. But how much longer could she hang on to sanity? she would ask herself. How long before she became like all the others?

Sarah turned her head and looked toward the door. Soon Jennings would be coming, she thought, shuddering. He would ask her the question, the same one he asked every time he came. "What's your name?"

Her name? It was the one thing she could not remember. And Jennings, she knew, did not really want her to remember. It gave him just one more excuse, among many, to beat her.

The door opened suddenly, letting in a stream of bright light. Jennings entered, his whip, as usual, beneath his arm. With him, was the scarred man.

Jennings strode over to her. The question that she had been dreading came. "What's your name?" he demanded.

Wearily, she shook her head. "I do not know. I cannot remember."

"You goin' ter flog 'er?" the scarred man said eagerly. "Can I watch? May'ap you'll let me 'andle the whip? I'll tickle 'er up good for you."

Jennings frowned. "Nay," he said regretfully, "I ain't got no time ter flog 'er. There's been new orders give me. She's ter go into one o' the cages."

Mitford gave a high-pitched burst of laughter. "I done me time in one o' them cages. Serve 'er right. Le's see 'ow she likes bein' on show."

Sarah's heart lurched in panic. The cages? What were they talking about? What did it mean? A cage? She wasn't an animal!

Dimly, Sarah could hear the scarred man growling in disappointment. "She ought ter be flogged first," he was saying. "I was flogged afore they took me out ter the cage. Ain't right that she shouldn't be flogged."

Ignoring him, Jennings bent over her. She stared at him with disbelief as he unlocked her manacles and removed the iron bar from between her legs. Why? Where was he taking her? She longed to ask him, but she did not dare. Jennings was obviously drunk. His breath reeked of the alcohol he had consumed, his face was red and congested, and his hands fumbling and uncertain. One word from her, and he might forget that he had been given new orders. With the scarred man urging him on, perhaps, after all, he would flog her.

Jennings pulled a crumpled yellow garment from his pocket, "Get that smock on," he ordered, flinging it at her.

The garment was sleeveless and thin. It was filthy and it smelled bad.

"Tha's right," Jennings said, as she managed to struggle into it. "Now we got yer covered up all nice and respec'able for yer audience."

Mitford moved closer. "I don' like 'er covered up. I likes 'er naked."

Again Jennings ignored him. Mumbling beneath his breath, he pulled Sarah to her feet, then, abruptly, released her. She fell back against the wall. The dark hovel, sharply divided by the bar of sunshine that had penetrated the half-opened door, swung round her. Jennings's hands were upon her again, pushing her toward the door. She could not do it! Surely he did not expect her to walk without support? She had been forced to crouch for so long in one position that her limbs felt wooden, useless, as though they did not belong to her. Evidently Jennings did expect her to walk. Propelled by his hard hand, she stumbled forward, and then fell heavily to her knees.

"'Ere, wench," a thick voice said, "le' me 'elp you up."

Sarah looked up into the face of the scarred man, and again she was conscious of the evil that seemed to emanate from him. Her voice, rusty with disuse, acquired strength as she cried out, "Please do not touch me! Never touch me!"

Mitford's face contorted with rage. "Bitch!" he snarled, raising a clenched fist. "If I could 'ave you alone for a while, I'd make you sorry for that!"

"You shut up, Mitford!" Jennings's slurred voice sounded in Sarah's ears like a reprieve. "If you wan' ter go 'ome today, you'd bes' keep your 'ands ter yourself."

Mitford's face changed. "I wasn't goin' ter do nothin'," he mumbled.

"Then whyn't you go an' wait where you're supposed ter wait? If yer ain't ready when that ol' girl comes for yer, they'll likely 'ave an excuse ter keep yer 'ere. Ow'd yer like that, eh?"

Mitford seemed to be cowed by this threat. Watching him as he scuttled over to the door, Sarah knew that he was by no means cowed. He was evil, dangerous, and mad.

She forgot the scarred man as Jennings's foot prodded painfully into her side. "Get up!" he ordered.

Clawing at the wall, she managed to rise. Unaided, she took

one step forward, then another. The numbed feeling in her legs was giving way to an almost unbearable burning, throbbing, prickling pain as the blood began to flow unhampered. But she could endure this pain. Her legs were coming to life, and despite the agony, it was so good to be using them again. Forgetting everything but the joy of movement, she gained the door. She heard Jennings coming up behind her, then his hand was on her back, pushing her out into the blinding brightness of the day.

With a choked cry, she went sprawling once more. The light! It was too strong. It was blinding her! Jennings's face, bending over her, looked blurred, unreal. He pulled her to her feet again. "Walk!" his voice rasped in her ear. "Get over there."

Where? She could barely see! She had been in the darkness too long. Sounds rushed in upon her. The movements of many people, the rustle of gowns, voices, laughter. Sane voices. The laughter easy, not like those bursts of crazed laughter that had so terrified her. Too many people, too much life thrusting at her. "Where are you taking me?" she said in a trembling voice. She strained her eyes; through a gradually clearing mist, she saw people passing to and fro. Terrified, she turned to Jennings. "All those people, who are they?"

Jennings laughed. "Why, them's yer audience, sweetheart. Them's the public. They likes ter come an' watch the loonies perform."

She shrank back. "Perform?"

"Aye, sweetheart. I'm goin' ter put yer in a nice little cage 'o yer own. The public pays money ter come an' gape at yer, so watch out that yer performs good for 'em."

She tried to hang back. Jennings, losing patience, hustled her forward. Suddenly she was standing before the cage. It loomed large and terrifying before her eyes, its bars made of thick wood.

"No! No!" She fought him with all the strength she possessed. She had forgotten the watching people; she had forgotten everything but the horror and the indignity of being caged up like an animal. An animal that must perform for an audience.

Jennings swore as her nails raked his hand. "Get in there, you mad bitch!" he roared.

She felt herself lifted, thrown forward. The cage began to swing as Jennings slammed the door shut behind her. She crouched there on her hands and knees, her falling hair hiding her face. A violent shudder went through her. The wooden floor of the cage was stained and littered with food. Lumps of mouldy bread, pieces of rotting meat, around which the flies swarmed greedily. Squashed fruits, a half-eaten meat pasty, and various other scraps all mingled together in a revolting mess. The sun was bright and strong. She could smell her unwashed body, the decaying food, sweating humanity, all mingling together in a nauseating wave. She stared at her hands. They were filthy, the nails long and yellow and broken. They looked like claws! she thought in horror. She put up one hand to examine a lock of her hair. It was a dingy brown. She pushed her hair away from her face and rose slowly to her feet, looking for the first time at her audience. The gowns of the women were a bright blur of color. The men's clothing seemed equally bright. The faces surrounding the cage expressed various emotions. Some looked at her with shock, others with horror, and some with amusement. Only here and there was she able to detect pity. With these few exceptions, they were all enjoying the spectacle.

"I can smell her from here!" a child's shrill voice said.

Dully, Sarah listened. Another voice said in horror. "She's got lice in her hair! See there? Can't you see them crawling?"

"Look at her flashing eyes, the poor mad soul!"

"Gi' 'er a piece o' bread. Go on, make 'er jump for it."

Sarah watched them, her eyes bitter with anger. It would seem that to these people insanity was something to be laughed at. It was not something to be pitied. If you were mad, you were beaten and abused. Perhaps they hoped that in this way the devils would be beaten from the mad one. An impulse came to her to cry out to them. She wanted to explain that she did not belong in this place.

She jumped as a small boy poked a stick through the bars and jabbed at her leg. "Dance, loonie, dance!"

She screamed as more sticks poked through the bars. They stabbed at her legs, her arms, her stomach. One man with a longer stick than the others, aimed for her face. She grabbed for the stick, trying to snap it. Cursing, the man drew it back. He examined the end of the stick, and then poked it back through the bars.

"Stop it! In the name of God, stop it!" She flung herself against the bars. She was crying out to them for mercy.

The sound of her voice seemed to momentarily startle the people, for they drew back staring at her. One small girl, her round blue eyes fixed on the thin, wild-haired figure in the cage, said in a wondering voice, "I never knew that loonies could talk." The child turned to the woman standing beside her. "I don't like that loonie. Her face is dirty."

General laughter greeted this statement. Then somebody threw a piece of rotten fruit into the cage. A group of boys, fired by this example, began to scoop up handfuls of horse droppings. They flung the mess at the cage, spattering her with filth. Beaten, Sarah clung to the bars, her fingers whitening with the pressure. "Go away!" she cried in a breaking voice. "Please go away and leave me in peace!"

There was a sudden bustle of movement. A hoarse, authoritative voice said loudly, "You heard the lady. Throw away the stick, lad."

"Lady? What yer talkin' about?" a defiant voice answered.

"She's a loonie. Anyway, yer bleedin' swell, who's goin' ter make me throw this stick away?"

"Don't be dim-witted, lad. I am, of course. Joshua T. Sanders, at your service. I assure you that, if you do not drop that stick, I will labor that plaguey skinny behind of yours until you howl for mercy. Do you hear me, young sir, eh? Eh?"

"Can' 'elp 'earin yer, can I, what wi' the way you're abellerin' in me ear." The defiance gave way to indignation. "Ma, we was 'ere first. These 'ere three swells 'as only jus' come. Are yer goin' ter let that fat un' tell me what ter do?"

A woman's voice said in sharp reproof, "Tha's enough o' that, Billy! You 'ave a little respec' for the gen'leman. The gen'leman's a doctor. Can' yer see 'is white staff?'

"I don' care 'bout no bleedin' doctor!"

"Come along do!" Now there was a touch of anxiety in the woman's voice. "Yer gon an' made the gen'leman angry. We'll go along ter see one o' the other loonies, sir."

"A wise decision, madam," the hoarse voice said severely. "If that lad should be tempted to linger even for another moment, I will inflict such mayhem upon his unsavory person as would stagger the stoutest imagination."

" 'E's leavin', sir."

"A further warning, madam. If I should catch him tormenting another helpless creature, the results to himself will be as aforesaid. Do we understand each other, eh? Eh?"

"Aye, sir. Aye, we understands."

"Fat buttocks!" the boy shouted in a derisive voice as he was dragged away.

"Shut up, Billy."

"Ol' jelly buttocks!"

There was the sound of a scuffle, a slap, and the boy, roaring his pain at the top of his voice, was finally led away.

"An admirable woman," Sarah heard the hoarse voice say.

"A slap round the ear is precisely what I would have recommended." The voice changed. 'What the devil are you about, Peter? You silly young cub, are you going off into a swoon? Watch the lad, Jason!"

"By Gad!" a weak, trembling voice answered. "Indeed I cannot bear to look upon this poor creature! The stench of her is abominable! Never before have I seen a human creature caged, though for that matter, she scarcely looks human. I vow that my stomach is in a quake of revulsion!" The words were followed by a choking sound.

"Bah, you dainty-stomached ninny! These cages and their occupants are but a minor sight to what is in store for you. Bedlam Asylum has sights far more gruesome than this to offer, I assure you."

"I pray you to assure me of nothing further. If you have no objection, I will wait in the carriage."

"You will stay here. 'Twill do you good to see the sufferings of others. Mayhap it will cause you to value your own blessings."

"Yes, but I say, old lad, there are limits beyond which I cannot go."

"Nonsense! You will do as I say."

"Oh, very well. On your own head be it."

Sarah opened her eyes at a further stirring in the crowd. It was as if the presence of the newcomers had restricted them, made them uncomfortable, for the people, with backlong looks, were rapidly dispersing, leaving the three men in possession of the space before the cage. One, a short, stout man, with a preposterously long white wig, on top of which was balanced a tricorn hat, beamed at Sarah. "I have cleared them off for the time being, lass," he said, his gray eyes twinkling at her. "I cannot guarantee that they will stay away, but at least you will have a few moments peace."

There was a lump in Sarah's throat. She wanted to thank

him for his kindness, but she could not speak. Instead, she nodded at him and smiled.

The stout man turned to the tall, elegant man standing beside him. "You see, Jason, the lass understands me."

"It would appear so." The drawling voice that answered him sounded forced, as though his throat pained him.

Sarah stiffened. She knew that voice! It sometimes sounded clearly through her haunted dreams. Her eyes fastened upon his face. The Duke! He looked ill, for he was white to the lips, and the hand that held the swagger stick was trembling, but for all that, he had not changed. But she had, she had! There he stood, tall and arrogant, the man who was the cause of all her misery. He had brought her to this!

"I say, Jason," the third man said nervously, "it might be wise to step back a pace or two. I cannot say that I care for the way the creature is looking at you. By Gad! Look at her eyes. They are positively blazing!"

"Do not call her a creature, you cursed coxcomb!" the doctor snapped.

"Coxcomb? Well, upon my word, if that isn't the dashed limit! You are used to these sights, doctor, since you have visited Bedlam upon a great many occasions. But for myself and for Jason, I would have you know, this is a dashed shattering experience."

"Aye, I can see it has affected Jason, but unlike yourself, you ninny, he keeps his thoughts to himself. He does not blabber and dither as you are doing, sir."

"Jason is stoic, but I myself am of a sensitive nature."

The doctor snorted. "Lily-livered is the way I would put it. How can we stop these evils, if we ain't got the guts to stand up and face things as they really are? Tell me that, young Peter."

With a haunted look in his eyes, Peter nodded toward the cage. "Look here, kindness and charity of thought are very well, but you will admit that she looks as though she might go for the throat at any moment." He laid a trembling hand on Jason's sleeve. "What are your thoughts on the matter, old lad?"

"It is unbelievable!" Jason spoke like one slowly awakening from a nightmare. "I never would have believed such cruelty to be possible!"

"Yes, but look here, that is not exactly the point. The point I am trying to make, dear old lad, is—"

"Be quiet!" Jason snapped.

"Eh? Oh, very well, if you say so."

Sarah's thoughts were racing wildly. Witherley! My lord Witherley! He was staring at her, those vivid blue eyes of his slightly narrowed. He did not like what he was seeing. It made him uneasy. She made him uneasy. It was as if that intent stare sought to penetrate through the filth to the woman below. What was he thinking? It was obvious that he did not recognize her. Indeed, how could he, so terribly was she changed. Nay, he did not recognize Sarah Barry, whom he had condemned to hell. Sarah Barry? She gasped aloud, her hand flying to her mouth. Of course, that was her name. How easily it had come to the surface of her mind, as though it had only been lying in wait for something to release it. She was complete now. The last piece of the puzzle had fallen into place. Sarah Barry! Sarah Barry!

The timid, stylish dressed man blinked his brown eyes nervously. "I say," he said apprehensively, "should we not be on our way? I am persuaded that there is something about our appearance that is causing this poor unfortunate wench to undergo great excitement. I would not like to be the cause of —er—of bringing on an irritation of the brain."

The stout little doctor gave vent to a contemptuous snort. "An irritation of the brain! Bah! One more word out of you, Peter, and I vow that my fist will bring on an irritation of your plaguey nose! Bring on an irritation of the brain! Never heard such poppycock and balderdash in my life, damned if I have!" The doctor turned to Jason. "We had best be on our way, lad, before Peter succumbs to an attack of the vapors. Jason! Did you hear me? Why in the plague are you staring at the lass like that, eh? Eh?"

"It is very strange, but for one moment, I thought—" My lord Witherley broke off, his face flushing. "No, that is quite absurd, of course!" He hesitated. Then, without another word, he turned abruptly and strode away.

The little doctor stared. "Jason!" He hastened after the tall figure, with the timid man bringing up the rear. "You thought what?" the doctor's loud voice drifted back to Sarah. "Plague take it, man, will you slow down! You thought what?"

"I could not explain without telling you of something that has haunted me for quite some time," Lord Witherley's cool voice said. 'My thoughts at that moment, as I have said, were quite absurd. Let us speak no more on the subject. It is of no real importance."

Sarah's hands gripped the bars. Had my lord Witherley been startled by some fleeting resemblance to Sarah Barry? No. For that would mean that she was of some importance to my lord Witherley, and she could never be that. She was not the one who haunted him. But for all that there had been something about her that had made him uneasy. If only she could gain her release from this vile place! If only! It might be then that she would have her chance at revenge. She frowned. But she was a fool! Why did she try to delude herself? Even if she were free, what could she hope to do about it? How could any action of hers touch the great Lord Witherley?

She looked about her. The sun had gone behind a cloud. The sky was showing faint orange streamers. Soon the sun would set, and darkness would fall. Perhaps that was why the area was all but deserted. The people who had tormented her would no doubt soon be making their way to their homes. She began to wonder at the thoughts of the other poor wretches who were forced to exhibit themselves in the cages. What did they think about? Did they suffer the same anguish that she had suffered? Or, if they were truly insane, were they dead to all feeling? Somehow she did not think so. They lived and breathed; they felt pain. Surely the sane and reasoning people they had once been must cry out in silent terror and rebellion?

A sighing sound from the cage opposite to her caught at Sarah's attention. She pressed her face against the bars and stared at the woman crouched in the cage. She was painfully thin, so thin that the yellow asylum smock she wore hung in baggy folds. On her feet were black woolen slippers. Sarah looked down at her own feet. Her slippers were brown. Sarah's lips twisted bitterly. The slippers were the only things the lunatics were allowed to retain. With a sudden flash of ironical humor, she wondered if the Bedlam Asylum authorities, having stripped them of clothes, beaten and abused them in every imaginable way, actually worried that their feet might get cold. She looked at the woman again. Her black hair was wild, but the small, pinched face between the bush of neglected hair looked mournful rather than ferocious.

The woman looked up suddenly, and, for a moment, her eyes met Sarah's. She looked away again, then, startlingly, she began to sing in a small, sad voice—

"Where were you when I was young
Why did you never meet me?
When that great song of youth was sung
Why weren't you there to greet me?

Why didn't we meet in years gone by
Why were my arms without you?

I look for you along life's path
Becalmed in sorrow's aftermath
I'll find you, dear, some day, but how?
Where were you then? Where are you now?"

Tears pricked at Sarah's eyes. The little song, the voice singing it was unbearably poignant. What did the song mean to the woman? Had a love affair gone wrong? Was that why she was here, locked like an animal in a cage, still mourning for her lost lover?

Sarah turned her head away, forcing herself to think of other things. There was too much sorrow in this place. Too much tragedy. She stared unseeingly at the blue cloak lying across a wooden bench. Then, as the soft color caught her attention, her eyes changed to wistfulness. It was such a lovely blue, and it looked so soft and warm. She would like to wear pretty clothes once more; she would like to feel human again. In a gesture of frustration and despair, she flung out her arms. Her hand thrust at the door, and it swung slowly open.

Sarah stared at the open door, her heart racing so fast that she felt nauseated. If only she could go through that door to freedom. How wonderful to find herself on the streets again. Free! It was the most wonderful word in the English language. Jennings, so fuddled with drink, had forgotten to lock the door. Would he suddenly remember and come hastening back? But surely, she reasoned, had he remembered, he would have been back long since. Doubtless he was snoring somewhere, sunk deep in sodden, drunken sleep. Her eyes gleamed as an idea took shape. The door was open, and someone had been careless enough to leave a cloak lying across the bench. Why shouldn't she go through that door? A swift look around told her that the time could not be more perfect. There was no one in sight. Only the occupants of the cages would observe her actions, and most of them appeared to be sleeping. The woman in the opposite cage was still singing her song, lost in a world of her own. Her eyes returned to the cloak. Do it now! she urged herself. You will never have a better chance. If you hesitate, you are lost. Her legs felt much stronger. Would they bear her weight? She would make them work for her. She would will them to work!

There was nothing weak about the sudden leap she made for the door. Her feet, in the thin woolen slippers, stung when they hit the ground, but she scarcely noticed. Her attention was on the cloak lying across the bench. The short distance she had to travel seemed like miles. Then she was standing by the bench, and the cloak, the lovely soft cloak with its enveloping hood was in her hands. God bless the carelessness of an unknown woman!

Her escape was meant to be, she thought. For no sooner had she draped the cloak about her and pulled the hood well forward to hide her hair than she heard the sound of voices. She knew a moment of panic. Would the people notice the empty cage? If they did, would they make anything of it, or would they assume that the keeper had taken the lunatic away?

From the shadow of the hood, she stared at the advancing people. A stout woman, a market basket over her arm, was loudly scolding two lagging, crying children. "No good thinking to get around me with that crying. We're going home, and that's that."

"But we've not seen all the loonies. Why can't we stay?"

"Because I say so. Now come along."

"Jim and me wanted to feed 'em. Let's go and feed 'em, Ma."

"Nay, they get fed plenty. It's our taxes that go to feed those loonies."

"What's taxes, Ma?"

"Never mind. Now stop that whining, and hasten."

Sarah's gaze went past the woman and became fixed. Following was the peppery-tempered little doctor who had defended her. With him was my lord Witherley. Between them they were half carrying the drooping form of the timid man.

"Never saw such a pother in all my born days!" the doctor was saying testily. "The very idea, swooning away like some confounded delicate lass!"

"You must not be so hard on Peter, Joshua," my lord Witherley said in a mild voice. "There were a few moments, you know, when I felt like swooning myself."

"Bah! Fiddlesticks! The plaguey fellow don't eat enough good red meat, that's his trouble. We ain't seen the half of what I wanted you to see."

"I am content to wait, Joshua."

"Aye, and so is everybody else. That's why nothing ever gets done to aid these poor wretches!"

Sarah's heart had begun to race in that sickening manner again as she fell in behind the three men. She clenched her teeth hard against the threatening nausea. It seemed right that she should walk to freedom behind my lord Witherley, who had in the first place condemned her. Oh, God, let nothing go wrong. Let me be free! She was surprised to find herself praying to God, who, in her bitterness and misery, she had denied for so long. Would He listen to her? Or was He too angry because, in the face of adversity, she had lost faith? Do not be angry, her heart cried. Help me! Please, help me! Her mouth was dry with fear, her hair beneath the hood clung damply, and she was intensely conscious of the odor of her unwashed body. Would the asylum odor betray her? Faint hope stirred. Perhaps, if she kept her head lowered and her hands hidden, it might be thought that she was one of my lord Witherley's party. Why not? The cloak was of good quality such as a lady might wear. Her lips moving in silent prayer, she moved a little closer to the three men, closing slightly the gap between them. As they came nearer to the gates, she would move closer still. And she would pray. She would keep on praying until she walked in freedom. But, if she should be discovered, she would find some way to kill herself. She could not go back; she could not! She almost choked on the hysteria that rose at the very thought. Please, God, please! I will never doubt You again, never, never again! The words sang through her head as she walked on. Repeating themselves until they became a mere senseless jumble.

A moan came from the drooping Peter. "By Gad!" he exclaimed. "Oh, by Gad! What a frightful nightmare!"

"Ah!" the doctor said. "So you're coming out of it, are you, you poltroon?"

"No, no!" Peter protested feebly. "Assure you, my good doctor, when that great hulking fellow came toward me with his eyes simply staring out of his head, and those great corded hands of his twitching, I was quite sure that I was about to be done to death. By Gad, I've never felt such terror in my life."

"Nonsense! All in your imagination."

"You are not in a position to say that," Peter said indignantly. "You know well that you and Jason had walked on, leaving me alone to face horror and violence."

"There were keepers there, Peter," Jason said. "Had the fellow attacked you, he would have been speedily restrained."

"He would, eh? Perhaps, my good fellow, you failed to notice that the keeper in charge was so roaring drunk that he had fallen from his stool. And that, at the moment the fellow started toward me, the keeper's snores would have drowned out the trumpeting of a bally elephant, let alone my cries for help."

"Balderdash!" the doctor said.

Peter ignored the interruption. "A moment ago you called me a poltroon, but I thought I showed a great deal of spirit and courage. I tried reasoning with the fellow, you know, although I was positively wilting beneath the glare in his eyes. I said to him, 'Look here, my dear old lad, can we not talk this thing over? I mean to say, only paying a visit, you know. Wouldn't harm you, old lad, not for the world.' "

Stifled laughter came from Jason. "And what did he say?"

"But that's just the point, dear lad. He said nothing. His face twisted in a most frightful grimace. That was when I fell over the keeper's stool. The mad fellow was on me in a trice, just like a hound who had cornered the fox. That was when I heard you coming back. Surely, under the circumstances, you cannot blame me for losing consciousness. I mean to say, what would you have done?"

"I would have acted like a man, that is what I would have done," the doctor growled.

"All very well for you to talk, my good leech, but you were not staring death in the face."

"Don't you call me a leech, you puppy!"

"Do you hear him, Jason?" Peter said with a great deal of warmth. 'If you ask me, the dashed fellow is too unreasonable for words. Calls me all the names he can lay his tongue to, and then objects when I call him a leech. What do you make of him?"

"My heart bleeds for you, Peter. But as for the irascible doctor, I have long since given up trying to make anything of him. He is himself. One of a kind. You must take him or leave him."

Peter sniffed. "If it is all the same to you, old fellow, I would much rather leave him. Today's doings have convinced me that the fellow is a rank outsider."

The doctor looked at him with a wrathful face. "Outsider, am I? You'll regret that remark! If you have anything further to say, you milksop, you will say it directly to me. Understand, eh?"

Sarah huddled in her cloak, her breathing ragged as the

gates came in sight. "Please!" she begged silently. "Please!"

My lord Witherley was pausing at the gate. In his cool, autocratic manner, he addressed a remark to the man standing there.

"Yes, my lord," the man answered, "it has been a fine day." He stood aside, an unctuous smile on his face. "I recognized you at once, my lord. 'Tis an honor to have you visit us."

My lord Witherley nodded an acknowledgment. "Good day to you," he said.

This was the moment, Sarah thought, the moment when she would win all or lose all. Oh, hurry, hurry! Perhaps it has already been discovered that I am missing. At any moment someone might raise an alarm. For God's sake, hurry! Holding her breath, she moved forward. Then she was through! She could hear the man at the gate nonchalantly chattering with someone behind her. There was a pain in her chest from holding her breath so long, but she was through! Thank you, God, thank you!

Light-headed, her mouth half open to gulp in air that, even if tainted, was free air, and not quite knowing which direction to take, Sarah automatically followed after the three men. Her steps slowed as she saw my lord Witherley pause before a carriage. Then, as she saw the doctor and the timid man climb into the carriage, she hurried on, her only wish to pass them and to put as much distance between herself and Bedlam Asylum as possible. It was as she was passing my lord Witherley, who was about to enter the carriage, that a small, sharp stone pierced through the thin wool of her slipper. She gasped, stumbling slightly.

She felt a hand grasp her shoulder, and my lord Witherley's voice said softly, "Are you all right, madam? May I be of some assistance?"

He knew! Those all-seeing eyes of his had penetrated her disguise. He had trapped her again! What could she do? Rage swept over her as his fingers tightened very slightly on her shoulder. No! It must not happen again! With a hoarse cry, she tore herself free and fled down the cobbled street. Gasping, stumbling, keeping her feet by a miracle, she forced herself on. She did not dare to look over her shoulder, but in her imagination she heard the thud of pursuing feet.

My lord Witherley stood looking after the flying figure, his tawny brows drawn together in a frown of perplexity. He saw the small, cloaked figure disappear round a corner, and, shrugging, he entered the carriage.

"What was all that pother about?" the doctor demanded.

"I have not the slightest idea, Joshua. Women have reacted in many ways to my touch, but never before, I believe, have I struck terror in their hearts." He gave the coachman the signal to drive on, then leaned back in his seat and folded his arms. "Could it be, Joshua," he said, smiling faintly, "that I am losing my touch with the fair sex?"

"It would be a damned good thing if you were," the doctor grunted. "Never saw so many females hanging on to one fellow's coattails. And you enjoying their bodies, you bloody rogue, with never a bit of love, or even affection to offer the poor hopeful creatures."

"That is not quite true," my lord Witherley demurred. "I have a mild affection for some. But I do trust, Joshua, that you are not about to bore my ears by prating of love. If you imagine that I will ever find myself weakened with love for some simpering female, you had best think again. Love, in my opinion, is something fabricated by the poets and the ballad singers."

"Indeed. What then of your father and mother? Were they not in love? And is not your poor mother broken-hearted because of your father's untimely death?"

"The emotion that existed between my parents was, I will admit, something of a miracle. I do not expect, in my case, to experience its like." My lord Witherley closed his eyes, signaling an end to the conversation.

The doctor snorted. "Damned cynical dog!" Receiving no reply to this provocative remark, he snorted again, glared at the wilting Peter, and closed his own eyes.

Chapter Five

It was midnight, and still the oppressive heat of the June day lingered on. The heat was like a great smothering blanket, pressing down, making it difficult to breathe. Some people, hoping to catch a vagrant breeze, sat on the steps outside their homes. Others, who had taken to their beds, tossed and turned restlessly, mumbling, moaning, as they sought to find a cool patch on rumpled sheets.

Those beggars who, at nights, made Lilacgrove Street their headquarters, were drained by the activity of their day. Some of them who had stumps for limbs, or others who had open sores, skillfully kept open and festering by the application of a special powder, had now no ambition to show themselves or their afflictions to the chance passer-by. To do this, they would have to hold a torch above themselves, and the thought of the heat that would come from the flaring torch was not to be borne on a night like this. Grumbling, the beggars huddled down, some curling up in shop doorways, or stretching out beneath deserted market stalls, hoping to catch a few moments sleep. Those that were wakeful were rendered uneasy by a vague fear. The heat had come so suddenly, and, even for the month of June, such a wave of heat was unusual. It was feared that it might be plague weather.

A full moon rode high in the star-pricked sky and lent a mockingly cool illusion of beauty to Lilacgrove Street. Its rays silvered the overflowing gutter that ran the length of the street, lit up the quick furtive darts of rats who were busily scavenging among the filth and refuse, and played on two skinny cats who, with arched backs and angrily lashing tails, had begun a noisy spitting dispute over the ownership of a large fish head. But in Lilacgrove Alley, where the tall, shabby houses of lath and plaster and rotting timbers leaned crazily toward each other, the light of the moon could not penetrate.

To Sarah Barry, rapidly sidling along the alley, her fingers touching the sweating plaster of the houses to aid her on her way, the darkness was a friend. She welcomed the obscurity it gave her. Certainly the darkness held no fears for her, for she had lived in it for too long. She felt a fleeting regret for the woolen slippers that she had lost at some time on her flight. Beneath her bare feet she could feel the roughness of the cobbles, slimed, as usual, from the emptying of innumerable chamberpots, the contents of which were daily thrown from the windows by lazy and industrious housewives alike.

Sighing, Sarah sank down in a doorway. Strange, she thought, that she had not noticed the intensity of the heat when she had been put into the cage. But perhaps it was her terror, her rage, and her grief that had blocked out all other feeling. Frowning, she tried to calculate. It had been September when Fuller, carrying out the sentence imposed by the court, had had her branded and flogged. And presumably it had still been September when she was transported from Newgate Prison to Bedlam Asylum. The scorching heat would indicate that it was now high summer. But what was the month? And how much of her life had been lost in Bedlam Asylum? She turned her head, listening to a silence that was so intense that it hummed in her ears. But now her strained attention could make out small sounds. The squeaking of a bed frame, a sigh, a low mumble, and the ever-present rustling of the rats. Then suddenly, causing her to start, there came from an open window the shrill ranting of a woman. "Go get your own bleedin' bottle," the woman cried. "I'm your wife, not your slave, you scabby swine!"

An enraged male voice answered her. "You shut your row. One more word an' I'll kick your fat backside down them stairs!"

"You ain't man enough ter kick me nowhere. I'm sick o' you, you guzzling swine! Bleedin' good and sick o' you!"

Adding to the noisy quarrel, there came the fretful crying of a disturbed child, and, from the cats, who had momentarily subsided, a renewed battle of wills.

Sarah's slumbering terror awoke in full force. She no longer felt safe in the dark doorway. She tried to rise, but an overwhelming weariness of mind and body washed over her and she sank back again. After all, any hiding place was dangerous for a fugitive. Wherever she might go, discovery was probably imminent. She began to tremble, her frail body shaking with the force of her fear as she recalled that terrible moment when, suddenly, shocking in its unexpectedness, she had come face to face with the scarred man. She had been walking slowly along Bravington Avenue, hoping that her sedate method of progress would render her inconspicuous and, perhaps, if her appearance seemed strange, avert suspicion, and then, suddenly, the scarred man had been standing in front of her. He had been accompanied by several men, who, if they did not in their appearance terrify her so much, appeared to be fully as brutal. When the scarred man had blocked her progress, and she had looked up into his twisted face, she had thought that she was back in her nightmare. If it were not a nightmare she was experiencing, then how could he be there?

Mitford was only too real, she found, when he grabbed for her and thrust his face close to hers. When he spoke, it was with a trace of bewilderment, but the bewilderment was quickly succeeded by a note of savage triumph. "So I got you 'ave I?" he growled. "You're goin' ter pay, me fine lady, for insultin' William Mitford!"

She screamed aloud, kicking at him, when his fingers fastened brutally on her shoulders. In her despair, she had even thought of appealing to the people passing by. But she had realized the hopelessness of such an appeal. The people that resided in this particular district were, she knew, inured to scenes of violence and brutality. They were but part of everyday life. Doubtless, if they interfered, they knew that it would go hard with them.

It was when Mitford had turned to address a remark to his companions that her chance at escape had come. Unconsciously, whilst he was speaking, his grip upon her shoulders had loosened. For a second she had stared at him. His twisted face, illumined by the light of the flaring torches carried by the other men, had seemed to her unbearably hideous. Then she had torn herself free. She pushed at him, sending him stumbling into the other men. She flew down Bravington Avenue at a speed that taxed her small store of strength to the utmost. Round the corner into Jannix Street, her heart thudding, her lungs laboring. She left Jannix Street behind her. As she ran on, her cloak billowed out from her shoulders and exposed the yellow asylum smock. But she was past caring about her appearance. Her one thought was to get away from the man who seemed to her to be not only mad, but evil. She was across the wide King's Way now, and turning into Alterbury Cross. It was in one of the turnings that led off Alterbury Cross that she had finally managed to shake off their thudding pursuit. But whatever else the scarred man might be, she had the feeling that he was both cunning and clever. He would find her. Very soon those flaring torches would light up her hiding place. What could she do? She was not clever enough to outwit him, and she was too exhausted to run any more. But what did the man want with her? What harm had she ever done to him? If he caught her, would he take her back to Bedlam Asylum? Yes, yes, that must be it! He would take her back, and she would be forced into the cage again. Chance came only once to the driven and the desperate. She would never be allowed to escape again, for she would be watched too closely. It must not be! She would die if she were taken back!

Tears welled into her eyes and fell down her sunken cheeks. Better by far to die than to spend her life helplessly caged. "Oh, God," she prayed fervently and silently, "before I am recaptured, let me die! Why must I be caged up like a wild beast, why must I be hunted? I am sane, You know it. And what have I ever done that is so evil that, as a punishment, I must be thrust into hell?"

Something moved near her foot. She jumped violently and put a hand across her mouth to stifle her involuntary cry. What had moved? Was it a rat? she thought, shuddering. Perspiration started out on her forehead, beaded there, and then ran down her face, stinging in her eyes. The weakness of her body seemed to intensify and, panting, she leaned back against the front door of the house. Slight though she was, the door creaked loudly. Be careful, be careful! The words scampered like frightened mice through her brain. Had the creaking door given her away? Would someone shortly emerge from the house and demand to know what she was doing here?

Closing her eyes, Sarah listened intently. Beyond the usual night sounds, she could hear nothing. The man and the woman had ceased their quarreling. The child was quiet, and the cats had apparently moved on. With the closing of her eyes, a certain peace came to her. She was so tired, so very tired! Her body slumped lower. As a deep sleep claimed her, her head fell heavily sideways.

Chapter Six

William Mitford halted at the head of Lilacgrove Alley. In the light of the torch he carried, he stared at his companion. It had been a long day, Mitford thought. He was tired, and he would like to roll into his bed and sleep. But he knew that he would not sleep, there were too many things on his mind. Bob Reid had elected to stay with him after the others had gone on their way, and he found himself wanting to tell Bob about his experiences in Bedlam Asylum. And then, too, if he was to resume his place as the leader of The Scavengers, there were many plans to talk over. He rubbed his forehead, trying to smooth away the throbbing ache that was constantly with him. The ache in his head was worse than usual, for the sight of the red-headed loonie had excited him. He cursed beneath his breath when he thought of how easily she had escaped him. They had searched for her for hours, until the others, with the exception of Bob Reid, had tired of the chase. But he would search for the bitch. He would find her too. And when he did, he would make her sorry she had ever been born. There was something about her, something he wanted to humble and hurt. Aye, he would like to hurt her. He would like to take his knife and slit lines in that thin skin of hers. He would enjoy seeing the blood bead around the cuts and then begin bubbling out in a red stream. The blood would flow slowly at first, then faster and faster. The pain in his head took on a new fury, and he moaned aloud.

Bob Reid started and looked at him nervously. Perhaps he

had been a fool to stay with Mitford after the others had gone. He had a queer look on his face. Suppose he became violent and turned on him? After all, he hadn't been placed in Bedlam for nothing. Mitford's old Aunt Liza believed him to be sane, but, looking at that expression on his face, he himself was by no means certain that this was so. Mitford moaned again, and Bob said in a halting voice, "you s—say somethin', Bill?"

"Nay," Mitford answered him abruptly in his rough, thick voice. "I don' think as I'm goin' ter sleep, so whyn't you an' me go in the 'ouse an 'ave ourselves a tankard o' ale. The ol' girl will 'ave been sleepin' long since, so we won' be disturbed none." He frowned as Reid showed no enthusiasm. "Come on," he added curtly, "you an' me'll 'ave ourselves a drink an' a talk."

"It's late, Bill," Reid said, "Maybe it's bes' if I get on me way."

"Don' matter 'bout late," Mitford said, glaring at him. "I said as I wan' ter talk, didn' I?"

Bob Reid's heart sank. Mitford might become violent if he refused. But this would teach him a lesson. In future, he would try never to be alone with the man. "All right," he acquiesced reluctantly.

Mitford grunted. Reid was weak, he thought scornfully. It would never do to have a weak gang member, not while he was the leader. He would have to think about getting rid of Reid. But not just now. He wanted to talk, and Reid, for all his weakness, was the only one available. "Come on then," he said abruptly. "Don' 'ang about."

Outside the door of the house where he made his home with his widowed aunt, Mitford halted. "By Christ!" His round blue eyes widened in triumphant amazement as he stared at the sleeping girl in his doorway. "Well what you know 'bout that, Bob? There was us a-'untin' o' the cow like a pack o' bloody fools, an' 'ere she is on me doorstep, asleepin' as snug as you please."

Reid shuffled his feet uneasily. "It's late, Bill," he mumbled. "Bes' not ter start nothin' now, eh?"

Mitford turned his head and stared at Reid with narrowed eyes. He was showing that weakness again. He would certainly have to go. He would take the matter up with the other boys in a day or two. Weakness could put the whole gang in danger. "You know me," he growled. "If I wan' ter start somethin', I will. I don' play by no one's rules but me own." He lowered the torch he had been holding over the girl. "Look at the dirty bitch," he went on. "Thinks 'erself a fine lady, do that one. I'll show 'er somethin, I will. Insulted me, the cow did. But I'm goin' ter show 'er that she ain't no better'n me. Ain't it a pity that the boys went off? I daresay as they'd 'ave liked ter join in the sport."

"Sport?" Reid gave him a quick, startled glance. "What sport you talkin' 'bout, Bill? You ain't forgot that you tol' me this 'ere wench is one o' the loonies from Bedlam? It don' do ter start nothin' wi' a loonie. Bleedin' dangerous, they are."

The prominent vein at the side of Mitford's forehead began to throb heavily. "You shut up, Reid! I was in Bedlam. Maybe you thinks as I'm dangerous too?"

Reid's heart plunged in panic. "O' course I don', Bill," he said in a pacifying voice. "Why'd I think a thing like that? You was in Bedlam, o' course, but you wasn't never a loonie, was you?"

"You ever try'n say I was, an' I'll slit your throat from ear to ear. You 'members that. Anyway, I can' 'andle 'er."

Forgetting his fear for a moment, Reid blustered, "You wan' a piece o' 'er, you 'ave it, but I don' want none." His nose wrinkled. "Smells, she do, 'sides being filthy."

"Pertic'lar, ain't you, Reid?" Mitford sneered. "Seems ter me that you don' smell none ter good yourself. Anyway, if I says as you're to 'ave 'er then 'ave 'er you will. That'll be a'ter me, o' course."

"I don' wan' nothin' ter do wi' 'er."

"I been voted back as the leader o' the gang," Mitford snapped. "That means that you do 'xactly as I says."

Nodding gloomily, Reid stooped over the girl and studied her closely. "Don' look ter me like no one's goin' ter 'ave 'er," he announced. "Maybe she'd dead. Or if she ain't, why'n't she woke up? We been talkin' loud enough ter wake 'er, ain't we?"

Mitford gave him a contemptuous look. "Why don' you use your eyes? Breathin', ain't she? 'Ow can she be dead if she's breathin'?" He handed the torch to Reid. " 'Old that. I'll soon wake 'er up."

"Go easy, Bill," Reid mumbled. "You never know what she might go an' do. It ain't safe."

"I don' worry none 'bout safe, Reid." Laughing, Mitford reached down and grabbed the girl by her hair. "Wake up!" he shouted. He gave her hair a vicious twist. "Come on, bitch, wake up. Your Billy's 'ere ter pleasure you."

"Who's that makin' all that row down there?" a voice demanded testily from an upstairs window. "Can' get no sleep wi' all that row goin' on!"

Candlelight began to bloom yellow in the windows of those who had been disturbed. Curious faces peered out. "What's up? What's goin' on?"

Mitford ignored the spectators. He gave the girl's hair another yank. "You sleepin', or 'ave you died? Come on, didn't I tell you that your Billy's 'ere?"

Sarah came back very slowly from the exhausted sleep that had been so deep that it was near unconsciousness. There was a pain in her head and she could hear a hoarse, thick voice commanding her to awaken. She whimpered a little as a hand pulled viciously at her hair. "Please!" Her lids lifted a little. "Oh, please don't! You are hurting me!"

"I'll 'urt you a lot more, if you don' do like I tell you. I's me, bitch, i's me! Come on, open up them eyes an' 'ave a nice long look."

Sarah came back to full consciousness. Her eyes opened wide and stared up at him in terror. "Let me go!" she screamed. "Take your hands off me!"

His fingers still tangled in her hair, Mitford jerked her to her feet. "Jus' as soon as I'm done pleasurin' o' you, I'll be takin' you back ter that comf'table asylum what you 'scaped from. Thank me pretty, now." He paused, then he thrust his face close to hers. "Don' you try tellin' me that you never 'scaped, 'cause I knows differen', see."

She could smell his sour breath. Frantically, she tried to pull away, but she was held fast. She began to scream. The chords of her throat strained as she went on screaming, screaming.

The wild, desperate sounds she made set the hairs at the back of Reid's neck prickling. "Why don' you let 'er go, Bill?" he ventured, though without much hope of success.

"Shut up, Reid!" Mitford kicked at the girl savagely. The screaming was causing his head to throb almost unbearably. "You shut up 'n' all," he snarled. "You 'ear me? Stop that bleedin' row!"

Above the uproar, a man's voice shouted from a window, "Well get on wi' pleasurin' 'er, then. We're all waitin' ter see the show."

"Wan' a show, do you?" Mitford shouted back. "Don' go 'way. I'm goin' ter give you a good un'."

"Billy!" A quavering voice called. "Wha's that you're doin' wi' the lass?"

Mitford looked up at the old woman staring at him from an upstairs window. "You go on back ter bed, ol' Liza," he commanded.

"Don' do nothin' bad, Billy," the old woman pleaded. "You

know what'll 'appen ter you if you do. It'll be back to the asylum wi' you."

"You ain't gettin' me back there, slobber-jaw!" Mitford's voice rose to a bellow. "Not you, nor no one. I'll kill anyone what tries ter take me back!"

"Let the lass go, Billy."

"'Old your row. You can stay an' watch, or you can go on back ter bed."

"Don' do it, Billy, lad!"

For answer, Mitford threw the girl to the ground. "I'm goin' ter do it. You jus' watch me, you ol' fool!"

Chapter Seven

Lady Margaret Witherley leaned back against the soft cushions of the carriage. She felt very tired. But there was nothing new in the feeling, she thought, with a wry lift of her fair brows. Since the death of her husband, the zest had gone out of life and she was constantly tired. She stole a look at her son. Jason seemed to be lost in thought. He was staring straight ahead of him, a slight frown between his brows.

Margaret sighed. She was fifty-four years old, not really so very ancient, and yet, without John, she might well be a hundred. Perhaps she was feeling sorry for herself, but these days she did feel very old and she was often unbearably lonely. Perhaps if she could see more of Jason, she might rediscover some purpose in life. But Jason, of course, was in almost constant attendance upon the King, who looked upon him as one of his best friends. Or, if he were not in attendance upon the King, he was in Gloucestershire, where he put much time into the management of the family estate. It might be that he felt guilty about his previous neglect of the estate and their tenants, but she wished that he did not feel that he must spend so much time there. Only this evening, he had mentioned that he might be returning to Gloucestershire very soon. As was usual on these visits, he would probably be gone for at least two months. As he had explained to her more than once, there was still a great deal to do. At the moment, there were new cottages in the process of being built for their tenants, to replace the tumbledown leaky-roofed dwellings they now occupied. There were also, he had told her, several other matters that required his personal attention. She was glad, she told herself firmly, that Jason wished to become a model landlord. Better a model landlord, beloved of his people, than a careless and indifferent one. And Jason, despite that something in his bearing, which, to those who did not know him, might be taken for cold arrogance, was beloved of all those little families who lived and worked on the estate. She had seen that for herself when she had paid a short visit. They went in awe of him, but nevertheless they loved him. They knew that they could always depend upon him to be just and fair. Margaret felt a rush of love for her son. Beneath his aloof, or, one might almost say, cold manner, there was much warmth, humanity, and kindness, it was simply that he did not seem to know how to express it. Here she was bemoaning her lonely lot, and yet Jason had several times urged her to travel with him to Gloucestershire. She could, if she wished, stay at the Manor House until his visit was terminated. But it was so hard to commit herself to a certain course of action. John's death had left her very uncertain, almost frightened.

Jason turned his head at that moment and smiled at her. The smile warmed his blue eyes and made him, it seemed to her fond eyes, look much younger than his twenty-eight years. "Are you feeling cooler now, Mother?" he inquired.

She smiled back at him. "Yes, indeed, darling. I am glad you insisted that I come for the drive. I imagine that the hour is quite advanced, but it is deliciously cool. The house seemed so hot and stuffy. Do you think this heat might break soon?"

"It is to be hoped so. However, Mother," Jason reminded her, "you do not have to stay in London, do you?"

Instantly she was flustered. She wanted to be with him, and yet she did not know if she could bring herself to leave the house on Twyford Street, which was so full of memories of her John, even for the two months Jason would presumably be gone. "Let me think about it," she said quickly. "I will make up my mind soon, I promise you."

"It is not good for you to stay cooped up in one place," Jason said. "It is true that you have your duties at the palace, but it is not enough for you at this time."

"The Queen is gentle," she said, smiling. "But there are times when she can be demanding."

"Nevertheless, you need a complete change. The Queen, I feel sure, will release you from your duties for a short while. When you are not at the palace, you spend all your time in the house. You must not do that."

"I know, darling, but pray do not lecture me."

"I am sorry you think I am lecturing you. I spoke out of love and concern for you."

"I know, darling."

Jason turned his face away. Margaret fell silent. Now she had hurt him. Dear Jason, who made his loving concern sound like lecturing. If only he could fall in love and marry. A loving wife would bring him, as his mother could not, from his shell of reserve. She sometimes wondered if that shell had grown because, when he was a little lad, she had shown, without meaning to do so, that his father came first with her in everything, her son second. She loved Jason devotedly, and yet she had the feeling that he did not quite believe in the strength of that love. Margaret thought of the portrait of her husband. It hung on the wall of the blue room. In that portrait, John looked as though he lived and breathed, as though he were just about to step from the frame. If only he could! If only he could somehow return to life. She bit her lip. She was being foolish, she must learn to face reality. John was gone, and no amount of longing and wishing would bring him back. The house on Twyford Street, where she and John had spent so many happy years, and where Jason had been born, was no longer home to her, not without John. It had become merely a house, and yet a house filled with so many memories that she could not bring herself to move away. To do so would be a too painful renunciation, like losing an arm or a leg. Everywhere she looked there were poignant reminders of John. Painful, yes. But somehow she preferred the pain to peace, however longed for, to another home that had never known his dear presence. She thought of the portrait again. It had been painted two years ago, in 1660, the year of the Restoration. In that portrait, John was relaxed and smiling, just as he had been on that terrible day that had taken him out of her life. Relaxed and smiling at one moment, the next, his face twisted in agony. Death had taken him out of her life, but it could never take him out of her heart and her mind. Each night she pictured him lying beside her in their big bed. Each night she spoke to him, saw his smile, and was held in his arms. Tears filled her eyes, and she hastily turned her thoughts away. Jason was not like his father either in appearance or nature, and she found herself glad of that. Had he been too like, it would have added to the pain. Jason's hair was a dark blond, rather like her own, but John's had been black, midnight black. John's eyes had been almost as dark as his hair. But Jason's eyes, again like her own, were dark blue. Only her eyes had never had the brilliance of Jason's. Her son, at twenty-eight, was fully as handsome as his father, but in a very different way.

Jason turned his head to study his mother from the corner of his eye. What was she thinking about? As if he needed to ask, he thought, answering his own question. She was, of course, thinking about his father. He was aware, since his father's death, that she thought of little else. This was perhaps natural, but must her eyes always be so far away, so remote from all that went on about her? Lost in dreams of his father, she did not seem to hear even when she was spoken to directly. Jason's hands clenched as he felt a swift pang of loss. He had loved his father, and he mourned him deeply and sincerely, but with his mother's increasing remoteness, he felt that he had lost both parents. Perhaps if he could speak to her, make her understand how he felt about her obvious retreat from life, something might be accomplished. Almost instantly, he pushed the thought from him. How could he speak to her? He felt deeply about so many things, and yet he had not the capacity to make himself understood. When he did speak, tried to express something of his concern, as he had done a few moments ago, he had succeeded, as always, in sounding cold and domineering. "Pray do not lecture me," she had said. Lecture her? It was the last thing he wished to do. His heart was full of things he wished to say to her. Loving things, gentle and compassionate things, things that told of his great concern for her welfare, so why must his words always sound the exact opposite of what he longed to express? Mayhap there was something lacking in him. And yet, for all that, he was popular with women. He could not complain of lack of tender attention from the sex. And yet he sometimes felt that they did not so much love him as they felt themselves to be challenged by his unfortunate manner, a manner that seemed constantly to hold them at arm's length. Perhaps it was fortunate that he had never been in love, for he felt this lack in himself deeply. The inability to express himself might have been the cause of much pain both to himself and the loved one. He doubted, however, when he thought over the various women of his acquaintance, that such a contingency was likely to arise.

He glanced at his mother again. She believed her life to be over, and yet she still had so much to offer to some fortunate man, if, of course, she could ever be brought to consider another man as a possible husband. She was a lovely woman, he thought proudly. Her hair was a shining blond, as yet only faintly touched with gray. Her eyes were very blue, and, when they were not lost in dreams of his father, still had a very youthful expression. Only the faintest wrinkles marred the smooth perfection of her skin. Tonight, he thought, she was looking exceptionally lovely. The gown she wore was almost the same color as her eyes, and so was her broad-brimmed velvet hat, embellished with curling green and white feathers.

To distract himself, Jason dismissed thoughts of his mother and began to think instead of the King. Charles and his women! A smile touched his lips. The good-natured and licentious Charles certainly had no difficulty in expressing himself. It might be that that warm and overpowering charm of his would get him into difficulties some day. Yet Charles was many men in one. Charles Stuart, for instance, despite his merry reputation, was often touched with deep melancholy. It seemed to Jason, considering the complex man who was King of England, that only he knew the real Charles. Even Catherine, Charles's adoring little Queen, did not know him half so well. They gave something to each other, he and Charles. Charles relied upon him, calling him his one indispensable friend. And he, in Charles's presence, would find himself less inarticulate than usual. Almost, it seemed, a restraint was lifted from his tongue, enabling him to speak of his thoughts and his dreams. But, then, perhaps it was not so very marvelous, for did not most people respond to Charles Stuart?

The carriage lurched around a corner, bumping over ruts in the road, the speed slowed slightly. A vile smell filled the carriage, causing Margaret's nose to wrinkle with distaste. Rising, she drew the leather curtain aside and peered out of the window. "Lilacgrove Street?" she questioned Jason in some surprise. "Why on earth has Bailey brought us this way? I have heard that this particular street is worse than any other for thieves, rogues, and other scoundrels of all descriptions."

"Lilacgrove Street certainly enjoys an unsavory reputation," Jason admitted calmly. "However, I told Bailey to come this way, since it is a convenient short cut to Twyford Street." The indulgent look that Jason believed he was turning upon her had so much of severity in it that Margaret was instantly subdued. "Do not let the district alarm you, Mother," he added. "You are perfectly safe with me."

"Of course, darling," Margaret said, sitting down again. "I am always safe with you. It was merely that I thought—" She broke off, turning her head toward the window. "Jason, someone is screaming. Do you hear it?"

"Naturally I hear it," Jason answered, shrugging. "In Lilacgrove Street you are liable to hear many such sounds." As Margaret sat forward in her seat, he said repressively, "I hope, Mother, that you are not thinking of interfering? You will not be thanked for it, I assure you, not even by the victim. It is best, I think, that we drive on."

"But, Jason, someone is in trouble," Margaret said, giving him a shocked look. "We cannot possibly ignore it. It is our duty to investigate." Rising again, she rapped sharply on the panel. "Bailey," she called, "pray stop the carriage."

Jason said nothing for a long moment. In the dim light shed by the carriage lamps, he could see that there was unusual color in her cheeks and a sparkle in her eyes. So someone else's trouble, it seemed, could bring her back to a semblance of life. He should have remembered that his mother was always drawn to the unfortunate, and, in aiding them, she invariably forgot herself. "Wait!" Jason said sharply, as he saw her fumble with the catch of the door. "If we must interfere, then it is best that I do the interfering. You will stay here, Mother."

"Jason! I do not wish to stay here. I am not afraid."

"Nevertheless, you will not stir."

Ignoring Bailey's proffered hand, Jason alighted into the rubbish-strewn street. "I think, Bailey, that 'tis best if you drive on a little way. I will catch up with you. But in case there is trouble, be prepared to get my lady Witherley away from here."

"Yes, my lord."

"Certainly not!" Margaret cried. "I am not a child that must be protected and guarded."

"I am aware of that, Mother. Bailey, you will do as I say."

With a quick glance at his indignant mistress, Bailey bowed his head. "Yes, my lord," he said again. He hesitated. "You will be careful, my lord?"

"I will, Bailey." Jason gave the man a fleeting smile. "Thank you for your concern."

"Let me go with you, my lord."

"Nay. It is your duty to stay with my lady Witherley."

Margaret waited only until Jason had disappeared from view, then she halted the driver, who had been about to resume his seat. "You will not drive on, Bailey. Instead, you will give me your hand and assist me to alight."

Bailey came back and peered at her gloomily. "But, my lady, my lord Witherley expressly commanded me to—"

"I know what my lord Witherley said," Margaret interrupted. "I cannot let my son walk into danger without making some move to assist him."

Bailey permitted himself a slight smile. "In that case, my lady, I will accompany you."

Margaret shook her head firmly. "Nay, but stay within earshot. I will call to you if assistance is needed. Your hand, if you please."

Bailey's smile vanished. His gloom increasing, he extended a white-gloved hand. "Very well, my lady. I hope you will not be sorry."

"I will not be. And pray do not look like that, Bailey. One would think you were expecting us to be murdered."

"It wouldn't surprise me none, my lady. What his lordship is going to say about this, I shudder to think."

Margaret placed her hand in his and jumped lightly to the ground. "If we are both to be murdered," she said, smiling at the man, "then neither of us will be in a position to say anything."

"My lady!" Bailey exclaimed.

"I do but jest, Bailey. All will be well."

"I hope so, my lady. I do indeed."

Leaning against the side of the carriage, Bailey watched her until she was out of sight. All well and good to order him to stay here, he thought. But if they were not back within the next ten minutes, it would be his duty to chance a knife in the back and go after them. A pretty thing when an honest working man was given two different orders. If harm came to my lady Witherley, he would probably be turned off from his comfortable position without a character.

Margaret's heart was beating uncomfortably fast. A louder scream than those that had gone before hastened her steps. At the entrance to the alley, she hesitated. Should she return to the carriage? Nay, she answered herself. It was she who had forced the issue. She must not be a coward.

"You will leave the girl alone!" Jason's abrupt, commanding voice came to Margaret. "Stand back, or you will be sorry!"

There was light ahead, and Margaret hastened forward. She stopped again, profoundly shocked at the scene before her. In the circle of light cast by a torch, she saw a naked, screaming girl. The girl was sprawled on her back on the dirty cobbles, and kneeling before her, his breeches about his ankles, was a heavyset man with a scarred face and a shock of wiry dark hair.

"If you're thinkin' o' savin' this slut," William Mitford said, looking up at Jason, "you'd bes' think again. There's more'n one o' us, my fine gen'leman." Calmly, Mitford rose to his feet.

Drawing up his breeches, he fastened them with the piece of rope that served him as a belt. His smile was insolent as his eyes traveled slowly over Jason's immaculate gray-clad person, lingering on the high stock at his throat, the lace edging his cuff, and the long, ringed fingers. "A real dandy, ain't you? What you think you c'n do agains' all o' us, eh?"

The expression in Jason's eyes was cold and dangerous. "You would be foolish indeed, my man, were you to allow yourself to be deceived by appearance," he said in a level, colorless voice. "If need be, I am quite capable of rendering you ineffectual. I think I can promise you that, at the very least, you will be nursing a split skull."

The coldness of his eyes, the calmly delivered words, caused Mitford's smile to die. He glared about him, hatred in his eyes. Then, as he caught sight of Margaret, who was edging nearer, his smile returned. "Now 'ere's a fine thing," he cried. "Not on'y 'ave we got a fine gen'leman come avisit' us, but 'e's brung wi' 'im 'is scented dressed-up whore."

Margaret wilted before the look that Jason turned on her then. She looked at him defiantly and continued to move closer.

Jason turned back to Mitford. "Open that filthy mouth of yours again, and I shall be obliged to—" His words broke off as he felt a tug at his ankle. "Sir," the girl on the ground said weakly, "please help me. Do not let him touch me!"

For the first time, Jason looked at her, and his eyes sharpened to keen attention. Somewhere, and quite recently, he had seen this bedraggled creature before. Repressing distaste, he said, "Lie still, wench. I will allow no one to hurt you."

Sarah stared up at him, and her terror was so great that she did not recognize him. She only knew that this tall, calmly assured man had come to rescue her. "Thank you!" she said. "Thank you so much!"

If Jason was surprised at the cultured voice that came from the girl, he gave no sign. But Margaret, frankly curious, bent over the prone figure. She shuddered inwardly as she saw the broken talonlike nails, the matted hair, and the open sores on the yellowed, unwashed flesh. The girl turned over on her side and hid her eyes against her arm. Margaret drew in a sharp, horrified breath as she saw the appalling lacerations on the thin back. The aversion she felt was instantly conquered by a surge of pity. "Oh, my dear!" Margaret said in a shaken voice, "I see that you have suffered greatly. Do not be afraid, for all is going to be well. My son will aid you."

The girl's shoulders quivered, and she made a muffled, wordless sound. "Jason," Margaret said in an unconsciously imperious voice. "You will please inform that—that creature that he will find himself in a great deal of trouble if he attempts to touch this poor child again."

"Don' you call me no creature," Mitford snarled, taking a menacing step forward. "You ain't stoppin' me from doin' nothin', nor the dandy ain't. I c'n do as I like wi' this wench, see. She's an escaped loonie from Bedlam Asylum, tha's what she is. An' that bein' so, she ain't no more 'uman than what a cat or a dog is."

Margaret saw that Jason had stiffened at these words. His eyes went to the girl, and the expression in them was one of profound shock.

Mitford stared at him, his smile gloating. "Ah, tha's give you a shock, ain't it, me bleedin' dressed-up swell?"

Jason looked back at him, his expression unreadable. He said nothing. Margaret waited for a moment, then, giving him an exasperated look, she stooped over the girl again. Catching one of her hands, she tried to assist her to rise.

"Oh, no you don'!" With a grunt of fury, Mitford tore the hand from Margaret's grasp. "You try anythin' else, you whore, an' I'll bash your bleedin' face in. I'll—" His words broke off in a strangled gasp as Jason's hand grasped him by his ragged shirt-front. " 'Ere, what you think you're doin'? Reid! You bas'ard, don' jus' stan' there, get 'im! Get 'im!

You take your 'ands off me, you bloody swell!"

"Certainly." Contemptuously, Jason flung the man from him. Mitford, with a hoarse bellow of alarm, staggered and fell heavily, his head striking against the cobblestones.

For quite some time there had been a confused babble of voices coming from the people standing at every available window. Suddenly, a woman's voice screamed out, "I tell you it's 'im! It's the Duke! Look, 'Arry, ain't that the Duke? You down there, don' you know 'im?"

Reid, who had doubled up his fists and taken a few uncertain steps forward, allowed his hands to drop. This man, this tall, elegant-looking swell was the Duke? He had heard much of him, but he had never seen him. He looked up. The faces at the windows were a blur, but he felt the menace that came from the watchers.

Mitford lumbered to his feet. "Wha's the matter wi' you, Reid, you bleedin' coward?" he raved. "Go on, lan' the bas'ard a bash!"

Reid flushed as he met Mitford's glaring eyes. "Don' dare ter touch 'im," he mumbled. "This 'ere swell is the Duke."

"What you talkin' 'bout? I don' care who 'e is!"

"You jus' better care," a man's voice shouted. "The Duke's a frien' to us. Lay one finger on 'im, an' we'll string you up from a post!"

Mitford gaped in bewilderment as he met Jason's coolly amused eyes. "I dunno what the mad bleeders is talkin' 'bout. Who are you, then?"

Reid saw the movement away from the windows, and he went quickly to Mitford's side. "They're comin' down, Bill. We'd better get in the 'ouse." Seeing Mitford's mouth opening to continue the argument, he began to explain rapidly, "This 'ere swell is well known to 'em, see. Seems that 'e's done 'em a lot o' good, an' they think as 'e's a perishin' saint. Touch 'im, an' they'll tear us ter bleedin' pieces. Now'd you un'erstand?"

"No!" Mitford shouted. "No, I tell you, I don' un'erstand nothin' o' this. I ain't never 'eard o' 'im!"

"Tha's 'cause you been away. But the Duke's well known, 'e is. We'd bes' get in the 'ouse."

Bewildered, his face contorted with rage, Mitford allowed Reid to take his arm and jostle him past the people who were pouring from the houses. They went unnoticed, so eager were the people to surround the Duke.

"Jason!" Margaret pushed her way to his side. "What does this mean? Why do they call you the Duke? Have they mistaken you for someone else?"

"No, Mother." For once, meeting Margaret's eyes, Jason had lost much of his air of calm assurance. He looked almost embarrassed. "I will endeavor to explain at a later date."

"But, Jason—"

"I pray you to say no more."

"The Duke called the lady Mother," a woman said in an excited voice. " 'Ere, this lady's 'is Ma."

Hands touched Margaret, friendly faces beamed at her. "Don' you worry, my dearie," somebody said. "Nobody ain't goin' ter lay a finger on our Duke, nor on 'is Ma."

Margaret flushed. "I am happy to know that you are our friends." She indicated the girl who was still lying on the cobbles. "She, too, would have been grateful for your friendship."

"But she ain't nothin'," a man said, looking at Margaret in puzzlement. "Loonies don' feel nothin'. They ain't got feelin's like you an' me."

"Nonsense!" Margaret snapped. "She is a human being."

Jason frowned and moved quickly and protectively to Margaret's side. He knew well how quickly a friendly mob could turn ugly. "Ladies and gentlemen," he said, raising his voice so that it could be heard above the babble, "my mother and I thank you for your goodwill."

Highly delighted, the people pressed closer. "Can we do anythin' for you?"

Jason inclined his head. "Aye, you may escort us back to our carriage." He took Margaret's arm. "Come along, Mother."

Margaret hung back. "Jason," she looked at him pleadingly, "we must take that poor child with us. We cannot leave her here."

"Certainly not! If it will ease your mind at all, I will make arrangements for her care. But that is all I am prepared to do."

Margaret shook her head stubbornly. "I will not go without her."

Jason looked at her. There it was again, that suggestion of life and animation. Perhaps she needed to care for somebody. But that creature in the house! "Mother," he began, "I think—"

"I have told you, Jason. I will not leave her here."

"It's up to the Duke," a round-faced woman cried. "Well, sir, will you take the loonie in your fine carriage?"

"Jason!" Margaret touched his arm pleadingly.

"You really want this?"

"I do. Come, Jason, do not try to pretend that you are hard and selfish, for I know that you are not." She nodded at the cheerful crowd. "It is evident to me that they know it too."

Abruptly, against his better judgment, Jason capitulated. "Very well. I hope that you may not regret it." He turned to the expectant people. "Will you aid the wench, please? I pray you to handle her gently."

Margaret looked on with awe and pride as they rushed to obey his command. Smiling faces were turned his way, and some of them looked at him with actual love. Margaret shook her head. It was evident that there were depths to her son of which she knew nothing. "Jason," she looked up at him, "why do these people hold you in such esteem?"

"It is nothing, Mother. You must not imagine there is a

mystery," Jason said stiffly. "I have been able, in small ways, to aid them from time to time. They are grateful, that is all there is to it."

"That is all? But, Jason, I think perhaps there is more to the story. There is love in their eyes when they look at you."

"Nonsense! You are imagining it."

"I do not think so."

A young woman came to Jason's side and touched his arm. "Sir," she said in a shy voice, "I wan'ed you ter know that my little wench is much better. If it 'adn't been for you gettin' the bes' of care for 'er, she'd 'ave died. Thank you kin'ly, sir."

Jason nodded stiffly. He did not look at Margaret.

Margaret's eyes were shining. "I think I begin to see, my darling. Oh, Jason, I love you, and I am so proud of you!"

He turned to her with his most forbidding expression. "I pray you, Mother, not to let your imagination run away with you. If you are imagining me to be some kind of saint, you are vastly mistaken."

"Not a saint, darling, no, but a kind and caring and warm-hearted man. Do you know, Jason, I am your mother, and yet I feel that only now am I beginning to know you."

He looked at her with an air of exaggerated patience. "May we now have done with this conversation?"

"Darling, why are you so afraid of showing your true feelings?"

"Possibly because I have no adequate way of expressing them. Come, Mother, do not look so bewildered. You know me as well as anyone can."

"I am ashamed to confess it," Margaret said, "but I think not. Perhaps if we could talk more. If you would tell me of the things you feel and think."

"Would you really listen, Mother?" he said dryly.

"Yes, darling, indeed I would!"

His tawny brows rose, and he said in a lightly mocking

voice. "I would like to think so. But I fear you have made it difficult in the past."

Hurt struck deeply. 'Have I been a bad mother?"

"Nay. I would not change you." He took her arm and began to lead her away. "The conversation has become much too intense. Let us change the subject."

Margaret bit her lip, but she said no more. It would be useless to continue when he wore that closed expression.

Startled out of his gloomy thoughts, Bailey watched wide-eyed as the laughing crowd of people approached the carriage. My lord Witherley and my lady Witherley walked in front of the strange procession. The torch-bearers, who walked on both sides, raised their torches higher, and Bailey gasped as he saw the creature who hobbled along behind his master and mistress. The girl, for girl he supposed the wild-looking creature to be, was wearing a short, torn, yellow smock. Bailey's lips tightened. He recognized that smock. What in the name of God were his master and mistress doing with a lunatic from Bedlam? The girl's hair surrounded her small face in a matted bush, and the parts of her body he could see through the rents in the smock were filthy. She was very thin, and her legs, which might have been shapely in normal circumstances, were badly swollen. Bailey's heart sank as he saw my lady Witherley turn her head and smile reassuringly at the creature. What was my lord Witherley about to permit? My lady Witherley had obviously taken it into her head to do one of her good deeds. In the past, her husband had restrained her more impetuous actions, and now it was surely for the son to do. Bailey stiffened to attention as they drew abreast.

"Bailey," Margaret said. "Give me your cloak, please." She indicated the wild-looking apparition. "This lady must be decently covered."

Bailey frowned. His cloak? Never! He met my lord Witherley's eyes. Jason shrugged. "As you can see, Bailey, I am not wearing a cloak. The honor, I think, is yours."

Margaret looked at Bailey incredulously. "Why do you hesitate? Surely you have some charity in your heart?"

"No, my lady," Bailey answered, "not if my cloak is to be used to cover that—"

"I will see that you have a new cloak," Margaret cut him off swiftly. She held out an imperious hand. "Come, Bailey, give it to me. Afterwards, when she is decently clothed, we will burn this one." She smiled coaxingly. "You need have no fears of contamination."

"Have I a choice, my lady?"

"I believe that your kind heart will give you the answer to that question."

Bailey was not proof against her smile, so rarely seen these days. Reluctantly, but obediently, he untied the ribbons and surrendered the cloak. My lord Witherley, standing by, appeared to have nothing to say for himself, so Bailey, with the privilege of an old and trusted servant, ventured a protest. "My lady, surely you are not proposing to allow that creature to ride with you in the carriage?"

"Bailey! You will not call her that creature. I am ashamed of you!"

Again Bailey glanced at my lord Witherley. Receiving no help there, he said stiffly, "I am sorry, my lady. May I ask what I am to call the loonie?"

Margaret's eyes flashed angry reproach. "Most certainly not that, Bailey!" she snapped. Turning to the girl, she draped the cloak about the thin, bowed shoulders. "There. That is much better."

Sarah kept her eyes lowered, but she was very much aware of the silent man beside her. The Duke! Would he speak at any moment? Was he even now planning to hand her over to the authorities? She clutched at the collar of the cloak with trembling hands. To think that she had not recognized her enemy when he was so close to her! To think that she had actually pleaded with him to rescue her from the scarred man! She felt shriveled inside with hatred. Even in her desperation, she should have recognized this man who was responsible for all her misery. But she knew him now! Her enemy, so handsome that he looked like a blond god! Perhaps that was why one tumbled so easily into sin, because it came disguised in perfection of face and form.

"My child?" Margaret said in soft inquiry.

Poised still for flight, Sarah managed to whisper, "Thank you. I—I had a cloak, but he—the scarred man, t—took it."

"Never mind," Margaret soothed. "Let us try to forget that most unpleasant creature."

Sarah's fleeting upward look was full of suspicion. This woman was the mother of her enemy. Had she not heard the people call her so? "Why are—are you being so kind to me?" she asked.

"Perhaps because you are in great need of kindness." Margaret's tone drove some of the suspicion away. "Tell me, my dear," she added, "do you remember your name?"

Jason saw the girl's hesitation. He saw those hands with their dreadful ragged nails tremble. For some reason the beat of his heart accelerated as he waited for her to answer. That voice of hers, with its soft, pleasant tones, it went so ill with her appearance, yet surely he had heard it before. That slight, almost imperceptible lisp when sounding some of the words made the voice distinctive. He had heard it before. But where? He knew, of course, beyond any doubt, that this poor creature was the same girl he had seen in the cage at Bedlam Asylum. He was remembering now in some bewilderment that, when he had first seen her, his natural feeling of sick horror had quickly been succeeded by an almost devastating pity. Then he became conscious of another feeling that was not in the least natural. He had felt, staring at her, that beneath the dirt and the pitiful evidence of cruelty and neglect, there lay someone he had seen before, in the world outside the asylum. A grotesque travesty of that person to be sure, but someone he had felt he should know.

The girl's eyes were full of tears. They ran down her cheeks, making pale paths in the grime. Lifting her hand, she wiped the tears away. "Yes, madam," Jason heard the hauntingly familiar voice say. "I remember my name. Why should I not? I beg you to believe me when I tell you that I am not and have never been insane!"

"Let us discuss that later." Margaret said gently. "Will you tell me your name, please?"

"My name is—" Sarah hesitated for a moment, then her eyes lifted and looked straight at Jason, shocking him with their expression of implacable hatred. "My name is Sarah Barry, madam."

Jason started. Sarah Barry! That voice, with its slight, fascinating lisp, saying, "Let me go, please! You are quite mistaken in believing me to be a thief." His own reaction. "Nay, wench, I think not. A strange combination, the voice of a lady, but a thief for all that." His anger that, upon reflection, seemed out of proportion to the incident. "It may be that a spell in Newgate Prison will effect a change of heart. If it does not, it will at least soften your brazenness." Despite her bold defiance, he had seen the terror looking from her eyes, and yet he had ignored it. He had strode away, leaving her to her fate. Why? It was as she had reminded him—"If you go slumming, you must expect to be forked." She was right, he had expected it, and it had happened before. Why then, had he expended the full force of his anger upon her?

He drew a deep, unsteady breath, remembering another day. Sarah Barry, a small, pitiful figure, hobbling into court to hear the charge against her. Her wrists and her ankles had been weighted down with iron fetters, and he had seen the terrible change in her. What had happened? What had occurred to send her to Bedlam Asylum?

"Jason," his mother's voice, "what is it? Are you unwell?"

"I am perfectly well, Mother. I think, however, that no purpose can be served in lingering here. Let us be on our way."

Margaret gave him a puzzled look. What an enigma was this son of hers. Evidently the silent people, looking on, thought so too. For she saw the exchange of puzzled looks. This man, so cold, so remote, so apparently indifferent to the misery that confronted him in the person of the girl, was far removed from their adored Duke. Frowning, Margaret looked at Bailey. "Did you hear the name?" she asked.

Bailey's face was wooden with disapproval. "I heard, my lady."

"Very well. In future, when you have occasion to refer to this lady directly or indirectly, you will call her Mistress Barry."

If he had occasion to refer to her! Did that mean that my lady Witherley intended her act of charity to be a permanent thing? Bailey inclined his head stiffly in acknowledgement. "I will remember, my lady." Again he glanced at my lord Witherley. Why did he not speak? Surely he would not allow his mother to indulge in such folly? Who knew, with such a creature about, but that they would not all be murdered in their beds?

To Bailey's intense disappointment, my lord Witherley turned to his escort, and, after giving them a brief smile, thanked them, and bade them on their way. "The hour is late," he said. "You have need of your sleep."

Bailey watched as the people, laughing, and with many good-natured ribald comments, went on their way. Then, with a shrug of his shoulders, he mounted to his seat. It was, after all, nothing to do with him. But the ways of the gentry were very queer. He heard my lord Witherley's voice bid him to drive on. With another expressive shrug, he gripped the reins firmly, and clicked softly with his tongue to the horses.

Inside the carriage, Jason sat stiffly upright. "I think, Mother," he said in that stiff and unfriendly voice, "that Mistress Barry will understand that my words are not prompted by malice or unkindness when I tell you that perhaps you should not sit quite so near to her. Through no fault of her own, it may be that she has picked up some disease."

"Jason!"

"The gentleman is quite right, madam," Sarah Barry's low, steady voice said. "You should not sit so near. But only because I am aware that my person is disagreeable. Apart from that, it is not, I think, diseased."

Margaret, rather shrinkingly, patted the girl's rigid arm. "I am sure not, Sarah. By the time I have finished with you, you will not know yourself. As for my son, I pray you not to be hurt by his words. His concern is naturally for me, but I know well that he did not mean to hurt you. By the way, let me make myself known to you. I am Lady Margaret Witherley. My son is Jason, my lord Witherley."

Sarah bowed her head. "My lord, my lady." She looked at Margaret. "If you would instruct your coachman to set me down somewhere, I will trouble you no longer."

Before replying, Margaret looked quickly at Jason's averted face. "No, Sarah," she said, an unconsciously defiant note in her voice. "I will not set you down. I mean to befriend you."

Sarah drew in a sharp, startled breath. My lady Witherley meant to befriend her. Did that mean that she would be constantly under the lady's care, and under my lord Witherley's hostile surveillance? No, it must not be! He was her enemy. "My lady," Sarah said quickly, "you are very kind. But I think it would be better if you were to set me down."

"Nay, Sarah, you are in need of care." She saw the girl

glance quickly at Jason, the undisguised terror in her eyes. "Sarah, you must not fear my son. It is not easy for him to show his feelings, but he feels compassion for your plight, even as I do. Come, do not tremble so! My son will not hurt you."

Jason turned his head and looked directly at Sarah. "My mother is quite right, Mistress Barry. I will not hurt you. I believe that you have been hurt enough."

Sarah averted her eyes. For a moment she thought she had read a plea in his eyes. Then, remembering the unfriendly tone of his voice, she told herself that she had been mistaken. How could she trust him? How could she believe in anybody or anything? Even this woman, who appeared to be so kind, might be readying a trap for her. But what was the use of fighting? She was so tired, so very tired! Let my lord Witherley do his worst. If he meant to see her imprisoned and caged again, there was nothing she could do about it. She was too tired to fight.

She was silent for so long that Margaret looked at her anxiously. "You have heard my son," she said in a hesitant voice, "and you know now that you have nothing to fear, do you not?"

"I hope that I have not, my lady."

"Then perhaps, if you are not too tired, you will tell me a little about yourself. Obviously, you are well educated. How come you to be in this sorry pass."

"Mother!" Jason's voice was so sharp that Margaret started. "Your good intentions toward the wench do not give you the right to pry into her life."

"I have nothing to hide, my lord Witherley." Sarah turned to Margaret. Her intention was to tell her as little as possible, but, before she could stop herself, the words came pouring out. She told of her family, of their move to London, of the disaster that had overtaken them. Only when she came to the part that Jemmie Taylor had played in her life did her voice falter.

Then, her voice gathering strength, she spoke of Jemmie's domination over her and of the mock marriage. She was aware that my lord Witherley was listening intently. He was waiting, she supposed, for a mention of how he himself figured in the sorry coil of her life. Perversely, not really knowing why she did so, she omitted any mention of him. Merely remarking that, her luck failing her, a gentleman had caught her with her hand in his pocket and had had her sent to Newgate Prison.

When her voice trailed into silence, Jason leaned back against the cushions, his brow furrowed in thought. Had he only imagined that he saw hatred in her eyes? Was it possible that she did not recognize him? He felt a curious relief at this last thought. Annoyed by the surge of relief, he tried to tell himself that the punishment she had suffered had been right and just. He looked at her again. She was so dreadfully altered, so worn down. Nay, the punishment did not fit the crime. No human being should suffer such degradation. And if she spoke the truth, then, to have sent her to Bedlam Asylum had been a terrible miscarriage of justice.

In his dingy room in Lilacgrove Alley, William Mitford walked up and down in impotent fury. From the moment he had seen the red-haired loonie, he had wanted her. All his life he had been dogged by ill luck, and it was just another example of that ill luck that, just as he was about to enter her struggling body, the high-nosed swell should have happened along to prevent him. But he would have the loonie yet! Somehow he would have her!

Seated in a chair by the table, Reid watched him uneasily. The loss of that ugly, skinny loonie seemed to have driven him quite frantic. He had been pacing up and down, mumbling to himself, for the last hour or more. His face was heavily flushed, his eyes glaring, and there was something about him that gave one the cold shivers. He should never have been released from

Bedlam Asylum, Reid thought, for if ever he had seen madness, he was seeing it now. He jumped as Mitford suddenly yelled out. "I'll 'ave that bitch, you jus' see if I don'! I'll rape 'er first, an' then I'll take me knife an' I'll carve 'er up!"

Reid shivered. "But why, Bill? What's the loonie ever done ter you?"

"She's laughin' at me!" Mitford tapped his forehead. "She is, I can 'ear 'er laughin' in 'ere. But she ain't goin' ter laugh long at Bill Mitford, by Christ she ain't! No one laughs at me, no one! An' no one don' get away with nothin' either. I'll 'ave 'er, I tell you!"

"But 'ow? 'Ow you goin' ter find 'er?"

"I'll find 'er."

"Why'n't you forget 'bout 'er, Bill? It ain't too likely as you can get your 'ands on 'er now."

With a sudden movement, Mitford drew a knife from his pocket and flung it on the table. Ignoring Reid's words, he began to laugh. "That loonie won' look too pretty a'ter I begin carvin' on 'er. What you got ter say ter that, Reid?"

"I say it ain't worth it. But you'll 'ave your way no matter what I say. If that lady an' gent what took 'er off wi' 'em is goin' ter be lookin' a'ter 'er, you ain't goin' ter be able ter do nothin'. Bes' forget it."

"I ain't forgettin', don' you worry none 'bout that. If I say I'm goin' ter do it ter 'er, then I am. I'll fin' 'er."

"The loonie don' look none too strong." Reid uttered a further weak protest. "If you rape 'er, an' then mark 'er up, like what you said, you'll likely kill 'er. What if you was ter get caught? You'd 'ang for it."

"'Ang!" Mitford looked outraged. "What, me 'ang on account o' a loonie? Don' be a bleedin' fool! 'Sides, I ain't goin' ter get caught."

"Do as you like." Anxious only to be gone from this atmosphere of frightening malice, Reid rose to his feet. "I'll be gettin' along," he mumbled. "It ain't far off daylight."

Mitford made no attempt to stop him. "Go on, then. But you 'member this. You say one word to anyone 'bout what I plans ter do ter the loonie, an' you ain't goin' ter live long!"

"I won' say nothin', Bill, not a word. It ain't no business o' mine what you do."

"You 'members that, Reid, an' you'll be safe."

Safe? Reid thought, running down the rickety stairs. Was anyone safe with that madman on the loose?

Chapter Eight

Seated inconspicuously with the other servants behind a bank of flowers, in the darkest corner of the great ballroom, Sarah Barry made no effort to join in their low-toned conversation. She had the oddest feeling that she was dreaming the glamorous scene before her. It must be a dream, for it did not seem quite real. She herself was not quite real. She leaned back in her chair, both hands tightly clasping my lady Witherley's white velvet cloak. Absurd, she thought, to have this superstitious feeling that, if she did not keep a tight hold on the cloak, the quiet happiness she had known over the past few months would somehow vanish, never again to be recalled. And it had been a happiness, a vast contentment such as she had not dreamed possible. Even the frightening menace of my lord Witherley had been removed. For the very next day, after her arrival at the house on Twyford Street, he had traveled into Gloucestershire, where, it seemed, he had pressing matters concerned with the family estate to engage his full attention. To her great relief, he had not returned to London until recalled by the King. He had arrived at a late hour yesterday. Without too much difficulty, she had succeeded in keeping out of his way. When my lady Witherley had explained to him that Sarah Barry would be accompanying them to the ball at Whitehall Palace, as a servant in waiting, he had looked faintly surprised, but had made no comment. When she had entered the carriage, he had given her a brief, disinterested glance, and had again said nothing.

Sarah frowned faintly, wondering why she should feel this sense of pique because he had not appeared to notice the change in her. What did it matter, she asked herself now, whether or not he noticed her? In the security of my lady Witherley's growing trust and affection for her, her fear of him had all but vanished. His opinion of her, or of her appearance, if indeed he had any opinion at all of someone as insignificant as herself, was supremely unimportant. Even her hatred of him, she realized, had dwindled to a dull resentment. But, she was honest enough to admit, the resentment could flare into active hatred if he attempted again to interfere in her life.

Disturbed by the trend her thoughts had taken, Sarah hastily dismissed my lord Witherley. Instead, she allowed her thoughts to dwell on the strangeness of life that had moved her to Newgate Prison, to Bedlam Asylum, to the happy security of the house on Twyford Street, and, finally, had brought her here as an observer of this colorful ball at Whitehall Palace. Naturally, as a servant, she had no part in this gaiety, and she was content that it should be so. She would ask nothing more than that her life should remain exactly as it was now. She could visualize no greater happiness. Her mind dwelt with pride on her altered appearance. Her body was clean and fragrant, as it always used to be before the nightmare. Her hair, restored by frequent washings to its original red-gold, shone with health, and her nails were pale, perfect ovals. She would never be plump, but her wasted figure had filled out sufficiently to show slight but satisfactory curves. The scars on her back and on other parts of her body would, of course, always remain with her, but they were now only pale ridges. As for her apparel, the attractive green gown she wore, originally Lady Margaret's, was well suited to her particular coloring. Yes, she was very different from the grotesque creature who, accompanied by my lord and lady

Witherley, had shuffled into the huge entrance hall of the house, full of terror, suspicion, and foreboding. That pathetic creature belonged to another time, another life, and had nothing to do with the Sarah Barry of today.

A murmur of excitement from the assembled servants brought Sarah back to her immediate surroundings. The girl who had been seated on a chair beside her was now on her feet. Her face was flushed with excitement as she craned her neck to see over the blue and red and purple and white of the massed flowers. "Look," she said, "the king is dancing with my lady Castlemaine. Oh! Is she not beautiful?"

"Aye," another voice put in softly, "beautiful indeed. But I have heard that for all her great beauty, she is hideously bad tempered and spoiled. The King, people say, is besotted with her, and if that be so, I'll wager she leads him a merry dance. Do you see that man in the white satin jacket with the high gold collar? That is my lady Castlemaine's cousin, the Duke of Buckingham. 'Tis said that he and my lady are always quarreling."

"'Tis said! People say!" somebody else said mockingly. "All evil-natured gossip, I'll vow."

They were all standing now. Infected by the general excitement, Sarah rose too. With the scent of the flowers in her nostrils, her ears filled with the lilting music, she scanned the glittering ballroom floor and the figures moving upon it. She saw the King. Charles Stuart was a tall and impressive figure clad in scarlet velvet trimmed with silver lace. His long dark hair touched his velvet-clad shoulders. His ringed hands flashed with multicolored fires. A turn in the dancing brought the King into her direct line of vision. His face looked drawn, she thought. She had the impression that, despite his flashing smile, he was feeling ill. Dancing with the King was my lady Castlemaine. Sarah watched her admiringly. Her hair was a flame against the ivory satin of her gown. Her huge blue eyes seemed almost as bright as the wide diamond collar that adorned her slender throat. Diamonds flashed from her ears, from the buckles of her shoes, and from the diamonds that studded her high green heels there came little darting points of light. She seemed to be all light, all grace and beauty and charm. Yet, if gossip did not lie, she was of a shrewish and greedily demanding nature.

Seated on a chair on a red and gold draped dais was the Queen. Studying her, Sarah thought that she looked rather sad, as though she were not particularly enjoying the festive occasion. Her big dark eyes in a little pointed face followed the King's every movement. Queen Catherine was dressed in a gown of silver lace. The scallops of her emerald-green underskirt were bordered with tiny pearls, and there were rosettes of pearls on her silver and green slippers. Her dark hair, with its intriguing bronze lights, was swept high on her shapely head and held in place by a coronet of rubies and diamonds. There were matching bracelets on both thin, childish-looking wrists, and her fingers, like the King's, were ablaze with rings. Poor little Queen, Sarah thought pityingly. Her love for the King, open, unashamed, was well known. How then could she bear his constant amorous adventures?

Sarah's eyes found my lady Witherley. A smile touched her lips. To her, the kind and compassionate Lady Margaret was the most beautiful of all the women assembled there, perhaps because she saw her with the eyes of love and devotion. Lady Margaret was wearing a gown of sapphire-blue velvet. The low, square-cut neckline was embroidered with small silver flowers, and set in the heart of each flower, nestling there like a tiny drop of dew, was a diamond. Her blond hair was swept to one side, but two long curls touched her right shoulder. Sarah remembered that Lady Margaret had been a little concerned lest the style of her hair and her gown be too youthful. Quite the contrary, Sarah thought now. The hair style was suited to her particular type of features, and the gown gave her dignity while, at the same time, it made the most of her enduring beauty.

Standing to one side, my lord Witherley, clad in a severely cut midnight-blue satin jacket and matching breeches, a foam of lace at his throat and his wrists, his blond hair shining in the light of the myriad candles, was absently watching the dancers. With him was Sir Peter Baxter, a rather vacant-faced young man clad in purple satin, whose exquisitely cut jacket was heavily embroidered in a complex design worked with silver, green, and gold thread. Sarah's face flushed as she remembered the first time she had seen him. He was the timid man, as she had called him in her mind, who had been so overcome by the sights of Bedlam Asylum. When he had called at the house one day, inquiring when my lord Witherley might be expected to return from Gloucestershire, he had returned in answer to her curtsey a stately bow, but there had been no recognition in his eyes. What would he have said, what would his attitude have been if he could have guessed at her identity? A smile touched Sarah's lips. Would sheer horror have caused him to swoon? Watching the two men, she felt a sense of surprise that a man of my lord Witherley's particular nature should make a friend of such a foppish young man. Lady Margaret had told her that they had been friends for many years, and had played together as lads. So mayhap, she thought, it was a question not only of familiarity but of the attraction of opposites. She thought of the little doctor, who had, to the best of his ability, tried to befriend her, and her eyes softened. She would like very much to see him again. She had spoken of him to Lady Margaret, and had been informed that he had left London for a time, but would be returning shortly.

Jason too was thinking of the doctor, who was at this moment taking a well-earned rest at Witherley Grove, in Gloucestershire. At first, the doctor had declined the invitation to the Manor House. Jason frowned. His invitation to the doctor had been given in all sincerity, and with pleasure at the thought of his company, but, as usual, he had managed to make his offer sound grudging. "If you are thinking, my lad," the little doctor had said, glaring at him ferociously, "that I must come cap in hand, as a pauper guest, barely tolerated, to your Manor House, you are vastly mistaken. I have always paid my own way, my lord Witherley, and I will continue to do so. I decline to be the object of your charity!"

Absurd how hurt he had felt. "As to that, Joshua," he had answered coldly, "you are quite mistaken. But you must please yourself, of course."

A small silence had fallen. Then the doctor had said in a subdued voice, "Damn! Why do I always make the same mistake where you are concerned? Blister it, but I need my brains examined! I should know better, for I have known you long enough, eh? Eh?"

"Yes, Joshua, you should know better."

"All right. No need to heap coals of fire on my head, eh? Am I forgiven, lad?"

"You are."

"Then, if you will open up your best guest chamber, your best, mind, I'll be with you in a few days. Mayhap I can help you with some of that infernal work you are always prating about."

And help the doctor had, and a fine mess he had made of everything! Jason rubbed a finger across his forehead. His head was aching vaguely, and he was feeling bored. These Court functions, which he avoided whenever possible, always had this effect upon him. The last time he had attended a ball, the King, seeing his frown and his barely hidden impatience to be gone, had said, a hint of laughter in his dark eyes, "I would make of you a courtier, my lord Witherley, though well do I know the task to be hopeless. You are too blunt, too outspoken, and I fear you make more enemies than you do friends."

"Then why do you not abandon the task, Sire?" he had asked.

Charles laughed. "I have made of you my particular friend, whether you will it or no. Therefore, even if it be against your inclination, I would have you present yourself whenever I so command. I am not and have never been deceived by the severity of your manner. I know only too well, you see, that it does not correspond with the true feelings you would wish to express."

But at this time, Jason thought wryly, the severity of his manner, as Charles called it, was in perfect accord with his inner feelings. The air was redolent of perfume, and the many perfumes mingling, came to him in a heavy, cloying wave as the dancers whirled past. He looked about him. The usual tapestries had been removed, the walls were hung instead with wide panels of red and gold. Every third panel had been embroidered in colors as near to life as possible to depict a scene in the history of England. The galleries, hung with blankets of flowers, hid the musicians, who were at this moment playing a gay reel. White-wigged servants, resplendent in green and gold livery, moved among the guests, carrying silver trays on which reposed fragile crystal goblets filled with wine. Jason's eyes were drawn to that corner of the room where he knew Sarah Barry to be. From this distance her face looked very young and eager. But mayhap it was merely the effect of the candlelight, for on his few meetings with her, her face had never looked other than solemn. Her red hair, against the green of her gown, seemed to have taken on an extra glow. She had lovely hair, he thought. It was so bright, so vital. Tonight, when she had entered the carriage, he had been amazed at the transformation his mother had wrought in the girl. Her hair, curling against her white neck, looked like fire. He had thought her quite lovely. Sarah Barry! How the damned girl seemed to haunt him. He had so many mind pictures of her. Pale and desperate, her eyes terrified, but at the same time defying him to hand her over to the Watch. The grotesque, pitiful creature in the cage. Standing beside his mother, her eyes looking into his with hatred. And yet, it had seemed later, she had not recognized him as the author of her misfortunes. And that was a question that still exercised his mind. Had she or had she not recognized him? Then there was that other memory of her that still seared him with anger whenever he thought of it. Lying on the cobbles at the mercy of that hulking man with the scarred face. He could still hear her trembling, begging voice: "Please help me. Do not let him touch me!"

Jason pressed his lips tightly together. Why the devil must he continually brood over Sarah Barry? She was nothing to him! It was as though her very presence constituted a deliberate invasion of his peace of mind. She was always changing. He had left London with one picture of her, filthy, verminous, a wild-haired creature conjured up from neglect and brutality. And he had returned to find that another picture had been substituted. The dainty flame-haired girl who had entered the carriage and sat so demurely with downcast eyes, that girl with her soft white flesh, her deep blue eyes with the dark fringes of her lashes making little shadows against her cheeks, the delicate, haunting perfume that arose from her clothes and her hair, reminding him vaguely of roses, could have no possible connection with that other creature.

He looked across the room again, and found that she was watching him. For a moment he held her gaze steadily, then, with calculated indifference, he looked away.

"I say," Sir Peter Baxter's voice broke in on his thoughts, "that's a devilish pretty little creature, old lad! I do not blame you that your eyes stray in her direction. Pity she is only your mother's servant, eh, laddie?"

"My mother's servant?" Jason said the words so abruptly

that Peter jumped. "I have no idea what you are babbling about!"

Peter frowned. He did not like Jason's tone. He felt it too lacking in the proper friendliness that was surely his due. Damn, he had almost barked the words at him. A pretty pass indeed if a fellow could not feel himself to be safe in expressing simple admiration of a lovely face and figure. For a moment he had had the alarming thought that the dashed fellow meant to set about him. His frown lifted as a possible solution came to him. Could it be that Jason had marked that delectable wench for his own? The more he thought about it, the more convinced he became that this was so. He said brightly, trying to mingle renunciation with wistful regret, "Hands off, dear lad, I quite understand. It only remains for me to beg your pardon for my blunder. I would not poach, laddie. No, no, not for the world. Pray put my words down to a simple and reverent tribute to your good taste."

"What!" Jason turned on him in a flash. "You will kindly cease this idiotic babbling! I have scarcely noticed Mistress Sarah Barry. If, however, your interest is caught, you have my permission to inform her of this fact."

Peter backed away a step. He had his permission, did he? he thought bitterly. All well and good to say that, and the dashed fellow looking as though at any moment he would smite him down in his tracks. Better by far to skirt danger than to run headlong into it. After all, he did not fancy being torn limb from limb for the sake of a fleeting fancy. Mistress Barry was very pretty, one might say beautiful, but he was sincerely in love with the Lady Dorothy Prentiss. Lady Dorothy, at the moment, was the mistress of my lord Bainbridge, but for all that, she had shown a decided interest in his humble self. Dorothy, too, was a redhead, and her eyes were very deep and blue. He thought rather uneasily of my lord Bainbridge, who was doing now what he had been doing all evening, scowling blackly in his direction. There was not much to choose between the two men, Peter thought in a surge of self-pity. Witherley and Bainbridge looked like a brace of murderers, both of them out for his innocent blood.

Peter's relief was great when Jason said, in what was, to his mind, an offensively abrupt tone, "It is hot in here. I think I will step outside for a few moments."

Despite his relief, Peter felt that it was his plain duty to remind him of something he had apparently forgotten. "It's November, laddie. Snow on the ground, that sort of thing."

"I thank you, Peter. However, I am aware that it is November."

"Oh, well," Peter said, waving a placating hand, "Reminder, that's all. Duty of a friend, you know."

Jason gave him a long, hard look. "If I were you," he said, "I would refrain from imbibing any more wine. You have never had a head for drink."

"Oh, now look here, dear lad, you are surely not intimating that I am addled with drink?"

"I am."

"Yes, but I say, that's all very well—" His words broke off as Jason turned his back and strode away. "Well!" Peter's voice took on a generous wrath. "Well, upon my soul!" Drawing his kerchief from his sleeve, he flicked an imaginary speck of dust from the purple satin of his sleeve. A quick glance sufficed to show him that Mistress Sarah Barry was no longer in evidence. But Lady Dorothy Prentiss, for the moment alone, was sipping a goblet of wine and glancing invitingly in his direction. Bainbridge's attention had been claimed by a little brunette beauty in a flame-red gown. Peter hesitated momentarily, weighing the safety of such a move. Then, pinning his faith on the brunette to keep the odious Bainbridge occupied, he strolled casually toward Lady Dorothy. Lady Dorothy's piercing squeal of delight when he stopped before her caused his heart to sink. He darted a nervous look over his shoulder. Encountering Bainbridge's menacing eyes, he flinched. Hurriedly executing a low, graceful bow before Lady Dorothy, he mumbled a few nervous words and then went hurriedly on his way.

The music drifted faintly to Jason's ears as he strolled along the path in the direction of the King's Fancy, as the famous rose gardens had been named. In the moonlight, the frost on the path had a subdued glitter, like unpolished diamonds, he thought. The trees and the bushes, heavy with their burden of snow, turned the familiar grounds into a ghost world. It was too cold, he decided, for casual strolling, but for the moment he wished to be alone. It was overhot in the ballroom, and his threatening headache had now become a pounding reality. As he drew nearer to the corner bench that marked the beginning of the King's Folly, he was surprised to see a small cloaked figure seated there.

"My lord." The cloaked figure rose and dropped a curtsey.

"Mistress Barry! What are you doing out here?" Even to his own ears, his words sounded unnecessarily curt.

She looked at him, and he saw the flash in her eyes before she looked away again. "If I have offended you, my lord," she said coldly, "I ask your pardon. I was not told that the grounds were forbidden to the servants."

"You are scarcely a servant, Mistress Barry. You are, I believe, to give you your proper title, my mother's companion."

"It is simply a more delicate way of putting it, my lord. I am still a servant."

He was instantly annoyed, the more so because she had been on his mind. "In any case, Mistress Barry, I did not say that the grounds were forbidden to you. I merely inquired of you what you are doing out here?"

"I was hot," she answered almost sullenly. "I felt the need of air."

"You had best return immediately. You will not be of much use to my mother if you take a chill."

"I will not, my lord. I am stronger than I look." She lifted her head and looked into his eyes. "I have learned to endure most things. I had need to learn that lesson, did I not, my lord?"

Again the question raced through his mind. Did she or did she not recognize him? The harsh words were out before he could stop them. "I dislike implication, Mistress Barry. If you have something to say, say it outright."

"What should I have to say, my lord?"

"Why did you refrain from telling my mother the name of the man who had you sent to Newgate Prison?"

She shrugged, and half turned away. "What purpose would it have served, my lord?"

He gripped her by the shoulders and turned her back to face him. "I am the man who had you imprisoned. There, it is out! You need fence with me no more. Say outright, Mistress Barry, that you hate me. That you would like to see me suffer as you have suffered. Say it!"

"No!" she tried to pull away. "No, I will not say it!"

"Why not? It is true, is it not?"

"I am quite sure, my lord, that my opinion of you, whatever I may think or feel, is of little consequence to you. Please release me. You are hurting my shoulders."

For answer, his fingers tightened. "You will not say you hate me, Mistress Barry?"

"I will not, my lord. I have found it wiser to say nothing at all."

Afterward, he was ashamed of the impulse that came to him to hurt and insult her. But in that moment he was not thinking rationally. He saw the mockery in her eyes, her cool assumption that she was mistress of the situation, and he determined to teach her otherwise. Slowly, he drew her toward him. "Then, Mistress Barry, I must assume that you do not hate me. That you will not object if I do this." His mouth came down hard on hers. Her struggling, violent at first, died. She was passive in his arms.

He lifted his head and looked at her. "What have you to say now, Mistress Barry?" he said, putting her from him.

She lifted her hand and wiped the back of it across her lips. "Rather than submit to your kisses again, my lord, I will say whatever you wish. I hate you. There, now are you satisfied?"

Her voice so cold, so lacking in any kind of emotion, brought the hot blood flushing to his face. "I beg your pardon, Mistress Barry. My action was unforgivable." His eyes glittered in the moonlight. "I think, however, that I would prefer your hatred to your indifference." He bowed stiffly and turned away.

She watched him walk toward the palace. The very last emotion she could feel for my lord Witherley would be indifference. Nay, she could never be indifferent, the emotions he stirred were too strong, too violent. She put a hand to her lips, feeling a self-hatred because she had enjoyed his kiss. Slowly, her thoughts troubled and confused, she followed after him.

She had almost reached the entrance when she heard somebody scream. She ran forward, her heart beating very fast. Her eyes widened with dismay as she stared at the frozen tableau before her. The dancers stood like statues, their eyes turned to the center of the floor.

The tableau broke as a small determined figure began pushing the dancers aside. "Let me through!" the Queen cried out in a voice that bordered on hysteria.

The dancers parted like a colorful wave, revealing the crumpled figure of the King. Standing above him, wringing her hands in agitation, was my lady Castlemaine. The Queen gave her one burning glance, then she dropped to her knees beside her husband. "My lord King!" She managed to lift his head so that it rested in her lap. "Do not stand there staring!" she cried. "One of you send for the King's physician."

"I have already done so, Madam," my lord Witherley's voice said.

"My lord!" The Queen looked up at his tall figure, her mouth trembling piteously. "I am so afraid!"

"Nay, Madam, you must not be. Have courage." My lord Witherley smiled at her. Sarah saw that that smile altered his whole expression. She had not thought he could be tender, but his expression was tender as he sought to reassure the frantic Queen. "See, Madam," he went on, "His Majesty's eyes are already opening. Doubtless it was the heat of the ballroom that caused him to faint. His Majesty's constitution is remarkably strong, and I feel sure that this is but some trifling indisposition."

"So you feel that, do you, you cursed knave?" the King's weak voice said indignantly. "I would have you know, my lord, that I am feeling plaguey ill."

"Charles!" Catherine's voice was agonized.

"Nay, Catherine, worry not. I am not yet dying. Pray, Madam, dismiss our guests with our apologies. As for you, Jason, I would have you stay with me for a while."

Chapter Nine

Mrs. Trevallion looked thoughtfully at the girl seated opposite her. Sarah Barry sat gracefully in her chair, staring with far-away blue eyes at the leaping flames in the grate.

The housekeeper smiled to herself. What a world of difference there was in Sarah now, she thought. It was almost impossible to believe that she was the same shivering, miserable creature my lady Witherley had brought to the house six months ago. In her plain white gown with bandings of bright green at the neckline and the cuffs, her creamy skin, her slender well-tended hands, and her rich red hair shining with vitality, Sarah looked more like a daughter of the house than an escaped Bedlamite. Mrs. Trevallion felt a wave of indignation, for she had grown very fond of the girl. Insane? Sarah! If she were insane, then so were thousands of others walking the streets. Hers was a story of misfortune, nothing more. Why, had she herself been in Newgate, and treated as harshly and brutally as Sarah had been, she too would have flown at the sadistic warder. Aye, and if she could not have found a weapon to attack him with, she would have used her teeth and her nails, just as Sarah had done. There was a limit to endurance, and that poor child, when she had attacked the warder, had reached it.

Folding her plump hands in her lap, Mrs. Trevallion settled herself more comfortably in her chair. It was true that Sarah had been a pickpocket, which was something that one of her perhaps too prim nature could not approve, but in these hard times, she felt that she had been driven to it both by the wretched circumstances in which she found herself and by her misguided love for that man, Jemmie Taylor. Only later had Sarah found to her cost that it had not been love she felt for him at all. He had a certain brute attraction that had appealed to the senses, and that she, in her lonely desperation, had mistaken for love.

Mrs. Trevallion smiled faintly. Sarah was quiet, there was no denying that, but she had plenty of spirit. A temper, too, which was almost as fiery as her hair. She had seen an instance of Sarah's temper. The boy employed to clean out the stables had been caught thrashing one of the horses with a weighted riding crop. She had been walking with Sarah at the time, and they had come suddenly upon the boy. Sarah's face had turned very white, then, her eyes blazing, she had leaped forward and torn the crop from the boy's hand. She had boxed his ears so thoroughly that the boy, bellowing with pain and fear, had fled hastily away to the safety of the inner yard.

Afterward, Sarah had said in halting explanation, "I hope that I did not frighten you, Mrs. Trevallion. I have never been able to bear cruelty, and especially not to helpless animals. In the district in which I lived as a child I saw a great deal of cruelty. And later, both in Newgate and Bedlam, I lived through a nightmare of it." She gave a strained smile. "But, then, I suppose you must be thinking I was cruel to the lad?"

"Nay, not a bit of it," Mrs. Trevallion had answered her roundly. "The plaguey boy deserved what he got." But she had seen the fear in the lovely clear eyes regarding her, and she felt that she knew exactly what the girl was thinking. "Nay, Sarah," she assured her gently, "you must not fear that I will think you showed insanity. It was indignation and good, healthy temper, nothing more. Why, child, you must not be afraid to show your natural emotions. You must always be yourself, and a plague on those who don't like it! As for

Bedlam, you must try to forget about that place. It won't be easy, I know, but you must try. And don't be forever watching yourself and guarding your tongue. Nobody in this house believes you to be insane, I do assure you."

Sarah had begun to tremble then, with reaction, and the relief the housekeeper's words afforded her. "I am sure the Bedlam authorities must still be searching for me," she said in a low voice.

Because she wanted to comfort the girl, Mrs. Trevallion had answered her soothingly. "Nay, they'll have given up by now. In any case, I feel sure that Lady Margaret has arranged everything."

Of course she was not sure. How could she be? But she could not bear to see Sarah look so. She stole another look at her. Sarah was still staring into the flames. What was she thinking about? the housekeeper wondered. The fact that Sarah chose to spend so much time with her in her snug little sitting room both touched and pleased her, but she could not help thinking that it must be excessively dull for her. Sarah was, after all, barely turned twenty. How shocking it was to know that in her short life she had lived through so much tragedy. But she had emerged like a butterfly from the chrysalis, showing herself to be an extremely pretty girl with a most attractive and arresting personality. Did she ever wonder what life now held in store for her? Did she perhaps fear that she would once more find herself adrift in her former state of humiliation and misery?

Mrs. Trevallion's eyes softened with pity. Poor child! She would not like to be haunted, as she felt sure Sarah must. If only Lady Margaret would come home. She had been at Court for several days now. But it would seem that, with the King suffering from the spotted fever, the Queen, who had a great affection and trust for Lady Margaret, needed her support. My lord Witherley, too, was detained at the Palace by the King's need. Mrs. Trevallion sighed impatiently. There was nothing particularly dangerous about the spotted fever, if care was taken. And the King, of course, had every care. Why then could Lady Margaret not come home? Sarah seemed lost without her. She loved her and missed her tremendously.

Sarah was not thinking of Lady Margaret at the moment. She was thinking of the scarred man. Often, tossing and turning in her bed, her mind too alert to admit sleep, the old terror would seize upon her and carry her back to that dreadful night. Herself, lying terrified and helpless on the slimy cobbles of Lilacgrove Alley. And that man! That man with his cruel, twisted face! She remembered her own fervent inward prayer that if the man took her she would not survive it. She had nothing to live for, nothing to hope for, and she would be better off dead. And then, like a miracle, my lord and lady Witherley had been there. They had saved her from the scarred man then, but who would protect her from him in the future? She shivered, thinking of the number of times she had seen the scarred man loitering near the house. She knew, instinctively, that he waited for her. But how had he found her? Why would he not leave her alone?

Unaware of the housekeeper's startled look, Sarah's hands gripped the arms of her chair, her knuckles showing white. Several times she had started to tell Lady Margaret about the man's frequent appearances, and each time, before the words could be uttered, she had stopped herself. The man had appeared about a month ago, but how could she tell Lady Margaret of her fears. Perhaps she would look at her with wondering and pitying eyes. She might even believe that she had been mistaken in thinking her to be sane, and that it was her inflamed imagination that had conjured him up. She could not bear it if Lady Margaret began to doubt her. Even to her it did not make sense that the man should choose to come here and spend his time gazing at the house. He belonged in the gutters and stews of London, and he was out of his element in this select neighborhood. Only this morning she had seen him again. He had been standing on the other side of the street, his eyes fixed unblinkingly on the house. A passing carriage had momentarily hidden him from view, and when she looked again, he had gone. When she saw that man, all her newfound confidence deserted her. But sometimes her fear would give way to a blaze of anger. She would picture herself marching across the street and asking him outright what he was doing there. Sometimes she even got halfway to the door, but before she could open it, her anger would fade. She had not been long enough in this new life to face with confidence that menacing figure.

"What is it, Sarah?" Mrs. Trevallion's voice cut across her troubled thoughts. "Why are you shivering? How can you be cold with that great fire blazing in the grate?"

"I am not cold." Sarah looked at her with somber eyes. "I had not realized that I was shivering."

"Is anything wrong, child?"

Sarah hesitated, wondering if she might confide in the housekeeper? "Nay, Mrs. Trevallion, what could be wrong?"

Mrs. Trevallion eyed her dubiously, sure in her own mind that something was troubling the girl. After a moment, she said, "In any case, my dear, you are looking rather pale. I know 'tis not the thing for a young lady to walk unescorted, but, if you care to take a little walk, you have my permission to do so. I know you will not go far, and the air will do you good."

Sarah clasped her nervous hands tightly together. A walk was the last thing she wished to take. The scarred man might be there. He might follow her, attack her! "I would rather not. If you do not object to my company, I would prefer to stay here."

"As you wish. You know that I am always glad to have you. I expect you are feeling a little depressed with my lady gone, and the house so quiet. Never mind, I feel sure my lady will be returning soon, and then things will be a little brighter for you."

"But I like the quiet," Sarah assured her. "You cannot imagine what it means to me. But naturally I do miss Lady Margaret." She smiled. "However, with you for company, I have no cause for complaint."

Mrs. Trevallion suppressed her pleasure and gave a disparaging sniff. " 'Tis nice of you to say so, my dear, but I am an old woman and no fit company for a young girl. Doubtless my lord Witherley will return with Lady Margaret, and mayhap there will be a few entertainments given."

Sarah's lips tightened. "Yes," she said.

Mrs. Trevallion looked at her curiously. "Whenever Master Jason is mentioned, I have this strong feeling that you dislike him. Why is this, Sarah?"

Sarah thought of the kiss my lord Witherley had given her, and she turned her hot face away. She loathed herself. How could she have found even a momentary pleasure in that man's kiss? She said in a low voice, "It is not for me to like or dislike my lord Witherley. If, however, I have allowed my feelings to show, then I am sorry."

"Then you do dislike him? I knew it. Why, child?"

"I would—would rather not say."

"Then I will not press you. But do try not to judge Master Jason too harshly."

"You are very fond of him, are you not?"

"Aye. He's a good lad. I have known him from the time he was breeched."

Sarah hesitated, but the compulsion to know more of the man was too strong to resist. "Will you tell me a little about him?"

Mrs. Trevallion nodded. "I will, but it is a little hard to know where to begin. Master Jason takes a deal of knowing, I assure you. I know that he has a cold and forbidding air, but 'tis only surface. He is not really like that inside. He can be very stubborn; he always was, even as a little lad. Another of his faults is that he is inclined to judge too hastily, and repent afterward." She chuckled. "And, oh, my, when he is really offended, those blue eyes of his can fairly freeze you to the marrow."

Sarah said in a puzzled voice, "Perhaps you are not aware of it, Mrs. Trevallion, but you are making him sound most disagreeable."

"That he's not!" Mrs. Trevallion said indignantly. "Though doubtless, when you first met him, you thought so. People do tend to do that. I told you he takes knowing." Her face softened. "But I can tell you this, Sarah. You will find, when you really get to know him, that your first impression was quite wrong."

"Will I?"

"Aye. And there is no need to look so doubtful."

"I am sorry," Sarah hastened to soothe the old lady. "In any case, since I am not a member of the family, I am unlikely to have much to do with my lord Witherley."

"You are Lady Margaret's companion. Master Jason is certainly not neglectful of his mother, so it is likely you will see a great deal of him."

Sarah smiled faintly. "Companions, I believe, are supposed to retire into the background. To become, as it were, part of the furniture."

"How can you say that," Mrs. Trevallion looked at her reproachfully. "You know well that Lady Margaret is extremely fond of you."

"I do know that. Her kindness is such that she treats me as she would a daughter. But I cannot expect my lord Witherley to view me in the same light. I am sure 'tis best if I become as inconspicuous as possible."

Mrs. Trevallion laughed. "Inconspicuous? With that flaming hair of yours? You are as pretty as a picture, child, and you couldn't be inconspicuous, no matter how you try. You will, I know, take Master Jason's eye."

"I do not want to take his eye. I would far rather that he did not notice me at all, Mrs. Trevallion," Sarah's voice, slightly uncontrolled, rose. "Not all are as kind and trusting as Lady Margaret. I cannot imagine that my lord Witherley feels the same toward me as his mother. I am very much afraid that he will send me away. D-do you think that he w-will?"

Mrs. Trevallion's thin gray brows drew together in a worried frown. "Let us not borrow trouble, lass. Master Jason is a just lad."

"But I could not bear it if he—if he—"

"If he what, Sarah?"

"If he should send me back to th-that place. Do you not see?" Sarah said brokenly. "I am an escaped Bedlamite. As such, I am at the mercy of people. They may raise me up, if they so choose, or they may d-dispense with my l-life."

Mrs. Trevallion leaned forward and patted the girl's quivering hand. "Nay, Sarah, stop it! Now you listen to me. I know well that you are not insane; Lady Margaret knows it too."

"But will my lord Witherley know it?"

"Aye. If you conduct yourself in such a way that your sanity will not be in question."

Sarah stared at her for a moment, then she nodded. "You are right. I will be as quiet and as careful and as neat as possible. And mayhap, if I do not irritate him or bring myself to his attention in any way, my lord will learn to endure me."

Mrs. Trevallion frowned. "Nay, Sarah, be yourself. I know well that Master Jason likes a fighter. If you show some spirit, he is much more likely to consider you favorably."

"What if he should mistake spirit for insanity?"

"Bah! Master Jason is no fool. Think you he cannot tell the difference between spirit and a good, healthy temper, and insanity?"

Sarah's mind again went back to that scene in the royal gardens. "I do not think I would dare to show him temper," she said slowly.

Smiling, Mrs. Trevallion leaned back in her chair. "And why not, I should like to know? Master Jason can be very trying at times."

"Mrs. Trevallion, I am not a daughter of this house. I am a servant."

"I also am a servant. But for all that, Master Jason has had the rough edge of my tongue many a time. No, Sarah, I know that he cannot abide a crushed or a timid female."

"You really advise me to be myself?"

"I do, child."

Sarah's chin lifted. "Very well, I will trust your advice. My lord Witherley shall meet the real Sarah Barry, and not a pale imitation of her."

"Good girl!" Mrs. Trevallion yawned. "I'm sorry. I do believe all this talking has tired me."

Sarah rose at once. "I have some tasks that I have been neglecting. You close your eyes for a while."

Left alone, Mrs. Trevallion tucked a few straying wisps of gray hair beneath her white cap and composed herself for sleep. At the back of her mind, driving sleep away, was a small worry. She believed that her advice to Sarah Barry was the right advice, and yet there was a faint doubt. Master Jason could be blind when he did not wish to see. But surely he would realize that Sarah did not belong in Bedlam Asylum? She found her thoughts drifting back to that time when Lady Margaret had first brought Sarah to the house. She could see it all so clearly. Bailey standing there, his face set and disapproving. Master Jason, expressionless. And Lady Margaret, concerned and anxious for the girl. Aye, that cringing, filthy girl.

With the privilege of long service, she had cried out in protest, "My lady, what have you done now? Who is this creature?"

"The girl is in sore need of help, Trevallion," Lady Margaret had answered, smiling at her. "I have brought her home so that she may be safe for a while."

"But, my lady, surely you have recognized by the smock where she comes from? She is from Bedlam Asylum!"

"I know that, Trevallion. But she is not insane."

"Not insane?" Scandalized, Mrs. Trevallion stared at her. "How can you possibly know that, my lady? Look at the poor creature. Cannot you see that she is beyond help?"

Lady Margaret ignored her. She had taken the girl's dirt-encrusted hand in hers and said in her soft and beautiful voice, "I have decided, Sarah, on this very moment, that this will be your home from now on. You will be safe here."

"Mother!" My lord Witherley, at his most forbidding, spoke curtly. "I have thus far given in to your whim, but I forbid you to commit yourself irrevocably."

Lady Margaret gave him a pleading look. "Jason, darling, she has had such a dreadful life. Be kind, as I know you can be."

"It is not a question of kindness, Mother, but of common sense. She may stay for a while, since your heart is set on this folly, but I cannot allow it to become a permanent arrangement."

Mrs. Trevallion had tried one more protest. "I feel quite sure, my lady, though your intentions are compassionate, that there is nothing that you can do for the creature."

And then Sarah Barry had spoken for the first time. Her drooping head lifted and she looked steadily at the housekeeper. "Pray do not call me a creature, ma'am. I would have you know that I am not insane, and that your mistress is as safe with me as she would be with you. My name, if you wish to know it, is Sarah Barry."

Mrs. Trevallion, to her annoyance, had felt suddenly ashamed. She stared at the girl for a long moment, then she said in a low voice, "Aye, lass, I was rude. You do right to rebuke me."

Remembering, Mrs. Trevallion smiled to herself. Though sometimes pausing to wonder at herself, she had taken the girl under her wing. Aye, she thought, with satisfaction, and she had never had cause to regret it. She still marveled at the way Sarah Barry had repaid her time and trouble. Bathed, those terrible nails cut and trimmed, her hair washed and cleansed of lice, dressed in a cast-off gown of Lady Margaret's, what a joy it had been to see the pale but pretty girl who had emerged from terror and privation. And the wonder of Sarah's hair! How amazed she had been when the filthy matted mass had washed a rich red-gold. In the days and weeks that followed, Sarah's personality likewise emerged. There were many facets to that personality, she had found. Sarah was quiet, yet spirited; she had a keen wit and a certain fascination, Lady Margaret called it charm, that bound people to her.

She herself, though she was but the housekeeper, was by no means as trusting as Lady Margaret, but little by little she had abandoned her suspicious watchfulness. After a month had passed, she could leave the girl alone with Lady Margaret without feeling the smallest twinge of alarm. If Sarah Barry was insane, she told herself firmly, then so was she, so was Lady Margaret. There was no doubt now in her mind that a great injustice had been perpetrated against Sarah Barry.

Mrs. Trevallion's faint worry vanished. Master Jason hated injustice. Aye, why concern herself. All would be well. On this last thought, she fell asleep, a smile on her lips.

Chapter Ten

The snow had given way to freezing rain. It had been raining for the past two hours, the first light drizzle rapidly increasing to a soaking downpour. Rain dripped from the eaves and ran down the fronts of the houses like dirty tears. Wide fans of muddy water sprayed from the wheels of passing carriages, soaking the odd pedestrian, who invariably retaliated with curses of an extremely pithy nature. The gutter, which ran the full length of Twyford Street, overflowed with its extra burden of water and sent a collection of fish scales, meat bones, offal, cabbage stalks, paper, and sundry other rubbish to wash over the uneven cobbles. A fat ginger cat, yowling piteously, sought shelter beneath the carved and gilded archway of one of the tall dwellings. The more ambitious of the hawkers who daily strolled the select residential area of Twyford Street and the adjacent Laburnham Crescent, shouting their wares in cheerful raucous voices, had long since abandoned their efforts. Though the old woman, her grizzled hair straggling from beneath a shabby black bonnet, had thrown her shawl over her basket of wilting lavender stalks and a collection of carved wooden dolls. Following the example of the cat, she was huddled beneath an archway. She divided her time between looking over her shoulder at the door of the house, obviously fearing to be sent on her way, and peering anxiously at the lowering sky, hoping for a cessation of the rain.

William Mitford, standing behind the tall, dripping bushes which lined the edge of the Common opposite the house he had watched so tenaciously for the past month or more, was oblivious to discomfort. He was used to being abroad in all conditions of weather. Looking at the spewed-out mess from the gutter, he reflected with a sour satisfaction that the gutters of the rich were not, after all, so very different to those of the poor. There was the same all-pervading stench, the same slime and filth as washed over Lilacgrove Street and the neighboring Lilacgrove Alley. The difference was that the gutters of the rich were cleaned out more frequently. And the rat-catchers, generously rewarded from well-lined purses, were more assiduous in their duties.

Mitford rubbed his head, wishing that the throbbing would subside. When the ache in his head became very bad, he would think fearfully of Bedlam Asylum. It was because of this ache in his head, because of the things it made him do, that his uncle had had him committed to that place. His lips stretched into a snarl. At least, his uncle had said that he did those things, but he did not believe him. The old man had hated him, and it was easy enough for him to make up lies. If he had done half of the things of which he was accused, he would remember doing them. No, the old man had lied, God curse his black soul! And he had been condemned to the agony of the lash, the cage, and the small, dark, stifling hole in which they thrust the rebellious patients.

To distract himself, Mitford began to think of the people who dwelt in these houses in Twyford Street. Aye, the people were grand now, but when they died there would be no distinction between a rich corpse or a poor. Death was no respecter of persons. The same worm-infested earth that covered the cheap coffins of the poor would be thrown over their expensive carved caskets. The same black crows would hover over their graves, hoping for pickings. and the worms would eat them with the same gusto.

Mitford's lips curled. But in life, the swells always survived.

It was the poor and wretched who went down. No chance for them, ever!

Mitford's mood lightened as he thought of his own little place in Lilacgrove Alley. There was nothing grand about it, like these great houses, but it was snug. There were still the rats, of course, and the bedbugs which sucked his blood, leaving little raised red bumps on his skin, but after Bedlam Asylum, it was a palace. He glared across at the house he had been watching. No bugs in their scented sheets, he thought bitterly. By Christ, but he hated the swells!

Frowning, he shrugged his heavy shoulders. Hate the swells he could and did, but at this moment he had other things on his mind. From a break between the screening bushes, he stared steadily at Number 52 Twyford Street. In his opinion, it was one of the fancier houses in a very fancy neighborhood. The front of the house was scrolled and gilded, and the great oaken front door was fretted in an intricate pattern and embellished with a lion's-head knocker. On either side of the short driveway, lawns stretched out. The grass was frost-seared now, but he could imagine how velvety and green those lawns would be in the spring and the early summer. The hour was early yet, but candlelight glimmered golden from the numerous velvet- and satin-draped windows, keeping at bay the gray murkiness of the weather.

Forgetting that he was hidden by the bushes, Mitford stepped back a startled pace as he caught a glimpse of a slender hand drawing the drapes closed at one of the upper windows. Just before they closed fully, the owner of the hand peered from the window. He saw red hair and the white blur of a face beneath it.

Mitford moved restlessly. He came here day after day. In his mind, he could still hear the loonie laughing at him. And his desire for revenge was a burning obsession. It had taken him a long time to find her, but when he had found out that the man who was called the Duke was, in reality, my lord Witherley, it had been easy. Nothing now could deter him. He would not be baulked. So each day he came to stand before the house. Sometimes he stood in full sight, wanting the loonie to know that he was there. Waiting! He took pleasure in the thought of her terror. Other times, as now, he hid himself behind the tall bushes. She must not glimpse him too often, or her fear might keep her indoors beyond his reach. But time was passing, and he had got no nearer to her. For all that, he was determined not to give up. He had seen the girl on the outside several times, but she had always been accompanied. The first time the loonie had emerged from the house, walking gracefully by the side of my lady Witherley, he had not recognized her. But gradually, as he followed them at a safe distance, his ears straining to catch scraps of their conversation, he had come to realize that the girl with the slender, prettily curved figure, the shining wealth of red-gold hair framing a lovely face, was the one he sought. Whenever she came from the house, he would, from the concealment of the bushes, stare hungrily at that face and figure. His obsession deepened, strengthened, became a part of him. For this obsession, hc neglected everything else that had once occupied his time. One day he would have the loonie. He would! He must! It was the only way he could stop the pounding in his head.

The rain had returned to its original light drizzle when the black coach with gilded side panels came bowling around the corner of Laburnham Crescent and drew up before Number 52. Mitford, watching intently, saw my lady Witherley emerge first. She was followed by a tall swell, with dark-blond hair showing beneath a wide-brimmed scarlet plumed hat. Mitford drew in his breath sharply. My lord Witherley! That interfering swine! He seemed drunk, Mitford thought, or maybe he was ill. Whatever the cause, he was swaying. He saw my lady

Witherley take one of his arms, and beckon to the coachman to take the other.

Irritably, my lord Witherley disengaged his arms. "Thank you," he said in the curt, arrogant voice that Mitford remembered so well. "I am not in need of assistance. I am neither crippled nor helpless, and I am perfectly capable of walking alone."

"I know, darling, as you have done all of your adult life," Lady Witherley's soft, distressed voice said. "But this time it is different, Jason, for you do need help. Come, pray do not be difficult."

Mitford gritted his teeth together in a spasm of hatred as the arrogant voice answered: "I have no desire to be difficult, Mother. And I inform you now that I will not be treated as a child."

"You are my child. Though most of the time you choose to forget it."

"As perhaps you have done on occasions, Mother." There was a short silence, then my lord Witherley said in a voice that shook slightly, "Forgive me, that was unworthy."

"I understand, darling. Perhaps I deserve it."

"Nay. But if we must argue on such a trivial subject, then pray let us do so in a decent privacy."

"Jason! It is not a trivial matter to me. Oh, very well, I will say no more, for I see that you are determined to make things as difficult as possible." Sighing, my lady Witherley lifted her green skirts clear of the wet cobbles and walked to the door of the house.

With a mixture of resentment and interest, Mitford stared at the dressed-up flunky who opened the door. Bowing, the footman stood to one side, allowing my lady Witherley to pass him.

With malicious amusement, Mitford noted that my lord Witherley was not quite as sure of himself as he would have the lady believe. He faltered, and then placed a thin, ringed hand on the coachman's shoulder. Aided by this, he reeled to the entrance in such a fashion that, had he not looked ill, Mitford would have thought him to be bosky with drink. Reverting at once to his usual bitter cynicism and his profound hatred of the upper classes, he assured himself that the swell was certainly bosky. Drink could give you that same ghastly pallor. This idea being one more to his taste and understanding, he grinned to himself.

When the carved door had closed behind them, Mitford came out from his shelter. Cursing beneath his breath, he at last became conscious of the discomfort of the rain. For a moment he stood there irresolute, wondering if the loonie might yet appear. A moment's thought told him that she would not be coming out in this rain. He was just wasting his time. His face brooding, he pulled up the collar of his tattered jacket and slouched away. He would come back tomorrow; he would come again and again. And one day he would find that she was alone. He would make sure that the loonie had good cause to remember William Mitford.

My lord Witherley entered the hall. His feet did not seem to belong to him. He had tried not to show it, for he hated to admit to a weakness, but he was feeling dazed and very ill indeed. Obviously he had contracted the spotted fever from the King. Strange. He had not thought the illness to be quite so contagious. Frowning, he stood still in the center of the hall. His head was swimming and he could not seem to collect his thoughts. He looked about him, not quite sure where he was. He looked toward the stairs and saw a girl standing upon the landing. Sarah Barry! The name sprang clearly into his fuddled mind. Sarah Barry! It would seem that the wench was fated to haunt him. He shook his head. But was she really there, or did he only imagine it? She seemed to be floating in a grayish light, and the only thing that stood out clearly from the mist was the red-gold nimbus of her hair. She was floating toward him now, first looming large before his eyes, and then rapidly dwindling until she was no more than a tiny, insubstantial figure. The white and gold tiles of the hall rushed up to meet him and swirled dizzyingly about him. He clutched at his cravat which suddenly seemed to be strangling him. "Damn you, Sarah Barry!" he said in a thick voice. Darkness closed in on him, and, with an inarticulate cry, he crumpled to the floor.

"Jason!" Lady Margaret sank to her knees beside him. She leaned over him anxiously, little dribbles of rain from the brim of her green bonnet fell on his colorless face. She looked up at the startled footman. "My lord Witherley has taken the spotted fever. Find Trevallion," she bade him. "Tell her that she is needed urgently." Her eyes turned to the coachman. "Bailey, go and tell Hawtrey that he is to help you carry my son to his room."

Sarah stood very still, watching. "Damn you, Sarah Barry!" he had said. Did he hate her so much, then? She had thought of the first time when, perhaps, she would find herself alone with him. She had thought of the kind of questions he might ask her, and she had planned how she would answer him. If his attitude prove to be hostile, she would be cool, perhaps haughty. But never defensive, never pleading. In those rehearsed and imaginary conversations she had with him, she had always managed to convince him that she was a thinking, feeling human being much like himself. "I have a heart, and I have feelings that are capable of being hurt," she would tell him. "I am not somebody who must be regarded with horror, or turned from your door like a leper."

Looking at him now, his last words still in her ears, she was convinced that he would never regard her with anything other than aversion and hostility. She took a step downward, and then stood still again, trying to remember how much she hated him. But he looked so white. So pathetically vulnerable in unconsciousness!

"Sarah!" Lady Margaret called to her impatiently. "Why do you just stand on those stairs? Cannot you see that my son is ill and that he needs our help?" She turned her head, beckoning. "Come here, child, loosen his cravat. I will go and hurry Bailey, for I have no doubt that he is loitering."

Looking thoroughly distracted, Lady Margaret rose to her feet. She hesitated for a moment, and then swept away with a rustle of silken skirts, leaving a trail of delicate perfume behind her.

Sarah hesitated no longer. She ran swiftly down the stairs. Kneeling beside my lord Witherley, she put to one side the hat that had fallen from his head. Gently she withdrew the sapphire pin and unfastened the satin cravat. He was breathing in shallow gasps, and her fingers trembled as she worked. On an impulse, she touched the damp blond hair and smoothed it back from the forehead.

She thought that he stirred very slightly, and panic touched her. Scrambling to her feet again, she almost fell over her skirt. She ran to the couch that stood between two long, velvet-draped windows. Snatching up a cushion, she returned to his side. She found that her nervous trembling was increasing as she lifted his head and inserted the cushion beneath. Would he open his eyes? Would he perhaps order her to leave his house at once? She bit her lip. Nay, she was being foolish. Even if he wished, he was far too ill to issue orders.

He stirred and moaned. It was as if her agitated thoughts had penetrated the veil of unconsciousness, for the thing she had been dreading happened. He opened his eyes, eyes that were confused and fever-bright.

'M-my lord." Sarah placed a soothing hand on his shoulder. "Pray to lie still."

For a moment he stared at her vaguely, then his face tightened to grimness. "You!" he exclaimed. "Why do you keep changing? Why do you follow me around?"

What did he mean? "Hush, my lord!" she whispered. "Hush!"

His head turned restlessly, and she could see the glaze of perspiration on his face. "Think not to gull me, wench. I am not so easily taken in."

"My lord, I am not trying to deceive you. I—"

Her words broke off and she gave a frightened gasp as his hand shot out and gripped her wrist with surprising strength. "You slut! Will you go of your own free will, or must I put you out?"

Sarah snatched her wrist free. "Do not trouble yourself, my lord, I will go."

His eyes turned to her again. "Sarah Barry?" he said in a voice that had lost its cold authority. "Is that you, Sarah Barry?"

She stared at him in bewilderment. Obviously he was delirious. Perhaps he had not meant his words. It was a frail hope, but she clung to it. "You must be quiet, my lord. You are very ill."

"Sarah?" he said again. "Is that you?"

"Yes, my lord, I am Sarah."

His tawny brows drew together. "Sarah? I will not have it, Mother! It is madness, I tell you!"

Sarah started as a hand was laid upon her shoulder. "My poor lad looks bad, Sarah," Mrs. Trevallion's voice said. "I had a feeling that he would take the disease from the King. Master Jason will not like being ill. He cannot abide what he believes to be a weakness."

Sarah looked up into the housekeeper's wrinkled and anxious face. "I am sure he will dislike it," she said crisply, "but he will have to learn that we are all subject to the weaknesses of the body. Does my lord Witherley believe himself to be so far above other men that he alone will remain untouched by human ills?"

Mrs. Trevallion was taken aback by the unexpected sharpness of her tone. She stared at the flushed and angry face for a moment. "Now, lass, whatever ails you? I only meant that Master Jason has ever been impatient with illness. His own, perhaps I should say. For when illness afflicts others, he can be quite astonishingly patient and gentle. I know. He was so with me when I took an ague."

"I am not impressed with your excuses, Rexham, or with your tales of the ill luck that constantly dogs you," my lord Witherley's slurred voice said. "If, after tomorrow, I find you still on this estate, I cannot answer for the consequences to yourself."

Her lips tight, Sarah rose to her feet. "Forgive me, Mrs. Trevallion, I know you are fond of him, but I cannot believe that there are any gentle or finer feelings in my lord Witherley."

"You are wrong, lass."

Sarah turned away. "Will you stay with him, Mrs. Trevallion? Lady Margaret will be returning shortly with Bailey and Hawtrey. If you will excuse me, I will go and see that my lord Witherley's bed is prepared."

"Of course I'll stay." With some difficulty, Mrs. Trevallion squatted down beside him. She touched his cheek gently. "Quiet, lad, quiet. All is well." She turned her head. "Sarah, mind you warm the sheets. He has a fever, and I am not wanting him to get a shock from cold sheets."

"I will see to it," Sarah answered. As she went up the stairs, the slurred voice seemed to follow her. "Sarah? Is that her name? Nay, Mother, I will not have the female near me!"

There were tears in Sarah's eyes as she entered my lord Witherley's bedchamber. He was cruel, callous!

She turned her thoughts in a more practical direction. Whatever my lord Witherley might be, she would not dwell on it now. She looked curiously about her. She had seen most of the rooms, but she had never entered my lord Witherley's bedchamber before. It was a big room, surely the biggest room in the house, she thought. It was decorated in tones of amber, green, and silver. The two big windows were draped in heavy amber velvet, the drapes looped back with twined green and silver cords. On the amber carpet, which, Mrs. Trevallion had told her, was a recent import from France, sat two easy chairs upholstered in a thick, lustrous green satin. Against the wall, nearest to the door, was a long couch upholstered in pale-green velvet, with several colorful cushions in various shapes scattered along its length. Beneath the windows was a large oval table, bearing a rather tattered quill, a leather-bound book clasped in gold, and a silver-framed painting of a much younger Lady Margaret. To the right of the room was another door, which, Sarah thought, must lead into a dressing room. But the dominant feature of the room was the bed. It was very wide and deep, with a rearing carved headboard and a tester in the same amber velvet embossed with small silver figures of children, goats, horses, and other animals. One of Mrs. Trevallion's favorite stories was that my lord Witherley had had this tester as a child, and had firmly refused to part with it. Somehow, Sarah found it hard to believe that he had this soft and sentimental streak in him.

Smoothing the sheets over the bed, and running over the cool linen with the warming pan, Sarah suddenly felt furiously angry. She knew what was in my lord Witherley's mind concerning herself, for his rambling words had betrayed him. He had already condemned her. Obviously he did not intend to give her the courtesy of a hearing. She thumped the two plump pillows into shape and wished that, instead of the pillows, it could be his arrogant head.

She stood back from the bed as the door opened and Bailey and Hawtrey came into the room. To her surprise, my lord Witherley was walking between them, supported only by their grip on his arms. Other than the fact that his face was now heavily flushed and his eyes too bright, he seemed to be in his normal senses. He glanced briefly at Sarah, and then sat down heavily on the bed. "You may go, Mistress Barry. And thank you."

She turned away from him. "I will go, my lord," she murmured, "but first I must finish making the bed."

"I beg your pardon? Look at me, if you please, Mistress Barry. I dislike to talk to the back of a person's head."

She turned quickly to face him. "Very well, my lord, now I am looking at you."

"I did not hear your previous remark, Mistress Barry. Pray repeat it."

"I said, my lord, that I will go. But first I must finish making the bed."

He thought he heard a challenge in her voice, but he felt too tired and too ill to pursue it. His senses, as they had done before, were beginning to haze over. To cover his weakness, he spoke more harshly than he had intended. "Either Bailey or Hawtrey will finish the task. Doubtless, Mistress Barry, you and I will converse at a later date. For the moment, however, you may leave me."

"Yes, my lord, we will, as you say, converse at a later date. I have no doubt that you will find a great deal to say to me." She dropped him a barely sketched courtsey. "I wish you a speedy recovery, my lord."

At the door, Bailey, who had grown quite fond of Sarah, bent his head and whispered rapidly, "Now don't you be looking so worried, Mistress Barry. 'Tis naught but an attack of the spotted fever. My lord, if nursed carefully, will quickly recover."

She stared at him. Bailey actually thought she was concerned about that man! "I assure you, Bailey," she answered him in a low voice, "I am not in the least worried."

Bailey looked at her with concern. It was his opinion that little Mistress Barry was on the verge of tears. "Don't you be put off by his lordship's manner. He don't mean nothing by it. When you get to know him, you'll find he's not such a bad sort. A little bit stiff and abrupt, but not so bad as you may think."

"What the devil are you whispering for, Bailey?" my lord Witherley demanded.

Sarah did not wait to hear Bailey's reply. Picking up her skirts, she fled along the corridor. She was about to descend the stairs when she saw Lady Margaret mounting, with Mrs. Trevallion puffing heavily behind her.

"Oh, Sarah, there you are!" Lady Margaret's hands fluttered out in a gesture of appeal. "I am so glad you are here. Jason must be nursed, but I am afraid he will be a very difficult patient for us to manage."

Sarah stared at her. "For us, Lady Margaret?"

"Why, yes. You will help me, will you not?"

"But, my lady—"

"Sarah! Surely you will not refuse me? You see, I irritate the poor boy so much, though I assure you that I do not mean to do so. And poor Trevallion, you must know, cannot take on an extra burden."

Mrs. Trevallion bridled indignantly. "That I can, my lady. He's my lad!"

"Dear Trevallion!" Lady Margaret gave her a vague, sweet smile. "Of course you will help. But Sarah is young and strong and willing. Are you not, my dear?"

Defeated, conscious of the great debt she owed this woman, who, until this moment, had asked so little of her, Sarah nodded. "I will do what I can, my lady."

"Splendid! I knew that you would." In her relief, Lady Margaret smiled radiantly. "Naturally there is Meadows, Jason's man. He will be here soon. He was following us with the baggage. But after all, there is only so much one man may do. Meadows will be willing, I know, but illness needs a woman's tender touch. Do you not agree, Sarah?"

Sarah looked at her sharply. This Lady Margaret, so fluttery and vague and helpless, was a very different woman to the one she was accustomed to. "I do agree," she answered slowly. "But in this case, does it not need a mother's touch?"

Sighing, Lady Margaret met Sarah's eyes. "I will never make an actress, I fear, for I can tell that you have seen through me. I thought, you see, if I appeared helpless, that you would not refuse me."

Sarah smiled. "I am sure that you must know that I could not refuse you anything. But why the pretense, my lady?"

Lady Margaret flushed faintly. "You see, child, you have grown dear to me, and I do not intend to lose you. I thought, if Jason were to see a great deal of you, that he would understand my feelings in the matter. Oh, my dear, do not look so stricken! I know that I put things badly, it has always been a failing of mine. I would not, in any case, allow him to send you away. But it would be nice if all could be easy and amicable."

Sarah released her caught breath. "Very nice," she said wryly. "But I fear that I will not grow dear to my lord Witherley. Or, for that matter, he to me. But I promise you that I will do my best."

"Sarah! Do you feel that you cannot like my son?"

"I should not have said that, my lady. I do not know him, do I? Therefore 'tis impossible to tell."

"Of course. But I feel sure, when you do know him, that you will grow excessively fond of him."

Sarah was certain that she could never, under any circumstances whatsoever, feel the smallest fondness for my lord

Witherley. But she was saved the necessity of replying when Mrs. Trevallion said in an amused voice, "Ah, my lady, there speaks the doting mother."

Lady Margaret turned on the housekeeper such a look of indignation that Sarah's lips twitched into an involuntary smile. "You are quite mistaken, Trevallion. I love my son, but I most certainly do not dote. I hope that I am able to see his faults as well as appreciate his virtues. My son may seem to be difficult at times, but he is a dear boy. You cannot deny it."

Mrs. Trevallion drew her plump figure up in haughty offense. "Nor would I dream of denying it, my lady, as well you know. He is my lad, and only an addlepate would suggest, or even remotely imply, that I do not love and understand him."

Lady Margaret laughed. "And I am an addlepate, Trevallion?"

Mrs. Trevallion sniffed. "If the cap fits, my lady."

"Aye, it does," Lady Margaret answered, patting her shoulder. "Come with me, Trevallion. We will go together to see our lad." She turned her sweet smile on Sarah. "I have told cook to prepare a warm drink for Jason. 'Tis just some healing herbs, on which I place great reliance, mixed with a little cordial and hot water. I think that it cannot harm him. Will you bring it up when it is ready, please?"

Lady Margaret turned away, drawing the housekeeper with her. "And, Sarah," she added, "pray see that he drinks it. Do not on any account allow him to refuse you. He can be very stubborn, but I am sure you will be able to deal with that."

"But, my lady," Sarah said in dismay, "Perhaps it would be better if you gave him the drink."

Lady Margaret began to walk away. "Nonsense, Sarah," she called lightly. "He is used to Trevallion and I. But he will think twice before venting his temper on you."

Full of doubt and misgiving, Sarah went slowly down the

stairs. She paused at the bottom, deep in thought. She did not at first notice the pale-faced little man advancing toward her. Only when he stood there, his expression polite, did she notice him, and realize that he was waiting to ascend the stairs.

Sarah stood aside. "I beg your pardon." At her glance of inquiry, the man introduced himself. "I am Thomas Meadows, ma'am. My lord Witherley's valet. I have just arrived."

There was nothing in him at first sight to inspire confidence. Meadows's eyes were brown and mournful, and even his lips turned down in the same mournful manner. Yet, for some reason, Sarah's heart lightened.

"My name is Sarah Barry," she answered. "I am lady Witherley's companion."

The respect in his manner did not decrease, but his mournful eyes warmed very slightly. Sarah Barry, though obviously an upper-class servant, was nevertheless a servant, and he unbent still more. He said in a confiding voice, "His lordship was quite irritable when he left the Palace. Is he perchance making himself difficult?"

Listening to the precise voice, Sarah wondered how well this man knew my lord Witherley. "I do not know," she said, smiling, "but I am to have the opportunity of finding out. I am to aid in his nursing."

Meadows nodded his head approvingly. "I am glad that it is not all to be left to me. For I don't mind telling you that his lordship can be the very devil!"

"I would imagine that he must be very difficult to work for," Sarah said sympathetically.

For the first time, Meadows smiled. "Aye, 'tis like I said, he can be the very devil." He tightened his grip on the bag he was carrying. "But for all that, he's a champion. And don't let no one tell you any differently."

Moving away, Sarah found herself deeply puzzled. It would seem that my lord Witherley could inspire many emotions, and none of them insipid. Who was my lord Witherley? Which one was the real man? The Duke, who had the respect and love of the humble people? The cold-eyed arrogant man who had shown her no mercy? Mrs. Trevallion's beloved lad? Lady Margaret's kind and gentle son? Meadows's master, whom he called devil at one moment, and "champion" the next? Would she have a chance to know the real man before he recovered and, perhaps, send her away? Frowning, Sarah pushed open the door of the kitchen. Why did she bother herself with trying to puzzle him out? She knew well that she could never like him. And certainly she was not interested in penetrating his guise, if guise it was.

Chapter Eleven

Doctor Joshua Sanders entered the house like a brisk wind. With his white staff clasped in one hand, his huge bag in the other, he stood in the hall, beaming upon Lady Margaret and Sarah. "The lad's bad, is he?" he said in a hoarse chuckling voice. "Seems I returned to London just in time, eh? Now then, Maggie, my girl, don't you be showing me that cursed long face. Jason, damned ruffian that he is, will be as right as a trivet. I'll see to that."

Amazed to find that she could remember him in such detail, Sarah looked at the little man with affection. His white wig and his tricorn hat were still askew and his muslin cravat still pulled to one side. Only the snuff stains beneath his nose had changed. They seemed to have taken on a slightly deeper hue. Naturally she had not expected him to recognize her, and for a moment she was tempted to remind him of their last meeting. But better not. This was not the time or the place.

Lady Margaret smiled as the doctor marched purposefully up the stairs. "I really love that man," she said to Sarah. "Normally, I detest being called Maggie, but somehow it sounds different when he says it. He is a very clever doctor, you know. Much more so, in my opinion, than any of the King's physicians. Indeed, I believe him to be far in advance of most doctors."

Ten minutes later Doctor Sanders came down the stairs. He had lost his smile. His wide mouth was pressed tightly together, and his round face looked almost austere. "I tell you,

Maggie," he began, "there is no doing anything for the lad." At Margaret's gasp, his grim expression relaxed slightly. "Nay, nay, I am not meaning that he is about to slip his anchor. The illness is progressing very well. But there is no talking to him, for he'll not listen to a word of advice, and that's a fact. Pigheaded is his lordship, and always was. Aye, always was." He shook his head sadly.

Lady Margaret laid an appealing hand on his crumpled sleeve. "But is there nothing you can do for him?"

"Eh? Eh? What a question! There's plenty I can do for him. But I'll not come here to be insulted, and I tell you so to your face, my lady."

"He doesn't mean it, indeed he does not. You would not desert him?"

Doctor Sanders snorted. "What rubbish you women will talk. Of course I'll not desert him. But I'll give my advice to someone other than his lordship." His sharp eyes fell on Sarah. "Who's that, eh? Eh?"

"This is Mistress Sarah Barry. She is my companion. She is going to help nurse Jason."

"More fool her, then. Still, she looks the sensible sort, for all she's so pretty and fine." His plump fingers came out to pinch Sarah's cheek. "Are you sensible, me dear?"

"I hope so," Sarah answered.

The doctor's beam returned. "Got a temper, have you? Maybe one to match that red-hot mop of yours?"

Sarah smiled. "Unfortunately, I do."

"Unfortunate nothing! Just what the lad needs. Serve him right, and may the devil fly away with him! I'll give my advice to you. Now attend me well. He's to be kept warm. He is not, as he did just now, to fling his coverings to the floor. Give him plenty of hot cordial. And he is to have those drops I left on every fourth hour. Understand, eh?"

"Yes."

"Lass of few words, eh? That's the kind I like. Wish I could say the same for me wife, curse her jabbering jaw! Now harkee. You're to take no nonsense from his lordship. We're sailing this ship, lass. Aye, you and I, and we'll take no scurvy mutiny, eh? Eh?" Without waiting for an answer, he turned to glare at Margaret. "And we'll have no mutiny from you either. You're a fine woman, but you're as much use in the sickroom as a sparrow in a hurricane, As for that fool Meadows, he's to take his orders from Mistress Barry. Dithering and pottering about the room the way he does, what i' plague use is he? And I'll not have Mistress Trevallion cosseting the lad. She's too soft with him."

"You'll not have this and you'll not have that!" Sarah cried. She looked at him pleadingly. "Is it all to be left to me?"

The doctor turned to look at her. Poking her with a plump finger, he said, "You're a mite scrawny, lass, but you can do it. Aye, of course you'll have help. There's that ninny Meadows to attend to his lordship's needs. Those needs that don't require brains, that is. Never you strike your colors, lass. I can see by the set of your jaw that you'll handle the lad." He flapped his hands at her. "Now then, don't you be standing there moping and mowing at me. 'Tis time for his lordship's drops. Give 'em to him in a sip of cordial. I am in great hopes that the taste'll curdle that devilish cutting tongue of his. Up with you, up!"

Lady Margaret seemed to be torn between apprehension and amusement. Meeting Sarah's eyes, she said gently, "Please child!"

Sarah took a deep breath. "Am I to understand that my lord Witherley is entirely in my hands? He is to obey me?"

The doctor nodded, causing his wig to slide forward over his eyes. He thrust it back with an impatient hand. "Said so, didn't I? He doesn't come to heel, he doesn't get fed." He gave his fat chuckle. "Not that the rascal feels much like eating now. He will later, though. We'll have him by the heels, then, lass, eh?"

Hesitating, Sarah looked at Margaret. Margaret smiled at her reassuringly. "I will leave you to do as you think best. I know you will be kind."

"Kind!" the doctor snorted. "Small chance she'll have of being kind, for he's a tongue on him like a cursed blade. Firm, that's what she's got to be. Now go, lass. And never forget that my money's on you, for I can tell you're full of fight and ginger."

It was a very different Sarah who approached my lord Witherley's bedchamber. Her shoulders were squared and there was a bright gleam in her eyes. Full of fight and ginger, the doctor had said. Was she? Time would show. She only knew that she acted with the full approval of the doctor and Lady Margaret, that her fear was temporarily in abeyance, and that, in a curious way, she even felt excited at the prospect of dealing with the recalcitrant my lord Witherley.

He was sitting up in bed, his back supported by pillows, when she entered the room. He had obviously been suffering, for his face was drawn, and his brilliant eyes seemed to be sunken. She was to find, however, that there was nothing wrong with his spirit or his tongue.

"Well, Mistress Barry?" he demanded. "What do you here?"

She felt a quiver along her nerves, but she answered in a steady voice: "I am to be your nurse, my lord."

His brows drew together in an ominous line. "You are quite mistaken, Mistress Barry. Meadows here, is the only help I require."

"May we discuss that later, my lord?" Turning her back on him, she addressed Meadows, who was hovering nervously in a corner of the room. "How does his lordship, Meadows?"

"Mistress Barry, since you seem to wish for a bulletin on my health, you will ask me, not Meadows."

Sarah looked at him over her shoulder. "Then tell me, please."

"It's none of your infernal business! You will oblige me by leaving this room."

Sarah's heartbeat accelerated, but she said calmly, "I will do nothing of the sort. Now, Meadows?"

Meadows's eyes flickered. "I told the doctor, Mistress Barry."

"And now you will tell me, if you please."

Avoiding my lord Witherley's kindling eyes, Meadows wrung his hands together in agitation. "My lord has had some vomiting and some wandering of his senses. He—"

"Meadows, you will kindly close that chattering mouth of yours! My health is of no concern to Mistress Barry."

"But she asked me, my lord. And if she is to nurse you—"

"Be silent, fool!"

As though he had not spoken, Sarah said quietly, "I have no doubt that the drops that the doctor left will relieve the nausea. I will give them to him now." She smiled at him. "You may go."

"Hold your tongue, Mistress Barry. Meadows, you will stay here."

"M'lord!"

"You may go," Sarah repeated.

"If you leave this room, Meadows, I can promise you that you will be very sorry."

Before Sarah's astonished eyes, an amazing change came over the man. His nervousness appeared to have quite vanished. "My lord," he said in a clear but colorless voice, "I hope I have enough dignity to forbid me to be bandied about between yourself and Mistress Barry. You tell me to stay, Mistress Barry says go. With all respect, my lord, I think I will make up my own mind."

Jason fixed him with a pair of glittering blue eyes. "Well, my good idiot, make up your mind, then. However, I advise you to remember that I employ you."

Meadows's dignity increased. "I am not an idiot, my lord, as you would very well know, were you in your right senses?"

"What! You dare to say that I am out of my senses?"

"Your lordship is not quite himself!"

"Confound your insolence! You will leave my employ at once."

"Yes, my lord." With an inclination of his head, Meadows walked over to the door. "I will pack my things."

"Meadows!"

"Yes, my lord?"

"You may not be aware of it, but you are trying my patience rather high. Go to your room and stay there until I send for you. You are not dismissed from my service. It would ill become me to turn loose on an unsuspecting world such a nincompoop as yourself."

Sarah saw the little smile flickering at the corner of Meadows's mouth. "You have ordered me to leave your service at least a dozen times, my lord," he said softly. "I knew well that I was not dismissed."

"The next time I say it," Jason said grimly, "I will mean it."

As the man bowed and opened the door, Jason stopped him once more. "Meadows. In future you will remember that you take your orders from me, not from this-this—" He gestured toward Sarah. "Not from this lady."

Sarah had caught the hesitation, and angry color flared into her cheeks. She thought that she knew what he meant to say. As the door closed behind Meadows, she turned on him furiously. "Why did you not say what was in your mind, my lord?"

He folded his arms across his chest and subjected her to a long, appraising stare. "Do you then number mind-reading among what I am sure are many accomplishments? Interesting, if so. Will you not relieve my curiosity, Mistress Barry, and tell me what was in my mind?"

He was laughing at her in his cold and hateful way! Her hands gripped the bed rail as she answered. "You know very well!" she cried. "Did you not mean to tell Meadows that he will take his orders from you, and not from the lunatic?"

For a moment the habitual severity of his expression changed to blank surprise. But before she could remark it, it had vanished. When he spoke, it was in such a mocking, drawling voice, that she found herself longing to strike him. "Did you know that strong emotion quite becomes you, Mistress Barry?"

She tightened her shaking hands on the bed rail, ignoring this remark with a scornful toss of her head. "Do you deny that you meant to say that to Meadows?"

"My dear young woman, I will neither confirm nor deny it. You know little about me. If you knew more, you would quickly realize that I am not in the habit of explaining my meaning. And most certainly not to you. If you believe that of me, then you must continue to do so."

His words, so cutting and so coldly delivered, were like a slap in the face. For a moment an angry retort trembled on her lips, then her anger was succeeded by a surge of dismay. There had been no perceptible change in his voice or expression, and yet she had the oddest feeling that her words had both angered and hurt him. "If-if I have misjudged you, my lord," she stammered, feeling very foolish before those suddenly inimical eyes, "then I-I ask your pardon."

He smiled at her. But since the smile did not warm his eyes, she thought that it was quite the most disagreeable smile she had ever encountered. "Come, Mistress Barry, you must not apologize to me. You would surely not wish to spoil my illusion."

"Illusion? I don't understand."

"Do you not? At the request of my mother, and, I would imagine, that pompous old bore Doctor Sanders, you have been appointed my personal dragon. Is it not so?"

Again the hot blood rushed to her cheeks. Confused, she said the first thing that came into her head. "Doctor Sanders is not a pompous old bore!"

"He has won your approval, then, Mistress Barry?"

"Yes. He is a kind and gentle old man. Which you—" She broke off, biting at her lower lip.

His eyebrows rose in sardonic amusement. "Which I am not, perhaps you meant to say?"

"You are certainly not old, my lord. As for the rest," she said, mocking him with his own words, "If you believe that of me, then you must continue to do so."

He lowered his eyes, aware of a sudden inclination to laugh. An insolent but spirited chit, this. She was quite lovely, too. He raised his eyes and gave her a long, searching look. Nay, he could swear there was no insanity in her. But if that were so, then how in the name of God had she come to be locked away in Bedlam Asylum? He thought of several questions he would like to have asked her, but almost immediately he decided against it. Now was not the time. He felt weak and ill, and the talking had exhausted him, but he was determined not to show it. "In the matter of Doctor Sanders," he said in a slightly slurred voice, "you are quite right, wench. Ofttimes he can be pompous and boring, and I have repeatedly told him so to his face, but he is a good man. I am really quite attached to him."

This surprised her, and once again she spoke without thinking. "Why," she said in a wondering voice, "you can be nice!"

"Oh, excessively so," he agreed at once. "I can be a veritable angel."

He was mocking her again. She answered him in the same vein. "That, my lord, I take leave to doubt." Unexpectedly, she smiled, and he saw the deep dimple in her left cheek. "I think, however, that without too much effort you can be quite insufferable."

Her words were delivered without particular malice, and he knew it. " 'Tis all part of my charm, Mistress Barry," he said.

Even as he said it, he was aware of amazement. His illness must surely be affecting his brain. He was actually indulging in light banter with the wench! He had often envied this ability in others, but it did not come easily to himself. He was fully aware of his own unbending stiffness of manner, yet he knew of no other way to be. In his love affairs, if you could call them so, he took, but he could find in himself nothing to give in return. Not even words of tenderness to soften that which, under the circumstances, became a purely animal act. He had tried to bring such words to his lips, but he could not. Perhaps there was no tenderness in him. It might have been kinder, in some cases, to pretend, but he had always found it impossible. Without the wish to do so, he put people at a distance. This knowledge did not please him, for he felt there was a serious lack in himself. His inability to communicate had inevitably led to misunderstandings, as well as to unhappiness and loneliness for himself. There were some, he knew, who gave easily of their warmth and tenderness and love, their laughter, but, unfortunately, he was not one of them. But why did he persist in this dissection of himself? It had become a bad habit, and it changed nothing.

He turned his face away from Sarah Barry's searching eyes. Confound her! Why did she look at him in that way? From the moment she had so disastrously entered his life, the wench had disturbed him. It disturbed him even more to realize that there was something about her that made him want to talk and talk. He had the feeling that he had but to open his mouth and the words would flow easily. His lips tightened in the old habit of repression. Stupid folly, this urge he had to reveal himself to her, to tell her of his hopes and dreams and longings. Did he really imagine that she would be interested in anything he might have to say? Nay, her hatred of him was evident. He tried to summon anger, and that cold dignity that had always cloaked his deeper feelings, but instead, he found himself trying to think of something to say that would bring that angry flash to her eyes again, and the hot blood to her cheeks. "Mistress Barry," he began. "I think—" he broke off with a gasp as the room darkened and tilted about him.

"My lord!" Sarah went quickly to his side. "What is it?"

The sense of ease and relaxation had abruptly deserted him. "What the devil do you think it is?" he snapped.

"I imagine, my lord," Sarah said calmly, "that you are feeling nauseated again." She picked up the small bottle from the bedside table. "If that is so, then these drops will help you."

The darkness was lifting. "Mistress Barry," he said in a freezing voice, his eyes on the bottle in her hand, "if you imagine that I will allow you to pour that vile stuff down my throat, I must beg you to disabuse yourself of any such notion."

"You will not allow it, my lord?"

"Have I not said so. I refuse to take any of your vile medicine. Do I make myself understood?"

"You do, my lord. You will, however, take these drops."

"Get out of this room. Leave me!"

"Pray do not be childish, my lord."

He looked at her with smouldering, dangerous eyes. "I think, Mistress Barry, that you forget yourself."

"I ask your pardon, my lord." Carefully, Sarah read the label of instructions. Then, ignoring his fury, she carefully measured the drops into a small pewter cup. "The drops may be taken with or without cordial, my lord," she informed him in a bright, yet soothing voice. "Which do you prefer?"

He turned his head away. "Since I have already informed you that I will not take it at all, the matter is easily settled."

"Nay, my lord, I think not," Sarah said, moving round to the other side of the bed. "When I was a little girl, and I refused to take my medicine, do you know what my mother would do?"

"I do not," he said through gritted teeth, "nor am I interested. I have only one thing to say to you, Mistress Barry. Get out of this room!"

"Since I am a servant in this house, my lord, you need not call me Mistress Barry. Will you not call me Sarah, or Barry, if you prefer?"

"Nay," he spoke quietly, but she could sense the undercurrent of violence. "I will not call you Sarah, or Barry, or any other cursed nonsense. However, since you have reminded me that you are a servant, I, in my turn, remind you of your duty to obey. Get out!"

Sarah answered him very slowly. She was afraid that if she did not space her words, her voice might begin to tremble, and she was determined not to show fear. "I believe, my lord, that Lady Margaret is my employer. I am bound to obey her, and in this I do but carry out her orders." She took a deep breath to steady herself. "But I was telling you about my mother. When I refused to take my medicine, she would pinch my nose until I was forced to swallow."

There was a silence pregnant with disbelief and anger. "Do I actually understand you to mean, Mistress Barry, that you are proposing to follow your mother's example?"

"Yes, my lord, if necessary."

"By God! You go too far. I will not tolerate your insolence!"

"Then drink, my lord." With a steady hand, she held the cup to his lips. "Come, the sooner you drink, the sooner will you be rid of me."

With an exclamation of rage, he seized the cup from her hand and hurled it across the room. "That, whatever your blasted name is, is my answer!"

Sarah turned away and crossed the room to retrieve the cup. She had a great desire to fly from the room, never to set eyes on him again. This battle of wills was wearing her down. She was too much aware of him, and the indifference she had so painstakingly mustered was fast slipping away. But how could one help being aware of this man? she defended herself. Hate him or love him, but you could never ignore him. Her hand clenched round the cup. Love him? Nay, that would be an impossibility. He would freeze love, repel it!

Measuring out the drops again, she wondered what would happen to her when he was once more in command of himself. Would he remember these moments against her?

"My lord, please!" Once more she held the cup to his lips, then, on an unconsciously pleading note. "Please drink it."

He looked at her for a long moment, and some of the anger died in his eyes. "Very well, wench, since you beg me," he said in a cool voice, "I will take it to please you." He took the cup from her hand, hesitated, and then drank the contents. At his look of horror, she found herself smiling.

"Is it so very bad, my lord?"

"Damn!" he answered in a strangled voice. "I will break your infernal neck before I allow you to force any more of that stuff upon me. What is it, poison? It is burning my cursed throat!"

Hesitantly, half afraid that he would repel her, she patted

his shoulder soothingly. "The taste will fade," she said in a soft voice. "All will be well in a moment, you will see."

Shuddering, he closed his eyes. She thought she saw a faint smile touch his lips, but it was gone so quickly that she told herself she had imagined it. She jumped when he spoke suddenly. "Have the goodness, Sarah," he said in a weary voice, "not to treat me like a child."

"Yes, my lord."

He made no reply. Sarah, she thought. How pleasant her plain little name had sounded on his lips, it had sounded very different to the way others spoke it. She stood there motionless, looking down at him. His hectic flush had faded, and he was very pale. There was a drawn look about his mouth, and deep shadows beneath his eyes. She wondered if he were aware of her eyes on his face? If so, he gave no sign. He continued to lie there, very still, his eyes closed against her. His breathing deepened, and she guessed that he had fallen asleep. There were beads of perspiration on his face, and his hair clung damply to his forehead. Touched by his helplessness, she had, for the moment, forgotten her hatred. Sitting cautiously on the side of the bed, she drew her kerchief from her sleeve. Fearful of waking him, she dabbed at his face with feather-light touches and smoothed back the damp tangle of his hair.

His eyes opened, startling her. "What are you doing?" he demanded.

"I-I am sorry. I thought you were asleep."

"I was not asleep."

"I was t-trying to make you more comfortable."

He regarded her sternly. "Sarah," his deep voice said, "you are treating me like a child again."

"Oh, no, my lord, no indeed. I was only trying—"

"To make me more comfortable," he finished for her. "Yes, Sarah, I know."

She rose to her feet as he closed his eyes again. "I will leave you to your rest, my lord."

Without opening his eyes, he said abruptly, "You will do nothing of the sort. If you would make me more comfortable, then oblige me by seating yourself again."

Wondering if he might be wandering again, she perched herself once more on the side of the bed. "Very well, my lord. I will stay, if it pleases you."

"For the moment it pleases me. But I shall not forget that you are a troublesome, insolent, irritating, and domineering wench. Be assured that, when I am able, I will deal with you."

"Yes, my lord, I feel sure that you will."

"See that you remember it."

She was still sitting there when the door opened and Meadows crept quietly into the room. She flushed as she met his surprised eyes.

With exaggerated caution, Meadows moved nearer to the bed. "I waited for his lordship to send for me," he whispered. "Then, when he did not, I wondered if he might have taken a turn for the worse, so I thought I would come along and see. Did he give you any trouble?"

Sarah shook her head. "Nay."

"Sarah Barry," my lord Witherley said in a clear voice, "you are a liar."

Meadows put a dismayed hand to his mouth. "I am sorry, my lord, I did not mean to wake you."

"Since I was not asleep, you could hardly wake me, Meadows." My lord Witherley opened his eyes and looked at Sarah. "You may go now, Mistress Barry. However, if it pleases you to bedevil me, you may return later."

"Yes, my lord." Sarah rose quickly to her feet. "I will return when it is time for you to take the drops again."

His eyes met hers. "Mistress Barry," he said in a calm voice, "may the fiends seize you and your cursed drops."

Chapter Twelve

The weather had taken another of its inexplicable turns. It was snowing now. Sarah stood by the window, her back to my lord Witherley, her eyes on the frozen scene below. But she was not really seeing the thick coating of virgin snow that masked the lawns, and disguised the ugliness of the open gutter in the center of the street. The leafless trees below the window swayed in a bitter wind, tapping skeletal branches against the front of the house. The wind, suddenly rising to a new high, drifted the snow, sending up thin, sparkling white veils. The shrieking of the wind, mingling with the mournful, restless sighing of the trees, filled the warm bright room with sound and fury. But Sarah was aware of nothing but her own misery and bewilderment. Her mind was back in the past that had contained Jemmie Taylor and all the horror that her association with him had set in train. She was trying now to conjure up his face. The dark, straight hair, the sharp eyes set in a square, lightly pocked face, but somehow she could not get a clear picture of him. As for the feeling she had once had for him, she knew now that it had never been love. Compared to the feeling that possessed her now, her feeling for Jemmie had been nothing. Nothing at all!

Sarah pressed her hand against her mouth. What had she felt then? An animal attraction? Yes, that was what it had been. Now Jemmie came clearer. She saw the lust in his eyes, that first time he had possessed her, after the false marriage. She shivered, remembering the touch of his hands on her body and her own ardent responses. Once more his arms were lifting her from her feet. He carried her across the room and set her down on the sagging bed with its gray, unwashed sheets.

"Jemmie!" Her voice trembling. Her hands touching him. Wanting him desperately, yet a little afraid of this new experience. "Jemmie, be gentle."

"Gentle, Sarah, girl? Gentle is for them that's got water in their veins 'stead o' blood. I'm a rough lover, wench, but you'll like it, I promises you."

His lips burned against her breast. They touched every part of her body, his tongue exploring, touching off sensations that she had not believe possible. And then her voice again, high and shrill, begging him for that final sensation. He had taken her then, roughly, brutally, hurting her so much that she moaned in agony.

Each night after that, he had taken her in the same way. And, as the agony died, she had coupled with him with a fierce satisfaction that, in its own way, was as brutal and as demanding as his own actions.

Remembering, the hot blood scorched her cheeks. Animal attraction? Yes, it had been only that. But not love. Until this moment, she had never known the meaning of love.

Sarah tightened her lips. She had been well served for that interlude with Jemmie Taylor. It mattered little now that she had thought herself to be his wife. She, thief, convict, branded before the eyes of an uncaring world as a lunatic, she had fallen in love with my lord Witherley. Of what use to remind herself that he was the scion of a noble house, the intimate friend of the King. The man for whom scheming mothers with marriageable daughters set their caps, she was in love with him, her beloved enemy, irrevocably, forever! And he? He scarcely knew that she was alive. If he knew of her love for him he would certainly consider her to be insane.

In the days that had followed her first encounter with him

in his bedchamber, my lord Witherley had been by turns exacting, autocratic, icily polite, and cuttingly sarcastic. Because of his bewilderingly variable moods, she had not seen the danger to herself. When she did realize that she was falling in love with him, she tried to remind herself of the past, the part he had played in her life. He was her enemy. He had condemned her to misery. Again and again she would go over in her mind all that she had suffered because of this man, but it did not help. It was almost as if he knew of the struggle that raged in her to shut him out of her heart and mind, for suddenly he would be gentle.

Once, in that gentle mood, he had smiled at her, and said, "Come here, Sarah Barry. Sit beside me. I would know what thoughts go on behind that serene brow of yours."

How could she say to him, "I am not serene. I want to hate you, but I cannot. I can only love you!"

Averting her eyes, she had answered him in a cold, flat voice, "I think of nothing in particular, my lord. Save perhaps will the weather be fine enough for walking. Will Bascombe allow me to help in the kitchen when she tries out one of her new recipes? Or should I put lace on one of my plainer gowns?"

When she looked at him again, she had the feeling that she had disappointed him in some way, for those expressive eyes of his had clouded. But of course she had not disappointed him, how could she? Certainly he had no interest in Sarah Barry, other than as one who ministered to him in his sickness, who smoothed his pillows, bathed his fevered face and hands, and who forced him, through a display of temper and a will as stubborn as his own, to swallow the medicines that the doctor left. The only small consolation she had was that he could not possibly know or suspect her love for him. Nay, she was safe enough from detection. For he roused her temper to such a degree that, in sheer defense, she was able to summon and maintain a like harshness. Knowing herself so well, she knew that her emotions were always clearly reflected in her eyes, and she was glad that it was rage he saw in them, and not the foolish, hopeless love she felt for him. A dozen or more times a day she would remind herself that he was a cold man, a man who knew not the meaning of love and tenderness. She would force herself to think of Lady Margaret, whose nerves my lord Witherley had so exacerbated that she now only came once a day, usually when he had fallen asleep, to inquire after his welfare. But nothing she could tell herself, not all her memories of Newgate Prison and Bedlam Asylum, helped her. She was in love with him. She could not reason or force that love to leave her.

Jason watched Sarah's slender green-clad figure through half-closed eyes. The wind's force, he noted, had dwindled considerably, and a pale, wintry sun breaking momentarily through the massed gray clouds touched her hair to brightness. What was she thinking about? he wondered. What did she find in the bleak view outside to interest her? He had been awake for some time now, and not once had she moved away from the window.

He frowned. He thought of her far too much. She baffled him, angered him, and touched off strange and unfamiliar emotions. He would deliberately provoke her to anger, and yet, when she looked at him with hatred in her eyes, he would feel such a strong regret that he could no longer bring himself to look at her. Those times when he would pat the side of the bed and invite her to sit down, she would obey him reluctantly. "I would as soon sit in a chair, my lord," she had said more than once.

"And I wish to see your face when I talk, Mistress Barry."

"Aye, my lord, so that you can clearly note when the shafts of your sarcasm strike home."

"Curb your insolent tongue, Mistress Barry, and be seated."

When she had perched herself on the side of the bed with the air of one poised for immediate flight, he would set himself the task of driving the suspicion from her eyes. He would talk to her, telling her small incidents of Court life, or of the work he was doing at Witherley Grove. It was as he had felt from the beginning. He could talk to her without restraint, and he was surprised at how easily his words came.

Gradually she would relax, and she would begin to question him eagerly, and to add her own little ideas for the comfort of his tenants on the Witherley Grove estate. Sarah, the enigma, he thought. Once, her suspicion of him apparently forgotten, her face changed from sullenness to smiles, she touched his hand to press home a point she was making. Then, on that instant, she changed. It was as though she felt that the touch of him had contaminated her. Snatching her hand away, she rose from the bed and looked at him with all the old hostility. "I must go, my lord. I promised Lady Margaret that I would walk with her this afternoon, and I am already late."

Unreasonably, he was hurt. "Go, Mistress Barry," he said coldly. "Go at once. Do not trouble yourself on my account. I daresay I can make shift for myself."

"You have Meadows, my lord," she had reminded him. "And indeed, you must know that you are so much better that you no longer have need of my full attention."

"That is for me to say, Mistress Barry, is it not? I alone can know how I feel."

It pleased him to see that uncertainty was now mingling with hostility. "Are—are you saying that you feel no better, my lord?"

He folded his arms, feeling a perverse satisfaction in the faint trace of anxiety in her last words. "Do not trouble yourself for a moment on my account, Mistress Barry. I am quite sure that nothing I may have to say could be of the slightest interest to you. Walk with my mother, enjoy the air. Let your conscience be at rest in the knowledge that you are leaving me alone with only that fumble-fingered fool of a Meadows to attend me."

Her cheeks flamed scarlet. "My lord! You have a cruel tongue!"

Coldness turned to anger. "Go!" he said in a goaded voice. "I am sick of the sight of you!"

Her hand clenched at her sides, she took an impetuous step toward the bed. "How dare you!"

"How dare I? I am not accustomed to choosing my words, Mistress Barry."

"You would remind me, I imagine, my lord, that I am a servant in this house. But even so, I am surely entitled to your courtesy. I have noted your many faults, but I had thought you to be a gentleman. It would seem that I was mistaken."

"By God, wench, do not drive me too far! There are times when your insolence goes beyond all bounds. I will not endure it!"

"If, as you say, my lord, it goes beyond all bounds, then it cannot matter if I add to that insolence. I hope you have a relapse!"

Turning her back on him, she walked over to the door. He saw her hesitate there, her shoulders drooping. "My lord," she said in a quiet voice, "I did not mean that. Pray forgive me."

Before he could reply, she wrenched open the door. It banged behind her, and he heard her running footsteps along the corridor. Suddenly ashamed, and not liking the feeling, he told himself that she was right. At the very least, she was entitled to his courtesy. He was changing, he was becoming an ill-mannered boor. What had made him speak to her like that? What was there about Sarah Barry that brought out his worst instincts? She troubled his conscience, of course. He had been within his rights to turn her over to the Watch. But even so, when he thought of the suffering she had endured through his action, he found himself wanting to apologize. Only a reluctance to stir up those old, bad memories had caused him to refrain. How she must hate him! How she must resent the task of aiding him in his weakness! It surprised him to find how much that thought hurt him.

Watching her now at the window, he wondered why, whenever she was in the room, he was so tinglingly aware of her. Whenever, in the course of her duties, she had occasion to touch him, it was like a shock along his nerves. Was this strange effect she had upon him because he was in need of a woman? If that were so, he could, when he was on his feet again, choose from many to assuage this particular need. There was Frances Beverley, for instance. Frances was beautiful and most accommodating, and for a long time she had been his favorite mistress. He was easy with her because she did not pester him or ask him to explain the various moods that beset him. She simply disrobed, and fitted her soft, sensuous body to his need. Frances was a baggage, but an unashamed one. She lived for the pleasures of the body. He had long known that he was not her only lover, but it did not disturb or anger him to know this. He had no deep feeling for her. He had never, in fact, had deep feelings for any woman.

He looked at Sarah again. Could it be that his illness had made him dependent on her? This morning, when she had not arrived at her usual hour, he had been astonished and annoyed at the strength of his disappointment. Calling Meadows to his side, he had bade him seek out Mistress Barry, and to inquire of her whether she intended to neglect her duties for this day.

"But, my lord, you are much improved," Meadows ventured. "I believe, if you wish, that I can now entirely relieve Mistress Barry of her duties."

"Perhaps, Meadows, you are becoming hard of hearing. I told you to go at once and seek out Mistress Barry."

Meadows drew himself up and looked at him with strong disapproval. "There is nothing wrong with my hearing. I will find Mistress Barry, if your lordship so desires. But, if you will forgive me, I would point out that she is not above two minutes late."

"I will not forgive you, Meadows. Mistress Barry is quite twenty minutes late. Pray do as you are told!"

When Meadows, his small body stiff with offense, had gone on his way, Jason lay very still, staring up at the gilded ceiling. He was so full of unreasonable rage, as well as a mixture of incoherent feelings that he could not put a name to, that he found it impossible to relax.

When Sarah finally came into the room, he did not look at her at once. "Good morning, my lord," she said in a bright voice.

He turned his eyes away from contemplation of the ceiling and looked at her coldly. "I see nothing good about the morning. It is chilly in this room. Why has the fire not been built up?"

Sarah looked across the room at the blazing fire. "I believe, my lord, should I attempt to build it up more, that the chimney would be ablaze."

"You have no apology to offer me, Mistress Barry?"

"Apology, my lord? For what?"

"You are late."

"I am sorry. I did not think you would have immediate need of me."

"My dear young woman, I have repeatedly told you that I have no need of you at all. Nevertheless, I would hear the explanation for your tardy appearance."

" 'Tis easily explained. Bascombe burned her hand. I was aiding in the preparation of your—"

"I believe, Mistress Barry, that your employment in this house does not include aiding the cook."

"But, you see—"

Again he cut across her words. "It may have escaped your notice, but we have three kitchen servants. You, wench, are not one of them."

"Quite true, my lord," she answered him crisply. "However, since your lordship had complained these last few mornings of the way your breakfast was prepared, I thought, to avoid additional complaint, I would do it myself. Meadows will be bringing it to you in a moment."

"I do not understand you, Mistress Barry. I have made no complaint."

"Indeed you have! You have complained several times."

"Nonsense! That is beside the point. In any case, I am not interested in food. I am not hungry this morning."

"Oh!" Bright color stained her cheeks. "Then perhaps, my lord, you will be interested in the news that Sir Peter Baxter will be calling on you at ten o'clock?"

"Baxter? Again! Damn! He has called every day for the past three weeks. I would thank the cursed fellow to leave me in peace!"

"Doubtless he calls because he is your friend, my lord," Sarah answered with a trace of sarcasm. "I would imagine that he is naturally concerned with your health."

"Indeed. When I wish for your opinion, Mistress Barry, be sure that I will ask for it."

"I merely made a suggestion, my lord."

"I must tell you, Mistress Barry," he said coldly, his brows drawing together in a formidable line, "that I do not care for, or appreciate, your argumentative attitude."

"I am sorry. I should have remembered that my lord Witherley is not accustomed to argument from his inferiors."

"I beg your pardon!"

Deliberately misunderstanding him, Sarah said in a mild voice, "No, pray do not beg my pardon, my lord. I understand your illness oft places you in a dark mood." She saw the danger signals in his eyes, and she hurried on. "I had thought your lordship enjoyed Sir Peter's visits."

"I might enjoy them, Mistress Barry," he said in a sardonic voice, "were I sure that he came to see me."

"I do not understand your meaning, my lord."

"Do you not, Mistress Barry? Simpering innocence ill becomes you."

"My lord!"

"Baxter finds many excuses to summon you back into the room, does he not? And you, of course, are always within convenient call. Think you that I have not observed you ogling him like some damned tavern slut? If you do, you are much mistaken!"

Taken aback by the savagery of his attack, she could at first find nothing to say. Then her heart began to hammer with angry resentment. "Your imagination does you credit, my lord," she said in a tight voice. "But you need not fear. Sir Peter is quite safe from the designs of the lunatic."

He felt as if she had slapped him in the face. There was a sudden rush of blood to his head that left him feeling dizzy. Losing his temper completely, he shouted at her, "Confound you, you little fool! How dare you call yourself a lunatic? You will not do so again in my presence. Do you understand?"

"I am sorry, my lord, but I believe that is how you must view me."

Now was the time to explain. To apologize for his part in her tragedy. He opened his mouth, but the words would not come. Instead, he heard himself saying in an icy voice, "I have no views on you at all, Mistress Barry. Therefore your belief is of no importance."

So he had no views on her at all. To him, she was probably of less importance than an insect. There was bitter hurt in her voice when she spoke. "Then perhaps you would care to explain your meaning, my lord?"

"I am not in the habit of explaining, Mistress Barry. However, in the case of Baxter, I must tell you that you have entirely misinterpreted my words."

"Then what did you mean?"

He gave her a frowning look. How could he answer her? He had not the faintest notion what he meant himself. He only knew that her friendly attitude toward Peter, and Peter's obvious interest in her, confused and angered him. But he could hardly tell her that. Were he to do so, the stubborn wench would believe that he made reference again to Bedlam Asylum. Changing the subject, he said abruptly, "It is past the hour of eight o'clock, Mistress Barry. Be good enough to give me the physic that Doctor Sanders left for me."

Her expression changed to one of amazement. "Are you telling me, my lord, that you will take it voluntarily?"

"Certainly. I am not in the mood to battle with you this morning."

So she had given him the black and bitter medicine, and he had been forced to swallow it. What was the matter with him? He was behaving like a petulant child. She was smiling when she took the cup from his hand, and he had said acidly, "I am glad that my suffering amuses you, Mistress Barry."

"Are you, my lord? I am happy that I have made you glad."

Later in the morning, when Peter, his dog snuffling at his heels, put in an appearance, his temper had grown progressively worse. Peter could not seem to sit still. His eyes kept straying to the door, and he found any number of excuses to call Sarah back into the room. But when she entered, he could not seem to remember why he had called her. Looking at his beaming face, listening to the flow of inane chatter with which he regaled Sarah, Jason's fist clenched in a longing to strike him.

At last, unable to endure more, he had curtly requested Peter to take his leave. "I have a headache," he informed him, "which your presence has not improved. Be so good as to leave me. I wish to sleep."

Sir Peter, his eyes on Sarah, answered him absently, " 'Pon my soul, Jason, you are a cursed friendly knave. It does my heart good to know that you have found my visit so enjoyable." Smiling at Sarah, Peter added, "But if my lord Witherley has the headache, Mistress Barry, we must not add to his discomfort for another moment, must we? Will you accompany me to the front door, my dear?"

Jason's mood was by no means improved when she had readily agreed. They had stayed so long in the hall that he wondered what they were finding to talk about. He had sat up in bed, his ears straining, but he could hear only a low murmur. Then Sarah laughed, and his imaginary headache became fact. How dare she laugh? How dare she leave him here neglected while she listened to Peter's prattle? When Sarah entered the room again, he demanded to know what it was she had found so amusing.

She smiled at him. "Sir Peter was telling me of the time when he accidentally fell into the Thames."

He had been with Peter at that time, and he had found the incident highly diverting. But now, with Sarah's eyes upon him, he refused to say so. "I find nothing amusing in it, Mistress Barry," he said severely. "One should not laugh at another's misfortune."

"No, of course not." Her lips twitched. "It was the way he told it, I suppose."

"Aye, he has a way with words. Always providing that one's wish is not for intelligent conversation."

His biting tone drew from her a more concentrated attention. "You look flushed, my lord. Is anything wrong?" She came nearer to the bed. "Mayhap your fever has risen again."

"Nothing is wrong, unless it be your incessant chatter. You will please be silent."

"I will leave you alone, then, my lord."

"I have not dismissed you. You will remain until I see fit to do so."

"Yes, my lord."

Ignoring her, he turned over on his side and closed his eyes. He had not meant to fall asleep. He had no notion of how long he had slept, when he awakened to find Sarah standing by the window. Something about her rigid figure suggested unhappiness, and he was filled with remorse for his own part in that unhappiness.

"Sarah," he called to her softly.

She turned. "Yes, my lord?"

"Come here, please."

With only the smallest hesitation, she came to him. "Is there something you need?"

He shook his head. "Sit down, please. I have something I wish to say to you."

She seated herself on the edge of the bed. "Yes?"

"I think, Sarah, that we must talk a little of the past."

She started. "No, my lord. I would rather not."

Without thinking, he possessed himself of her hand. "Sarah, that day when you—when you attempted to pick my pocket, I was angry at your defiant attitude. But I did not, in the beginning, intend to turn you over to the Watch."

She snatched her hand away. "I know. I drove you to it. It is over, my lord, must we speak of it?"

"I think we must. When I saw you in the courtroom that day, I wanted to stop it. But things had gone too far. Those things that happened to you. I did not know how it would be, Sarah. Now I can find in myself only one need, and that is to apologize to you."

"You wish to apologize? To me!" At her expression of

astonishment, he felt himself flushing.

"You may well look so, Mistress Barry. Not often in my life have I apologized for my words or my actions. Mayhap I should do it more often, it might serve to humble me."

"Nay!" she spoke so sharply that he was surprised. "It is the last thing I would desire."

"You would not care to see me humbled?"

"No, my lord."

"Why not?"

"I know not. I only know that I would not care for it at all."

"There are many who do not share your opinion. I know well that I am a devilish bad-tempered and arrogant fellow. Sarah, do you hate me? I would not blame you if you did."

"Oh, no, my lord!"

"That is the truth?"

"Yes, it is the truth. Oh, I did hate you. But—but now that feeling is gone."

"You are magnanimous. Were positions reversed, I do not think I would find it easy to forgive."

Now, oddly, she wanted to reassure him. "It is over, my lord. The kindness and generosity of your mother has more than made up for my sufferings."

"But not my kindness and generosity, Sarah. I know only too well that you are a stranger to that. Do you really forgive me, wench?"

She looked at him. His eyes were anxious, almost pleading. "My lord," she tried to speak lightly, "I have told you that I do not care to see you humble. I forgive you freely. Is that what you wish to hear?"

"Only if it is the truth."

"It is."

"Thank you, Sarah." He smiled at her, and that smile, so rarely seen, made him look much younger than his twenty-eight years.

"Do not distress yourself more, my lord," Sarah's voice trembled slightly. "This is not the time for serious discussion. You have been very ill, you know."

"I know." His smile faded, and he frowned. "I have used you badly, Sarah. Nay, I do not now refer to the past. I fear that I cannot use illness, however severe, as an excuse for my bad manners. Yet I do assure you that it is unlike me to lose control of myself. I do not, as a rule, show temper."

She smiled. "Nay, I would imagine you instead as very correct. Perhaps icily polite." She gave a mock shiver. "I think, my lord, that I prefer your temper."

"You make me sound a very dull dog."

His words were without rancor, and suddenly she felt almost giddy with happiness. "That is one thing you could never be, my lord."

"Not dull?" His eyes smiled into hers. "Then insufferable perhaps? As I remember, you called me so once."

She laughed. "I did. I remember. But never will I admit to dull. If I may believe Lady Margaret, the many ladies of your acquaintance find you far from dull."

"My mother should hold her tongue," he said with a faint return to his old manner. "But I thank you for your good opinion of me, little as I deserve it. You know, little Mistress Barry, I had thought 'twas you who bedeviled me. But now, looking at you, I fear that the devil is inside myself."

Her happiness receded as it came to her that she was afraid of him in this gentle mood. It might be that it would cause her to betray herself. "I think, my lord," she said hastily, "that I should also make apology to you. There are times when—when I have been very rude. I should not have been."

He surprised her again. "You have," he agreed instantly. "I have found you to be a most insolent and bad-tempered baggage. But I will allow that you had cause to be. No one could call me an exemplary patient." He took her hand and carried it to his lips. "Friends, Mistress Barry?"

At the light touch of his lips against her hand, she started so violently that he looked at her searchingly. "What is it? It was not my intention to offend you. But if I have done so, I beg your pardon."

"Oh, no, no. Indeed you have not offended me. It is just that I suddenly remembered that it is time for your broth. If you will excuse me, I will go and fetch it."

"No, Mistress Barry, I will not excuse you. Let us forget the broth for today. I am not hungry for that thin and unpalatable mixture, I assure you."

"Nevertheless, my lord, it is good for you." She drew her hand away and rose to her feet. "Mrs. Trevallion says that it will build your strength."

"Must you really go?" he said mildly. "Trevallion and her crack-pot notions have ever been the bane of my life. Come, Sarah, sit down again, I want to talk to you. When you told your story to my mother, I was not listening intently, and I do not fully understand how you came to be sent to Bedlam Asylum." He saw her painful flush, and he added quickly, "Whoever sent you there, must have been a likely candidate himself. Will you tell me again, please? And this time, I promise, you will have my full attention."

She was shaken by the continuing gentleness of his tone, and by the suggestion that he, without question, believed her to be entirely sane. But she was in a fever to be away. "I—I will tell you anything you desire. But not now, please. I must go and get your broth."

He laced his fingers behind his head, smiling at her. "Very well, if you feel that you must. Do not look so frightened, Sarah, I will not harass you with innumerable questions, for such is not my way. You shall tell me only as much as you wish to tell."

She backed toward the door, trying to smile at him. Oh,

please don't be gentle, she thought, or you will make my foolish tongue blurt out things that are best hidden. Be rude, arrogant, but do not be gentle! She paused by the door, then, seeing that he was expecting an answer, she said, "I will return shortly."

But it was, after all, quite some time before Sarah returned. My lord Witherley, waiting impatiently, grew increasingly irritable with the strong desire he was experiencing to touch her, to know the feel of her in his arms. It was not merely a wish to bed her, though she was desirable enough to make any man's thoughts turn in that direction. No, it was more than that, and he could not as yet put a name on it.

When she entered the room again, he had the dismayed feeling that she had been crying. The thought pained him.

"You must drink the broth while it is hot, my lord," Sarah said, carefully placing the blue pottery bowl on the side table.

He gave the bowl an impatient glance. "Yes, yes." Then, abruptly, "Mistress Barry, you have been crying. Why?"

She looked away from him. "You are mistaken, my lord."

"I am not mistaken. I know the marks of tears when I see them. Is it because I asked you to tell me your story again?"

"No, of course not."

"Then why were you crying?"

"I have not been crying," she cried out in a shaken voice. "Please, my lord, do not persist." Turning away from him, she walked over to the window.

All his good resolutions were forgotten. "And now, I suppose," he said in his old curt way, "you intend to spend more time gaping out of that infernal window? I cannot imagine what you see out there to interest you."

Her mouth trembled. She had thought him to be sleeping. But apparently he had been watching her. "There is nothing to interest me," she answered. " 'Tis a habit, I suppose."

"Come over here."

She heard the note of command in his voice. "No!" she blurted out the word, trying to resist him.

"You will not say no to me, Mistress Barry. I have told you to come here."

"I can tell you my story as well by this window, as I can standing before you," she answered stubbornly.

"Mistress Barry, you will either walk over here, or I will leave my bed and fetch you." His voice softened to a mocking drawl. "Pray let me know your choice."

She whirled round to face him. "My choice, my lord? Have I one? It would seem to me that your mood of repentance has quite vanished."

"But then you expected nothing else, did you, Mistress Barry? So I have not disappointed you." Smiling, he crooked his finger and beckoned. "Come. I am waiting."

"Very well!" She ran to the side of the bed. "Can it be that your lordship believes, if you do not see every expression that crosses my face, that I will lie?"

"That is a great piece of nonsense, wench, and it requires no answer." He patted the side of the bed. "Sit here, please."

"I will not. If you do not object, my lord, I would rather stand." She turned away.

"But you must know, Sarah Barry, that I object most strongly. Pray do as I have told you."

She kept her back to him. "No."

"A pity, for I deplore violence." With a sudden movement, he leaned forward and seized her, toppling her backward across his knees.

Her cry of protest died as she found herself looking into his brilliant eyes. "My lord, please," she whispered. "Allow me to rise."

He did not seem to hear her, for he made no response. He was looking at her as though he had never seen her before. He touched the long, slender line of her throat with his finger, and then traced the outline of her full, soft mouth. "Sarah?" her name on his lips was a question. He stared at her in a puzzled fashion. What the devil was the matter with him? What was he doing? He made a movement, as though he intended to release her. Then, as if he could not resist, he put his arms about her and drew her close. "Sarah!" he pressed his lips to hers.

For a moment she was rigid, then her lips warmed beneath his and parted, and she returned the kiss fiercely.

"Sarah!" he said after a long moment. "I did not know."

Common sense came back, chilling her. "Please, my lord," she said in a toneless voice, straining against his arms. "This is not the first time you have kissed me against my will. Do you intend making a habit of it? I must beg you never to do it again."

His arms tightened. "Was it against your will, Sarah? Do you imagine that I did not notice your response?"

"You—you are an attractive man," she said in a choked voice. "The kiss w-was taken against my will, but I-I did enjoy it. Nevertheless, you must not do it again."

"Why not?"

"Because I say so. Whatever you may believe, my lord, I am no whore to be used as you please."

"Be silent! Have I called you a whore?"

"Nay, not yet. But if your intention is that I shall warm your bed, you have made a mistake."

His brow quirked mockingly. "Perhaps, Mistress Barry, you should wait until you are asked."

"I know what is in your mind!" she cried. "Indeed, my lord, your action speaks for itself."

"Does it so? You are lovely enough to make any man lust after you. But does it not occur to you that I might have another reason for my action, as you call it?"

"You could have no other reason, my lord," she said, deliberately trying to court his anger. "Unless you consider me to be a complete fool, do not try to tell me differently."

He disappointed her. There seemed to be no anger in him. "You are a strange wench, Sarah," he murmured. "You look at me with hatred now, but a moment ago I could have sworn you shared my feeling."

"And what feeling is that, my lord?"

He spoke in the tone of someone who was trying to reason something out. "You have always had the oddest effect upon me. You have roused things in me that I have never felt before, and, indeed, never hoped to feel." His eyes held her compellingly. "But until I kissed you, Sarah, I swear that I did not know I was in love with you. And until you returned my kiss, I did not know you returned my love."

"You are dreaming, my lord!" It was an effort to draw her breath, so deeply did pain stab, but she would not let him use her to gain his own ends. "I? In love with you?" She began to laugh on a note of hysteria. "My lord," she gasped, "I would not so presume!"

"Stop that infernal laughing!" he snapped. "I would have you answer me in a sensible fashion. You are a woman, not an hysterical child. I am in love with you. What have you to say to that?"

"Only that your illness has obviously unhinged your reason." She saw him flinch, and she desperately wanted to take the words back. But she could not. If she allowed herself to believe him, she shuddered to think of the pain that would be hers. Had she not been hurt enough? "My lord," she went on in a calm voice, "I know that you do but jest with me. But I assure you that I do not appreciate the jest."

"No, Sarah Barry, believe that if you will, but it is no jest. I am very sure that I am in love with you."

"Stop it, please. I will listen to no more."

"Do you, then, find it so hard to believe?"

"Naturally, my lord. In all honesty, did you really expect me to believe?"

"Look at me, Sarah."

"No."

"I said look at me!"

Slowly, unwillingly, she looked into his eyes. "Well, my lord?"

"I want you to tell me now, while you are looking at me, that you do not love me. If you can do that, I will let you go. I will never speak of the matter again." His fingers gripped her chin. "No, do not turn your eyes away, you must keep looking at me. Now, Sarah, tell me."

Tears filled her eyes, so that she saw his face through a wavering mist. "I cannot!" she cried. "You know that I cannot! Are you pleased, now that I have made a fool of myself? Is your vanity satisfied, my lord?"

"I am pleased. I am well satisfied." He kissed her quivering mouth. "I love you, Sarah! I have no notion of when it began to happen. But I do love you."

"Please!" she struggled to free herself. "Let me go!"

"Let you go? Nonsense! Of course I will not let you go." Suddenly losing patience, he glared at her in a manner that was far from tender. "You have admitted that you love me. I have said that I love you. So what in the plague is the matter with you?"

"My lord, I do not believe in your protestations of love. I do not wish to go on with this farce."

"You will listen to me, Sarah," he said in his most repressive voice, "and you will listen well. I have many faults, but I am not in the habit of lying, and especially not about something like this. I have never before told a woman I loved her. But I am telling you. If I say I love you, then I damned well do! Do you understand me? Though why in the name of

God you should find it so hard to believe, is quite beyond me!"

"Is it really, my lord?"

"It is. I have said so, have I not?"

"Have you forgotten who you are? Who I am? What I have been?"

"Sarah, since you came into my life, I have discovered that I am possessed of the devil's own temper, so I beg you not to try me too far. I care nothing for what you have been. I care only for what you will become. My love! My one and only love! You little fool! Cannot you understand anything? I want to marry you."

"M-marry me?"

"I do. And pray do not repeat everything after me."

"But it is impossible! I am a convicted thief. For this crime, you yourself had me imprisoned in Newgate!"

"I was under the impression you had forgiven me for that."

"Of course I have, but—"

"Then why do you bring it up again? I would prefer that, instead of talking, you kiss me."

"No! It is obvious to me that you have not thought."

"Do as you are told, Sarah, my darling."

"Please! I beg you to let me go!"

"What! Do you mean to say that you have the infernal impudence to doubt me still?"

"Yes. For you have not thought. You cannot mean it!"

"By God! But this is too much. What the devil must I do to convince you?"

"My lord, you could never convince me!"

He gripped her so fiercely that she cried out in pain. "I warn you, Sarah, you are going too far! I am not a patient man!"

"But—" She stopped short as a knock sounded on the door. "That will be Meadows. Let me go, please!"

Shrugging, he took his arms away. "Very well, if you will have it so." He waited until she had got to her feet and straightened her rumpled gown, then he called in a sharp voice, "Come in."

The door opened, and Meadows entered in his usual dignified fashion. "I regret to disturb you, my lord, but Sir Laurence Shields is below."

"Laurie? What does he want?"

Meadows took one look at his scowling face, and pursed his lips disapprovingly. "Sir Laurence did not confide in me, my lord. At this moment he is talking with my lady Witherley, but I have no doubt he will soon be mounting the stairs."

Jason smiled faintly. "I imagine, remembering his own attack of spotted fever, last year, he has come to gloat."

Meadows looked shocked. "I have always found Sir Laurence to be a kindly gentleman, my lord. I feel sure that he would not take pleasure in your discomfort."

"Would he not?" Jason answered, his eyes on Sarah's face. "He is, as you say, Meadows, of a kindly nature. But this visit, I believe, would be more in the nature of revenge. When he suffered his own attack, he was not satisfied with the sympathy I showed. Or, as he put it, my lack of sympathy."

Meadows turned his face to the door. "I hear Sir Laurence on the stairs, my lord."

Sarah started for the door. "Pray to excuse me, my lord."

A thoughtful gleam came into Jason's eyes. "Remain where you are," he ordered. "Sir Laurence is an old friend of mine. He is an interesting character, and I should like you to meet him."

"I think it would be better, my lord, if I—"

"I said remain, Sarah."

The gentleman who came into the room, with Lady Margaret beside him, was big and bluff and hearty of manner. He wore a jacket and breeches of a particularly startling shade of red, which went ill with his high complexion. Quantities of lace foamed at his throat, and cascaded over his plump, ringed hands. From beneath a wide-brimmed hat plumed in green, white, and purple, long dark hair fell to his shoulders. Small dark eyes in the plump mound of his face were crinkled with merriment, and his mouth was curled into a wide grin.

With a smile in Sarah's direction, and an appraising look, Sir Laurence strode over to the bed. "Well, well," he said in a loud voice that might almost be described as a bellow, "and how is our delicate patient today? What's that you say? Oh, better are you? In that case, Witherley, you lazy hound, why are you still lounging in your bed?"

"All right, Laurie, I deserve it, I know. You may have your laugh. But lower that plaguey voice of yours. It cuts through my head like a knife."

"Your apologies are duly noted, lad," Sir Laurence said in a slightly lowered voice. "He who laughs last, you know. You know that old saying, do you not, lad?" He turned to Margaret. "Is the lad malingering, think you, my lady?"

Margaret smiled. "Nay, Laurie, you know him too well. He is of far too impatient a nature to keep willingly to his bed."

"Hmm!" Sir Laurence's twinkling eyes turned to Sarah. "Now there is a little beauty, by Gad! Will you not introduce me?"

"Mistress Sarah Barry," Margaret answered. "She is my companion."

Sir Laurence strolled forward and extended his hand to Sarah. "Would that you were my companion, damned if I don't!"

Sarah smiled as she placed her hand in his. "You are very kind, sir."

"And would be kinder, if given the opportunity."

Sarah started as Sir Laurence, releasing her hand, touched

her cheek with a caressing finger. "Were you mine, sweetheart, we would make some merry sport."

"Laurence!" Jason's voice was a whiplash. "Take your infernal hands away. Mistress Barry and I are going to be married."

"Married?" Sir Laurence's large pink mouth dropped open in astonishment. "You, Jason? Married! I never thought I would live to see you captivated by any lass, no matter how beautiful." Recovering, Sir Laurence took Sarah's hand once more, and bowed over it. "I wish you very happy with the cursed disagreeable fellow, sweetheart." Bending closer, he whispered in her ear. "Nay, pay me no attention. Jason is a good lad, for all his high-nosed attitude. You'll make him human, will you not, lass?"

Sarah could not speak, Jason's announcement had stunned her. Over Sir Laurence's bowed head, she met Margaret's eyes. They were blank with shock. "It seems, Sarah, that I must congratulate you," Margaret said in a stiff, unfriendly voice.

"My lady, I—"

"Not now, Sarah," Jason interrupted. "Mother, I had not meant to break the news in quite this way. Later, we will talk more of this."

Sir Laurence glanced from Sarah's face to Margaret's. "Then you knew nothing of the romance, my lady?" He smiled. "Ah, hah, I scent a mystery."

"No mystery, Laurie," Jason answered quickly. "Had you not arrived at this particular time, my mother would already be acquainted with the news."

Sir Laurence shrugged. "No mystery, then. Pity, for I thrive on 'em. Anyway, I approve your choice, lad." He grinned. "I have a confession to make. This is not the first time I have heard Mistress Barry's name. That feather-top of a Baxter is forever singing her praises. So you see, my visit had a double purpose. To see how you did, lad. And to meet

Baxter's beauteous Mistress Barry."

Jason frowned. "Baxter is an affected puppy and a prating fool!"

"Nay, lad, you judge him too harshly. He believes himself to be in love with Mistress Barry. In any case, I thought him to be your friend."

Jason smiled ruefully. "Well, so he is. But Peter has believed himself to be in love a hundred times or more. 'Tis not long since that he was ogling Lady Dorothy Prentiss, Bainbridge's mistress."

"And still ogles her, lad. Peter has ever believed in having more than one iron in the fire. I'd not be surprised if Bainbridge challenges him one of these days."

"How does the King?" Jason said, changing the subject. "Is he fully recovered?"

Sir Laurence's eyes twinkled. "Aye, Old Rowley is fully recovered, and randy, lad, randy!"

Sir Laurence wandered over to the bed. Seating himself casually on the edge, he engaged my lord Witherley in light conversation. As he talked, he found himself intrigued by the expression on Mistress Barry's face. What, he wondered, had brought that look of horror to it? Could it be that the marriage was distasteful to her? If so, he felt sure that Witherley, with his fierce pride, would not hold the lass to it.

It was not horror that Sarah felt, but an angry confusion. Why had my lord Witherley placed her in such a position? He must know that such a marriage could not be. All this, together with the talk of Sir Peter Baxter's love, or supposed love, for her was a little too much for her to absorb. Even so, she felt joy trying to break through the anger. He must love her, or else he would not have made such a rash statement before such witnesses as Sir Laurence and Lady Margaret. If only she were in a position to accept such happiness! But she was not. She found herself remembering my lord Witherley's words. "What the devil must I do to convince you?" It would seem that he, in his imperious way, a way that admitted of no obstacles, had determined that she should be convinced. But the obstacles were too numerous, and one of them was Lady Margaret. Margaret, regarding her so stonily, might have been a hostile stranger, rather than the kind and good friend she had proved herself to be.

"My lady," Sarah whispered, taking a step toward her. She placed her hand on Margaret's rigid arm, "pray do not look at me so. For indeed, I assure you, it is not as you think."

Margaret drew her arm away. "You know nothing of my thoughts, Mistress Barry."

Sarah flushed at the coldness of her tone. "But I would know your thoughts, my lady," she whispered urgently. "I would do nothing to hurt you. And it is important to me that I keep your affection and your trust."

"My affection and my trust?" Margaret gave her a contemptuous look. "You ask a great deal, do you not? I did have affection for you, I did trust you, and how have you repaid me?" As though she could no longer bear the sight of her, Margaret turned away. "For the moment, Mistress Barry, I have nothing further to say to you."

For the first time since she had known her, Sarah felt anger toward her benefactor. The marriage was impossible, of course, and Lady Margaret must know that she would never go against her wishes. But did she have to look at her as though she were some loathsome crawling insect? Need she have shown her horror and revulsion quite so plainly?

Margaret blinked tears from her eyes. How could Jason so far forget what he owed to his name, his heritage? He must not be allowed to make this marriage with a girl of lowly parentage. A girl moreover who had not only been imprisoned in Newgate but who had been an inmate of Bedlam Asylum. Nay, it was unthinkable! She glanced at Sarah, and, at the sight of her distressed face, she felt a twinge of shame. Perhaps she was not being fair to the girl, perhaps it was unjust to blame her. Who could stand out against Jason when he was determined to have his way? He had always been arrogant and strong-willed, who should know that better than herself? Had she not fought many battles with him, and always lost? And now, if he truly believed himself to be in love with Sarah, he would certainly brook no opposition. No matter what she had said to Sarah, she was still fond of her. She did not want her to be hurt. But she must be made to see that a marriage with her son was quite unacceptable. But what of Jason? Could he be brought to see his folly? Her heart quailed as she faced the knowledge that she had never yet been able to bend him to her will.

Jason, replying to Sir Laurence's remarks, his attention apparently fixed on that affable man, was thinking of Sarah and his mother. What had they been whispering about? He had seen the cold and haughty look his mother had bent upon Sarah, and he could guess at the direction her conversation had taken. His hands clenched on the sheet. He would not allow Sarah to be hurt. He loved her. As for his mother, he desired her happiness as he felt sure that she desired his. If that were so, then, in this particular matter, she must refrain from criticism. Nothing in his life had been quite so important as this. He would marry Sarah no matter what his mother or the society in which they moved might say or think. He was no green boy. Love had come to him unexpectedly, and he had no intention of losing it.

Sir Laurence regarded him for a long thoughtful moment. There was more in this situation than he had thought for. Jason scarcely looked like the happy bridegroom-to-be. Mistress Barry still had that strange look on her face, and as for Lady Margaret, she looked almost ill. Curbing his curiosity with some difficulty, he rose to his feet. "A plague on you and that cursed scowl of yours, Jason," he said without rancor. "You are a surly dog.'

Jason smiled. "Nay, Laurie, not surly, merely thoughtful. Are you leaving?"

"Aye, 'tis time I took my departure. Have a care for yourself, lad." Sir Laurence looked at Jason critically. "You have taken the fever lightly. A pity, that. I had hoped to see you suffering as I suffered."

Sir Laurence took a cheerful farewell of the ladies, and then sauntered slowly from the room. Once outside the house, he hastened his steps. He was anxious to spread the news of Witherley's intended marriage.

Chapter Thirteen

Sarah stood with her back pressed against the door. When Lady Margaret had called her into her small sitting room, she had been prepared for her opposition, but not for the anger she was displaying.

Margaret's eyes swept over the girl. "I see that you are dressed for walking."

"Yes, my lady. I need to think. I thought the air would help to clear my head.'

"Think? What is there to think about? Have I not made it clear to you that you cannot marry my son?"

"Yes, my lady, you have made it abundantly clear. But is it clear to my lord Witherley? He is not a child. You cannot order his life as you see fit. He must—" She broke off, the color rising in her cheeks. Why had she said that? What did it matter? She still had no intention of marrying Jason.

"I see." Lady Margaret's eyes were hard with suspicion. "So you do have some thoughts on the matter?"

"I believe I have told you my thoughts, my lady. I can only repeat that I will not marry your son."

"I wish I could believe you, Sarah. But in encouraging him in his folly, you have proved yourself unworthy of my trust."

"That is not true!" Sarah cried. "You cannot truly believe that?"

Lady Margaret ignored her protest. "Do you see yourself as my lady Witherley, is that it? A girl like you!"

"A girl like me," Sarah said bitterly. "How contemptuously

you say that. What kind of girl do you believe me to be?"

At the look on Sarah's face, Lady Margaret was stricken with remorse, but she was determined not to show it. "Why, you know," she said coldly. "Surely I do not need to put it into words."

"I know, my lady. I see now that, in your eyes, I am little better than trash. I would be better off dead, would I not?" Sarah turned blindly and opened the door.

"Sarah! What are you saying? I did not mean—"

"No more, my lady. I know exactly what you mean."

Margaret stood in the center of the room, her hand pressed to her mouth, her eyes dismayed. Why had she been so cruel? Sarah had assured her again and again that she would not marry Jason. Why had she continued to harry her? Sarah deserved better from her. She heard Sarah's hurrying footsteps, the slam of the front door behind her. Where was she going? What had she driven her to? With an exclamation, Margaret flew to the window. She was relieved when she saw Sarah cross the road to the Common. She sighed. Sarah's favorite walk, and one on which either she or Trevallion always accompanied her. Margaret's brows drew together in an uneasy frown. What should she do now? She had not seen Jason since yesterday, when he had made his dramatic announcement. Should she go upstairs and confront him? A quiver went through her at the very thought. No, better to go after Sarah. She would ask the girl's forgiveness for her cruelty. Mayhap they could talk, perhaps end the matter of Jason, but still keep some kind of friendship between them. She was very fond of Sarah. She must make her realize it.

The fresh covering of snow that had fallen during the night crunched sharply beneath Sarah's feet as she made her way across the Common. "A girl like you! A girl like you!" The words kept repeating themselves. She had not needed Lady

Margaret to add to her misery. This morning, when she had sought the interview with Jason, had in itself been more than she could bear. When she had entered the room, Jason had been standing by the window. Hearing her, he turned, smiling, and held out his arms. "I thought you would never come, Sarah. I had almost made up my mind to go in search of you."

She could not look at him. She stood there, her eyes downcast. "Good morning, my lord," she said in a low voice. "I am happy to see that you are well enough to leave your bed."

He laughed. "I see that my Sarah is still wearing her closed look. What is it, my darling? Are you angry because I made my announcement without first consulting you?"

How different he sounded. How different from the aloof and unbending my lord Witherley. She stole a quick look at him. His face was slightly flushed, and his blond hair was rumpled. He looked almost boyish. "Nay, my lord," she said quickly. "I am not angry."

"Then what is it? I had great hopes that I would see you looking happy this morning."

She raised her eyes and looked at him steadily. "How could I possibly be happy?"

He frowned. "You are allowing my mother's disapproval to affect you, is that it? I must tell you now, Sarah, that no amount of disapproval will stand in our way. I am the head of this household and answerable to no one. I love you. I am going to marry you. There is no more to be said."

"No! I cannot marry you. It is quite impossible!"

He crossed the room in three strides and pulled her roughly into his arms. "What nonsense is this?" he demanded.

"Oh, please, my lord! It is not nonsense."

"My mother has spoken to you, is that it?"

She shook her head. "My lord, you know my story. Can you not see for yourself why a marriage between us is impossible."

"A pox on your story! I am tired of hearing of your past

life. It is over, Sarah, over! The future is before us, and that is all that counts. As for all that you have suffered, what can I say except, 'My poor darling, Sarah!' Come, do you not see that you are being foolish to allow old ghosts to stand in our way?"

"I cannot marry you," she insisted stubbornly. "I will not."

"Sarah, you are trying my patience again. I promise you that I will take very good care of you. Nothing harmful shall ever touch you again."

"No!" She drew away from him and turned to the door.

"Sarah!" He caught her before she could open it. Turning her to face him, he said in a furious voice, "Have we not played this game long enough? I would remind you of certain words you said to me. As I recall, you admitted that you loved me. If there is love between us, then nothing else matters. Not birth, or convention, or any of the other rubbish with which society and one's family seek to bind about one. We are a man and a woman, Sarah, and we love each other. We are not puppets to be moved at someone else's will. Cannot you understand that?"

He was sincere. He really believed that now. But later, when his infatuation had died, he would be ashamed of her. And because he was ashamed, he would grow to hate her. "I am afraid, my lord," she said in a steady voice, "that it is you who do not understand. Yesterday, I did but play a game. When I said that I loved you, I meant it not."

"You lie, Sarah!"

She heard the note of uncertainty in his voice, and she pressed home her advantage. "I do not lie, my lord. So let us have done with the matter. If—if you must know, I care for somebody else."

"Someone else? Who?"

"Does it matter?"

She sensed his withdrawal. She was prepared for his coldness, but not for his actual words. "Baxter? Is it Baxter?"

She stood there mute. Sir Peter? That fop! But let him think it. There must be a complete severance between them. It was for his own good.

"I see," he said at last. "Your silence tells me that I have guessed correctly. He is more to your liking, eh, wench?"

"Stop it!"

He grasped her roughly, his fingers digging into her flesh. "Stop it, you say. For God's sake! Do you now seek to play the injured innocent with me? You shall speak. You will tell me in so many words if it is Baxter. Tell me, or I will shake the truth out of you!"

"Believe what you will," she cried desperately. "If you say it is he, then it must be so!"

He looked at her with eyes that had grown narrowed and cruel. "I am, unfortunately, new to this game of love. But of this much I am certain. Had you loved me, as I believed, you would have let nothing stand in our way. Therefore I am compelled to recognize that you speak truth. I wonder if you really love Baxter, or if you love more his possessions. If that is so, wench, you should have thought to better purpose. I am far richer than he."

This pain was more than she could bear. She had to end it. Now! "If you have quite finished, my lord, be so good as to let me go."

He stared at her for a moment. That cold, clear, steady voice of hers. Nay, she had never loved him. She had told him the truth. "Aye, I'll let you go, Mistress Barry!" he said savagely. He flung her from him so violently that her back jarred against the door. "Get out! Do not let me set eyes on you again, or I might be tempted to break every bone in your body!"

Not daring to look at him again, she had fled from the room. It was some time later, on her way out, that she had encountered Lady Margaret.

"A girl like you!" The words began ticking in her brain again. Yes, but my lord Witherley had said: "We are a man and a woman, not puppets to be moved at someone else's will." Who was right? She caught her breath in anguish. Had she been a fool to turn aside from love? If Jason truly loved her, was she not condemning them both to misery? Perhaps she should go back, explain, tell him all that was in her heart and mind? In sudden uncertainty, she stumbled, almost losing her footing. Perhaps it was not too late. Jason loved her, she was certain of it now. And she? She could not love him more than she did. He was everything to her. Yes, she would go back. But not yet. She must think about it a little more. This, after all, was the first chance she had had to think clearly. The miserable doubts began tearing at her again. If he married her, would he grow to regret it? She must think. She must not allow herself, and her longing for him, to push her into a hasty decision. She must think what was best for him.

William Mitford smiled as he watched Sarah walking toward him. He had always known, if he were patient, that his moment would come. Her blue and white cloak sailed from her shoulders in the icy wind, the white plumes of her bonnet made a gay flutter. Mitford's face flushed as he stared at her slender hips and the high, rounded curve of her breasts clearly outlined by her wind-plastered gown.

She was much nearer now. But she must not see him yet. He stepped behind the concealing trunk of the tree against which he had been standing. In the afternoon, just as she was doing now, she always took a walk across the Common, but this was the first time she had been unaccompanied. He could scarcely believe his luck in finding her alone. Berkton Common, though starting in this rich district, was shunned by most of the swells. It was definitely not a popular promenade, but the loonie seemed to like it. The Common spread out a far distance, going all the way to Tipton Green, with great gloomy stretches in between. Those parts of the Common, not visible to the passer-by, were wild and overgrown, and, save for an occasional hardy walker, always deserted. It was these deserted stretches, which he found so suitable to the plan he had in mind, that the loonie always frequented.

Mitford grinned to himself. Fortune seemed to be with him. Only last week, he had found the little summer house. It lay just beyond the high bushes at his back. It was apparently never used, for it was all but hidden under a burden of ivy, and he had almost missed it. It would do very well, he thought. He peered cautiously from behind the tree trunk. His eyes sharpened in annoyance as he caught sight of another woman plodding along in the distance. He cursed beneath his breath, wondering if his luck was changing. Why should the woman have chosen this day of all days to walk where none usually came? He began to hope that the strong wind and the chill in the air would discourage her. If she came too near, she might prove to be a problem. His frown cleared. Nay, she was unimportant. He'd have the loonie in the summer house before she noticed and raised a cry. No one would hear her, and if it came to it, he would soon silence her. He fingered the scarf in his pocket. If the loonie set up a great screaming, he'd use the scarf to gag her. Beneath the scarf there was a knife in a leather sheath. Mitford's fingers touched it almost lovingly. How would the loonie like it when everybody shuddered at the sight of her mutilated face?

He frowned thoughtfully. Even with a deserted place like this there was always the odd chance of discovery. That unknown woman, for instance, if she came too near. When he'd done with the loonie, he would waste no time in getting away. But before he did, he'd tell her his name, just so that she would always remember him. Aye, and he'd tell her about the dose of pox he'd caught. Let her worry about that too. Once away, he'd never be found. There weren't many who were foolhardy enough to venture into those rabbit warrens in the district he inhabited. The swells rarely came near, they were too afraid of getting their precious throats slit. Though they sometimes passed through in their fancy carriages, on their way to the King's Theatre, the Duke's Theatre, or some other place of amusement. But if somebody wished to avenge the loonie, whoever that somebody might be would have to search on foot, that is if they hoped to find him. Nobody would give him away, not even if they were paid to do so. They wouldn't dare! They knew only too well what the street gang would do to them.

Still walking fast, her mind preoccupied, Sarah was only vaguely aware of a dark shape near the tree. When the man stepped forward suddenly, she almost collided with him. Swerving, she murmured an apology, then, her thoughts still with Jason, she walked on.

"Not so fast, you!" a voice said.

Before she could turn, a hand was clasped across her mouth. An arm circled her waist, tightening painfully. "It's me," a rough voice said in her ear. "Billy's come back to his pretty loonie."

Sarah stood perfectly still. She could feel the warm gusts of his breath on her neck. She did not need to see his face. She knew who stood behind her. Because she had not seen the scarred man for some days, she had allowed her caution to relax. She had, she realized now, forgotten all about him. How could she have been so foolish? Her first sensation of blind panic was rapidly succeeded by fury. All the tricks that Jemmy had taught her, in case she should ever be caught, came back to her now. Struggling in his hold, she kicked backward at his shins. The vicious blow landed, and Mitford gave a stifled exclamation. The hand he had placed over her mouth, loosened. Instantly she sank her teeth into his flesh, biting down savagely.

"Christ!" Mitford howled. "You bleedin' whore!" Cursing, he doubled up his fist and aimed a violent blow at the back of her neck. Sarah's head jerked forward, and for a stunned moment she believed that her neck must be broken. She knew it was not when, still cursing, he caught her by the hair and dragged her head up. His hands fastened over her nose and mouth, cutting off air. Hoping he would ease the pressure, she went limp against him. She began to struggle again as he dragged her toward the bushes. She managed to jerk her head free for a moment, and she screamed loudly.

His hands stifled the sound. "Shut up, you bitch! One more sound out o' you, and I'll land you such a clout that your 'ead'll ring for weeks!"

Margaret blinked the wind induced tears from her eyes. Above the howl of the wind, it seemed to her that she had heard a faint cry. Now she could see the blue flash of Sarah's gown. There was somebody with her. A man. Her heart began to pound. The man was struggling with her. Oh, God! How many times had she told the girl that this deserted stretch of common was not safe? Even as she watched, the man dragged Sarah out of her sight.

"Sarah!" Margaret ran forward. Sliding over the snow, she did not see the raised tree root that loomed in her path. She stumbled and fell headlong.

Mitford's hard hand slapped Sarah's face first one side and then the other. "That'll teach you!" he snarled. "That'll keep you quiet, you loonie bitch!"

Keeping his gloating eyes on her, Mitford began to disrobe. He kicked off his breeches and the grubby underdrawers, then drew his shirt over his head. Standing over her, posing, he exulted in her terror. His face was red with exertion and filmed over with perspiration. Her nostrils caught the stench of his body.

Mitford grinned down at her. "Like what you see, do you, wench?"

With a sudden spring, she was on her feet and running for the door.

Mitford captured her easily. "Oh, no you don't!" He threw her to the floor, laughing as she cried out in pain. "Banged your 'ead, did you? Ain't that a shame."

She glared at him. Words came to her lips, words normally alien to her. "You bastard! God rot you, you filthy stinking swine!"

He began to laugh again. "Ah, you can curse as good as any gutter whore, eh?" He fell to his knees beside her, and began to tear at her clothes. "Can't you, me little darlin'?"

"Let me go!" Her nails stabbed at his face. "You scum!"

He ripped the gown from her body, and then began to tear at her petticoat.

Rearing upward, she clawed at him viciously, sank her teeth into his arm, and aimed for his eyes with her sharp nails.

His clenched fist struck her in the mouth. He grunted with satisfaction as she went limp again. "I'll bet that's loosened some o' them nice white teeth o' yours." He tore the rest of the petticoat from her body. "You turned out to be a proper little beauty, you did! Billy's going to enjoy dipping in your little pot o' honey."

His voice was a rumbling sound, the words meaningless. There was a swirling darkness before her eyes, and a salty taste of blood in her mouth. She moved, still struggling to fight him off, but it was as though she did everything in slow motion. Her arms lifted, but they felt so heavy that she could scarcely bear their weight. She pushed at him, striking out again with her nails. His next blow sent white hot pain exploding through her head. Only half-conscious, she was quiescent beneath him.

Margaret got to her feet with an effort. She had struck her

head when she fell, and it was throbbing painfully. Once more she became conscious of rising agitation. Sarah? She must find her, help her! She ran forward, her eyes searching wildly. It was more by accident than luck that she found the summer house behind the tall bushes. Approaching the door cautiously, she peered inside. Sarah! She put her hand over her mouth to stifle her cry. Sarah lay on the floor, her face so bruised and bloody that it was almost unrecognizable. Above her was the man, his gross body poised as he prepared to enter her. Sarah's eyes were closed, and she was unmoving.

Margaret's head whirled. Dear God, she must stop him! But how, how? She saw the man's carelessly scattered clothes, and lying beside them, a knife in a leather sheaf. Silent-footed as a cat, hardly daring to breathe lest she alert him, Margaret crept forward. Stooping, she picked up the knife and drew it from its sheath.

Mitford was angry. A plague on the cursed whore! In fainting, she was cheating him. He wanted her to be fully conscious and aware of every stroke of his body within hers. He began to slap her face again. "Wake up, you loonie!"

A shadow fell across him, and he turned his head sharply. It took only that flashing glimpse to recognize my lady Witherley. Fury rose in him in a hot tide. So she was here again? But this time she would not interfere! His eyes dilated as she drew the knife from behind her back and held it out menacingly. With an angry bellow, he bounded to his feet and closed with her.

Her lips pressed together in a grim line, Margaret fought him with all her strength, but she was no match for Mitford. She went white with pain as he gripped her wrist and twisted viciously. Her fingers opened, and the knife thudded to the floor.

Pushing her away, Mitford snatched it up. He thought he had subdued her. He was not prepared for her next move when, in sheer desperation, she launched herself at him once more. Holding the knife in his right hand, confident of his strength, he endeavored to hold her off. He swore as her nails tore a furrow down his cheek. In that moment, when his attention was not fully on her, it happened. With no thought of the carelessly outthrust knife, Margaret made another lunge. Mitford winced at her gasping scream as the knife entered the upper part of her arm.

The mists of rage clearing from his brain, he found himself remembering just who it was he dealt with. Appalled, he stepped back hastily. The instincts of self-preservation rising strongly within him, he opened his mouth to warn her not to remove the knife. Before he could get the first word out, she had wrenched the knife from her arm. Shuddering, she flung it from her.

Automatically, never taking his eyes from the blood staining her white silk sleeve, Mitford stooped and picked it up. Holding the knife clutched in his sweating hand, he knew the taste of fear. What if she died of the wound? This was a different matter from raping a loonie and cutting her up a bit. She was unimportant. But this woman was very important. If she died, and if the loonie gave his description, he would be hunted down. He would hang! The fear-induced silence of his neighbors would no longer protect him, for he knew well they would be made to talk. They would never rest until they found him. The murder of my lady Witherley would be no small thing. And it would be called murder. For a brief moment he hesitated, wondering whether it might not be safer to make an end to the loonie. It would be easy to slit her throat. He shook his head to clear it. Nay, he had always been one to believe in his luck, and he would take his chance. He could tell from the look in my lady Witherley's eyes that she had recognized him, but as long as she did not die, it would not matter. It might well be that the wound was not too serious.

Margaret's trembling legs would no longer support her. Holding one hand over the wound, she sank to the floor beside Sarah. Almost indifferently, she watched as Mitford snatched up his clothes and ran for the door. The scarred man! The words beat monotonously in her brain. The scarred man. The man from Lilacgrove Alley! But how had he found Sarah? What madness brewed in his brain that even now he sought her out?

Margaret took her hand away from the wound. Rolling up her sleeve, she looked at her arm. The bleeding had stopped. It was not after all, very deep. She had seen from the scarred man's expression that he had feared she would die. Well, she was far from dying, and she must help Sarah. Drawing out her kerchief, she dabbed at the blood on the girl's face. To her great relief, she found that the injuries were not as serious as she had first believed. Sarah's face, to be sure, was very bruised, but bruises healed. The blood had come mainly from the cut above her eye and from her split lip. It was the cut above her eye, from which the blood now came sluggishly, that had given her face the horrifying appearance of being a mask of blood. But the blood from her lip had already begun to dry and to form a brittle crust.

It seemed to Margaret to be a very long time before Sarah stirred and opened her eyes. For a moment she stared uncomprehendingly into the face bent over her, then her dulled eyes gradually grew bright with terror. "That man!" she gasped. "The scarred man. He—he r-raped me!"

"He is gone now," Margaret hastened to soothe her. She opened her mouth, meaning to tell Sarah that he had not succeeded in raping her, but, after a moment's thought, she decided against it. Let Sarah believe that he had succeeded. If she knew anything about the girl, nothing then would induce her to marry Jason.

Sarah closed her eyes again. She felt soiled and degraded.

That man! That terrible animal of a man! She wanted to ask Lady Margaret how she came to be here, but she felt too tired. The only thing that mattered was that she had not arrived in time to prevent the rape. If she had done so, she would have told her.

Margaret felt heavy with guilt as she stared at Sarah's drawn face. But still she could not bring herself to say the words that would relieve part of the anguish she must be feeling. No, she had done the right thing. The right thing for Jason. "Sarah," she said, "do you think you can manage to get to your feet? We are both in sad case, I fear, and we would be better off at home."

Sarah's eyes opened again. For the first time she noticed Margaret's blood-stained sleeve. "Your arm?" she whispered. "He-he did that?"

"He had a knife. It happened when I tried to take it away from him."

"He might have killed you!" Sarah shuddered. "What if he should come back? What if he should seek us out again?"

"Do not think of that, Sarah."

"He had been watching the house for a long time. Watching and waiting! I know, I have seen him."

"You said nothing to me," Margaret said sharply.

"I was afraid you might think that I had imagined it."

"Oh, Sarah, poor child!" Feeling like a Judas, Margaret took her hand. "You should have told me."

"I thought of it." Sarah pulled her hand free and struggled upright. "But I know now that it would have served no purpose." Her voice rose hysterically. "Only yesterday, when my lord said he wished to marry me, your shock was for more than my lowly birth. I saw your eyes, my lady, and I knew then that you genuinely believed that at one time I had been insane. You thought, did you not, that there was a possibility my madness might return?"

"No, Sarah! No!" Margaret's shock was genuine. Such a thought had never entered her head.

Tears welled and ran down Sarah's face. "I know it is true. I tell you, I saw it in your eyes. I knew what you were thinking! I love your son, I will always love him. But I will not marry him, and especially not now. I have already told him so, and there need be nothing further to worry you. But you should have trusted me. I would never have hurt you!"

"I know, Sarah, I know." Margaret drew the trembling body into her arms. "Hush, my dear, hush! Listen to me, I want you to know that never for one moment did I doubt your sanity. I pray that at least you will believe that. As for the rest, it is simply that I do not think that a marriage between two people of such very different backgrounds would be very wise."

"I know. And after a time, my lord will know it too. But even had it been possible to marry him, I could not do so now. Th-that m-man has made me dirty."

Margaret made no answer, but she continued to hold Sarah close. She was a wicked woman! But she did not do this thing for herself. It was for Jason.

Sarah was wondering how she could bear the pain of never seeing Jason again. Her lips tightened. It was no use whimpering, she had to learn to bear the pain. There was no other way. Certainly she could never return to the house. For no matter how bitter my lord Witherley might be feeling toward her, if he saw her in this condition, he would demand an explanation. It would all come out, then, the whole sordid tale. She would not be able to hide from him how the scarred man had used her. Her past, she felt sure, would matter to him then. He might even think she had encouraged the man. In her imagination, she saw his eyes grow cold with contempt. If he should think that of her, believe her to be as soiled as she now felt, it would kill her! All those qualities that had hitherto held her calm and steady and able to face life again, would crumble before his hatred and contempt.

"Come," Margaret's voice said. "We must go home. If we remain here, it is likely that you will take a chill."

"A chill? Oh, my lady, does it matter? I would like to die!"

"Sarah, pray do not talk like that! Things will seem brighter soon."

"Not for me!" Sarah drew herself from Margaret's arms. "Never again for me! You are kind, my lady, but my troubles must not any longer be allowed to concern you. It is better if I do not return to the house with you. You see that, do you not?"

"Let me think for a moment, child." Since Sarah had already told Jason that she would not marry him, it might be best if she went elsewhere. She would be sorry to lose her, of course, but it would be wiser. If Jason did not know where Sarah had gone, and he would not know from her, then he could hardly seek her out. Given time, he would forget about her.

Margaret stirred uneasily. But would he forget Sarah? Had she ever been able to forget her John? No, and she never would! But she had truly loved John. Surely Jason could not really love Sarah, a girl so different in breeding and background, so different in every way? It was simply that he was bewitched by her now, and he was incapable of seeing that such a marriage would be disastrous. At the same time, she could not cast Sarah completely adrift. There must be a way she could help her. Suddenly, she thought of Opal Sunderland. The cheerful, vulgar, but big-hearted Opal Sunderland had, at one time, been one of the King's mistresses. The affair had lasted only a short time, but Opal had not suffered because of that. Charles was always generous to his discarded mistresses. Margaret, who could not help liking Opal, had befriended her. She saw her quite often, so she knew that Opal had recently purchased a home in Brondesbury Square. If Sarah could stay with Opal for a while, it would be an immense help. It was true that the house was in London, but it was not in a fashionable district. It was doubtful if Jason, though he had met Opal on several occasions, would think of seeking for Sarah there. The more she thought of it, the more suitable the idea seemed. Opal, good-hearted and generous to a fault, would not refuse her help.

"Sarah," Margaret said, suddenly brisk. "Listen to me. You must come home with me tonight. Yes, child, you must, so do not shake your head. Tomorrow, early in the morning, I will take you to Mistress Sunderland, who is a good friend of mine. You will like her. She will shelter you for a time. Later, I will seek out a pleasant situation for you. I wish to remain your friend. So please have no fear that I will abandon you."

Sarah's smile was mirthless. "It might be better to abandon me, my lady. I do not wish you to feel indebted to me."

"Nonsense, Sarah. I want to help you. You must know that I am very fond of you."

But not fond enough. Sarah could not prevent the sudden bitter thought. You could never see me as a suitable daughter-in-law. "If you wish to help me, my lady," she said quietly, "then please take me to Mistress Sunderland tonight."

Margaret shook her head firmly. "Neither of us is in a fit condition. Tomorrow will be better."

"Please! I would not wish to encounter my lord Witherley."

"I understand. You shall not encounter him. But we must be sensible. You may safely leave everything to me."

Margaret rose. Ignoring the pain in her arm, she got Sarah to her feet. She helped her to dress in the rags of her petticoat and the torn silk gown. Taking her cameo brooch from her lace collar, she pinned gown and petticoat securely at the back. The blue and white cloak was fortunately whole. Draping it about Sarah's shoulders, she tied the strings beneath her chin and drew the hood well forward. "You must carry your bonnet, Sarah," she told her. "If you do not lift your head, your face cannot be seen."

Sarah was apathetic. Let Lady Margaret direct and control her movements. Why fight? Nothing mattered anymore!

To Margaret, the walk back to the house seemed endless. Although her own wound was not serious, she nevertheless felt a little weak from the loss of blood, and her arm was growing increasingly stiff and painful. As for Sarah, it was as if she could not see very well, for her steps kept wandering. Several times she fell, and she made no attempt to get to her feet. More time was wasted as Margaret dragged her upright again. She did not seem to want to get up, and Margaret had the uneasy feeling that, if she were to walk away from her, Sarah would continue to lie there in the snow, uncaring. Concern grew in Margaret as she unwillingly faced the fact that something essential seemed to have snapped in the girl. She had the guilty thought that it was not only the scarred man who was to blame for this frightening change. She, too, was to blame, perhaps Jason as well. Each, in different ways, had combined to bring Sarah low.

She had never been so thankful when she saw the house loom up before them. Dismissing guilt, Margaret stepped briskly across the street, drawing Sarah after her.

The door was opened to them by Cransford. The footman's eyebrows rose as he took in my lady Witherley's disheveled appearance. For a brief moment, he allowed his eyes to dwell speculatively on Mistress Barry's drooping form. As is common with most household servants, who have their own mysterious ways of gathering information, he was already aware of the situation between my lord Witherley and Mistress Barry. His curiosity was further piqued when my lady, after telling him to send Mrs. Trevallion to her at once, took Mistress Barry's hand and led her along as though she were a blind child. Shaking his head and pondering on how he could find out what was amiss now, he walked with majestic stride toward the housekeeper's quarters.

When Mrs. Trevallion entered Margaret's sitting room some moments later, she was looking flustered and indignant. Margaret guessed that Cransford, momentarily allowing his curiosity to overcome his dignity, had been questioning the old woman. Margaret had few secrets from Mrs. Trevallion, and, after only the briefest hesitation, she told her exactly what had occurred. Cutting short the woman's distressed exclamations, Margaret cautioned her to keep what she had told her to herself, and to send somebody immediately for Doctor Sanders.

Doctor Sanders had been out when the messenger arrived at his house. It was therefore almost an hour before he put in an appearance. He entered the room in his usual tempestuous fashion, his beaming smile giving the lie to his peppery treatment. His smile faded as he caught sight of Sarah. She was lying on the couch, her eyes closed. She did not stir as he came to stand over her. "What's this, eh?" The doctor turned an accusing glare on Margaret, who was crouched in a chair, her hand over her throbbing arm. "Who did it, eh?"

Margaret's smile was weary. "Pray, do not glare at me, doctor, I assure you that it was not I. Indeed, I have need of your attention myself."

"I will hear who is responsible first, if you please, Maggie?" He puffed out his cheeks. "Who, eh? That cursed fellow upstairs?"

At this mention of her son, Margaret sat up indignantly. "Certainly not! How can you say such a thing? I am aware that you do not like Jason, but to say—"

"Rubbish! Don't gabble! I like the blasted fellow. Always have, and you know it. And if you think differently, Maggie, my girl, then you're the damned feather-top I have always thought you. I just wanted to see if you were attending me."

Understanding that the doctor's words had been more in the nature of an attempt at humor, designed to lighten a grim situation, Margaret subsided. "Oh," she said weakly. "I see."

The doctor was unforgiving. 'Are you a lady or a fishwife, eh? Eh? It ain't ladylike to scream, as I am forever telling that nag that I call wife." Placing his bag and his white staff on a nearby table, he turned and gave Margaret another severe look. "I see from the blood on Mistress Barry's face, and the same on your sleeve, that there's been dirty work afoot. You had best tell me about it." Removing his tricorn hat as an afterthought, he tossed it on top of the bag. "Been walking across the Common again, ain't you, eh?"

"Well, you see, it—"

His snort cut across Margaret's halting words. "Thought so! Blasted females! Never did come across one that wasn't queer in her attic. I could have told you that the place abounds with rip-tops and scoundrels. In fact, I have told you. What do you mean by it, eh? Eh?"

Wilting before the ferocious glare in his gray eyes, and knowing that he would not proceed until she had explained, Margaret wearily began her story again.

Except for the doctor's occasional grunts, which varying in tone, expressed a variety of emotions, he heard her out in silence. When her voice faded, he became a whirlwind of activity. With quick deft movements, he cleaned Margaret's arm, smeared a pink paste over it, bound it, and then recommended her in a curt tone not to be such a blithering idiot to go walking again without a man in attendance. "For I don't mind telling you, Maggie," he concluded, "that all the cursed females I have ever met, and I mean every blistering one of 'em, should be in leading strings, and that's a fact. Not a brain among 'em!"

Having delivered himself of this biting denunciation, the

doctor turned his attention to Sarah. His manner in odd variance with his words, he laid a gentle hand on her head. "Now then, my pretty, open up your eyes. Let's see if we can't bring back some of that fire and ginger of yours."

Sarah opened her eyes obediently. To some of his more outrageous remarks, she managed a wavering smile. But not all his efforts could bring forth a voluntary remark. She was submissive under his ministrations, too submissive, the doctor thought uneasily, and, although it must have pained her a great deal, she winced only slightly when he cleansed her face, and finally smeared it with a soothing balm.

"Thank you," Sarah said in a toneless voice. "You are very kind."

"Kind, nothing! Doctor, ain't I? I can't say you'll be a pretty sight for a day or two, lass, but there, 'tis only your bedsheets that will be seeing you, eh?"

His rumbling laugh encouraged her to laugh at this witticism, but Sarah nodded to show that she had heard, and then closed her eyes again.

Sighing, the doctor picked up his hat and clapped it on top of his white wig. "I don't like it, Maggie," he said, picking up his bag and his staff. "Nay, I don't like it one bit. There's no life in the wench, no cursed ginger. I'll thank you to give me a full description of the bloody dog who attacked her, a full one, mind! I'll expect it when I look in on you tomorrow. I'll be setting some inquiries afoot. We'll see what can be done about tracking down the scoundrel, eh?"

"Wait!" Margaret's voice halted him as he stumped over to the door. "I must tell you that Mistress Barry will not be here tomorrow."

"What's that?" The doctor whirled round to face her. "What in the name of common sense do you mean by that, eh? Eh? Won't be here, be damned! That little wench must keep to her bed for a time, or I'll not be responsible. Do you hear me, you damn fool woman!" Snorting through his nose, he turned upon her his most ferocious glare. "What's the meaning of this, eh? Frightened she'll contaminate his lordship, are you? Him that has deflowered many a wench to my certain knowledge. Don't she suit you and your respectable household now, eh? Is that why she's to go?"

"How can you be so unfair!" Margaret cried. "It is simply that I feel that Mistress Barry is in need of a change."

"Change, bah! Where's she going?"

"I fail to see that it is any of your business."

"Hoighty toighty! That nasty temper will get you into trouble one of these days, Maggie."

"My temper?" Margaret said weakly. "Well!"

"Aye, yours. Never could stand a liverish female. As for the rest of the claptrap you've just been spouting, I'll have you know it is my business. Her doctor, ain't I? Yours too. You're up to something, Maggie."

"No, you are mistaken."

"Now you listen to me, Maggie. I've known you a number of years. Helped bring you into the world, in fact. And if I say you are up to some mischief, then you are." He pointed his staff at Sarah. "I'll not have that lass turned out on the streets to shift for herself."

"How dare you! How can you believe that I would do such a thing?"

"Well, if you wouldn't, then there's no need to be standing up to me like a fighting cock and telling me that it ain't my business, is there? Now then, where are you sending the lass, eh? Speak up!"

"Oh!" The angry scarlet in Margaret's cheeks subsided as she met his twinkling eyes. "You are very clever, are you not? I should have known that I could not stand out against you. If you must know, she is to stay with a friend of mine."

"Who?"

Margaret bit her lip. "Mistress Sunderland."

"What! Opal Sunderland? That brazen trollop!"

The twinkle in his eyes had grown more pronounced, and Margaret gave him a reproving look. "You are a very wicked man to call poor Opal a trollop."

"Nonsense! Had it from her own lips that she's one."

"Opal told you that?"

"Certainly she did. A point in the wench's favor, I thought. Never could abide a hypocrite. She enjoys men. Says so. What's wrong with that?"

"She—er—she has a little weakness for men, but you can hardly call her a trollop."

"A little weakness! Balderdash! I'd not be saying no if Mistress Opal would consent to warm my bedsheets, and so I tell you. Better by far than that collection of whining bones I've got now."

Margaret smiled. "You should think shame of yourself for describing your poor wife in such terms."

"Never mind." The doctor's eyes sharpened. "Whatever Opal's weakness, as you call it, she's a great-hearted woman, and kind as the day is long. I know well that Mistress Barry will come to no harm with her, but that ain't the point. Why can't she stay here?"

"For one thing, she does not wish to stay."

"Oh? Why not?"

"There are many reasons," Margaret said, summoning dignity to her aid. "But I do not propose to go into those reasons now."

"Mind my own infernal business? Is that what you're telling me, eh, Maggie?"

"Yes, if you please."

The doctor hesitated, obviously minded to say more. Meeting Margaret's eyes, he changed his mind. "I'd like well to know what you are up to, but I can see that you have resolved not to tell me. No matter, I'll find out."

He turned to the door again. "See that the lass gets to bed. Oh, by the way, where is Mistress Sunderland living now?"

"Opalhall, Brondesbury Square," Margaret said unthinkingly.

At the sight of her dismayed face, the doctor gave a little chuckle of triumph. "Didn't mean to tell me that, eh, Maggie? Well, no need to be flushing and biting at your tongue, I could have found out in time. Just taken me a little longer, that's all. So Opal's no longer living with her fancy protector, what's his name, the one with the face like a sick cod?" He grinned. "Opalhall, now there's a damned silly name for a house!" He glanced at Sarah. "Tell the lass, Maggie, that I'll be paying her a visit."

After he had taken his departure, Margaret stared at the door, wishing that she had not allowed him to trap her into saying so much. But after a moment, she relaxed. So the doctor would visit Sarah at Opalhall, but what of that? He was a good-hearted little busybody, who meant well, and he would undoubtedly try to pry. But she would warn Sarah to say nothing. Were she to do so, he would go straight to Jason, and Sarah would not want that. The doctor would make nothing of distinction and class, and he would see nothing incongruous in such a marriage, for he had ever been, under that thorny exterior of his, an incurable romanticist. As for Jason himself, pride alone would forbid him to confide in the doctor or anyone else something of so personal a nature. Nay, if Sarah guarded her tongue, all would be well.

She went over to the couch. "Come, Sarah," she said gently. "I will see you to your bed."

Sarah opened her eyes. Like a docile child, she took Margaret's extended hand. Rising to her feet with some difficulty, she was led from the room.

Chapter Fourteen

It had stopped snowing, but the clouds, looking like huge puffs of dirty cotton wool, were massed together, giving a promise of another fall to come. The thickly concealing mask of ghostly beauty that the snow had laid over everything had turned now into icy, trampled mud. Rivulets of this mud, mixing with the unsavory contents of the gutter, swirled about the steps of the houses on Twyford Street, making the way hazardous and extremely unpleasant for those forced to go out. These were mostly servants, with errands to run, and the indefatigable hawkers, who, hands chapped and purple with cold, breath steaming out in a white cloud, cold-shrivelled faces bound about by scarves, bawled their wares in voices of undiminished cheerfulness.

My lord Witherley, seated in a chair by his bedchamber window, seemed unaware of Mrs. Trevallion, who was seated next to him. For the last hour he had sat there unmoving, his eyes staring unseeingly outside. Only when a bare branch tapped sharply against the window, sending down a deluge of drops, did he start out of his abstraction. December was almost finished, he thought. The Christmas season had come and gone, unmarked by any particular festivity on his part, since he had been confined to his bed. Christmas! Sarah, trying to smile, to make things a little gay. She had put a little wreath of holly over the fireplace. He frowned, refusing to think of Sarah for the moment. Tomorrow, it would be the first day of January. He had always hated the month of January. He thought of it as a somber month, heavy with the ghosts of things that had gone and could never be recovered. Sarah, for one. Again he pushed the thought of her aside. He did not, like most people, think of January as a new beginning, but as a poignant ending. When he had been small, he had ached inside with the wish to hold on to the vanishing year. He had been unwilling to allow the happiness that each year had contained to become past joys, or delicate memories to be looked back upon yearningly. His mouth twisted cynically. It seemed that there was nothing in this life that one could hold on to. This year had contained Sarah and, for him, a first-time love. What would 1663 hold? But since he no longer had Sarah, did it really matter?

His hands gripped the arms of his chair as he thought of his mother's visit last night. Her manner had been evasive, and not once had she made mention of his declaration of love for Sarah. Perhaps she was already aware of Sarah's repudiation of him. But if so, why did she remain silent? The visit had been uncomfortable, the air heavy with things that must be said, but were perhaps better left unsaid. It was he who had broken the silence. "You have not said, Mother, but I take it that you do not approve of my wish to marry Sarah?"

For the first time she had looked at him directly. "No, Jason, you must know that I do not."

"Why?"

"I think I do not need to tell you the reasons. You would not, I imagine, wish me to enumerate them?"

He thought that she looked pale and ill, and it crossed his mind to wonder why she kept clasping her arm. "Is anything wrong? Have you hurt your arm?"

Her reaction to this simple question surprised him. She looked frightened. "No," she answered him hastily. "A little accident, nothing more."

Concern for her was swept to one side by the stabbing of his pain. "Your reasons for objecting, Mother, would, I imagine, be duty, family, one's position in life, what is expected of one?"

She winced a little at the sneer in his voice. "Exactly. Can you really tell me that these things are not important to you, my son?"

She caught the hint of restrained violence in his voice as he answered. "They were. But then, you see, I had not met Sarah. Tell me, Mother, had my father been of a different class to yourself, would you have given him up to embrace duty and convention, and all of those things that are apparently so dear to you? Would you, Mother?"

For the first time, Margaret felt doubt. Was she doing the right thing in withholding her approval, in doing her best to keep them apart? Jason looked so strained, he sounded so bitterly hurt. Confused, she said the first thing that came into her mind. "You will forget, Jason. After a while, you will understand that it was for the best."

"For the best!" he mocked her. "If you can say that, then I think that you can never really have loved my father."

The accusation was like a stone in her heart. "How dare you! Never say that to me again!"

"I regret if my words have disturbed you." His eyes watched her, brilliantly blue, savagely mocking. "But you speak as though all is settled, Mother. Can it be that you already know that Sarah has refused to marry me?"

"Yes, Jason. When I saw her this morning, she—she told me."

"And did she also tell you the reason?"

"No, there was no need. The reason is apparent."

"Is it? But somehow, Mother, I do not think she refused me for the noble reasons you have in mind."

"Nonsense! I know Sarah. There could be no other reason."

"So, from your point of view, the affair has come to a satisfactory conclusion. You must be congratulating yourself, Mother."

"Jason! You sound as if—as if you hate me!"

"No. I do not hate you. It is simply that I am sick of people, and of interference. But mostly, I am sick of myself!"

"I understand you to mean by that that I have interfered in your life. I am sorry that it had to be so, but you were not thinking straight. How could I help but disapprove of such a marriage? It would not have led to happiness, Jason. I know it. And you must know that your happiness is my only concern?"

The strange considering look he gave her frightened her. What was he thinking? Oh, God, don't let him hate me! Before she could say anything, he said quietly, "And now my happiness is quite secure, is it not, Mother? But why do you look so distressed? Sarah has refused to marry me, so all is well."

"Jason, please! I know you are hurt by my attitude. Pray try to forgive me."

He changed the subject abruptly. "Where is Sarah now?"

"She is—is in her room. She was not feeling very well. I suggested that she go to bed."

"I see. I hope that she is suffering from nothing serious."

His icy formality hurt her more than his anger. "Nay," she said wearily, "it is nothing serious."

"I am happy to hear it. And now, if you do not mind, Mother, I will go to bed myself. I am sure you will understand when I tell you that it has been a long day."

Later, lying in his bed, he found himself tortured by doubt. His mother had been so sure of Sarah's reason for refusing to marry him. Could it be that she had no thought in her mind of Baxter? Had she lied, in a mistaken belief that it was for his own good, when she had told him that she cared for somebody else? He heard her voice again, when he had questioned her. "Believe what you will," she had cried out. "If you say it is he, then it must be so!" But if it were not Baxter, then whom?

The doubt grew stronger, and with it came a rekindling of hope. If he found that she had rejected him for some foolishly noble reason, then he would pursue her. He would never let her go! When he rose the next morning, he had determined to send for her. He would have done so, had not Mrs. Trevallion come to him with the news that Sarah was unwell and did not wish to see anyone as yet.

He looked at Mrs. Trevallion. So deeply had his thoughts been engaged, that he had almost forgotten her presence. Sitting in the chair, her eyes were downcast and she was very quiet. Was she not too quiet for such a normally garrulous woman? She looked worried, he thought, her face was much paler than usual, and she looked as though she had not slept very well.

Staring down at her folded hands, Mrs. Trevallion was wondering how she could bring herself to tell Master Jason that Mistress Barry was no longer in the house. My lady Witherley had told her, if Master Jason should inquire, that she was to say that Sarah had gone away for a while. But she had not been able to say it, and, instead, had told him that Mistress Barry was unwell. After all, it was not fair of my lady Witherley to expect her to give him such a message. He was still far from well, and it would be a blow to him. Hoping that he would not mention Sarah again, she tried to think of some excuse to leave the room. Master Jason, after telling her to be seated and saying that he was in need of company, had apparently forgotten she was there. She glanced toward the door. If only Meadows would return, it would give her the excuse she needed.

She started as Jason's voice said, "What is it, Trevallion? Is anything wrong?"

She looked at him with a nervous smile. "Gracious, lad, no. What could be wrong?"

"Trevallion, I have known and loved you for a very long time. I have always been able to tell when something was worrying you. So out with it!"

"It is nothing, Master Jason, I swear it!"

"You lie, Trevallion. So do not swear, else, I fear, will you imperil your immortal soul." He was silent for a moment, then he said abruptly, "Is it something to do with Mistress Barry?"

"I—I—" Her eyes shifted nervously as she groped for a way to answer him. Despising herself, she lied again. "You are not to concern yourself, Master Jason, it is simply that S-Sarah has been taken with the spotted fever."

"What!" He half rose from his chair, and then sank back again. "Is it serious?"

"Nay, 'tis a very light attack. She will be over it in no time at all."

Jason forgot bitterness and doubt in a sudden rush of love. "I think I will go to her room and see for myself."

"Nay, lad," Mrs. Trevallion said sharply. "At this point, she would not wish to see anyone."

"Oh?" His eyes bored into hers. Such uncomfortably, penetrating eyes, she thought. "That is very strange, is it not, Trevallion?"

Having committed herself, Mrs. Trevallion plunged on valiantly, "There is nothing strange about it, Master Jason. Sarah is not looking her best, and she has a woman's natural vanity."

"I see." Jason relaxed. "You are sure it is a light attack?"

"Certain. I have nursed many cases of spotted fever in my time."

"She has seen the physician?"

This much was true, and she could say with good conscience that Sarah had indeed seen the physician. She trembled to think of what he would say and do if he knew the real reason. "Aye, lad, she has seen Doctor Sanders."

Jason was silent. The urge to see Sarah was overwhelming. More than ever he felt that he had let her go too easily, that he had made a terrible mistake. Sarah loved him. He had seen it in her eyes, heard it in her voice. She had lied to him, and he, of course, being so new to love, had leaped to the conclusion she wished. Let them but talk it out and all would be well. He would overcome Sarah's foolish stubborn resistance to the marriage. He would point out to her that he could never be happy without her. Sarah and Baxter? Nay, he did not believe it!

"Trevallion," he said, "I think, vanity or no vanity, that I must insist on seeing Mistress Barry. Pray go to her and tell her that, if you please."

At the unmistakable note of command in his voice, Mrs. Trevallion stared at him in dismay. Anxious only to be gone, she rose hastily to her feet. "Y-y-yes, Master Jason," she stammered. "I will tell her. I will look in on you a-again as soon as possible, Master Jason."

She was hurrying to the door, when his voice halted her. "Who is looking after Mistress Barry, Trevallion?"

"Who?" She could only think of Jane Trevor, my lady Witherley's maid. "Jane, Master Jason," she blurted out. "Jane Trevor."

"You will send Jane to me, please."

She was fairly caught. Jane had accompanied my lady Witherley in the carriage. My lady had left the house so early that Jane, who was devoted to her mistress, and proud of her appearance, had insisted upon accompanying her. She wished, she said, to make my lady Witherley's toilette upon the moment they arrived at the home of Mistress Sunderland. She had wondered at the time how my lady Witherley would explain to Jane that she did not wish Mistress Barry's whereabouts to be known. Her face flushing scarlet, she turned slowly to face him. "I cannot send Jane to you, Master Jason."

"Why can you not?" he drawled.

She was afraid of that drawling voice. It meant, she knew, that he was aware that she was lying. She had the suddenly disconcerting feeling that those eyes of his could see right through her. She was a poor liar at best, and, on the very few times she had lied to him, Master Jason, as she feared he was doing now, invariably caught her out. Nevertheless, she tried again. "Jane r-refuses to leave Sarah's side."

"Does she indeed. That is a most admirable devotion, is it not?" The ruby ring on the middle finger of his right hand flashed a red fire as he beckoned her forward. "Come here, please, Trevallion."

Like a guilty child, she went to stand before him. "Yes, Master Jason?"

"Sit down, please."

She seated herself. "I-I should hurry, Master Jason. I have to see my lady Witherley on a matter of some importance."

There was a cold glitter in his eyes, but the smile he gave her was almost amiable. "So you must see my mother, must you? I wonder why I do not believe you, Trevallion?"

"Well, I'm sure I don't know," she said, feigning indignation. "Why should you find it hard to believe?"

He studied her intently. "Let us say it is because my intuition tells me that you are lying. That you have lied to me repeatedly. Why would that be, Trevallion?"

"Why should I lie?"

"I have not the least idea." Leaning forward in his chair, he laid his hand over hers. "Trevallion," he said in a dangerously gentle voice, "shall we go together to see Mistress Barry?"

"No!" she snatched her hand away. "I have told you that she wishes to see no one."

"I remember. Nevertheless, I think we should go."

"Please," she said desperately, "you have been very ill. I cannot permit you to traverse that long corridor."

"You feel, perhaps, that I will faint from the exertion?" His voice bruised her with its sarcasm. "I think, if you will lend me your strong arm, that the strain will not be too great. You will lend me your arm, will you not, Trevallion?"

He was playing with her. He was the cat, she the mouse. Obstinately, she still refused to tell him the truth. His mother must do that. "Master Jason," she burst out, "my lady would never forgive me if you suffered a relapse."

He put his hand over hers again, his fingers tightening painfully. "And now, if you please, Trevallion, be so good as to tell me where Mistress Barry is."

"I have told you!"

"I think not. Indeed, dear Trevallion, I fear that you begin to try my patience to a dangerous degree."

"She is in her bed."

His fingers tightened yet more. "Why, Trevallion? Why are you lying?"

"Master Jason, please!"

"Where is Mistress Barry?"

It was no use, she could not go on lying to him. But she would tell him as little as possible. She swallowed, then said in a difficult voice, "She has gone."

She saw his quickly controlled flinch. "Where has she gone?" he asked in a calm voice.

"I do not know."

"Why has she gone?"

The glitter in his eyes frightened her. "Master Jason, I did not wish to tell you. It is for your mother to do."

"My mother, I see." The lazy note in his voice did not match those hard eyes. "Where and why, please, Trevallion?"

"I can't tell you where, Master Jason, but I can tell you

why. Sarah said she needed a change, and that she wished to go away for a while."

He patted her hand. "Poor Trevallion, that was a very hard thing for you to tell me, was it not?"

Had she not known better, she might have thought him to be unmoved. Then she noticed the tightness of his jaw muscles, and the light gleam of perspiration on his forehead. "Yes, Master Jason," she said softly, her heart going out to him. "I did not wish to tell you."

A silence fell between them. Now the strain was apparent in his face. Mrs. Trevallion, who knew him so well, guessed at the fury that boiled beneath his calm outer surface. Why could not my lady have refrained from interfering in his life? Master Jason was a man, not a child. He knew what he wanted. And if he wanted Sarah for his wife, why could she not have accepted it with good grace? Even now the lies would go on and on, for my lady would only tell Master Jason that she had driven Sarah to a place where she might pick up a public conveyance. If she could help it, she would not even tell him that much.

She was astonished when Jason said, "Will you tell my mother that I would like to see her, please." She had thought he had guessed that Sarah had left the house with my lady Witherley.

"As soon as she returns, Master Jason."

"She is no doubt off on one of her shopping sprees?"

She nodded helplessly. "No doubt, Master Jason. I will tell her as soon as she returns."

Watching him, she thought, with the first real bitterness she had ever felt toward her mistress, that my lady would be only too happy to deny all knowledge of Sarah's departure.

As though following her line of thought, he said suddenly, "You said, I believe, that it was for my mother to tell me? Does she know that Mistress Barry has left the house?"

"Master Jason, how can I know?"

"Then what did you mean?"

"I meant that when she—when she realizes that Mistress Barry has gone, if she is not already aware of it, she would be the one to tell you."

"I see. Is there perchance anything else you would like to tell me, Trevallion?"

"No, Master Jason."

"Mistress Barry was meeting somebody, is that it?"

What did he mean? "Not to my knowledge."

"Thank you, Trevallion. You may go."

Outside the door, Mrs. Trevallion leaned against the wall and closed her eyes for a moment. She liked nothing about this situation. There was my lady Witherley, usually so gentle and kind, not caring apparently if she destroyed two lives with her blind and stubborn belief that she was doing the right thing. No, that was not quite right, Mrs. Trevallion amended, anxious to be fair. She did care, but in the wrong way. But how in the name of heaven could she have so far forgotten her own love for her husband that she could not recognize a genuine case of love when she saw it? Then there was Sarah, gone off with God only knew what thoughts filling her mind, and with a look in her eyes that filled her with terrible misgivings. What would happen to the girl, spiritless and broken as she now appeared? Where would she end? There was the way Master Jason had taken the news of Sarah's departure. He had been calm, much too calm. He was hurt and he was angry, for his calmness had not deceived her. Why had he asked her that question: "Mistress Barry is meeting somebody, is that it?" Quite suddenly she felt that he had had a certain somebody in mind. As the possible significance of this struck her, she began to tremble. Master Jason was in love for the first time in his life. His feelings were raw with the sequence of events. But surely he could not think that Sarah had gone off with another man? She tried to dismiss the notion, but the more she thought of it, the more she became convinced that he had thought just that. She pulled herself together with an effort. It would not do to stand musing here. Her brow furrowed with anxiety, she went slowly on her way.

Meadows, who had been about to cross the hall, drew back into the shadows and waited for the housekeeper to disappear about her duties. He did not care much for Mrs. Trevallion. Her tongue could quickly turn acid and cut down his own sense of self-importance. And those eyes of hers, old, but still keen, seemed to see through all his pretenses. He frowned. He had been gone overlong, and my lord Witherley would doubtless be annoyed with him. It was only a few minutes walk to Sir Peter Baxter's house, in Laburnham Crescent, where he had gone to deliver a message from his master, but it had been a temptation to linger with Barton, Sir Peter's man, and exchange various views on their respective employers.

Mounting the stairs, Meadows grinned to himself. Barton certainly had a poor opinion of Sir Peter. "All he thinks about are the wenches," Barton had said. "He's fancied himself madly in love at least a dozen times to my certain knowledge. Then it's off with the old love and on with the new. What a man! There's no relying upon him, not so far as wenches are concerned. And now, if you please, he's gone careening off to the country with yet another wench. Be gone for a few days, he said. So it seems like your master's message will have to wait."

Pausing outside the door of the bedchamber, Meadows felt a tremor. My lord Witherley could be very nasty indeed when he was angry. As a rule it was a quiet, self-contained anger, not bursting all over the place as was the way with some gentlemen. But his anger, for all its quietness, was somehow more deadly than a good healthy explosion. Meadows shrugged ruefully. Not only had he been gone an excessively long time, but he had failed to deliver the message. But still, the latter was no fault of his, he could hardly be blamed for that.

Mentally girding himself, Meadows entered the bedchamber. My lord Witherley was lying on top of the bed. Meadows, who had expected to be met with anger, was disconcerted to find the blue eyes fixed upon him with only the faintest query in their depths. Before he could speak, Jason said pleasantly, "You have certainly taken your own confounded time. Did you enjoy your chat with Barton?"

Meadows was highly suspicious. "I apologize for the length of time I have been gone, my lord," he said, drawing upon a dignity of manner that he hoped might serve him. "But Barton was—"

"Unusually hospitable," Jason finished for him. "And, in the absence of his master, he pressed you to stay. Pray take note, my good man, that I am familiar with all your excuses."

Meadows looked at him in some surprise. "Why, yes, my lord, you are right. He did press me to stay, and Sir Peter was from home. May I inquire how your lordship knew that?"

"Merely a guess," Jason answered him lightly. "Did Barton perchance say when Sir Peter would be returning?"

Meadows gave him a sharp glance. The uneasy suspicion came to him that my lord was a little too casual, a little too quietly amiable. He pursed his lips. He did not like it. It might well be the prelude to that quiet and deadly anger of his. "He won't be back for a few days, my lord," he answered cautiously. "Barton thinks that Sir Peter might possibly return on the Friday of this week."

"Is it so? I will be able to visit him personally, then, will I not? I think, however, it is very strange that he did not take Barton with him. He is usually so particular about his clothes and his general appearance."

Meadows's suspicion deepened to certainty. There had certainly been a very nasty ring to my lord Witherley's voice. He hesitated, wondering if he might delay the inevitable by passing on some of Barton's gossip. My lord was not one to listen to gossip, but it might serve to distract him temporarily from his anger. On the other hand, it could earn him a severe rebuke.

In that uncomfortable way my lord often had of reading his mind, he said softly, "Yes, Meadows, you were about to say?"

Meadows's expression became prim. "Yes, my lord, I was about to say something. But now I am not sure that I should."

"You intrigue me, Meadows. Will you not endeavor to force yourself?"

Meadows gave him another keen glance. My lord Witherley's dark-blond hair fell in untidy curls over his forehead, giving him a much younger look. His face was flushed, his eyes glittered brightly, and he still looked far from robust. Compunction smote Meadows. In spite of many quite spirited disagreements with his master over the plain mode of dress he chose to adopt, he was really quite devoted to him. Filled with good will, he bustled over to the bed. "Now, my lord," he said, his plump, well cared for hands smoothing the bed covers beneath Jason, "do get into bed properly, and let me make you more comfortable. In your weak condition, you'll not be wanting to listen to a lot of nasty gossip. Particularly when it is not my place to criticize Sir Peter." He put his hands on Jason's shoulders. "If you will just sit up for a moment, my lord, I will arrange your pillows."

"Meadows," Jason said in that same pleasant voice, "you may not be aware of it, but you are trying me rather high. You will remove your confounded hands at once, like the good fellow you are."

Offended, Meadows straightened up. "I am sure I am very sorry, my lord. Perhaps your lordship would care to suggest something I might do to aid your comfort?"

Jason smiled. "Why, yes, Meadows, there is one thing I can suggest. You have my permission to step out of your place this once. I find myself uncommonly interested to hear this nasty gossip."

"My lord!"

"The request offends your sense of what is fitting, Meadows?"

"It is not my place to be offended, my lord."

"Ah, we are back to that again."

"If you insist, my lord, I will tell you what I have heard."

"Make your mind easy, Meadows. I do insist."

"In that case, my lord, very well. It is Barton's opinion, if you will excuse the liberty, that the members of the female sex are a little too much on Sir Peter's mind."

"Interesting," Jason murmured, "though hardly surprising. Is that the extent of the gossip?"

Meadows, looking primmer than ever, took a deep breath. "No, my lord. Sir Peter has gone off to the country, taking with him, if I may use Barton's words, a wench. Shocking, if I may say so."

"You may not say so, Meadows," Jason said in a lazy voice. "Was Barton acquainted with this female's name?"

Wondering a little at this unusual interest, and more than a little inclined to take offense, Meadows answered him in a frosty voice, "He is not, my lord. It is not Barton's place to pry into Sir Peter's business."

"And you, in your turn, are putting me in my place, are you not, Meadows?"

"I would not dream of doing so, my lord."

"But of course you would. Since first you entered my service, your one aim in life has been to do just that."

The tone was good natured, and Meadows, perceptibly thawing, permitted himself a faint smile. "Your lordship is pleased to joke?"

"Not at all, Meadows. 'Tis a simple statement of the truth. Tell me, did Barton approve of Sir Peter's taste in females?"

Meadows withdrew again. He was unsure of my lord Witherley in this unfamiliar mood. He preferred him cool and withdrawn, one knew where one was then. He answered hesitantly, but none the less firmly, "It is not for Barton to approve or disapprove. In the case of this latest young lady, he did not see her. She arrived at the house early this morning. He tells me that Sir Peter took her up the front stairs. Soon after that, they went off together. Barton did hear her voice. He said it was low and pleasant.

Jason frowned. Low and pleasant? He would have described Sarah's voice in those terms. He sat up abruptly. "You may arrange my pillows now, Meadows."

Meadows started a little at the harshness of his voice. Complying with the request, he thought bitterly that one never knew where one was with my lord. One moment he would be sarcastically amiable, and the next he would freeze you. He was looking decidedly strange at this moment, and a possible explanation came to him. "My lord," he inquired solicitously, "are you feeling nauseated again?"

"Yes, Meadows, quite considerably so. But not, I think, in the way you mean." With this cryptic remark, my lord Witherley settled back against the pillows and closed his eyes. "I think I will sleep for a while."

Going quietly about his duties, one half of his mind on the annoying plainness of my lord Witherley's wardrobe, the other half on the man himself, Meadows could not help wondering what he was thinking about to bring that look of suffering to his face. It might be the lingering effects of his illness that made him look so, but one thing was certain, he was not sleeping. He could tell that from the constant restless movements he was making. With his eyes shuttered, his mouth drawn into a straight, grim line, he no longer struck Meadows as looking youthful. If anything, he looked gaunt and considerably older than his years.

It is coincidence, nothing more, Jason was thinking. No, Sarah would not go to Peter! And yet she had left the house early this morning, possibly at the same time Peter was greeting the wench. Had it been Sarah of whom Barton had spoke? He clenched his teeth tightly together. He had always had a vivid imagination. It was an injustice to her to think this way. Then where was she? Where had she gone? His mother, disapproving, would be unlikely to help her. Sarah, if she now found herself homeless and without friends, would remember Peter's publicly declared love for her, and where else could she go? Sarah and Peter! He must find out, he could not go on in this uncertainty.

Meadows's voice broke in upon his tortured thoughts. "I know you are not asleep, my lord. Are you sure there is nothing I may do for you?"

Jason opened his eyes. "Yes, Meadows, there is one thing you may do for me. You may take your irritating presence from this room. You will not return until I send for you. I trust we understand each other?"

Jason studied the droop of the man's shoulders as he crossed over to the door, and he was suddenly contrite. "Meadows," he said, "I am an ill-mannered boor. You meant well, and I am fully aware of it. Pray to forgive me."

Meadows's shoulders straightened. Turning, he beamed like a benevolent father upon an erring child. "But of course, my lord. Don't I always forgive you?"

"Meadows, go to hell."

"Yes, my lord. Certainly." Grinning, Meadows left the room.

Chapter Fifteen

Sarah sat on the window seat looking out over the sodden grounds. It was almost March, she thought, which meant that she had been at Opalhall for two months. In that time it had rained on and off. And it would seem that they were still not done with the rainy season. The first hopeful flowers of spring had been battered by the lashing rain, and some hardy winter specimens that had somehow survived long after their season was done drooped shaggy dispirited heads and showered the ground about them with a confetti of browning purple, pink, white and bronze petals. The frail daffodils, their slender stalks snapped, lay with their frilled and curling yellow petals bogged in the mud. The trees lining the short driveway showered water from branches and from barely unfurled leaves, and a rising wind sent the ever-present rain slanting in cold, gray lines. Over everything, the weeping sky pressed down like a smothering blanket, and, even when the clouds were scattered by the wind, there was no trace of blue.

It seemed to have rained forever, Sarah thought, as she rose from the window seat and wandered over to the fire. She stared into the flames, her hand gripping the edge of the white and gold overmantel. What was Jason doing now? What was he thinking, feeling? Had he looked for her, would he? It was more probable that he had dismissed her from his life. Tears rose in her eyes. She brushed them away impatiently. She had turned her back on the dazzling chance of happiness he had offered, because she felt that it was not fitting or right to grasp it, therefore it was foolish to indulge in this continual self-pity. But she was so tired of being courageous and practical. Why could she not be like the handsome and effervescent Opal? Opal savored every drop in the cup of life, and she loved not once and forever, but many times. She had loved the King deeply and sincerely, and she loved every man whom she took to her bed and held in her generous arms in the same way.

Moving away from the fire, Sarah sat down in a winged chair. As always, her thoughts, drawn by a horrible fascination, reverted to the scarred man. Would she ever feel clean again? she wondered. At first she had feared that she would bear that man's child, and she had called on God for mercy. At that time, she wondered why she called on God. Had He not turned His face from her long ago? Where was He when she had needed Him so desperately? She had determined, should she find herself pregnant, to kill herself. And she had wondered what God would do about Sarah Barry then. Would He have pitied her, understood, forgiven? But He had heard her, for, shortly afterwards, she found that she was not after all to bear the scarred man's child. She hoped that God had forgiven her for her time of doubt.

She leaned her head against the back of the chair and closed her eyes. Almost instantly Jason's face came to erase the vision of the scarred man. But Jason was looking at her coldly, as he had done on that first occasion when she had entered his bedchamber. Now his voice, soft and tender: "I love you, Sarah! I have no notion of when it began, but I do love you." Now, again, the smile was gone from his eyes. She saw the spasmodic clenching of his hands, she felt his fury and his violence. "Get out! Do not ever let me set eyes on you again, or I might be tempted to break every bone in your body!"

She had done that to him. She had lied, because it was the only way, and she had seen his love and his tenderness replaced by hatred. She had done the right thing, surely she had.

She dared not, even now, allow her mind to dwell upon the hurt that his hatred must cover. She could bear anything else, but not the thought of his hurt.

Trembling, Sarah forced herself to think of Mistress Sunderland. Never would she forget her first glimpse of the beautiful and the magnificently proportioned woman. For Opal, though built on heroic lines, was extremely beautiful. When she came into the room, her presence was almost overwhelming. In her pink gown, the bodice cut so low that most of her full white breasts were revealed, she was like a bright bird. Her gypsy black hair hung loose about her shoulders, her green eyes were bright with life, and her wide red mouth was curved into a radiant smile. She sparkled, she glowed, and one felt that inner generosity that was so much a part of her instantly reach out, embracing, gathering you close. She was eternal woman, eternal mother, she was magnificent!

For all her size, Opal could move swiftly and gracefully. Sarah smelled the clove sweetness of her perfume as she swept past to fling her arms about my lady Witherley. "Margaret!" she cried in her rich voice. "How happy I am to see you. I do love company!"

She reminded one of a large, happy, and slightly mischievous child. Then her eyes had fallen upon Sarah, and, again like a child who is easily moved to tears or laughter, their bright green had clouded. Opal could never bear to look upon unhappiness, and her heart was quickly touched to compassion.

Opal did not even hesitate. In a second she had moved to Sarah's side, and her comforting arm was placed about her shoulders. "Margaret, this child is unhappy!" There was real distress in her voice. The tip of her finger touched Sarah's bruised face. "Who has done this? Who has hurt her?"

Sarah was pushed gently into a chair, while Opal gave her full attention to my lady Witherley's story. Dear Opal, who even now could not understand why she had been forced to refuse my lord Witherley's love. Who, without question, had taken her into her heart and home.

Sarah witnessed Opal's rare rage, which, she was to find, could be brought forth by injustice and unkindness. There was nothing mean or petty or conniving in her own nature, and she had an intolerance of it in others. Facing my lady Witherley, her green eyes flashing, her hands planted on her ample hips, she fought for the happiness of a girl she had met only a few moments ago. "I just do not understand you, Margaret." The rich, melodious voice that, like a finely tuned instrument, could express a whole range of emotions, was now expressing shock and horror. "Why are you doing this thing to the little wench? She has had so much misery in her life, so much that you and I could not even begin to conceive of it. Oh, Margaret, be kind! Now is the time for happiness."

"You do not understand, Opal. There is more to be considered than the gratification of love."

"Margaret, you must not interfere in their lives, you simply must not!" Opal pushed the gleaming black mass of her hair away from her flushed and angry face. "Love is everything! Love is all that matters! What more could there be?"

"Opal, please! It is better if we do not discuss these matters in front of Sarah."

The comforting white hand with the sparkling rings on every finger touched Sarah's shoulder. "Look at her, Margaret. Can you not see that she is too dazed, too hurt to understand anything we say?"

But she had heard, every word, Sarah thought. And she had understood. But for all that, she could not bring herself to speak. She could only sit there, her heart feeling as heavy as a stone, while they talked on and on.

"Margaret," Opal's voice was slightly lowered. "Is your son in love with this little Sarah wench, or is he not?"

"He believes himself to be." Margaret's answering voice was stiff, slightly resentful.

"Well, then?"

"Opal, you must know that I care a great deal for you. But there are some things you cannot be expected to understand."

"Why? Because I am called whore? Is that why you think I cannot understand?"

"Dear, Opal, no! Have I even implied that you are a whore?"

"Yet I suppose that is what I am. But I will tell you something. I have never taken a man to my bed whom I could not love. I have never sold my body for money." She raised her arms, and the jewels on her fingers flashed. "I have jewels, a comfortable home, a good living, but none of these things was given to me because I demanded them. All that I have was given to me out of love."

"I know, Opal. I have always known that."

"Will you reconsider, Margaret. Will you admit that love between a man and a woman is the only thing of importance?"

"No. I cannot. Not in this case."

The eager light faded from Opal's eyes. "I had thought that you understood love, but I see now that you do not." She turned her back on Margaret. "I will be glad to have Sarah stay with me. That is what you came to hear me say, is it not?"

"Yes, Opal, and thank you. It will only be for a short while, though. Just long enough for me to find her a suitable position."

Again Sarah smelled the clove sweetness of Opal's perfume as she whirled to face my lady Witherley. "Margaret! What has happened to you? You make me think that I have never really known you. You offer this child a position instead of the love and happiness that should be hers? Shame on you! I think perhaps you had better go. Pray do not let me keep you."

"Opal!" There was real anguish in Margaret's voice. "Surely we are still friends?"

Some of the high color faded from Opal's face. "Friendship is not so easily forgotten. It is simply that I cannot like you quite as much. What are you going to tell your son? Will he know that Sarah is here?"

"No! For I intend to tell him that I was not even aware that she had left the house."

"Margaret! Surely you cannot bring yourself to such deception."

"I can. I will! I am not good like you, Opal."

Opal's green eyes opened wide. "Good? Nay, Margaret, you are mistaken. I am human, that is all."

Margaret shook her head. "You are all heart, all goodness, and you make me ashamed. Yet, I have set my hand to this course, and I cannot do differently."

Opal's eyes were pitying, as she said quietly, "Shall I ring for Daventry to show you out? Or do you prefer to find your own way?"

"There is no need to trouble Daventry. I really must go now. Jane, my maid, has been waiting for me for some time."

"And if Jane should talk?"

"She will not. She is devoted to me."

"Jason is a man, Margaret," Opal warned her. "He will look for Sarah. I am sure of that."

"No. He believes Sarah to be in love with another man. Ask her. She will tell you. That being so, Jason's pride will forbid him to search for her."

Again there was that flash of pity in Opal's eyes. "It will depend upon how much he loves her. I have often known pride to take second place to love."

"Not this time. You do not know Jason."

Opal smiled faintly. "You know, Margaret, I rather think that I know Jason. Aye, very well indeed."

"You mean—"

"My meaning does not matter."

Margaret gave her a stricken look. Then, without another word, she turned on her heel and went out of the door.

Opal stood there for a moment, then she turned to Sarah. She dropped to her knees beside the chair and touched the bruised face gently. "Sarah, poor little girl, do not look like that!" Opal took her cold hands and held them firmly. "I will look after you, never fear. But at this moment, bed is the place for you. We will talk again tomorrow."

"Thank you, Mistress Sunderland. You are—are very kind."

"Nay, you must not say so. I vow you will turn my head. But will you not call me Opal? When you say Mistress Sunderland, I feel that you are talking to somebody else."

Sarah smiled. "Opal, then."

"Sarah," Opal said hesitantly. "There are things that go on in this house that perhaps you might not understand. I am—I am not a virtuous woman. There will be gentlemen who will come acalling. Sometimes they will not leave. Do you understand what I am trying to say?"

"I understand. A little while ago you told my lady Witherley that love is everything. But kindness is everything too." Sarah's voice choked a little. "A-and you are very kind, O-Opal."

"Bah! You scarcely know me."

Sarah gave her a wan smile. "A few minutes sufficed to tell me that."

In the days that followed, Sarah felt something that was almost akin to happiness. Had it not been for the constant ache of loss, the longing to see Jason that, while she lived, would never leave her, she could have been entirely happy.

Opal, though only seven years older than Sarah, was like a mother to her. A safe, warm, loving presence that helped to drive some of the chill of her misery away. It took only Opal's tread on the stairs, her voice calling her, and Sarah's black mood would lift.

When Opal was not occupied in her big bedroom with her gentleman friend—the current one was Bruce McGregor, a brawny Scot, with riotously curling fair hair, small, twinkling blue eyes, and an adoration for Opal that was apparent in his every word, look and gesture—her time was spent with Sarah. Opal had an amazing variety of gowns in the jewel tones best suited to her brunette beauty. She had lavishly embroidered shawls, gloves, shoes, bonnets, satin and silk petticoats trimmed with imported lace, painted fans, feathered fans, perfume from France, and any number of other treasures that she delighted in showing Sarah. Frustrated by Sarah's firm refusal to allow her to spend her money on her, Opal, with that air of a mischievous child which was so hard to resist, insisted upon altering many of her gowns to fit Sarah's slighter figure. In vain did Sarah protest, in this, Opal insisted upon having her own way. She was quite overwhelmed by Opal's astonishing generosity, her genuine pleasure in dressing her up, that it drove her objections away. And so she found herself the awed possessor of six gowns, a peacock-blue feather fan, six cloaks, and six bonnets, which, Opal insisted, were necessary to go with the gowns. Had it not been for the fact that Opal's feet were larger than her own, she would have found herself with shoes to match. Opal deplored this lack in her wardrobe, and only with the greatest difficulty was she prevented from buying new shoes for her little friend, as she called Sarah.

Much enjoyable time was spent in a frank discussion of Opal's many lovers, for all of whom she still retained the deepest affection. Sarah, listening to these lovingly told tales of the King, and many other notable personalities, and their prowess in the bedchamber, would almost feel that she knew them. She heard of Opal's one true love, Johnny Bestford, a boy of sixteen, who had courted a fifteen-year-old Opal. Johnny, upon leaving her one night, had been involved in an accident. A carriage, bowling along the dark country road, had struck him down. His skull had been smashed beneath the trampling hoofs of the frightened lead horse. Opal, telling this tale, as she often did, would sigh for her lost Johnny, the innocent love of her springtime. With tears filling her green eyes, she would assure Sarah that, had her Johnny lived, she would not now be a lonely woman who was forced to take many lovers to fill the void in her life. Sarah would nod sympathetically, but she did not really believe this last statement, nor did she think Opal really believed it herself. Opal loved her life, she adored each and every one of her men. She would not, Sarah felt sure, have been so happy as the faithful wife of Johnny Bestford. She would have made a wonderful mother, but she was not cut out for domesticity.

Sarah rose from the winged chair and walked over to the door. Opal had gone for a jaunt with Bruce McGregor, and the house felt empty without her.

Going up to her room, the house seemed to her to be overwarm, almost stifling, and she had a sudden longing for fresh air. She hesitated, looking doubtfully at the rain-blurred window panes, but the longing would not be denied. Putting on her cloak, she left her room and ran swiftly down the stairs. The carved front door resisted her efforts to open it for a moment, then it blew back with such force that she was startled.

Once outside, she noticed that, in the last hour, the weather had worsened. The rain, driven by a high wind, soon reduced her gown and her cloak to coldly clinging impediments. Bending her head against the force of the wind, she walked on steadily. Turning left, she made her way down the little rough-cobbled path that led to Opal's particular pride, a small artificial lake. "Except for this season," Opal had told her, "flowers grow beside the lake all year round."

At the moment the lake and its surroundings looked very bleak. Standing on the edge, Sarah looked down at the disturbed water and tried to imagine how it would look in milder seasons. She narrowed her eyes and pictured flowers flaunting their reds and yellows, their purples and whites and blues against the weathered gray of the flagstones. The weeping willow would brush cool green fingers over the water, providing trembling shade for the ducks and the swans who mingled there in amity. But at this time, the poor creatures bobbing on the heavily rain-dimpled water looked unutterably dejected.

Turning away, she sat down on a rustic bench. As much as she would like to do so, she thought, she could not stay here with Opal forever. Opal had said that she would be glad to have her and, indeed, she had frequently spoken of the possibility of Sarah making Opalhall her permanent home. But pride would not permit her to accept the offer. Opal, throwing out lures, had hinted that she was in need of a companion, but of course she was not in any such need. Kindness alone had prompted her to intimate this. She was entirely self-sufficient and happy with her way of life. Sarah frowned. When would my lady Witherley come to her with the news that she had found her a position? She had been here with Opal for two months now. Tomorrow would see it slipping into three, and in that time she had heard nothing. Could it be that my lady Witherley had forgotten about her?

Sarah sighed, her thoughts turning, as ever, to Jason. Each day that passed without a sight of him was like a year. If only she could cut him out of her memory! If only they had never met! Sarah tightened her quivering lips. But they had met, and she loved him. Useless to try to forget him, she could not do it, no matter how hard she tried. She would love him always!

She moved restlessly on the bench as she tried to force his

image away. Of what use to sit here in the rain bemoaning her fate, nothing would change. If my lady Witherley did not come soon, perhaps she could find a position for herself. Or mayhap Opal, when she realized that she was determined to be independent, would help her. She had many friends, many contacts, Sarah's eyes went to the lake and lingered there. Or, as an alternative, and one infinitely to be preferred, she could die. Suicide! Her mind played with the thought and could find in it no horror. Indeed, at this moment, the thought of it held an almost sensuous pleasure. Better death, far better, than a life without Jason. Growing old, with only a memory to cling to. Death would be an end to misery, an end to the constant stabbing pain of loss. Why not? What would it be like to die, to be no more? She began to shiver, not with fear of the act, but because it seemed to her that she could almost see the sternly rebuking face of God. Would He forgive suicide? Would He allow her to be with Jason in that other world? What if He would not forgive? What if she, through her own act, be forever condemned? Alone! Always alone, with Jason lost to her as surely as he was on this carth!

For some time she continued to sit there in the deluging rain, the shuddering chill of her body matched by an inner chill. At last, she put aside the thought of death, relinquishing it reluctantly but finally. She could not destroy her chance of seeing Jason in that other world. She rose to her feet and walked away without a backward glance at the temptingly beckoning waters of the lake.

Nearing the house again, she saw that the door stood open. Opal had returned. Laughter drifted out to her, and she heard Bruce McGregor's deep voice say, "Then I will leave ye for the noo to your company, Opal. Do not be keeping me waiting frae too long, my lass."

Opal turned as Sarah stepped into the hall, greeting her with a smile. Beneath a little red bonnet embellished with curling green and white feathers, her face was rosy and sparkling. There were dark spots of rain on her red silk gown, and raindrops, shining like diamonds, spangled her black curls.

"Good gracious, Sarah," Opal exclaimed, "you are as wet as if you had been diving in the lake."

Sarah smiled. "I did not go quite that far. I have been sitting by the lake, however."

Opal clicked her tongue. "Foolish child. Do you want to be taken with a lung fever?"

Sarah shrugged. "It is all one to me."

Opal's face clouded with distress. "Well, it is not to me. You have not spoken in that fashion for some time now. It hurts me, Sarah."

Sarah came close and laid her hand on Opal's arm. "I did not mean to say it, it just slipped out. Please forgive me."

"Of course I forgive you. Now, child, I want you to go and change into something dry. You have a visitor."

A visitor? Jason? Opal, reading her thoughts. looked at her sadly. "No, Sarah, it is not Jason. Though, if you would not be so stubborn, if you would but allow me to seek him out and tell him that you are here with me, it could be Jason."

Sarah shook her head. "No, Opal. In any case, I doubt that he would forgive me. Who is the visitor?"

"My lady Witherley. Hurry now, Sarah, I do not wish to be too long alone with her."

"My lady Witherley is your friend, Opal. Do not, because of me, destroy that friendship."

Opal made an impatient gesture. "I am still her friend. But I will not tell her so until she relents."

"I am sorry to hear that, Opal, for I know that she will not relent."

"We will see." Opal flapped her hand. "Go! Go!"

Opal watched Sarah run lightly up the stairs, then she turned and walked into her small, cosy sitting room.

My lady Witherley, seated in a chair by the fire, turned her head and smiled at her. "I heard voices. Were you talking to Sarah?"

"I was."

Margaret sighed. "You sound so cool. You are not at all like my warm and generous Opal."

"And you are far removed from the woman I thought I knew. For I know well, from the expression on your face, that you have not come here to take Sarah back to Jason."

"Please, Opal, let us not quarrel. When you offered me a ride in your carriage, I had hoped that you had relented just a little."

"Nay, nor will I relent. When you told me that you were on your way to Opalhall to visit Sarah, it seemed foolish to allow you to continue standing in the rain while you waited for your own carriage. Margaret, I do not like unhappiness, and it would seem to me that you have caused a deal of it."

"I have told you, Opal, that their parting was by Sarah's own wish. God's life! Do you think I wrenched her away from Jason?"

"In a manner of speaking, yes. Had you been kind and understanding, had you but remembered your own love for John, I doubt not that they would be together now."

Margaret's hands clenched on her blue velvet-clad lap. In the shadow cast by the brim of her blue bonnet, her face looked pinched and white. "Do not speak of my love for John, Opal," she said in a cold voice. "There is no comparison."

"Is there not, Margaret? Do you tell me that only the high-born can know love? Do you also tell me that the humbly born are devoid of all feeling and emotion?"

"Opal! You know well that I am not telling you that."

"Well, then?"

"The girl has been in Newgate and Bedlam. How can you expect me to overlook that?"

Opal shrugged. "I am beginning to think that I can expect nothing from you. For the crime that sent Sarah to Newgate, she paid a high price. But it is over, Margaret. As for Bedlam, that was a mistake. You know well that she is no more insane than you or I."

Margaret bowed her head. "I do know it, Opal, but I cannot bring myself to overlook it."

"Those things matter little to my lord Witherley. Why must they matter to you?"

With a sudden movement, Margaret stripped off her gloves and held her trembling hands to the blaze of the fire. "Jason is besotted with her."

"Besotted, Margaret? But do you not see, that is only another name for love? Tell me, how is my lord Witherley taking Sarah's departure?"

Margaret hesitated before answering. "He has had little time to think. Shortly after Sarah left, he suffered a relapse. He does not seem to pick up his strength."

Opal momentarily forgot the issue in a wave of sympathy. "A relapse? Margaret, I am so sorry!"

"Thank you, Opal. However, he is much better now. All but recovered, I think. He—he does not say much about Sarah."

Opal saw the pain in Margaret's face, and she said softly, "And he does not say much to you either. Is that it, Margaret?"

Margaret turned her face away, but not before Opal had glimpsed the tears in her eyes. "He seems to have retreated. I told him that I knew nothing of Sarah's movements, that her leaving the house was a great surprise to me, but I think that he does not believe me. Sometimes there is a look in his eyes that frightens me."

"He is unhappy, Margaret," Opal said gently. "Surely that does not surprise you? I think, as soon as he is able, that he will look for Sarah."

"He will not. He believes her to be in love with another man."

"If I know him at all, and I think I do, he will want to make quite sure that it was the truth Sarah told him."

"Really, Opal! You must permit me to know my own son."

"Bah! When a man is in love, he changes. You should know that."

"And I tell you, that his pride will not permit him to go in search of her."

Opal's fingers toyed with the diamond necklace about her full, white throat. "You know, Margaret, this necklace that I am wearing means a great deal to me, because it was given to me by the King. But I will willingly wager it. I say that you are wrong. Jason will search for her."

"I am not wrong! I know him."

"I wonder if you really do, Margaret? I would not like to be standing in your shoes when he finds out your part in this coil."

Margaret looked so stricken that Opal said compassionately. "Go to him, Margaret. Tell him everything. Once he has his Sarah, he will understand and forgive. Go on, it is not yet too late."

"Nay, Opal, I cannot." Margaret shook her head firmly.

"Then, in that case, I fear you are laying up a great deal of sorrow for yourself. Tell me, why, actually, did you come here."

Margaret averted her eyes. "I-I came because I have found a position for Sarah." She gripped her hands together and began twisting them nervously. "It is not precisely the position I would have wished for her, but I think she will be content."

"I see. Where and what is this position?"

Color scalded Margaret's face. She turned her head and, with some difficulty, met Opal's eyes. "The position is in

London. In Briar Street. She is to be apprenticed to Madam Gilbert."

Opal's green eyes opened wide. "Madam Gilbert? The same Madame Gilbert who makes gowns and bonnets for the quality?"

"The same."

There was a moment of pregnant silence, and then Opal's rare rage exploded into heated words. "I would not have believed you to be so sly, Margaret. You could not risk Sarah being a companion to one of your friends, could you? You feared that it might get back to my lord Witherley, did you not?"

"Opal, please! It is not like that at all."

"Is it not? But there is one little thing you have forgotten. What of the ladies who go to Madam Gilbert, some of whom, I am sure, must know Sarah by sight? Are you not afraid that your son, through them, will hear where he might find her?"

"No, I am not afraid of that." For the first time, Margaret displayed a flash of genuine anger. "Sarah's job will be in the back room. She is therefore quite unlikely to come into contact with Madam Gilbert's clients. And, even were she to do so, she is not known to them."

"You have thought of everything, I see. And what exactly will Sarah's job be?"

"She will learn to make the gowns and to fashion the bonnets. Occasionally she will be sent out to other places of business. It will be for the purpose of matching ribands and laces. That sort of thing."

"And with that position, you will have her well and truly buried. I congratulate you, Margaret. My lord Witherley will never think to look for her in Briar Street. But what of myself? Do you really trust me that much?"

Margaret paled. "What do you mean? Opal! You would not tell Jason?"

"Nay, I cannot, for, foolishly, I gave Sarah my word not to approach him on her behalf. But had it not been for that, I would go to him without a second's delay." Her eyes were contemptuous as she saw Margaret draw a deep, relieved breath. "Aye, you might well sigh with relief, for you know well that I never break my word. In this particular case, however, I am truly sorry that I have such scruples."

Opal rose abruptly to her feet. "I will go and see what is delaying Sarah. I am sure you will wish to give her the wonderful news that she is to be apprenticed to Madame Gilbert."

Margaret held out a pleading hand. "Dear, Opal! Please try to understand."

"I will never understand what gives you the right to interfere and ruin two lives. But I will tell you this. If Sarah does not wish to take this position, I will not have you trying to force her into it."

"How can you say that? Of course I would not attempt to force her. But if she does not, what will she do?"

"She may stay with me. For good, if she wishes."

"I think, Opal, that Sarah will not consent to such an arrangement. She has a great deal of pride."

"And so do you, Margaret. Only yours is an arrogant pride. Stiff-necked, destructive!" Opal whirled about and ran to the door. "I will fetch Sarah."

Margaret heard her light footsteps on the stairs. Sitting there, she felt bleak and unbearably lonely. From the look she had seen in Opal's expressive eyes, she felt sure that she had lost her friendship. The thought hurt. Somehow, without her realizing it, she had come to regard the impetuous, generous Opal almost as a daughter. And, for her added pain, she had come to love Sarah too. But there was still Jason, whom she loved above all others.

Margaret's teeth worried at her lower lip as, just for a moment, she felt her firm conviction that she was right to part Jason and Sarah wavering. Was she wrong and Opal right? Was love all that mattered? She sat up straighter in her chair, pushing doubt from her. Love did matter, but it must be the right kind of love. In no way could Sarah be considered good enough to wed with her son. There was too much that was sordid in her past, too much that might rise up to confound Jason, to wound his pride. And what then? Would his love for Sarah be strong enough to surmount all obstacles if the world he moved in continually brought home to him unpleasant facts? How could she know? And because she did not know, how could she take that chance? She would fight with every weapon at her command for Jason's future happiness.

Margaret rubbed her aching forehead. In her confusion of mind, it did not occur to her that she was viewing Jason as a little boy, and not as the strong man he undoubtedly was. He was a man who, ruthless in many ways, knew exactly what he wanted, and would not rest until he had obtained it. Jason in love was a stranger to Margaret, and she was endowing him with weaknesses of character that he did not possess. In her maternal love and her anxiety on his behalf, she made him less than he was.

A man's voice cut in on Margaret's troubled thoughts. "Is that my Opal? What are ye doing, lass? Hurry now, for I have something for ye."

Opal's voice, oddly strained, with the lilting, laughing note gone from it, answered him, "I cannot come yet, Bruce. But I will be with you as soon as possible."

"What's wrong wi' ye, lass?"

"Nothing. Sarah, my lady Witherley is waiting to talk with you."

Margaret closed her eyes. She tried to tell herself that she had done a great deal for Sarah. But a persistent voice inside her kept whispering: "And a great deal against her, Margaret."

As Sarah came into the room, Margaret managed to silence the voice. She flashed a bright smile at the girl. "Sarah, my dear, how good to see you! Sit down, please. I have some wonderful news for you."

Chapter Sixteen

On Laburnham Crescent, the quiet thoroughfare that adjoined Twyford Street, the tall, narrow houses leaning forward to touch eave to eave had been built and decorated by the master hand of Sir John Fortescue. The timbered and plastered fronts bore an amazing variety of patterns. There were gilded loops, bows, sprays of flowers, cherubs sporting with goats, and, on one house, Satan was depicted complete with horns, tail, pitchfork and writhing victim, all done in glaring red and gold. John Fortescue, always in keen competition with Christopher Wren, had made the building of these fancy houses on Laburnham Crescent his first major project. Wren, who liked pure clean lines, sneered at these houses with their ornate facings and called them "The same old fire traps as of old". This, however, did not worry Sir John one jot. His clients, who had plenty of money with which to indulge their tastes, were loud in his praise. Even the King, who had finally given in to Sir John's importuning, had been prevailed upon to view the newly built houses, and had been heard to say in his light, faintly mocking voice, "They are remarkable pleasing to the eyes, Sir John. Be sure that I will bear your undoubted talent in mind."

If Sir John made aught of the twinkle in the King's dark eyes, he put it down to his sovereign's pleasure in seeing such an imposing collection of buildings. His pleasure was completed when my lady Castlemaine, who had accompanied the King, said in her high, clear, slightly imperious voice, "It would greatly please me, Your Majesty, if I might have one of these houses for my very own."

To Sir John's keen disappointment, he did not hear the King's reply, but it was enough for him that the King's whore approved. My lady Castlemaine, in common with most of the wenches who caught Royal Stuart's roving eye, had a way of wheedling him to her point of view. The lady, he told himself, might be well worth cultivating. Could he but gain the royal patronage, it would be a distinct facer for Wren. Sir John, elated beyond reason, met Wren, who was out walking with Samuel Pepys and the blind poet, John Milton. Approaching Wren, Sir John stated in a confident voice that it would be he, not Wren, who would be given the task of designing several new buildings for the beautification of the city of London.

To this, Wren merely smiled and inclined his head. But Samuel Pepys, who disliked Sir John and blamed him, unfairly, as it happened, for the loss of a rounded and extremely luscious wench upon whom he had had his lascivious eyes, snorted out indignantly, "Fiddle faddle! I tell you, fellow, those trashy houses of yours are naught but a laughing stock. Who but fools would live in them? Out of my way, you plaguey, treacherous hound!" With a last glare at the discomfited man, Pepys settled his wig more securely on his round, shaven head, and strode off in high dudgeon.

On the last day of March, with the sun smiling at last and a brisk wind blowing, one of the fools so scathingly mentioned by Samuel Pepys, opened the door of his gilded monstrosity, the one depicting Satan, and stepped out into the fresh air to take a leisurely stroll along Laburnham Crescent. This gentleman was not concerned by the squabble between the two master builders and designers, though both were his very good friends. And both had asked him to state his opinion concerning their respective talent. But Sir Peter Baxter, who never gave an opinion if he could possibly help it, preferring to be friends with all, had managed quite nimbly to evade the issue. In Sir Peter's view a building was a building. Why fatigue oneself by getting excited about a rubbishy thing like that? Excitement, as everybody knew, caused bad humors within the body. Before you knew it, you had to be calling on the plaguey leech for a blood-letting. He was more concerned with sensible matters, like the set of his coat, the cut of his breeches, or the latest wench to catch his fickle fancy.

On this particular morning, having returned from a long and pleasant stay at his country home, he was, although it annoyed him faintly to be out of touch with London affairs, feeling at peace with the world. He was particularly pleased with his latest acquisition, for which he still owed his patient and long-suffering tailor. It was his view that his handsome lime-green satin jacket with its silver embroidered lapels and stiffly embroidered skirts, to say nothing of the elegant matching breeches, were well suited to his particular style of looks, which, complacently, he designated as handsome above the average. His lime-green tricorn hat beplumed with orange and laced with silver, sat jauntily atop his flowing black wig. A fall of silver lace tied to the knees of his breeches with green satin ribands, brushed frothily against green stockings clocked with silver, and showed to distinct advantage his green silver-buckled shoes with their three-inch red heels.

Bowing to acquaintances as he proceeded along Laburnham Crescent on his way to Twyford Street, with the intention of calling upon Mistress Sarah Barry and dazzling her with his glory, his brown spaniel dog, a gift from the King, trotting at his heels, Sir Peter was pleased to see his old friend, my lord Witherley approaching. It was well over two months since he had last seen him. Beaming, he stopped and waited for him to come abreast. Jason, Peter noted, with a critical lift of his brows, was clad in a plainly cut suit of black silk, edged at the neck and the wrists with a narrow ruffle of white lace. A black cloak swung from his shoulders, and his own hair gleamed darkly blond beneath a wide-brimmed hat decorated with a curling white feather.

Sir Peter felt a throb of alarm as Jason stopped before him. He did not like his look at all. And when he considered the fact that it was well known that Witherley could be a dangerous and difficult fellow, his alarm increased. There was a saying that he found himself recollecting. "When Witherley forgets to smile, there is danger in the air." Witherley was definitely not smiling, and Peter began fervently to wish that he had not encountered him.

"So you have returned at last, Peter," Jason began without preamble, and in what Peter could only think of as an unpleasant and distinctly offensive manner. "I was just on my way to your home to inquire after you. I think that you and I must talk."

Peter, feeling threatened, gave him a blank, brown-eyed stare. "By all means, my good fellow. Delighted."

"Delighted, are you? We will see!"

"Come, come, my dear good fellow," Sir Peter protested with rising dismay. " 'Twas a perfectly innocent remark. What i' plague is ailing you that you must bark at me so?"

"We will talk at your home, Peter. As for what is ailing me, I think you already know."

Peter feverishly searched his mind for the action or words that might have given offense. Finding none, he teetered agitatedly on his high red heels, and cast a glance of dislike at the brown spaniel dog. It occurred to him that the animal was far too tame. In this moment, he could have wished that it were a more ferocious brute, one inclined to snarl and show its teeth when danger threatened the master. As it was, it merely squatted there, long ears drooping, a silly expression on its face. Then, as if to add insult to injury, the animal rose and approached Witherley with every sign of amiable friendship.

After first sniffing at him, the dog made a snuffling sound that seemed to betoken approval, looked up at him with mournful, liquid brown eyes, and then settled contentedly at his feet.

Conquering an increased surge of dislike for the faint-hearted and spiritless animal, Peter said nervously, "Splendid animal, is it not?"

Jason gave him a long considering glance. "Splendid, as you say. But I did not seek you out to discuss your dog. Perhaps I should warn you, Peter, that it will go ill with you if you seek to practice evasion with me. You have known me long enough, I think, to realize that it will not work."

"Eh? 'Pon my soul, Jason, I can't think what has come over you. Damned if I know what the devil you are talking about." Meeting Jason's steely glance, he visibly wilted. Then, deciding to assert himself, he cleared his throat loudly. "I wonder you do not take more pride in your appearance, Jason. I don't mind telling you that I simply cannot approve of that coat. 'Tis positively shabby, old lad. And I also see that you are still insisting upon wearing your own hair. How many times must I tell you that 'tis not fashionable to go wigless?"

"Nonsense!" Jason answered him shortly. "Let us be moving on to your house."

Suppressing a craven desire to take to his heels, Peter reflected that it was precisely this that he wished to avoid. "In a few moments, dear lad," he protested in a faint voice. "I feel sure you will wish to stroll with me for a while longer."

"I have no such wish."

" 'Tis true there is a keen wind," Peter persevered rather desperately, "but nevertheless I find it pleasant and most invigorating. It—er—is good for the lungs, don't you know."

"A plague on the weather! You will cease this senseless dallying at once, if you please."

"Oh, yes, indeed." Alarmed by the abrupt tone, Peter hastened to agree. "Certainly, certainly. And as you say, dear fellow, a plague on the weather."

"Then we are in perfect agreement. Shall we be on our way?"

Seeing no help for it, Peter sighingly acquiesced. The dog, basely forsaking the high red heels, trotted contentedly beside Jason.

Arriving at the house, the gilded door was opened to them by Barton, Sir Peter's man. Jason, glancing at the red and lavishly gilded satan, remarked in a cold voice, "Most apt, Peter."

"Well, upon my word!" Peter said in a goaded voice. "Your attitude completely baffles me, Jason. What the devil do you mean by that last remark?"

When Jason made no answer to this, Barton, bowing, filled the awkward silence by remarking smoothly, "A good morning to you, my lord. I am happy that I see you well."

"Thank you, Barton."

The aggrieved Peter noted that Jason's voice was almost warm as he replied to Barton. And the dashed man, he reflected bitterly, instead of wasting his time answering the door, should have been looking after his clothes. Many of his garments were wrinkled and in sore need of the smoothing iron.

As though sensing his thoughts, Barton turned his eyes to Peter. "I could not be about my usual duties," he confided in a low but nonetheless carrying voice. "The lady has awakened. She is now in your room, Sir Peter, lying on your bed. She has been asking for you repeatedly. Shall I inform her that you have now returned, sir?"

Peter avoided Jason's penetrating eyes. Flushing, he said haughtily, "Nay. I will go to her myself, later. You need not wait, Barton."

"Yes, sir." Barton bowed again. Then, walking with a slow, measured tread, he withdrew.

Turning to Jason, Peter winced beneath his steady regard. Nervously, he twisted the front curl of his wig. "Well, well," he babbled, "so here we are, eh?"

"Here we are indeed," Jason answered in a quiet voice. "I am interested in Barton's mention of the lady occupying your bedchamber. I am sure you will wish to introduce me to her?"

Astonished at this breach of good taste, Peter gaped at him. "Nay, Jason, dear lad," he protested. "Have you taken leave of your senses? You know well 'tis not done."

For the first time, Jason smiled. Peter, instead of being relieved by this, became increasingly agitated. There was something in Witherley's eyes that he could not like. It was a hard glitter, and it seemed to go through him like a sword. As he had for the dog, he felt a sudden dislike for this cherished friend of his childhood. He could not think why it was said that when Witherley forgot to smile there was danger in the air. It was a complete and utter fallacy. After all, Witherley was smiling now, but he found that it brought him little comfort.

"Come, Peter," Jason said in a drawling voice, " 'tis scarcely a breach of etiquette involved in this instance, for I have good reason to believe that I am quite well acquainted with this particular lady."

"No, no, I give you my word, Jason. You—you are quite mistaken. The lady is not known to you."

"Is she not? But you seem very nervous, Peter. Could it be that you are trying to keep something from your old friend?"

Not for the first time, it occurred to Peter that Witherley was really a very dangerous man and would make a relentless enemy. He was a man who played with words in that icy voice of his, putting you off guard before delivering the death thrust. "Wh-why would I keep anything from you, dear lad?" he answered, giving him a hunted look. "I tell you that the wench is of no importance. You do not know her."

"I see." Then, with a bewildering change of front that set Peter's head reeling, Jason said lightly, "Where is your courtesy toward a guest in your house, Peter? Why are we still standing in the hall?"

Peter started. "Barton should have conducted us." He glared about him, as though expecting to see Barton standing in the shadows. "I vow that the man is getting beyond his duties."

"Indeed? I had thought Barton's duties were to see to your wardrobe, and to yourself. And Parson's duty to open doors."

"Aye, Parson," Peter exclaimed. "Where the devil is the man anyway? He's doubtless gone sloping off to dally with the kitchen maid. He's another who is getting beyond his duties. I will speak to him most severely about this neglect." Meeting Jason's eyes, he concluded pettishly, "Oh, confound you, Jason, you have me in a devilish ravel! I believe you are deliberately trying to confuse me. Come into the cursed sitting room."

Looking apprehensively over his shoulder in the manner of one expecting to be attacked from the rear, Peter minced across the hall, his heels making a clatter on the polished wood floor. Leading the way into a small, comfortably furnished room that was decorated in tones of red and gray, he bade his guest to be seated. "I will ring for Parsons and tell him to bring wine and biscuits," he said, smiling uneasily.

Leisurely, Jason seated himself in a chair upholstered in heavy red silk and decorated with numerous gray tassels. "Not for me, thank you," he answered politely. "I did not come here to drink wine. I think, under the circumstances, it would ill behoove me to do so."

Ill behoove him? What did he mean? The palms of Peter's hands felt uncomfortably damp. From the time they had played together as small boys, Jason had always had this gift of awing him. And, as he was doing now, had ofttimes filled him with guilt of a deed of which he had no knowledge. He sat down on the sofa, his brown eyes blinking rapidly. "Well, then, why did you come?"

"Shall we say that I came for a friendly chat."

A friendly chat? It was too much! Now indeed he had gone too far, Peter thought indignantly. He sat there in that chair, those blue eyes of his boring into him, and still holding that glitter that could not but cause him much concern, and had the supreme audacity to say he had come for a friendly chat. It was more than flesh and blood could be expected to stand. "Now look here, Jason," he burst out, "I don't mind telling you that I do not at all appreciate your attitude, which is dashed menacing. I would be a fool if I did not realize that something is wrong, but I—" He broke off to scowl down at the dog who, apparently taking grave exception to his tone, had bared his teeth in a most unpleasant snarl. "Oh, damn," he went on bitterly, "even my plaguey dog is against me!"

"You must know why I am here," Jason said quietly, toying with one of the gray tassels. "So why do you play the innocent, Peter? For your own good, and in the friendliest of spirits, I assure you, do not provoke me too far." He smiled, and that smile, so cold and glittering, cut through the other man like a knife. "Your green coat is most elegant and vastly becoming to you," Jason went on, "so 'twould be a shame to soil it with your own blood, would it not?"

Peter shuddered. For a hopeful moment he wondered if he might not be experiencing a nightmare. He was a peaceful man and he detested violence. Opening his eyes again, he came to the regretful conclusion that he was awake. "I say, Jason," he said in a fainting voice, "must you smile at me in that deadly way? In all truth, my nerves simply cannot stand it. How have I offended you? What is it you want of me?"

Jason sighed. "Now indeed you do begin to provoke me, Peter. But if you would please me, and I feel sure you would wish to do so, you will furnish me with a description of the lady secreted in your bedchamber."

"A d-description?" Peter said, goggling at him anxiously.

"That is what I said. For instance, might I inquire the color of the lady's hair?"

Peter longed to tell him that he might not inquire, but he did not dare. "Her hair?" he repeated the words in a hollow voice. Looking sharply at Jason, the unwelcome and disturbing suspicion came to him that something must have broken down in the fellow's head. Shifting uneasily on the sofa, he glanced longingly at the door. Then, seeing the ominous narrowing of those blue eyes, he burst into hasty speech, "Her hair, you say? Yes, yes, quite, her hair." In assumed nonchalance, he crossed one leg over the other. "Well, the truth of the matter is, dear boy, I would rather not say."

"You would rather not? I see. I quite understand."

The words were pleasantly spoken. But Peter, who had seen Jason's thin fingers clench convulsively, was in no wise reassured. Beads of perspiration gently dewed his forehead. It now began to seem to him that there was a great deal more in this matter than met the eye. Had Jason come here on Bainbridge's behalf? If so, why did the fellow play with him? Why did he not come right out with what he wanted to say? His eyes wistful, he glanced again toward the door. His alarm now was tinged with bitterness. Damn, but the trollop was not worth all this trouble! He had thought that he had conducted his affair with the lady in admirable secrecy, for both he and Dorothy had given different, but devilishly clever reasons, for wishing to leave town. She to go to the bedside of her sick aunt. He to retire to the country for a well-earned rest. But God's life! If Bainbridge had found out, he shuddered to think of the consequences to himself.

Jason's drawling voice prodded at him again. "Would you say, Peter, that the lady's eyes are blue?"

Surreptitiously Peter lifted his hand and wiped his damp forehead. Suppose Jason had not come on behalf of Bainbridge. In that case, might it not be best if he humored him? If there should happen to be something gone wrong in his head, it would be better not to get him all excited, for one never knew what might happen. With this thought in mind, he beamed sunnily upon his tormentor. "Blue, that's the color," he agreed eagerly. "A lovely shade for eyes, I always say."

"Is that what you always say, Peter. I would imagine that you have looked into this particular pair of eyes quite often?"

Peter's beam faded. It was all very well to humor the fellow, but one must draw the line somewhere. He said with a cautious trace of heat, "Look here, Jason, I don't know what this cat and rat game is that you are playing with me, but I assure you that I do not like it." Emboldened, he drew himself up haughtily. "If there is something on your mind, I pray you to speak out. All this fencing about is making me extremely nervous."

"But then, Peter, you so easily become nervous."

With a vague feeling that he had been insulted, Peter made to rise. "This is—is pointless."

"Pointless or not, oblige me by sitting down."

Feeling boneless, his nerves twanging, Peter sank back again. He was not noted for his quick thinking, but staring into that blandly smiling face, he thought he had the solution. But who would have believed it of Witherley? Eager to disperse the strong aura of menace that seemed to threaten his life and limb, he said placatingly, "Had I known you felt so deeply for the lady, I would not have started the affair. I ask you to believe that, Jason, dear old lad."

The lines of Jason's face seemed to sharpen, giving him a gaunt look. His eyes, Peter noted with sick dismay, looked positively dangerous. "You lie," Jason said softly. " 'Twas you who first suspected how I felt about her."

"Eh?" Peter cast about in his mind for his meaning. Finding none, he said weakly, "No, no. Assure you that I don't know what you are talking about. Word of a gentleman!"

Jason did not seem to be listening. His eyes had dropped to the tassel in his hand. "This room is tastefully decorated," he said, pulling at the silken strands. "Who makes your furniture?"

Peter's jaw dropped. Damned if he knew what to make of the cursed fellow. "W-Westing Stockle and Harris of Bolton Court. Fine craftsmen, very fine."

"I will bear those names in mind." Jason's eyes rose to meet Peter's. "You will now conduct me to the lady."

Defiance stirred. It was hardly fair of Jason to make him believe that the discussion was terminated and then to so abruptly return to it. The fellow was mad, quite, quite mad! He had his code. What would she think of him if he went clumping into the bedchamber with a companion? His name would be blackened beyond repair, for he had no doubt that she would find a subtle way, without implicating herself, to see to that. After she had finished with him, for he had found to his cost that Dorothy, though dainty and delightful of appearance, could be extremely vindictive, it was doubtful if he would be able to lure another wench into his bed. There were, of course, females of the lower order who would be glad to accommodate him, but he had a distaste for such females. He had never been able to understand how the King could so demean himself as to bed with actresses, and others of the ilk. The exception, he had found, was Sarah Barry, for whom he had a decided tenderness. Becoming aware that Jason was waiting for an answer, he shook his head. "Nay, Jason, dear lad, it positively cannot be done."

"Can it not?" Jason rose. "I do not need to be conducted to your bedchamber, Peter. I have been there often enough before. You may therefore accompany me, or you may stay here. It is just as you please."

Peter jumped hastily to his feet. "This is an outrage!" he spluttered. "Damned if I'm not of a mind to call you out!"

"If you are so minded, I will be happy to accommodate you."

He must be cautious, Peter thought, staring at him in dismay. He? Face Witherley's blade! A man would have to be tired of life to do so! "You deserve that I should call you out," he countered in a feeble voice. "I would do so, believe me. But the thing is, dear lad, I am not too handy with the sword."

"A pity," Jason said, striding over to the door. "I had hoped I would not be deprived of the pleasure of killing you."

"Jason, dear fellow!" Peter fluttered after him, an agitated blur of green and silver. If he could but calm this madman for a few hours, long enough, before the fellow's brain took another twist, for him to get over to France, all would be well. Bitterness rose. After all, what had he done? How was he to know that Witherley had set his heart on the lady? Life was so damnably unfair, for he only wished to live in peace and harmony, friends with all. And how had he been served? Damn! That red-headed baggage wasn't worth all this agony of mind. It was true that she was good in bed, but what would that benefit him if he were lying stark and cold in a grave at Elder Green?

Arriving at the door of his bedchamber, Peter grasped Jason's arm and began to pat it soothingly and affectionately. "Jason, lad, do not put yourself about, I beg of you. She is very beautiful, I grant you, but getting just a little overblown for my taste. Such types go off early, you know. So you see, there's surely no need of all this pother between friends. You may have her, lad, and my sincere blessings upon you both."

"Thank you, Peter," Jason drawled, "your offer is most generous." Almost casually, he reached out and grasped the unfortunate Peter by his silver embroidered lapels. "For those words you have just uttered, I could shake you like the little rat you undoubtedly are, or I could knock you down. Which would you prefer?"

Trying unsuccessfully to control his trembling, Peter reflected that Witherley's eyes were much too close to his, and he could not like the message he read in them. The fellow was dangerous, and becoming more dashed sinister by the moment. He tried to smile, but instantly realized that this was a mistake. "If it's all the same to you, Jason, dear old lad, I'm not frightfully enamored with either idea. Come, be reasonable. Have I not offered to give her up to you? W-what more can I do or say?"

With an exclamation of disgust, Jason flung him from him, and Peter's head struck the wall hard. With a little bleating cry of despair, he sank slowly to the floor. Lying very still, keeping his eyes tightly closed, it occurred to him to wonder if the fellow would be such an out and out blackguard as to attack an unconscious man? He also wondered if it might be possible to make good his escape while that cursed madman was in the bedchamber?

Jason was not thinking of him at that moment. He stood there with his hand on the latch, and wondered what he was doing here? Why had he put himself in this ridiculous position? Was he then entirely devoid of that pride that had sustained him in other difficult situations? What would she say when he confronted her? She had deceived him with her protestations of love; she had made him look a fool. And here he was, preparing to make an even bigger fool of himself. He loved her still, no matter what she had done, loved her far more than he had dreamed it possible to love any woman. His hand tightened on the latch, and he felt a surge of such bitter anger that the blood drummed in his ears. Damn her! Curse her to hell, the little bitch! He'd like to kill her for this betrayal! He'd take her lover to her. He would throw him down on the bed beside her. If Peter was the kind of man she preferred, then she was welcome to him!

Peter gasped with horror as Jason's rough hands seized him. By God, but the fellow was unspeakable! He was going to murder a helpless and unconscious man! Were there no limits to which he would not descend? Terrified, his limbs too palsied to struggle, he was dragged to the door of the bedchamber. Terrified or not, he could not help giving a fleeting thought to his magnificent green satin apparel. It would be ruined, and he had not yet paid his tailor. With an anguished moan that came out as a fluting cry, he gave himself up to his fate. If he were to be murdered in cold blood, then his comfort must be that Simpson, his tailor, could not very well cut up stiff about an unpaid bill. One could not expect to get money from a corpse.

Jason lifted his foot and kicked open the door. "Madam," he said coldly, dragging the despairing Peter into the room, "here is your love, come to visit you."

"Is it so?" a sleepy, amused voice answered him. "A pox on your impudence, my lord Witherley. What in the plague have you done to Peter? God's eyebrows, but he quakes like a terrified green rabbit! Explain yourself, you bloody ruffian."

Jason, who was bending over Peter and holding him beneath his arms, froze. Lady Dorothy Prentiss's voice! What had he done? Abruptly, he let his victim fall. Tears came into Peter's eyes as his head once more made stunning contact with a hard object.

Jason turned to face Lady Dorothy. He bowed slightly, "My lady." His eyes went over her naked body which was only partly veiled by her beautiful red hair. "I did not expect to find you here."

"Ah, my lord, I think you did." Dorothy lifted a hand to sweep back her hair. "Look then," she said, her smile slightly malicious, "for I feel sure it is what you came to do."

"You are mistaken, my lady. Have I not said that I did not expect to find you here?"

Her eyes sharpened. "Who, then?"

"It is of no importance, my lady Prentiss."

Dorothy laughed softly, "I have heard rumors of your doting fondness for a certain little gutter brat, though I credited them not. But now I am not so sure. Oh, this is exquisitely funny! Can it be that you expected to find her in Peter's bed?"

Jason could not prevent his flush, but his voice was even and cold when he answered her. "Your imagination does you great credit, my lady. But we will not discuss Mistress Barry, if you please."

"So that is the wench's name. Have you indeed been tumbled from your cold and lofty pinnacle, my lord Witherley?"

Jason approached the bed and sat down on the edge. "As I have remarked, my lady, you have a most vivid imagination. Doubtless you are even now longing to be back at Court, so that you may tell your tale of the amusing fruits of your imagination. However, I cannot help wondering if Bainbridge will be equally amused when I tell my own tale."

Some of the high color left Dorothy's face. "Your tale? My lord, do you actually have the audacity to threaten me?"

Jason smiled, "Yes, indeed, my lady Prentiss." He lifted his shoulders in a shrug. "Bainbridge, though always overwhelmingly generous to his mistresses, will scarcely continue to keep you in luxury were he in receipt of certain damaging information."

"What do you mean?" Dorothy shouted, glaring at him. "There is nothing James could hear that would cause him to stop loving me."

Jason's tawny eyebrows rose in cynical amusement. "Come

now, my lady, you know better."

Dorothy gave him a sullen look. She was afraid of James. It would not be the first time he had beaten her and threatened to cast her out. It might be that Witherley, the icy swine, was bluffing, but she could not afford to disregard his threat.

"Well, my lady, have you thought well?"

Dorothy's eyes narrowed in sudden hatred of this man who had so often resisted her wiles, but she managed to force a smile to her lips. "Why, my lord, I vow you are as cold-blooded as a fish and as dangerous as a snake. Do not worry about your cursed secret, if secret it be, it is safe with me. I will not mention a word about the Barry creature."

"My lady Prentiss, lest you mistake me, I am not ashamed of my love for Mistress Barry. But it is as well that you keep a still tongue in your head. Were you to allow yourself to babble, the results might well be disastrous to yourself."

With a light of pure malice in her eyes, Dorothy cupped her breasts with her hands. "Has this Barry breasts like these to tempt a man? Has she a body like mine? Come, my lord, mount me. Let us see if there is fire beneath your ice."

"I regret, my lady," Jason's light voice stung her with its sarcasm, "that though I am well nigh consumed with desire, I must forgo the pleasure."

Angry color flooded Dorothy's face. "Get out!" she screamed. She turned her head to glare at the feebly moaning Peter. "And you may take that stupid creature with you. His cursed bleating is more than I can bear!"

Peter stopped moaning. He found himself scarcely able to credit the evidence of his own eyes. The impudence of the woman! How could he have ever thought he loved her? There she lay, in his bed, using his house as if it were her own. Why, he had lavished what amounted to a small fortune on her, and she dared to refer to him as that stupid creature! He was suddenly flooded with a vast self-pity. His day had been quite ruined, and it had started out so well. But mayhap Dorothy did not mean what she said, he thought, and despite everything, he felt the rising of hope. Indeed, how could she mean it? She who had rested so soft and yielding in his arms, her mouth opened like a ripe fruit beneath his own. It must be that she was distraught by the presence of that cursed madman. Opening his eyes, he stretched out a quivering hand. "Dorothy!" he moaned softly. "Dorothy, my love!" Encountering her furious glare, he paled, and hastily closed his eyes again.

"Do not dare to lie there bleating at me like a bloody sheep, you idiot!" Dorothy screamed. "I want both of you to leave this room at once!"

Jason rose from the bed. "In one moment, my lady. I must aid Peter."

"Nay, let me aid him," Dorothy panted. "You may believe me when I tell you that I will aid him well!" She leaped from the bed.

Peter half-opened his eyes as Dorothy fell to her knees beside the bed. He saw her scrabbling beneath it, and he heard the tinkle of china as her rings struck against an object, and a terrible and monstrous suspicion set his head reeling. She could not! Surely she would not? It would be inhuman!

"I will revive him for you, my lord," Dorothy said savagely.

Peter opened his mouth to say that he did not need reviving, and he gasped and strangled as the contents of the chamber pot hit him full in the face. It went down his throat, it splashed on the new green satin. My God! He was filled with a shuddering revulsion. The woman was lost to all decency! She was quite beyond the pale! And he had actually thought he loved her. Only a vile creature could do such a thing! Blinking moisture from his eyes, he looked up into Dorothy's face. "No, by God!" he croaked. "This is more than I can endure!"

"Bah!" she scoffed. "What is a little water, especially when 'tis your own?"

Drab! Trollop! Any man's whore! Peter wanted to scourge her with his bitterness, but he did not dare. She was a dangerous woman, and who knew what fresh horrors she might be planning. She was quite capable of seizing every chamber pot in the house and emptying them over him. He would put nothing past the vile woman! Feeling that honor demanded that he say something, he said in a voice that was meant to sting, "I hope you are satisfied, madam, now that you have quite ruined my coat?"

For answer, Dorothy's hard foot struck him a painful blow in his side. "Get up! Get out of my sight! How dare you continue to lie there like a sick frog, when I have told you to go?"

A sick frog? My God! What had happened to their glorious love? A broken man, Peter rose painfully to his feet. He would never forgive her for this, never in this world! He limped over to the door. "See what she has done, Jason," he said in a trembling voice. "This is imported material, and it cannot be matched. It will wrinkle! It will stain!"

Jason's mouth quivered as he fought to control his rising laughter. "Nonsense!" he said. Without looking at Dorothy, he propelled the dripping Peter through the door.

Along the corridor, down the stairs, and into the sitting room, Peter continued to voice his grievances. "I have been insulted in my own home. I have been set upon by that evil and disgusting woman. I have been spurned by my very dog! And I have been made to believe that I was at the mercy of a madman! And if all that were not enough, my lady Prentiss, on whom I bestowed a very handsome necklace, to say nothing of matching bracelets and earrings, has dared to call me a creature! A creature, mind you! I, whom she called her one true love!"

"Come, Peter, you must make an effort to pull yourself together," Jason said. "It is most distressing, I know, but you will rise above it. I am sorry for my part in it, but I was under a misapprehension." He pushed Peter into a chair. Looking at the dripping wig with the erstwhile elaborate curls now straggling in limp hanks over his forehead, the woebegone face and the crumpled jacket, the stern control he had imposed upon himself collapsed, and he was helplessly shaken with laughter.

Peter looked at him with unbelieving eyes. "You are laughing?" he exclaimed in outrage. "Do you tell me you are actually laughing? Oh, I see, now I see! It is a tragedy to me, but that means nothing to you. But I would not for the world reprove your levity, though it cuts me to my very heart to know you for a false friend! Go on, pray do. You have my permission to laugh."

Remembering all that had gone before, Jason was seized with a fresh convulsion. "D-damn!" he gasped. "I am sorry, Peter. I-I just cannot seem to h-help it. What color are her eyes? What c-color is her h-hair?"

Peter shuddered. "If you had only explained your meaning, instead of toying with me. You can have no conception of the agony I endured." He looked down at his coat. "Of the agony I am still enduring."

Jason's only answer was a fresh burst of laughter. Peter regarded him for a moment with kindling eyes, then he said with cold dignity, "Pray enjoy yourself. Do not let my outraged feelings concern you at all."

With a visible effort, Jason controlled himself. "I beg your pardon, Peter. I do not know what came over me. But I do know that I have not laughed like that in years."

"Indeed. Then I must congratulate myself on being the cause of your unseemly mirth, I suppose?"

"Peter, I pray you do not be dignified, or you will be setting me off again. I do most sincerely apologize to you for my unjust and, I am forced to confess, foolish suspicions."

Peter forgot the injury done to his dignity and pride in simple curiosity. "But who the devil were you expecting to find in my bed?"

"Sarah," Jason said briefly.

"Sarah?" Peter stared at him in astonishment. "Nay, Jason, though 'tis true I have a fondness for the wench, she would have none of me." He broke off, frowning, "But that you could believe me capable of the treachery of smuggling her into my house and my bed, after I had accurately guessed at your feelings for her, that goes beyond all bounds!" He collapsed back against the chair. "It needed only that final insult to complete the tragedy of my day!"

Sobered now, Jason regarded him with a touch of impatience. "I can only repeat that I am sorry. But pray do not expect me to grovel, for I fear you will be disappointed."

Peter gave vent to a bitter laugh. "Knowing you, Jason, 'tis the last thing I would expect of you." He paused, then added wistfully, "Though a little groveling, however, slight, would not come amiss." He touched the lapels of his coat. "Especially after what you have done to me."

"I did not do that," Jason reminded him. "However, since it was my actions that brought it about, I will pay for the clothes. Have your tailor send his bill to me."

Peter brightened. "My wig?" he said hopefully. "It, too, is ruined."

"It will dry."

"But not in the same shape. And how can you expect me to wear it with such a stench clinging to it? People will be crossing the street to avoid me."

"It does not occur to you to have your barber wash it?"

"Certainly not! It would never be the same."

"Very well. I will pay for a new monstrosity."

Peter beamed. Witherley might be awe-inspiring, he might

sometimes freeze a fellow, but there was nothing mean about him where money was concerned. His tailor would be more than satisfied to be paid so promptly, and it was no business of Simpson's where the money came from, greedy churl that he was. Peter began then to plan on an elaborate scale. He would set Simpson to work at once on that new puce brocade. As for the green satin, he had no doubt that it could be made to look as good as new. Simpson had his own special way of cleaning things, and he was magic with a smoothing iron. Filled with goodwill, he leaned forward and fixed Jason with sympathetic eyes. "My dear lad, was my guess correct? Are you really in love with Mistress Barry?"

Jason flushed. "Something like that," he said shortly.

The sympathy in Peter's eyes deepened, and seeing it, Jason gritted his teeth together in annoyance. But it was no use being angered with Peter, since it was his own folly and his obviously unwarranted suspicions that had placed him in this impossible situation. "And the wench will have none of you, is that it?" Peter said. "But my dear old lad, mayhap she wants you to woo her."

"I can scarcely do that," Jason said in a tight voice. "She has gone."

"Gone where?"

"Had I been in receipt of that information, I would not be here."

"True." Peter nodded his head. "Quite true, dear boy. I had not thought of that." He hesitated. "Where can she be?"

"How do I know!"

Peter was silent for a moment, then he said in a thoughtful voice, "Perhaps she did not very much care to be a man's mistress, even yours."

Jason's brows drew together in an ominous frown. "Watch your tongue!" he snapped. "It was not my intention to make her my mistress. I wished her to become my wife."

"Eh? No, I say! That's going a bit too far."

"And what the devil do you mean by that? Are you suggesting that Mistress Barry is not good enough to become my wife?"

"Steady!" Peter drew back in alarm. "It's just simply that she is—"

"She is what?"

"I say, no need to snap my head off. I only meant that she is of a different class to yourself."

"Rubbish! Do you think such a paltry thing could possibly matter to me?"

"It might not matter to you, old lad, but perhaps it did to Sarah. It would most certainly matter to my lady Witherley. I yield to no one in my admiration of the Lady Margaret, but she would not like it at all. Mayhap she prevailed upon Sarah to depart."

Jason gave him a long, thoughtful look. "So you think my mother will know where Sarah is to be found?"

"I'll wager you ten to one that she does. I remember the time when I became enamored of a kitchen wench. My mother found out about it, and she immediately sent the poor little girl packing. Never forgave her for a long time. Just like you, I was mad to marry the wench."

"Just like me? Nonsense! It is not the same thing at all."

"If you say so." Peter suddenly felt superior to the troubled man before him, and he found it to be a good feeling. "I'm surprised that you are so easily gulled, Jason," he said, giving him a pitying look. "I have had much experience with the ladies, far more than you, I dare swear, and I know how they think. Depend upon it, your mother sent her packing. She will know where Sarah is."

"If I thought that!" Jason's mouth set grimly. "You really think so, Peter?"

"Certain of it."

"Then, by God, I'll find out!" He rose to his feet. "I bid you good day, Peter."

"Good day, huh!"

"Once again I apologize. I freely admit that my actions were foolish, headstrong, and quite unforgivable." He smiled. "Pray to pardon me for my unworthy suspicions."

Under the influence of that rare and extraordinarily charming smile, Peter relented at once. "Oh, well, I suppose I pardon you. Next time, however, should there be a next time, oblige me by using your head." He sniffed. "I had not supposed you to be a fellow who is ruled by his emotions."

"Nor am I in the ordinary way. But we all have our weak moments, I suppose. Good-bye. I'll look in on you again. No, don't get up, or trouble Parsons. I can let myself out." With a wave of his hand, he departed.

"Should you find Sarah, dear lad," Peter called after him, "do wear something decent before presenting yourself. The ladies, bless 'em, when you come acourting, expect full dress before they will even condescend to let you kiss their little feet."

To this surprising cynicism on the part of the normally affable and good-natured Peter, there was only the slamming of the door to answer him.

Sir Peter removed his wet wig and gave it a sour look. "And it was the best hair, or so that damned old thief of a barber told me. The way it looks now, 'twas more likely made up of the cursed sweepings of the streets." Petulantly he flung the wig from him. "Thieves and robbers everywhere to plague an honest man," he grumbled, "to say nothing of vile trollops and madmen. As for Witherley and his situation, there's more in that than meets the eye. I think, Mistress Barry, from Witherley's attitude, that you likely gave him some pledge. If that is so, then you had better have a good reason for your flight, reason enough to satisfy Witherley. The plaguey fellow is not a man to be trifled with, I'm damned if he is!" His eyes brooded as he sought to work out the problem. He looked down at the brown dog for inspiration. "I wonder why the devil he thought Sarah was with me, Jasper?" He sighed. "The wench doesn't give a button for me, more's the pity. But I had thought, from a certain look I saw in her eyes, that she cared more than a little for Jason, curse his hide!"

Jasper snuffled. Raising those liquid brown eyes to his master's face, he growled disapprovingly.

"I should call you Judas," Peter said, looking at him sternly, "not Jasper. Get along with you! Don't you show your teeth to me, you infernal old flea bag. I have had quite enough for one day, thank you!"

Chapter Seventeen

In the long and narrow workroom at the back of Madam Gilbert's small and fashionable salon, complete silence reigned. The two girls, the only occupants of the room, worked industriously, heads bent in apparent meekness, for one never knew when Madam Gilbert might make a sudden appearance. Esther Tate seemed resigned, for her light-brown eyes seldom left her work, but Sarah Barry's heart seethed with rebellion as she thought of her employer. One would think them trollops, or perhaps not particularly bright children, she thought, remembering Madam Gilbert's cold, precise voice reciting her requirements. "If you are to work for me, Mistress Barry," Madam Gilbert had said, "you must be neat and clean at all times. You must be modest, honest, demure, and gentle spoken. If you should at any time come into contact with my clients, you must never speak unless spoken to. If you are sent out to match a length of ribbon, or perhaps, as you grow more proficient, to a private home to measure a lady for a gown, you will model your behavior in such fashion as to do me honor. And, since you will live in my establishment, as well as work here, you will keep your room in good order. I will inspect it once a day. One infraction and I will put you out on the street as casually as I would a stray cat or a dog."

Savagely Sarah twisted the length of light-blue ribbon with which she was attempting to trim the high crown of a pink satin bonnet. She was not very good at this kind of work, she thought, looking ruefully at her pricked fingers. As for the rules, it was not that she had any objection to them, it was the way they had been voiced that she hated. Just as she hated the tall and stately Madam Gilbert, with her smooth pale-blond hair and her hostile gray eyes. Hostile. Aye, that was the keynote to Madam Gilbert's character. The woman exuded hostility to those in a lower position to herself. Except with her customers, for whom she had a ready smile and an almost overpoweringly gracious manner, she was critical, carping, and perpetually afraid that something might be taken away from her. Especially was she afraid when it came to her son, Thomas Gilbert.

Frowning, Sarah tried to loop the ribbon in the way Esther had showed her, but only succeeded in tangling and creasing it. Thomas Gilbert! If only he would leave her alone. From the moment she had entered the establishment, he had pursued her. His gray eyes, so like his mother's, would be full of light as he furtively brushed against her, or, if she were not on her guard, his thick fingers would touch her breast and linger there. Once, when he had caught her between salon and workroom, he had dragged her into his arms and kissed her lips. She had cried out in protest and pushed him away fiercely. But Thomas, smiling disagreeably, had reminded her that his mother would never believe her if she should be thinking of complaining. Alone in her small bedchamber at nights, for Esther went home to her parents' house, it had reached the point where she must bolt the door to keep him out. What could she do? He was right. Madam Gilbert would never believe any complaints against her cherished son. She would be put out on the street, as Madam Gilbert had said, as casually as if she were a stray cat or a dog.

Tears came into Sarah's eyes as she tried once more to loop the ribbon. If that happened, what would become of her? She could not apply once more to my lady Witherley, neither could she throw herself upon Opal Sunderland's charity. Opal, of course, would not look upon it as charity, and she would take her in willingly and cheerfully. Nevertheless, she could not bring herself to impose on her good nature. She must learn to make her own way in the world. It was not good to be dependent.

Giving up temporarily on the blue ribbon, Sarah reached for a length of petunia-red, with which Madam Gilbert was expecting her to form roses. Roses! Anything she attempted in this line invariably turned into an ugly crumpled mess. She did not have Esther's talent, and Madam Gilbert would find that out soon enough. What then? Would she be put out on the street to fend for herself! Not that Madam Gilbert's establishment or her treatment of her workers was ideal, but at least it was a roof over her head. Her wages, five shillings a year, would at least be honestly earned. If, that was, she was still here when the wages, together with a bolt of rough cloth were presented. Esther had told her about the cloth. Madam did not like her girls to look shabby. They must therefore make themselves two new gowns a year. But Esther had also said that the material presented was shoddy and cheap, and that the new gowns were lucky to see the year out. Sarah looked at the gown Esther was wearing. It had been made from her last year's bolt of cloth. It was a drab, dark-green without trimming of any kind. There was a rip beneath the arm, which she had tried unsuccessfully to mend. Doubtless, Sarah thought, the rotting cloth would not yield to Esther's usually clever needle. Nonetheless, if Madam saw the rip, there would be trouble. Esther's excuses and explanations would be thrust aside, and she would be labeled clumsy and lazy.

Sarah looked down at the petunia-red ribbon. Already her fumbling attempts to form the flowers had reduced much of the ribbon's sheen.

Sighing, Sarah took up the blue ribbon again. Vaguely, she

became aware that she was hungry. Breakfast this morning had consisted of a slice of stale bread, thinly covered with dripping, and half a tankard of ale. Luncheon, of course, if she were to be allowed to partake, would be the same thin broth with the small pieces of fat floating on its surface, that they had had yesterday and the day before.

Sarah grimaced. Madam did not like waste. Yesterday, in the dark dining room, seated at her private table with her son, both of them consuming mutton, washed down with copious draughts of ale, she had made this very clear.

"That broth is good and hearty and strength-giving," Madam had remarked with her tight smile. "I have ordered the cook to make a sufficiency of this nourishing broth, enough to last for several days." She frowned. "Yet it does seem to me, young ladies, that you are not enjoying it. I must tell you that I do not like waste, and that it grieves me to know that you are ungrateful for my thought and care of you."

Esther, stirring the unsavory mixture with her horn spoon, had looked up to give Madam a nervous smile. But her own look toward Madam's plentifully supplied table, Sarah thought, had earned her a sharp rebuke. Madam's son, having finished with the mutton, was engaged in cutting into a meat pasty, and perhaps her eyes had lingered too long on his actions. "It would seem to me that you are ruled by greed, Mistress Barry," Madam said in an ominous voice. "With good food before you, you yet seem to covet more. Why is this?"

"Possibly because I am hungry for something other than this thin broth," Sarah had answered her in a cool voice. "I cannot say that I find this particular fare strength-giving."

Madam's face had flushed a dusky red. "So! It is apparent that you are not only ungrateful, Mistress Barry, but impudent too."

Sarah would have said more, had not Esther's nervous tug on her skirt stopped her. Madam, however, had not finished with her reprimand. With her pale-gray eyes fixed on Sarah's face, she said coldly, "It might be as well, Mistress Barry, if you forgo your noon meal on the morrow. Perhaps hunger will teach you an appreciation of good food, and, likewise, the joy of having an indulgent mistress."

Sarah bit down hard on her trembling lower lip. What did it matter, what did anything matter? Without Jason, her life could never be other than a dreary burden. She thought of his brilliantly blue eyes that had been so warm with love for her, his voice telling her that he loved her, and her breath caught on a sob.

At the sound that escaped Sarah, Esther Tate looked up from her work. Sarah Barry was an odd girl, she thought. She was beautiful, but lifeless. It was as though she did not care what happened to her. Madam Gilbert did not like Sarah, that much was plain. Given an opportunity, Madam would not hesitate to get rid of her.

Esther smoothed with a loving hand the rich blue and gold of the gown she was working upon. How she would like to wear such a gown! She continued to place her neat, all but invisible stitches, telling herself that it was no use crying for something she could never have. In any case, this particular blue would not be kind to her complexion. But Sarah now, with her red-gold hair, her luminous blue eyes, would look ravishing in this gown. Esther's thoughts reverted to Madam Gilbert. Madam was cunning. She would not get rid of Sarah yet, because she would not wish to offend my lady Witherley, who had recommended the girl to her. No, she would never wish to lose my lady Witherley's patronage, but just the same, the time would come when she would feel that she had sufficient reason to dismiss Sarah from her employment. Esther had seen the flame in Madam's eyes when her son Tom had pressed close to Sarah and had spoken to her in a low, caressing voice.

Esther grinned. Madam was a tigress where her precious son was concerned. There was not a wench living that she would think good enough for him. Esther shrugged. Madam could keep her son. Even if she were not small and plain, even if Master Tom had desired her, she would not want him. Tom Gilbert, with his heavy figure, his leering smile, and his hot, moist hands, did not appeal to her at all. Give her a real man, a man like her Jim. He was all man, was her Jim, not a milksop of a mother's boy like Tom Gilbert. Jim did not care about her lack of looks and her meagre stature. He loved her, he had said so, and she was still not over the wonder of that avowal.

Esther glanced quickly toward the door. Madam did not allow talking in her workroom, and, if she should be caught, it would mean that she would lose a shilling from her wages, but she must tell someone about her Jim, or she would burst with her happiness. "Sarah," Esther said in a hoarse, whispering voice, "I got something to tell you."

Sarah nodded, and smiled her vague, sweet smile. Esther found herself wondering yet again what had occurred in Sarah Barry's life to put that pained and wounded expression in her eyes? "What is it, Esther?" Sarah said in a low voice.

"I got me a sweetheart," Esther said triumphantly. "His name is Jim Hawkins."

"I am glad for you. Are you going to be married?"

Esther smiled warmly. For once Sarah had sounded genuinely interested. "Aye, 'tis likely," she answered, "for the great ninny is fair daft with love for me. He's big and rough and he's not what you would call handsome, but he—"

The words died on Esther's lips as the door of the workroom was flung open and Madam Gilbert came sweeping in. Her gray eyes darted suspiciously from one girl to the other. "I was standing near the door, young ladies," she said in a harsh voice, "and it seemed to me that I heard talking. Were you talking, ladies?"

Esther darted an imploring look at Sarah. "N-no, madam," she stammered.

Madam Gilbert's eyes turned to Sarah. "And what have you to say, Mistress Barry? Is Mistress Tate telling me the truth?"

Sarah kept her eyes lowered. "Esther has already told you."

"I am asking you!"

"We were not talking, Madam Gilbert."

"It is strange indeed, then, that I thought I heard voices. Perhaps you would imply that my ears are playing tricks on me, Mistress Barry?"

"I imply nothing, madam."

Madam Gilbert looked at the pink satin bonnet in Sarah's hands. "What are you doing, you clumsy wench?" she cried in an outraged voice. "Look at that ribbon! It is ruined!"

Sarah raised her eyes. Madam Gilbert, to her anger, felt herself flushing beneath that clear, steady gaze. "Well, Mistress Barry, what have you to say for yourself?"

"I am sorry about the ribbon, madam," Sarah answered. "I will try to do better. But I hope you will bear in mind that I am new to this type of work. In time, I feel sure, I will grow more proficient."

Madam Gilbert stared at her. What was the matter with the girl? Did nothing move her? Those eyes of hers, so mournful, so full of pain, made one feel quite uncomfortable. Then there was her indifference to everything that went an around her. But what if that indifference was only a cover to hide her real design? But sly Sarah Barry would not get Tom into her trap, not if she had anything to say about it!

Madam Gilbert snatched the bonnet from Sarah's hands and flung it on the long, scarred table. "So you think you will grow more proficient, do you? Well, let me tell you this. You have not the feeling for this work. You are as clumsy as a cow! If it were not that I value my lady Witherley's patronage, I would turn you away! There, what have you to say to that?"

"What can I say, madam?" Sarah clasped her hands tightly together. "If you truly believe me to be useless, then mayhap it will be better if I leave your service. I will make it plain to my lady Witherley that you are in no way to blame."

Tempted, Madam Gilbert's eyes narrowed in thought. But no, what was she thinking about? She did not trust the chit! It would not be wise to turn Sarah Barry away after so short a time. To do so would be to seriously offend my lady Witherley. "You will not answer me back, Mistress Barry!" she snapped.

"I am sorry. I was not aware that I had done so."

"You are clumsy and rude. But for all that, I am disposed to give you another chance."

"Thank you, madam."

The words were meekly spoken, but Madam Gilbert thought she detected a faint defiance. With furious spots of color burning in her cheeks, she said loudly, "I think you are trying to be impudent again, Mistress Barry! I warn you, that impudence is the one thing that I will not tolerate!"

Sarah said nothing. Madame Gilbert said in a quieter voice, "After yesterday's episode, you cannot expect to indulge yourself at the table. There will be no luncheon for you today. Therefore you will put on your cloak and bonnet. I desire you to go to Bettina's, in Tavistock Street. They have in a new stock of ribbons and laces. Do you think that, without your usual bungling, you can manage to match a length of lavender ribbon?"

Sarah rose from her chair, her face expressionless. "I will do my best, madam."

Madam Gilbert looked at her sharply. Barry's expression was much as usual, yet anger and violence seemed to emanate from her quiet person. So she could be stirred? Madam Gilbert opened her mouth to administer a rebuke, then, realizing that she was not certain what it was about Barry that she should rebuke, she closed it again.

Esther had been listening eagerly, her head bent over her work. Thinking of Jim, and forgetting the rule of silence, she burst out eagerly, "If it please you, madam, I will go. Sarah has never been to Bettina's, and it might be that she would have trouble in finding the place. If you would allow me to go, I would be there and back very quickly."

Madam Gilbert turned frozen eyes on Esther. "I was not aware that I had given you permission to speak, Tate. Perhaps it is more than my ears troubling me, perhaps I am also suffering a loss of memory. Tell me if it is so, Tate. Did I give you permission to speak?"

Esther's face flamed scarlet. Like a small animal hypnotized by a snake, she could not seem to drag her eyes away from Madam Gilbert's cold face. Her mouth twitched, and her small hands began to shake in a paroxysm of nerves. "N-no, madam, you d-did not give me permission. I only th-thought that I—"

"You will not think, Tate. You will say and do nothing until I say you may do so."

"Y-yes, madam."

Madam Gilbert eyed the twitching mouth with distaste. "Pray calm yourself, Tate. Your hands are shaking. If you are not careful, you will ruin the blue gown."

Esther began to cry soundlessly. Tears dribbled from her eyes, fell down her cheeks and splashed on the blue and gold brocade, making dark blotches.

Madam Gilbert turned to the door. "God preserve me from sniveling fools!" she said savagely. "Put on your things, Barry, and follow me into the salon. As for you, Tate, if that brocade is ruined, the cost will be taken from your wages."

Tying the strings of her gray cloak, Sarah thought of Madam Gilbert with hatred. Hatred? It seemed to be the only emotion she was capable of feeling since she had left the house on Twyford Street. But the woman was mercilessly cruel! Addressing them formally at one moment as Mistress Tate and Mistress Barry, and the next, when her vindictive anger and cruelty was roused, as Tate and Barry. But at least, Sarah thought, it served to show the climate of her mood.

Sarah crossed to Esther's side and put a comforting hand on her bowed shoulder. "Do not cry, Esther," she said gently. "You must not let Madam Gilbert know that you fear her, else will you play into her hands. She is a bully. In order to vanquish a bully, it is necessary to stand up for yourself."

Esther glared at her, her small, short-sighted eyes sparkling with tears and hatred. "It's all very well for you to talk!" she hissed. "You ain't got nothing to lose. You ain't got no human feelings. You don't feel nothing!"

"You are right, Esther," Sarah said. She walked over to the door. "I have lost all that I value and love, and to feel nothing is a kind of protection."

Esther stared after her as she went through the door, and she wondered what it was that Sarah Barry had lost? Momentarily, her curiosity was piqued. Then, as she thought of the lost opportunity for seeing Jim, she bowed her head and wept bitterly.

In the salon it was all luxury and brightness. Cream satin drapes appliqued with gold flowers and emerald-green leaves concealed the two big bow windows, which were the showcase for several tempting articles. In one window there was a high-crowned befeathered bonnet, and a clever copy of the blush-pink and silver-trimmed gown worn by Queen Catherine at the last Honors Ball. The other window held a display of small mesh purses, cut in various intriguing shapes, and some vivid and exotic flowered headdresses, the most recent imports from France.

The salon was carpeted in a soft green. Two long couches upholstered in heavy cream satin threaded through with gold, and several green and silver chairs, with deep cushioned seats, provided comfortable resting places for Madam Gilbert's distinguished clients. The high, arching ceiling was gilded, and carved with satyrs in various positions, sporting, making love, or reclining at their ease. That ceiling was Madam Gilbert's pride, and she did not fail to point it out to her new clients. If they appeared suitably impressed, she would then inform them that the satyrs had been carved by the master hand of Donelli. The walls were draped in alternating panels of cloth of silver, cream satin, and cloth of gold. The air was redolent of perfume. In the midst of all this splendor, the black-clad Madam Gilbert made a startling contrast. She had been called the high priestess of fashion, and this perfumed, luxurious bower was the perfect setting for a high priestess. To her clients, her smile was always gracious, her manner charming.

As Sarah approached she heard Madam Gilbert say in a cooing voice, "Dearest madam, that color will be simply ravishing on you."

"Do you really think so?" a familiar voice answered. "I have never worn that particular shade of green. You do not think perhaps that the effect will be too startling?"

Madam Gilbert moved aside, revealing Opal Sunderland, seated at her ease on the couch nearest to the windows. Sarah stood very still as she listened to Madam Gilbert's reassuring and flattering answer. Why was Opal here? She had never patronized Gilbert's before. She preferred the fashions of Esmeralda of Brooke Street. Had Opal come here purposely to seek her out? Had she news of Jason?

At that moment Opal caught sight of Sarah. "Sarah, darling!" She rose from the couch and ran forward, her face lit with a happy smile, both blue-gloved hands outstretched. "Sarah, love!" Seizing Sarah's hands, she held them tightly. "I was just about to tell Madam Gilbert that I wished to see you. Are you happy here? How are you liking your work?"

Sarah withdrew her hands gently, and shot a swift look at

Madam Gilbert. The woman's lips were pressed tightly together, and her attitude was one of sour disapproval. "I do very well, Opal," Sarah said in a low voice.

Opal turned her engaging smile on Madam Gilbert. "Sarah is a dear friend of mine," she explained. "I have been worried about her. I felt that I just had to come and see for myself that she was well and happy."

Madam Gilbert, forced to the unwelcome conclusion that the notorious Mistress Sunderland's query about the ice-green satin had been merely a ruse, became icily formal. "I believe, Mistress Sunderland, that Barry is quite well and content."

Opal's smile faded. She looked distressed, as she always did in the face of outright unfriendliness. "Thank you, Madam Gilbert," she said quietly, "but I would prefer Sarah to tell me that herself."

"Indeed. But if I heard correctly, Mistress Sunderland, she has already reassured you. I have no wish to appear inhospitable, so when Barry's duties for the day are finished, I have no objection if you wish to converse with her. But she has no time at the present. She is about to go on an errand for me."

Opal turned to Sarah. "Where are you bound, love?"

Sarah hesitated. Opal meant well, but Madam Gilbert was making it obvious that she was displeased with the intrusion. "I go to Tavistock Street," she said. "It is so good to see you, Opal, for I have missed you sorely. Pray forgive me, but I must go." She looked at Madam Gilbert. "May I have the ribbon, please?"

Madam Gilbert walked over to a long table that stood in the center of the salon, and whose gleaming surface held an enormous silver urn filled with spring flowers, and a silver figurine of a reclining woman. Opening a drawer at the end of the table, she drew out a length of satin ribbon. "Here it is. See that you make the right match. And, Barry, hurry, if you please."

Opal frowned uneasily. "I will take you to Tavistock Street, Sarah. My carriage is just round the corner."

"It is good of you, Opal. But I will walk."

"You will do nothing of the sort." Opal took Sarah's arm and hustled her over to the door. "Madam Gilbert cannot have any objection to you riding. With my own ears, I heard her tell you to hurry."

Fuming, Madam Gilbert watched them go. She did not approve of Mistress Sunderland, who, everybody knew, was nothing more or less than a high-class whore. Nor did she approve of her vulgarly low-cut gown of peacock blue, and the little white-plumed bonnet of the same hue that framed her vivid face and her mop of black curls. Nevertheless, she thought with a fleeting touch of regret, Mistress Sunderland was known to be generous with her money, and she was forever buying new gowns, sometimes as many as six a month, and she would have liked to number her among her exclusive clientele. What a triumph to take her away from Esmeralda, who was an odiously boastful woman. If that gown Mistress Sunderland was wearing was a sample of Esmeralda's work, then she need not fear competition. She frowned, suddenly remembering that her attitude had not been one calculated to tempt Mistress Sunderland to her salon. Very well, if Mistress Sunderland was lost to her, Barry should bear the brunt of her displeasure. When she returned, she would inform her that she was here to work, not to entertain her low-bred friends. "I am not accustomed to receiving strumpets in my salon," she would say. "And since you are so friendly with Mistress Sunderland, Barry, perhaps you yourself, at one time, practiced a whore's profession? Should I find this to be so, I will have no recourse but to inform my lady Witherley that I cannot have a prostitute in my workroom."

"Sarah," Opal said, as she settled herself in the carriage. "I do not like that woman. Nay, I do not like her at all. I think it better if you return with me to Opalhall. If you feel you must work, then I will find you something to do."

Sarah was tempted for a moment. Then, pushing temptation firmly from her, she shook her head. "No, Opal, I will not do that. It is very kind of you, but I cannot accept your generous offer."

Opal clicked her tongue impatiently. "I have missed you, Sarah. I want you with me at Opalhall. Why will you not come?" She hesitated, and then added softly, "I promise to see that my gentlemen friends do not bother you."

Sarah smiled. "You know well that your gentlemen do not bother me in any way, so pray do not pretend. You also know why I must refuse."

"Because of Jason? Come now, do you suppose he will ever visit Opalhall?"

"He might. He has visited you at your other home."

Opal gave a guilty start. "I must have been mad to tell you about that!"

"But I am not angry or jealous, Opal. His visits to your other home were made before he met me."

Opal's flush began to subside. "Well, he will not visit Opalhall. You must know that for yourself."

"Opal, listen to me. I know well that you want me to be happy. You would like everybody to be happy. I know, too, that you have given me your word that you will not go to Jason. But, dear Opal, in the cause of your friends, you can be devious. Without actually breaking your word, you would find some way to let him know that I was at Opalhall."

"Well!" Opal exclaimed indignantly. "What a thing to say to me! Could I not have let him know in some way, without breaking my word, as you put it, that you could be found at Madam Gilbert's? Come home with me, Sarah. I promise that I will neither tell him nor intimate where you are."

Again Sarah struggled with temptation. "Let me think about it," she said weakly.

"That's right, my love, you think about it. Promise?"

"I promise."

Opal giggled. "Do you know something. Jason suspects that Margaret had a hand in your disappearance, and that she knows where you are to be found. He will not let her alone for one moment. He keeps asking her the same question: 'Where is Sarah, Mother?' It is a wonder to me that Margaret does not break under the strain." Catching sight of Sarah's expression, she added triumphantly. "Oh, yes, I know all about it. I have my spies in that house."

"Opal, I am surprised at you! You seem to be enjoying all this. I thought that my lady Witherley was your friend?"

"I am very fond of Margaret," Opal said, sobering, "and despite what she has done, I always will be. But, Sarah, she has brought this on herself."

Sarah changed the subject. "Opal, pray bid the coachman drive on. I must get to Tavistock Street."

"Very well. And you will think about coming back to Opal-hall?"

"I will." But even as she said it, Sarah knew that she would not return.

Chapter Eighteen

Starting from the back of the house, the grounds spread out in spacious and green invitation, but my lady Witherley, who was not, as she often laughingly phrased it, an outdoor woman, seldom ventured into them. Today, because she felt old and jaded and very tired, the thought of a walk in the fresh air was very appealing. It might, she thought hopefully, help to restore her drooping spirits, and diminish some of the now familiar heaviness of heart.

She found it pleasant to walk along the winding pathway that led to a small orchard. The sun was warm on her head, and the scents of spring brought to her a sudden heady joy. With a touch of whimsy, Margaret suddenly thought of the grounds as a green and pleasant oasis, where the stench that hung over London was effectively barred from entering.

Oasis, Margaret reflected. Aye, she needed an oasis to escape from her son. Jason had searched for Sarah, but without success. And now he always seemed to be watching her with cold suspicion. It was as though he were waiting for some chink in her armor, something that would give him the clue he needed. A wave of self-pity washed over her. Jason made her feel guilty, for there was pain in his eyes as well as suspicion. But the sense of guilt was absurd, of course, since she had acted entirely in his interests. And so she continued to deny all knowledge of Sarah's whereabouts. But sometimes the urge to give in, to have the old loving companionship between herself and her son restored, was very strong.

Margaret stopped for a moment to examine the still tightly folded buds of a lilac shrub. She was so tired of fighting Jason, of feeling his strong will battering at her defenses. She touched one of the buds with a gentle finger. Even in her sleep, Jason's constant question intruded. Tossing restlessly in her bed, she would hear that demanding voice say: "Where is Sarah, Mother?"

Sarah! Sarah! She was tired of hearing her name. Wearied of a conscience that insisted upon showing her that last picture of Sarah, with her white face, her blank eyes, her utter lack of interest in what became of her. She had looked so, when she was led into the presence of Madam Gilbert. Margaret saw Madam's sharp eyes examining the girl, her look of doubt. She had taken Sarah reluctantly into her employment, and then only, she made it clear, because she wished to please a valued client.

Margaret had a sudden yearning to see again the Sarah who had looked at her with love in her eyes, who had run eagerly about the house, her cheeks flushed with returning health, her eyes shining, ready to do the slightest bidding of the woman who had rescued her from degradation and misery. But that Sarah was no more. She had killed her! If only she could hear Sarah's laughter again, the gay lilt in her voice, that way she had of singing in a low, pleasant voice as she worked at a task!

Sighing, Margaret walked on. She stopped again as she came to a bench. The bench was set beneath trees that, leaning forward from either side of the path, formed an archway above her head. She was tired again, she thought, sitting down. She was always tired these days. She looked up into the delicate pale-green mist of the new leaves, and without warning, hot tears filled her eyes and ran down her cheeks. Wiping them away with the back of her hand, she thought of a meeting she had had with another old friend, Lady Ellen Snowden.

She had known Ellen nearly all her life. They had played

together as children, and, when they grew older, had sometimes shared the same beaus. Ellen, seated in a chair, her rustling lavender skirts spread elegantly about her, had exclaimed at the sight of her white face. "What have you been doing to yourself, Margaret? You look positively ill!"

Ellen's eyes were kind, her expression one of genuine concern, and Margaret found that she could not hold back. As it had been when they were children, she found it easy to confide in Ellen. Conscience, the wish for Jason to start acting as a loving son again, and not the hostile stranger he seemed to have become, all gave force to her words. She told of Sarah Barry, the condition in which she had found her, her past history, and, finally, her gradual emergence into an attractive and beautiful girl. Only when she came to the part about Jason's love for Sarah, and his announcement that he intended to marry her, did her voice falter.

But even Ellen had failed her. She did not show horror at the thought of such a girl being united with Jason in marriage. Instead, she said in her soft voice, "Poor Mistress Barry. What a hard, grim life she has led."

"I know, and I would not have you think that I am not sorry for her. Indeed, Ellen, I grew very fond of her. But marriage with Jason! No, it must not be. You do see my point, do you not?"

"No." Ellen shook her head. "You were wrong, Margaret."

"Wrong?" She stared at Ellen in outrage, the color flushing her face. She had expected her understanding and support. Instead, she read in her eyes a hint of that same condemnation that was ever present these days in Jason's eyes. "Ellen! How can you say that I was wrong? I did it for Jason, because I could not bear to see his life ruined!"

"No, Margaret, you did it for yourself. Would it have been so very bad if they had married? After all, you did tell me that you are very fond of the girl."

"I am. That is the truth. But I cannot see Sarah as my daughter-in-law."

"And yet Jason sees her as the girl he loves. The girl whom, despite birth, position in society, he wishes to wed. Come, Margaret, be sensible. I know you love Jason, and that you wish him to be happy."

"Of course I love him," Margaret cried. "Why else do you think I had to make a move to prevent such a disastrous marriage?"

"Disastrous?" Ellen's finely arched dark brows rose. "They are sincerely in love, or so I gather from what you have told me. That being the case, I do not think it would be in any way disastrous."

"It would! And I am not the only one who thinks that way. Sarah believes as I do. She quite understood."

"Did she?" Ellen was silent for a moment, then she said slowly, "No doubt, loving him, remembering her past, she thought herself to be unworthy. Her reaction I can understand. But not yours, Margaret."

"You cannot?"

"I will amend that. I should have said your continuing reaction. It is only natural that at first you would have been shocked and disapproving. I quite understand that. But afterwards, when you saw how it was with them. No, that reaction I cannot understand."

In a spasm of anger, Margaret clenched her hands tightly together. "I was foolish to believe that you would understand, Ellen. I should never have told you!"

"Margaret, listen to me. If you would keep Jason's love and respect, you must tell him where she is. You must, with good grace, let him have his way."

"Let him have his way?" Margaret repeated bitterly. "I must let him ruin his life, you mean."

"I know Jason. I am, after all, his godmother. This is a

first-time love for him. And, if I am not mistaken in my estimate of him, a lasting love. Through this girl, he will begin to live as never before. Jason has always been somewhat stiff and unapproachable. He needs to love and to be loved."

"Many women have loved him."

"I do not doubt that. But he has not loved them in return." Ellen laughed. "I have told him many times that love will make him more human."

"It is easy for you to be wise, Ellen," Margaret said resentfully. "But how would you feel if it were your son who was contemplating such a marriage?"

"It is customary to marry into one's own class, therefore I would not care for the idea at first. But if William's heart was fixed, if I knew that the girl was decent, and that she sincerely loved him, then I would not wish to alienate him. I would withdraw all objection. I would support his bride with every means at my disposal. The power of love, you must know, Margaret, is a very hard thing to fight."

"There is more to life than love and romance."

"Did you think that when you were married, Margaret?"

"Oh, do be quiet! I—" Margaret stopped short. "Please forgive me, Ellen. I did not mean to shout at you like a fishwife."

"You are forgiven," Ellen said, smiling. "But please do take my advice. Tell Jason where Mistress Barry is to be found."

Margaret shook her head stubbornly. "No!"

"You have said yourself that Jason has too much pride to force himself upon her. Mayhap she will tell him once again that she does not love him. Should that happen your battle will be won, your conscience easy, and you will not stand condemned in Jason's eyes."

"No!"

"It may be that he will find her for himself. What then?"

"I doubt that he will. But if it should happen, I will at least have the comfort of knowing that I did my best."

"Poor comfort, Margaret, if your attitude parts you from your son. I have never thought you to be foolish, but now I am not so sure. If one cannot win, one should give in with a good grace. Accept the inevitable, and keep the love of your son." She looked into Margaret's stormy face. "But I see that you are not to be swayed. I will say no more."

Ellen had kept her word. Conversation had drifted lightly, touching subjects of mutual interest. Some time later, Ellen left, promising her to visit again on her next excursion into town. She had gone back to the peace of her home in the country, and to her uncomplicated son, William. William was sober and reliable. In time he would make a suitable marriage, and present Ellen with grandchildren. He would never, as Jason had done, turn his mother's life upside down. There were no dark depths in William, as there were in Jason.

A rustle in the trees brought Margaret back to the present. She listened for a moment to the shrill piping of a bird, then her mind, as always, went back to her problems.

William Mitford stopped short as he saw Margaret seated on the bench beneath the trees. He stepped behind a clump of tall bushes, his mind working furiously. The obsession to take revenge on the loonie was still with him, stronger than ever now. After the scene in the summer house, he had been too frightened to venture near the house again. But, as fear died, his mind dwelled increasingly on Sarah Barry. Two weeks ago, he had again taken up his stand before the house. He had had no sight of the girl, and he was beginning to wonder if old lady Witherley had turned her adrift. With frustration eating at him, he grew bolder. He was no longer content to stand in front of the house. After three days had passed, he decided to explore the grounds of the house. Since that time, he had not left the premises. At night, he made his bed in the small shed at the other end of the orchard. By day, he played his own game of tag with the gardener. Grinning to himself, he would dodge out of sight until the man, happily unconscious of his presence, had gone by. Then he would emerge, his ears alert for the gardener's return. The element of discovery and danger pleased him, and he had even been considering various ways of getting into the house. He would soon find his way to the loonie's side. If he could not get into the house, he would have to think of another way. When he had strolled through the gap in the hedge, to be brought up short by the sight of my lady Witherley, he had been wondering how he could find out if the loonie was still living in the house. It might be, of course, that she was ill. If so, he could wait. But not too long.

His eyes went over the figure on the bench. My lady Witherley was wearing a white muslin gown threaded with cherry-red ribbons at the bodice and the hem. Her blond hair was piled high on her head and held in place by four jeweled butterflies.

Mitford's lip curled. Her slender, graceful figure he at once designated as scrawny, and he did not like scrawny women. The loonie was scrawny too, but that was a different matter. Had he not determined that she must be taught a lesson, he would never have gone near her. He rubbed his forehead, feeling the beginning throb of pain. She had insulted him. She had to pay for that. There was something else too. It was she who caused this terrible pain in his head. It was no longer enough to rape her and carve up her face. He had to kill her now. Once she was dead, the pain in his head would stop.

His eyes went back to my lady Witherley, narrowing as they rested on the jeweled butterflies in her hair. If he could get his hands on those, he would not have to worry about money for a long time. He knew a man who would take them, and, asking no questions, would give him a fair price for the jewels. An idea came to him. A way in which he might fulfill both of his desires. The information he needed, and the jewels. Aye, he would have them both.

His eyes glittering with excitement, he glanced hastily around. There was no one in sight. Except for the sighing of the leaves and the shrilling of the birds, there was no sound. He would not be detected from the house. One must round two bends in the path before it came into view again. He drew his knife from his pocket. He would not kill her, he decided, unless she forced him to it. If she proved stubborn, he would slit her throat. But he did not want to kill her. She was a great lady, and there was still that fear in him that he would be hunted down. They did hunt you down if you killed one of the quality. Still, even his fear would not save her if she refused to tell him where the loonie was. He had to get rid of the pain in his head. He had to! Holding the knife in his left hand, he emerged from the bushes and began to edge cautiously toward her. He was right out in the open now. My lady Witherley had but to turn her head and she would see him at once.

Margaret shivered. The brightness of the sun could not penetrate this fragrant archway of green, and she was growing a little chilly. She stroked her throat with nervous fingers, wondering why she felt so uneasy. She had the strangest feeling that somebody, hidden from view, was watching her. Unseen eyes! She did not like the thought. But she was being quite ridiculous! Here, in the grounds of her own home, who would be watching her? All the same, perhaps she should think about returning to the house. Before rising to her feet, she glanced quickly over her shoulder, and she saw him. The creeping figure of the scarred man!

Mitford sprang forward, reaching her just as her mouth opened to scream. His right hand clamped brutally across her mouth, shutting off the sound. His strong fingers exerted a painful pressure on her cheeks. "No screamin', me lady, 'less you're awantin' ter get that throat o' yourn slit." He held out the knife. "Sharp, is this knife," he warned. "It'll cut through anythin'."

Above his hand, Margaret's dilated eyes stared into his. The terror in them pleased Mitford. "I'm goin' ter take me 'and away," he said, "but one scream out o' you, an' you won' live ter make another. You understan'?"

She managed a slight movement of her head. Cautiously Mitford withdrew his hand, his eyes never leaving her face. Margaret felt a wave of sickness wash over her. Insanity looked from his eyes. She had no doubt at all that he would kill her if she attempted to call for help. But he was a madman, she thought with an inner shudder, so perhaps he would kill her anyway. She moistened her lips. "What do you want?" she managed in an unsteady voice.

"Firs' I wan' them things in your 'air. Take 'em orf."

She stared at him for a moment, then she raised her hands and her quivering fingers began to remove the ornaments. A strand of her hair caught in the last one, and she tugged it free. "Here." She dropped the little jeweled butterflies into his outstretched hand. "Now go, please!"

Mitford grinned. "A real quality 'aughty lady, ain't you. No, me lady, I ain't goin' yet. There's one more thing what I wan'."

She knew the question he would ask her, and she braced herself to refuse him. "Now then," Mitford said in a rough voice, "where's the loonie?"

"Who?"

Mitford placed the sharp tip of the knife against her throat. "You know who I mean. The red-'eaded wench what I 'eard you call Sarah."

"I do not know." She jerked the words from her dry throat.

The knife pricked her skin very slightly. "Ah, but you does know, me lady."

"I tell you that I do not," she cried desperately. "She—she ran away."

For a moment Mitford hesitated. Then some instinct told him that she was lying. "I'm goin' ter ask you once more. If you don' tell me, I'll slit your throat. Aye, an' enjoy doin' it! Where's the loonie?"

Words swirled in Margaret's mind. "Where is Sarah, Mother?" And now this man, this madman! "Where's the loonie?" Where is Sarah, where is she, where is she! What was she to do? If she betrayed Sarah, it would mean her certain death. But perhaps she could get to Sarah first. Once she had given him the information, he would have to go on foot, for she knew that he could have no conveyance. It would therefore take him some time to arrive at Madam Gilbert's. By that time, she would have Sarah away to some safe haven. As for herself, she need not fear his threats. She would take good care that she did not come into contact with him again. Warmed by a glow of hope, her agitated breathing grew more even.

Impatient with her silence, Mitford grasped her hair and forced her head up. "You goin' ter tell me where she is? Or do I use my knife on that nice white throat o' yourn?"

Even though she knew it to be useless, Margaret nerved herself to make one last appeal. "Listen to me. I will give you money, more jewels. Sarah has done you no harm. You cannot really wish to harm her!"

Mitford's eyes glittered. "Money an' jewels ain't no good ter me, not 'less I get rid o' the pain in me 'ead. I got ter kill the loonie, tha's the only way ter rid meself o' the pain."

"Kill her! Oh, dear God! No!"

He stared at her blanched white face, her trembling lips. "'Tis the only way," he said again.

"But—"

"Shut up! Don' say no more 'bout savin' 'er. You jus' tell me where she is."

Margaret closed her eyes. "If I tell you, will you let me go free?"

"Aye, o' course I will. I ain't got no in'erest in you."

She could get to Sarah long before he did. It did no harm to tell him. "She-she has a position with M-Madame Gilbert," she said in a faint voice.

"Where's that?"

"In B-Briar Street."

"Ah, I know. I passed that place lots o' times. But if I fin' that she ain't there, me lady, I'll be comin' back ter kill you."

Keeping her eyes tightly closed, fearful that he would suspect her plan, Margaret nodded. She gave a sigh of relief as the sharp tip of the knife left her throat.

"Tha's better, ain't it, me lady? You feels safer now, don' you."

"Yes, yes! Please go!"

"Don' you wan' ter look at me firs'? Don' you wan' ter gi' me a little kiss?"

"No." Stubbornly, she kept her eyes closed. "Just go!"

Grinning. Mitford drew back his arm and sent his bunched fist exploding against her jaw. The force of the blow toppled her from the seat. Mitford looked down at her unconscious form. "Tha's for thinkin' William Mitford's a bleedin' fool, me gran' lady. You think as I never guessed what was in your min'?" He thrust the knife into his pocket. "The loonie'll be long dead by the time you get there." With a last look at her, he walked away.

Sir Peter Baxter, having been directed by Mrs. Trevallion, rounded a bend in the path, in search of my lady Witherley. He stopped walking to pull petulantly at his red silk stockings. They were positively baggy! he thought in distress. Tradesmen! There was not a one of them to be trusted. Never again would he buy his stockings from Bestley. This was the very last time! Bestley? Bah! It would be more fitting were the old man called Beastly. Either he was the thieving, unscrupulous rogue he had often been called, a rogue, moreover, who used the very shoddiest of materials, or else he must have entered his dotage to put out stockings like these. They might be a snug fit on a cursed elephant, but certainly not for a man. He tugged at the stockings again. A fine thing were he to present himself to my lady Witherley with his stockings absolutely ballooning about his legs. What would she say? And, if it came to that, how was he to get home? He would be a laughing stock! About to walk on, his eyes were caught by a bloom of dust on his elegant black and red shoes. Everything, he felt, scowling down at the shoes, seemed to be against him. Sighing, he removed his kerchief from his sleeve. Bending, and wincing a little as his tight corsets dug into his flesh, he proceeded to scrub at the offending dust. A whimper of pain escaped him as the corsets jabbed at him savagely. Really, if it were not that he suspected he was developing a belly, he would not wear the beastly things! But one must think of one's appearance. A pretty sight he would look with his belly protruding a mile!

He was thinking with some bitterness of Jason's scathing comments on the subjects of corsets, so when he became aware of the rush of footsteps in his direction, it was too late to straighten himself. Something hard struck against his shoulder, and he fell sideways from the path. Dazed, he lay there for a moment, his cheek resting against the grass. He moved his shoulder cautiously, and a little yip of pain escaped him. What had struck him? Was it a thunderbolt? He looked fearfully at the innocent sky. Thunderbolt? No, by God! He had heard footsteps. So, unless thunderbolts came equipped with legs, it could not have been that. He thought with sudden alarm of my lady Witherley. He sat up very carefully. Sometimes, the corsets had a habit of locking, and he could hardly investigate, crawling on all fours, like some cursed animal. Besides, it would very likely frighten my lady out of her wits. Relieved to find that the corsets had not locked this time, he rose painfully to his feet. He cursed softly beneath his breath as he saw that his fall had somehow managed to snap the heel from his right shoe. But he must not think of shoes now, he must find my lady Witherley. He paled a little. Who knew what horror he might find! Limping grotesquely, but determined, he made what speed he could along the path.

My lady Witherley lay on her back, her face upturned to the sky, and her disordered hair blowing in a slight breeze. "Oh, by Gad!" Peter exclaimed, gazing down at her. With a fluting cry of distress, he fell to his knees beside her. "Oh, I say!" He possessed himself of one of her cold hands and began to rub it feverishly. He thought of the rushing footsteps he had heard. "The beastly blackguard!" he cried, increasing his efforts to rub life into her.

His relief was enormous when Margaret opened her eyes, "Peter!" she said after a moment.

"Yes, yes," he babbled anxiously. "Oh, I say, thank God you are alive, Lady W! For a moment I feared that the rogue had done you to death!"

Alarm sprang instantly into Margaret's eyes. "Peter! It was the scarred man!"

"Eh?"

Wincing, Margaret put a hand to her jaw. "Oh, Peter, do not gape at me. You must go to Madam Gilbert's. You must stop him!"

She seemed to be wandering, Peter thought. "Oh, rather!" he said in a hearty voice. "Er—Madam Gilbert's?"

"Yes, yes, in Briar Street. Peter, he has a knife! He is going to kill her!"

A cold feeling clutched at Peter. She was not wandering. She was serious. "I will find Jason," he volunteered feebly.

"No. There is no time. You must go yourself. Somehow you must stop him!"

Peter put out a hand to assist her, but she thrust his hand aside. "Go now! At once! Do not bother about me. I am well able to find my way back to the house. Hurry! There is no time to waste!"

Catching some of her terror, Peter scrambled hastily to his feet and limped rapidly along the path. "Madam Gilbert's. Right." He was about to round the bend, when a thought struck him, and he was forced to return to Margaret. "Who?" he said. "Who is he going to kill?"

"Sarah. Oh, Peter, do go!"

"Sarah. Right." Once more he set off. Despite the broken heel, he fairly raced along. Gaining his carriage, he flung himself inside and bade the startled coachman to make all speed to Madam Gilbert's, in Briar Street. As the carriage started up, Peter thought with some bitterness that he was once more a pawn of fate. His jacket was covered in dust, there was grass in his wig, his stockings were sagging about his ankles, and he had lost the heel of his shoe. And now, more than likely, he was speeding toward a rendezvous with death. All his life he had avoided violence. And now violence had been thrust upon him. He closed his eyes and collapsed against the cushions of the carriage. So be it. He was resigned. He would fight no more!

Chapter Nineteen

The footman stood aside from the door to allow my lord Witherley to enter the hall.

"Thank you, Cransford." My lord Witherley handed his cloak and his hat to the footman. "Is my mother at home?"

"She is in the grounds, my lord. Shall I go in search of her?"

"No, thank you. If my mother should return to the house. You may tell her that I am in the library."

"Yes, my lord." Cransford hesitated, wondering if he should mention that Sir Peter Baxter had called. But my lord Witherley was already walking away.

Cransford laid the cloak and the hat on an oak chest. It was odd about Sir Peter, he mused. When Sir Peter had arrived at the house, he had been elegant in red satin trimmed with scallops of black lace. As always, his wig had been elaborately curled and in immaculate order. But later, when he had had occasion to go into the stable yard, he had seen Sir Peter again. He had been limping along at a dangerous speed, since he had lost a heel from his shoe. The remaining heel was a little over three inches high, and it had seemed to him, if Sir Peter did not slow down, that he would very likely break his neck. There had been a look of terror on his face, and he was altogether a sorry sight. Cransford rubbed his chin thoughtfully. What could have happened to set him fleeing like a terrified rabbit? Cransford chuckled. Sir Peter, with those brown eyes of his all but bolting from his head, had definitely reminded him of a rabbit.

But it was not for him to laugh at his betters, Cransford sternly reproved himself. Still, Sir Peter had been a comical sight. Cransford looked toward the closed door of the library, and his smiling face sobered. He was very fond of my lord Witherley, who, for all he could sometimes be very stern, was a good man to work for, and he did not like to see him looking so pale and strained. He had no doubt at all that he had been out searching for Mistress Barry again. These days he was like a man possessed.

Cransford rubbed his chin again. What could have happened to the wench? Little Mistress Barry had vanished as effectively as if the earth had swallowed her up. If my lady Witherley knew where the girl might be found, and sometimes he had the feeling that she did, she would not tell. Again, Cransford felt a twinge of sympathy for my lord Witherley. He was a cool, remote man, the type who would take things harder than a more excitable man, because of holding so much inside. The cook, confiding in him one day, had said, "I tell you, Cransford, my lord Witherley is so cold that he is scarce human."

Cransford frowned. In this frantic search my lord Witherley continued to make for Mistress Barry, he had proved himself to be very human indeed, and somehow a great deal more likable.

About to turn away, Cransford suddenly found himself remembering Doctor Sanders and the visit he had paid to the house on the night before Mistress Barry had vanished. The doctor was a very kindhearted man, but for all that he was an old busybody. He made it his business to know everything. If anyone would know where Mistress Barry had gone, it would be he.

As the idea came to him of presenting this thought to his

lordship, he began to tremble with a sudden attack of nerves. Did he dare speak out? And if he did, how could he put it? Cransford hesitated, and then he thought of my lord Witherley's strained face. He would do it, he decided. And the devil take the consequences. Taking a deep breath, he squared his shoulders and marched to the library. Tapping on the door, and hearing my lord's low voice bidding him enter, he was again taken with a spasm of nerves. He was forced to take another deep breath before turning the handle.

"Yes, Cransford?" my lord Witherley said in an abstracted voice.

Cransford opened his mouth to speak, then, looking helplessly at my lord Witherley, he closed it again.

"What is it, Cransford, why are you trembling? Are you feeling ill?"

"No, my lord," Cransford said in a husky voice. "I-I have something to say to you, and I d-don't quite know how to say it."

Jason looked at him consideringly. What had occurred to ruffle the usually calm Cransford? He appeared to be quite agitated. "I think, Cransford, that you should just say it. It is usually the best way."

Cransford's mouth twitched nervously. "Yes, my lord. But I fear it is not that easy."

"I see. I cannot imagine what can be so difficult." He stopped, frowning, then added in a quiet voice, "You are not afraid of me, are you, Cransford?"

"I-I-yes, my lord, I am."

Jason was startled. Repressing a twinge of hurt, he said stiffly, "Then I can only say, Cransford, that I am indeed sorry if I have given you cause to fear me. However, if you have a problem, I assure you that I will do my best to understand."

Cransford looked into the brilliant blue eyes that were regarding him so steadily, and his heart began to hammer. He moistened his lips. "It-it is not my problem, my lord." He got the words out with a visible effort. "It is y-yours. It touches upon a very p-personal matter."

Jason's tawny brows drew together in an intimidating frown. "Pray explain your meaning, Cransford."

"It is about M-Mistress Barry, my lord."

"Mistress Barry!" The two words were like dagger thrusts. "What of her?"

Cransford saw that my lord's eyes had narrowed. There was a grim set to his mouth that filled him with the most dire misgiving. He suddenly felt very sorry for himself. Why had he spoken? Why had he allowed his heart to rule his head? His only wish was to help. But my lord was proud. It was far more likely that he would resent a servant trying to meddle in his personal affairs. Maybe he would even be dismissed from his comfortable and secure position.

"Cransford," my lord Witherley's voice struck very gently on his shrinking ears, "I will make it easy for you. I am well aware that you, in common with the rest of the servants, are fully conversant with my affairs. Therefore, if you know where Mistress Barry is to be found, you may speak out without fear of consequences."

Cransford felt a touch of amazement that the icily correct and unbending my lord Witherley should invite him to speak out on such a touchy and personal matter. He must indeed be desperate to find the wench. He found his courage. "My lord, it is true that I did fear to speak. But I have known you a very long time, and, if you will pardon the familiarity, I am fond of you. I—"

"Thank you, Cransford," Jason interrupted impatiently. "Pray go on."

"Might I suggest, my lord, that you ask Doctor Sanders where Mistress Barry is to be found."

"Doctor Sanders? What has he to do with anything?"

"He was here the night before she disappeared. The night she was attacked."

"The night she was attacked! Cransford! What are you saying?"

At the look in his eyes, Cransford took a backward step. "My lord!" he exclaimed in dismay, "I thought you knew. I-I had the story from one of the maids. The maid told me that the night before Mistress Barry vanished, she was attacked. It happened on Berkton Common."

My lord Witherley rose to his feet and approached him. Cransford's heart leaped with alarm as my lord suddenly gripped his arm with steely strength. "My lord!" he protested.

The fingers tightened. "Do you know what you are saying, Cransford? This is not some garbled servant's story?"

"No, my lord, I believe it to be true. Your mother, my lady Witherley, was likewise hurt." He heard my lord's sharply drawn breath, and he felt relief when the gripping fingers suddenly released him. He said hesitantly, "I do not know the details, my lord. But I feel sure that the doctor will know. I believe, too, that he will know where Mistress Barry is to be found."

Jason turned away. "Thank you, Cransford," he said in a tight voice.

Cransford bowed and left the room quietly. My lord Witherley had not known about the attack on Mistress Barry, and now, with that expression on his face, he looked fit for murder. A flicker of movement caught Cransford's eye. He turned his head sharply. He was just in time to see the edge of my lady's white gown as she disappeared up the stairs. He hesitated, wondering if he should go after her and inform her that my lord Witherley was at home. Remembering the look on my lord's face, he hastily decided against it.

Entering his pantry, which was strictly speaking not his pantry but belonged more properly to the butler, the lofty

Trask, he poured himself a glass of wine. He felt that he deserved it, for the interview with my lord Witherley had been a severe strain on his nerves. He drank the wine in two gulps. He was just about to pour himself another, when he heard Trask's ponderous footsteps approaching.

Trask walked into the pantry, stopping short when he saw Cransford. "What are you doing here?" he said suspiciously. "If I find you have been at the wine again, I shall report you to my lord Witherley."

Cransford shot a look of dislike at the butler. "I haven't touched the wine," he answered, brushing quickly past him.

Cransford saw my lord Witherley leave the house, and he felt a touch of self-congratulation. He felt sure that the lead he had given my lord would prove fruitful. That old devil of a doctor seemed to know everything.

It was some fifteen minutes after that that my lady Witherley came rushing down the stairs. Catching sight of Cransford, she bade him have somebody bring her carriage to the door.

"Yes, my lady." Cransford bowed and turned away. What was happening in this house? he wondered. First Sir Peter, looking very unlike himself. And now my lady Witherley, white-faced and distracted. Her jaw discolored by a bruise. He pondered for a moment on that bruise. It was all very mysterious, but he did not doubt he would find out what it was all about. He always did.

Chapter Twenty

Doctor Sanders's face was red and congested with suppressed rage. He had had a very trying time indeed. Two of his patients, for both of whom he had had the highest hopes of eventual recovery, had disobeyed his strict orders. They had glutted themselves with rich food and wine, disdaining the light diet he had prescribed. It was therefore not too surprising, in view of this, that they had taken a turn for the worse and died. He had tried to explain this to the daughter of the stricken house, but, to his deep mortification, she had all but thrown him out. He did not care to dwell too deeply upon the vile names she had called him, it being his contention that no gently reared young lady should be acquainted with such epithets. Shortly after this unfortunate episode, he had been caught in a drunken brawl between three men. They should not have been drunk at that early hour of the day, and he had felt it to be his duty to tell them so. The three men, as though his interference had united them in a bond of friendship, had set upon him in a most vicious manner, with scant regard for his venerable years. The result of his well-meant intervention were some painful bruises and a rapidly swelling and quite agonizing eye. Then, in a dingy house by the docks, where he had gone to attend a sick child, a dog, apparently mistaking his intentions, had bitten him upon the thumb. And if all that were not enough to curdle a man, he had arrived home footsore and weary and in some considerable pain, and had been invited to sit down to a meal which any self-respecting person would have hesitated to serve to a mangy cur.

His bushy gray brows drawn menacingly together, he glared at his wife across the table. "What's this, eh? Eh?" He poked at the fish on his plate with a stubby finger. "Am I a cursed animal, that you must feed me scraps from the gutter?"

Mistress Sanders folded her thin arms across her meagre breasts. "Aye," she answered him calmly, "for you are an animal. And an evil-tempered one at that. Though, in deference to animals, I could think of many with whom I would rather live."

The doctor regarded her with some dislike. Her narrow face was quite impassive as she delivered these wounding words. Her brown eyes with their scanty lashes, expressionless. In her drab black gown with a narrow frill of lace at the high neckline, which did little to conceal her scrawny throat, and her straight, mouse-colored hair hidden beneath a white cap, she was, in his at present jaundiced opinion, an uninspiring sight. He moved uneasily as he saw the tip of her long nose twitch, for it was always a sign that she was about to deliver a lecture or a further insult. In an effort to circumvent her, he roared out in what was meant to be an intimidating voice, "You evil woman! Don't you dare start in nagging me. I'll not tolerate it!"

"Do not behave like a child, Joshua."

"I'll give you child!" He searched for further words. Finding none, he resorted to a familiar grievance. "And what is that plaguey thing you've got on your head, eh? Eh? What do you mean by it, affronting me eyes in such grotesque fashion?"

"As you very well know, Joshua, I have worn a cap for many years. Pray stop this braying and posturing, for you must know that it does not impress me in the slightest."

"Hah! We will see about that!" Leaning across the table, he clutched at the cap and flung it to the floor.

Mistress Sanders regarded him for a long moment. "You know, Joshua, you should not have done that. It was a most unwise thing for you to do. Several times you have removed my cap in a like ruffianly fashion. I have often thought, husband, that I do not care to be handled in this manner." She pushed back her chair and rose to her feet.

At the scraping of the chair, the doctor started, and the wrath rapidly faded from his face. Blinking in alarm as she approached him, he put up a weak bluster. "Dare to lay one finger on me, woman, and I warn you it will be the worst for you!"

Mistress Sanders ignored the warning. With a swift movement, she tore the wig from his head and rattled her sharp knuckles painfully upon his bare pate. "There," she said without heat, "let that be a lesson to you, you billy goat!"

Rubbing his head, the swollen eye winking rapidly and exuding moisture, the other looking wounded, he said in a hurt voice, "Am I to understand from this, Deborah, my precious pet, that you no longer love me?"

The grim line of Mistress Sanders's jaw relaxed and a certain tenderness softened her eyes. "Old fool!" she said. Bending, she pressed her thin lips briefly to the top of his throbbing head. "No more nonsense from you now, Joshua. You will eat your meal at once."

"Yes, my love. My primrose." Meekly, he obeyed.

He had just finished the meal and had accepted his wife's offer of a glass of wine, when a tap sounded on the door. "Enter," Mistress Sanders called.

The door opened and a little maidservant came into the room with a clumsy rush. There was a smut on her nose, her cap was awry, and her young face flushed with excitement. "Please, ma'am," she said, twisting a corner of her apron. "If you please, ma'am."

Mistress Sanders eyed her with disfavor. "Your face is

dirty, Mary," she said coldly. "And pray do not stand there goggling at me, child. What is it you want?"

"If you please, ma'am, my lord Witherley has arrived to see the doctor." She hesitated, and then burst out impulsively, "Oh, ma'am, he's ever such a handsome gent!"

Mistress Sanders's look changed to one of severity. "Handsome is as handsome does, Mary," she said in a repressive voice. "Show the gentleman into the sitting room. Inform him that Doctor Sanders will be with him shortly."

Doctor Sanders gave a long rumbling belch. "Ah," he said, "that's better! Aye, Mary, tell that young devil he can await me pleasure."

Mary giggled. "Oh, sir, please! I couldn't say nothing like that to him." With another giggle, and a fleeting look at the doctor's wigless head, she fled from the room.

"Joshua!" Mistress Sanders reproved her husband. "Have I not begged you on a great many occasions not to belch in front of the girl. 'Tis vulgar."

"Eh? Nothing of the sort, 'tis healthy. It shows that the juices are working well. Anyway, woman, if I cannot do it here in me own home, then where can I do it?"

Mistress Sanders looked at him with pained eyes. "I would much rather you did not do it at all, Joshua. It is surely not necessary, and I find it most distressing."

"Bah!" Giving her a defiant look, he deliberately belched again. Then, cutting off anything further she might have to say, he rose to his feet and bustled over to the door. "If you will feed me such rubbish," he said, lingering there, "what else can you expect. I'll be belching in your ear all night, you old bag of bones. And who's fault will it be, eh? Eh?"

"You have forgotten your wig, Joshua," Mistress Sanders said in a stern voice. "Pray to cover your pate, for I am bound to declare that you look perfectly hideous without your head covering."

"Not as hideous as you look in that plaguey cap." He came back to her side. Taking the wig from her hand, he clapped it carelessly on his head.

"Joshua," Mistress Sanders said in a sighing voice as he made for the door again, "I trust you will endeavor to restrain your gross vulgarity when in the presence of my lord Witherley?"

"Bah!"

Jason, who had been staring fixedly at a painting of two sailing ships above the empty fireplace, rose to his feet as the doctor entered the room. "Good afternoon, Joshua."

Doctor Sanders snorted. "Good afternoon, nothing! A fine rogue you are for a man to encounter after a hard morning's work." He seated himself. "Sit down, sit down." He waited until Jason had complied. "Now what is it, eh? I can tell that something is wrong, for you have a face on you as sour as a lemon."

"There is a certain matter I wish to speak of, and which I hope you will be able to help me with." Jason smiled faintly. "But first, would you care to tell me how you came by that quite exceptional eye?"

Doctor Sanders touched the swollen area with tender fingers. "No, I would not care to tell you. It's none of your infernal business, you young cub. Out with what you came to say, for I warn you that I have not—" He broke off to peer anxiously at Jason. "You are not suffering from a return of the fever, are you?"

"Nay, it is not a question of my health. I have come here to ask you some questions concerning Mistress Barry."

"You have, have you. Why?" The doctor gave him a sharp look. "What about her, eh?"

"You attended her, I believe, on the night before she left Twyford Street?"

"I may have done."

"Joshua, do not fence with me. Did you or did you not attend her?"

"I did."

"I wish to know what happened to her on that night."

"Why?"

Jason frowned. "I believe I have been kept in the dark about a great many things concerning Mistress Barry."

"And why not? What is she to you?"

Jason turned his face away. "Because I love her, and I wish to marry her."

"You do!" The doctor's jaw dropped. "Well, upon my soul!"

"I do," Jason said sharply. "Now be so good as to answer my question."

The doctor pressed his fingers together. "I think, young Jason, if that is the case, you will not be caring for my answer."

"Nevertheless, I would hear it."

The doctor sighed, and his eyes were pitying as he looked at Jason. Here was a fine kettle of fish! He hesitated for a moment, wondering how he could soften what he had to say, but he could think of nothing. "She was raped, lad," he said bluntly.

Jason's swiftly indrawn breath and the tightening of his hands on the stick he carried were the only signs of emotion he gave. "Go on, please," he said calmly.

The doctor stared at him. "Well, you're a cool one, ain't you?"

Jason met the doctor's eyes. Cool? Not he! There was murder in his heart. But he had come here for a certain purpose, and the doctor, if distracted, was like to ramble on at great length. He must get to the root of the matter, and at once. In an effort to hide his profound shock and anger, he said in an even voice, "I see no reason to waste time in venting fruitless emotions. You will tell me, if you please, who did this thing to Mistress Barry?"

Doctor Sanders flushed. He was about to deliver a tirade on the subject of cold fish who spoke of love, but did not know the meaning of it, when he saw the very real pain in the blue eyes regarding him so steadily. Aye, he thought, the lad was suffering right enough. How could he have thought differently? He was an old fool! God knows, he had known Jason long enough. He should have remembered that this cold stiff front he was putting up was just that, A front, a façade, to hide the real emotions that seethed beneath. He said gently, "I have no name to offer you, lad. Your mother, and later, Mistress Barry, spoke of a scarred man."

A scarred man? For a moment Jason failed to make a connection. Then into his mind flashed a picture of William Mitford's face. The scar pulling down his eye. That scene in Lilacgrove Alley. That man? Nay, surely it could not be! It did not make sense. He took a deep breath. "Go on, please, Joshua."

In as few words as possible, the doctor told him all that he knew of that night. "And I may say, Jason," he concluded, "that I did not at all like the idea of Mistress Barry removing herself from the house. The girl was in a state of profound shock, and I told your mother so."

"My mother?"

"Aye. 'Twas Maggie's idea. She told me that Mistress Barry was in need of a change. Stuff and nonsense! I told her so at the time."

"I see. And do you know where Mistress Barry is to be found now?"

"Perhaps. After all I have told you, do you still want the lass?"

"Want her?" Jason looked at him in genuine surprise. "What a question to ask! Of course I want her. Should my feelings change because of something over which she had no control?"

"Just a test, lad. There are some for whom it would change things."

"I find your test insulting."

"Tush! Don't climb on your high horse with me, young fellow." The doctor scratched at his wig, causing the erection of hair to slip sideways. "She's a fine lass, a pretty lass." A thought occurred to him, and he leaned forward and tapped Jason's knee with a pudgy finger. "Tell me, lad, this love ain't one-sided, is it? The lass does love you?"

Jason was silent for a moment, and the doctor saw his eyes darken. "I hope so," he said slowly. "I will go further. I believe so. If you know where she is to be found, it is my intention to find out for certain."

The doctor nodded. "Many things that puzzled me are beginning to come clear now." He hesitated, then, with an abrupt change of tone, he added, "And what of the scarred man?"

Jason's lips tightened grimly, and now the doctor could not complain of his lack of emotion. A dangerous flame flickered in the blue eyes. "I intend to find him," Jason said. "And when I do, I shall kill him."

"You will not, lad," the doctor said sharply. "You will hand him over to justice."

"We shall see. And now, Joshua, before my killing instinct extends to you, you will tell me where Mistress Barry is to be found."

"Will I?"

"You will," Jason answered calmly, "if you know what is good for you."

"You would threaten an old man, you bloody ruffian!"

"I would. Where is she?"

The doctor chuckled. "She made me promise to say nothing of her whereabouts to you, though she did not tell me why. That is why I have kept out of your way of late."

"Joshua." Jason spoke with an air of strained calm. "You do intend to break that promise you made to Mistress Barry, do you not?"

" 'Tis a sin to break a promise, lad."

"And a greater sin to lose your life over a foolish quibble. I give you a choice, Joshua. You may either tell me where she is, or I will place my two hands around your fat throat and I will choke it out of you."

"Now then!" the doctor said indignantly, "I'll not have remarks upon my personal appearance, and I'll not have violence!"

"For the first I apologize. But for the second, I can promise you violence in very short order."

The doctor rose to his feet. "A fine thing when I am threatened in me own home!" He glared at Jason. "Well, what are you waiting for? On your feet, lad, on your feet. I'll get my hat and we'll be on our way."

"There is no need for you to accompany me, Joshua."

"If you think, young Jason, me lad, that you're leaving me out of this little frolic, you may think again. Always did want to see my lord Witherley in love, damned if I didn't."

"You will be disappointed, Joshua. I do not wear my heart upon my sleeve."

The little doctor grinned. "Stuff and nonsense. Been wearing it on your sleeve for the past half hour, ain't you?"

"Dear me!" My lord Witherley's blue eyes regarded him mildly. "I see that I must endeavor to keep my emotions under firmer control. I have ever been told that too much emotion is a failing of mine."

"Eh?" The doctor gave a snort of laughter. "Blister you, you young devil! You got the better of Joshua Sanders that time, eh?"

“Aye, I think perhaps I did. Pray hurry, or my impatience will force me to prod you into action with this stick.”

“You’d not dare.” The doctor took a quick step forward as Jason lifted his stick. “Oh, aye, curse you for a knave and a blackguard, I see that you would. Wait for me, I’ll not be above a minute.”

Chapter Twenty-one

Sir Peter Baxter felt hot and tired and thoroughly distraught when the carriage finally pulled up in front of Madam Gilbert's. The journey had been a series of calamities. Clary, his driver, had somehow managed to get himself tangled up with another carriage. In the fracas that followed, with Clary and the other driver shouting the vilest of insults at each other, much time had been lost. No sooner had the carriage been extricated, and, after a last exchange of insults, the journey resumed, than a back wheel had come off the carriage. He had been forced to sit there fuming, while Clary chased after a group of young ruffians who, with shrieks of delight, had borne the heavy wheel away. Clary's will, in the form of several clouts round the ear, having won the day with the ruffians, the man then came panting back to the carriage to call upon him for aid. The wheel was heavy, he complained. It had gone down a slope, and he could not manage to bring it up alone. He was not a well man, he had added in a plaintive voice, "Or I would not dream of bothering you, Sir Peter."

Would not dream of bothering him! He had, of course, given Clary the length of his tongue, but in the end he had been forced to aid the man. Panting up the slope, with the ruffians hooting behind them, and making derogatory comments on his face, his clothes, and his wig, he had thought bitterly that this was the sort of thing that came of being a good-natured and tolerant master. Scrambling back into the carriage, his stockings ballooning, he was filled with the liveliest of apprehensions. What would he find when he arrived at this Madam Gilbert's? The man, the scarred man, as Lady Margaret had called him, might already have murdered Mistress Barry, and what on earth was he to do if he found this to be the case? Now, having arrived at his destination, he was trying to calm his shattered nerves and to force himself to descend.

Clary, walking with what Peter could only think of as an exaggerated limp, calculated to play on his sympathy, approached the carriage and poked a lugubrious face through the window. "We're 'ere," he announced in a funereal voice. "This 'ere is Madam Gilbert's."

"Yes, yes," Peter said testily. "I can see that for myself. I can read, my man."

"I'm sorry, Sir Peter," Clary put a hand to his back. "It's the pain, you see. Takes me something cruel in the middle of me back. I dunno what I'm saying."

Peter gave him a haughty look. "Stand aside from that door."

"Yes, Sir Peter."

Clary watched as his master, refusing his offer of aid, descended from the carriage and limped heavily to the door of Madam Gilbert's. Something's got him all in a lather, he thought with gloomy relish. I wonder what's up?

Madam Gilbert turned with a smile as the door of the shop opened. The smile froze as she saw the apparition who entered. Her cold glance went over the bedraggled clothes, the frowsy wig and the disgraceful shoes and stockings. Really! she thought, it was too much. First it had been the hideous man with the scarred face. He had entered her shop, and, in a truculent voice, had demanded to see Sarah. Just Sarah, no other name. When she had told him that Mistress Barry was on an errand and would not be back until much later, he had given her an extremely unpleasant look. Muttering something about, "I'll wait," he had slouched outside again. And now there was this man. Was she now to have the even tenor of her day interrupted by yet another odd character? It simply would not do! Her clients would very soon complain if they were confronted with such disreputable characters. Fortunately, as it happened, there was nobody in the shop for the moment. Lady Lyons, of course, was due for a fitting of her rose-pink satin ball gown. But she would not arrive for another two hours yet. As for Mistress Barry, when she returned, she would have one or two quite pointed remarks to make about the individual who had inquired for her earlier. She would certainly tell her that she did not intend to allow her to bring her disreputable friends to her exclusive shop.

The odd character approached her, his grotesque limping gait filling her with alarm. "I say," the man said in a hoarse voice, "is everything all right?"

"I beg your pardon?"

A frown fretted Peter's forehead. The woman did not seem to be listening. Surely he had made himself perfectly clear? "I said," he repeated in a louder voice, "is everything all right?"

"I fail to understand you."

"Oh you do, do you?" Peter said peevishly. "My good woman, I have not come here at breakneck speed, risking both life and limb, only to have you tell me that you do not understand. Where is she?"

Madam Gilbert darted a look toward the velvet curtain which masked the door to the back of the shop. Where was Tom? Why could he never be near when she had need of him? "Where is whom?"

"Mistress Sarah Barry, of course."

Madam Gilbert's fear fell away. So this was another of Mistress Barry's peculiar friends. After this, she would certainly dismiss the girl from her employment. She drew herself to her full height. "I see," she said in an icy voice. "Oh, yes, now I see!"

Peter laid a trembling hand on her arm. "She—she's not dead, is she?" he said anxiously. He advanced his face nearer to Madam Gilbert's, and, sinking his voice again to a hoarse whisper, he added, "I am in time, am I not?"

Madam Gilbert drew her head back, and haughtily jerked her arm free from the fingers that were now clutching at her. "I think, sir, that you must be insane. If you refer to Mistress Barry, naturally she is not dead."

"Insane!" Peter said in a bitter voice. "That is all you can find to say to me, after I have endured things that might well have broken a lesser man." He seemed about to add more in the same vein, but catching sight of Madam Gilbert's frozen face, which to say the least, was intimidating, he reluctantly reverted to the present dilemma. "That's all well and good for you to say," he said, trying to put an indignant warmth into his voice, "but if she's not dead, then where is she?"

"Are you a friend of Mistress Barry's?"

Peter's brow furrowed in concentrated thought. "Yes," he said at last. "Yes, you might say that. I damned well must be since I have risked everything in her service. Is she here?"

"She is not. Nor will she be for some time. Now, sir, I must ask you to take yourself from my premises."

"Yes, but I say, I am afraid you do not understand."

"And I have no wish to understand." Madam Gilbert tapped an impatient foot. "I wish you to go, please."

Peter wilted somewhat before the glare in her gray eyes. With something of an effort, he pulled himself together and shook his head firmly. "Madam, I fear I must issue a refusal to leave. I would like to oblige, I assure you of that, but it cannot be done. There is dirty work afoot, and I must stay." He looked nervously over his shoulder. "'Tis the only way," he mumbled.

The hapless Peter felt himself shrinking before Madam Gilbert's cold glance. "It is apparent to me, sir," she said, "that you are far gone in wine."

Peter gaped at her for a moment, then, as the insult registered, a generous wrath surged in his breast. "Far gone in wine?" he said haughtily. "Well, upon my soul, it takes only that! I would have you know, madam, that I have come here on a selfless mission. Not a drop of wine has passed my lips. Perhaps I should introduce myself. I am Sir Peter Baxter."

"Oh, yes?" Madam Gilbert uttered a derisive laugh. "Sir, I am fast losing patience. Please leave."

"Now look here—" Peter turned, looking rather like a hunted creature, as the door of the shop was flung open. "Lady W!" he exclaimed on a quivering breath of relief.

"Peter!" My Lady Witherley ran toward him. "Where is Sarah?"

"Not here," he answered her gloomily. A thought struck him, and he looked at her accusingly. "I must say, Lady W, had I known you were coming barging to the rescue, it would not have been necessary to have risked my very life."

My lady Witherley made an impatient gesture. "Peter!" she said curtly. "I must beg you not to talk such nonsense!"

"Nonsense! By Gad, I like that. There is gratitude for you! And when I think of all that has occurred today, I could—"

"Oh, Peter, pray stop raving!" My lady Witherley turned impetuously to Madam Gilbert. "Sarah does not seem to be here. Where is she, please?"

Madam Gilbert looked at her curiously. My lady's face was pale and strained, and there was a livid bruise on her jaw. Her curiosity aroused, she suppressed her growing annoyance and said in a reasonably civil tone, "May I know what is happening, my lady? You are the third person to inquire for Mistress Barry." She waved her hand toward Sir Peter. "There is this man, whom, I now apprehend, is indeed Sir Peter Baxter. I must confess that his appearance is distinctly odd and therefore quite misleading." She paused to bestow a gracious smile upon the glowering Peter. "Before Sir Peter," she went on, "there was another man making the same inquiry. And now, of course, there is yourself."

"This—this other man," my lady Witherley said in a trembling voice. "What did he look like?"

"Most unsavory," Madam Gilbert said. "He too had an odd appearance. There was this scar, you see. It made him look—"

"It is he!" my lady Witherley interrupted. "Where is this man now?"

Madam Gilbert shrugged. "How do I know, my lady. I told him that Mistress Barry would not be back until later. He muttered something about waiting. After that, to my great relief, he left my shop."

"But where did he go?"

"I have told you, my lady, I have no idea."

My lady Witherley wrung her hands together in agitation. "Peter! He must be lying somewhere in wait for her. You must find him!"

Peter's soft brown eyes bulged. "Me!" he exclaimed in a goaded voice. "By Gad, but this is too much to bear! How the devil do you expect me to find a cursed man I have never seen before."

"He is scarred, Peter. Quite badly scarred."

Peter waved his hands in a distraught gesture. "He is scarred, you say?" He gave a bitter laugh. "Am I then to go glaring into the face of every scarred man in London? Am I to say to every scarred man I meet, 'Look here, are you the scaly scoundrel who plans to murder Mistress Barry?' I would very soon have a frenzied mob on my heels, let me tell you. Insult one of those low-born bounders and they set their dogs upon you. I know, it has happened to me before."

Peter was prepared to go on at greater length, but my lady Witherley was no longer listening. With a moan of despair, she sank down on a satin-covered couch and buried her face in her shaking hands. "It is all my fault!" she cried. "That man will find her, and he will kill her. He is a madman! Oh, God! If only I had not interfered. Sarah would be with Jason. She would be safe. That terrible man would never have been able to get near enough to touch her. This is my punishment!"

"Ah!" Peter exclaimed triumphantly. "I told Jason that it was ten to one you were behind her disappearance."

My lady Witherley dropped her hands and gave him a bitter look. "How can you be so superficial?" she cried. "But it is true, all too terribly true! And now I am well served. I lied to Sarah, and I lied to Jason. If I could but have another chance, how gladly would I welcome Sarah into the family!"

Both Peter and Madam Gilbert were staring at my lady Witherley as she rocked to and fro in her bitter remorse, and they did not hear the door open.

"My lady Witherley," Sarah's quiet voice said. "What is wrong? Did I understand you to say that you had lied to me?"

Margaret started violently. For a moment she did not move, it was as though she could not quite believe that she had heard Sarah's voice. Then she turned her head and saw her standing in the doorway. "Sarah!" she cried. "Oh, Sarah!" Her face radiant with relief, she sprang up and rushed over to the girl. "Oh, thank God, my dear child!" Impulsively, she put her arms about the girl and drew her into her warm, scented embrace. "Sarah, can you ever forgive me!"

"For what, my lady?" Gently, Sarah withdrew herself. "You seem upset. What has happened?" She looked at Margaret with fear in her eyes. "It is not my lord? Nothing has happened to him?"

Tears brimmed into Margaret's eyes and fell down her

cheeks. "He is well, my dear. But he is very unhappy without you. I thank God it is not too late for me to make amends."

Sarah said nothing for a moment, then she turned hastily away. "Nay, my lady. I understand that you have now withdrawn your objections. But even so, there is too much in the way."

Margaret caught at her arm with frantic fingers and turned her about to face her. "Sarah, listen to me. There is nothing in the way. This is a very hard thing for me to say, but I let you believe that the scarred man had raped you. It was not true!"

"You did that!" Sarah withdrew her arm and stepped back a pace. "How could you!"

"Can you ever forgive me, child?" Margaret's eyes pleaded with her.

"You have made me suffer, aand now you ask me to forgive you? I think, my lady Witherley, that you ask a little too much." Sarah turned to Madam Gilbert. "I have matched the lace, madam. May I now return to my work?"

At a loss for once, Madam Gilbert made no answer. It was Peter who spoke. "No, Mistress Barry, you may not return to your cursed work. If you think I have endured all this suffering only to have you calmly sit down to your sewing, or whatever it is you do, then you may damned well think again! Why do you suppose Lady W and I are here?"

"I have no idea," Sarah said in a hard voice. "Perhaps you would care to explain?" She glanced at the weeping Margaret. "My lady Witherley appears to be overcome, so it is for you to do, Sir Peter."

"Aye," Peter cried bitterly, "everything is for me to do. Look at me! Look at the condition I am in! I paid a polite social call on Lady W, and see where it has got me. And where is that cursed Jason when he is needed? I am hounded by ruffians. I am forced to work like a damned lackey to mend the wheel of my carriage. I am driven, I tell you, absolutely driven! And where is Jason? Off galivanting, that's where he is! If I had my way—"

"Peter, will you be quiet!" Margaret turned a tear-stained face to Sarah. "I will tell you in a few words. You are in danger, Sarah. The scarred man knows where you are to be found, and he intends to kill you. There, I have put it baldly, but somebody had to do so."

Sarah's face had whitened. "But how did he find out? Why should he wish to kill me?"

"As for the first," Margaret said in her old brisk manner, "we will discuss that later. The man is mad, Sarah, that is all you need to know for the moment. He has already been here inquiring for you, so there is no time to be lost. You must come home with me at once."

Madam Gilbert's face flushed darkly. "Murder!" she said. "In my shop! I will not have violence here." She rounded on Sarah. "Get out, Barry! I have always known you spelled trouble. I curse the day I ever set eyes on you." She turned to Margaret. "As for you, my lady Witherley, your patronage is not so valuable that I cannot dispense with it. Get out of my shop, and take this slut with you."

"No one ain't goin' nowhere," Mitford's voice said from the open door. He strolled forward, smiling. "You was all bellerin' so loud, an' acarryin' on, that you forgot 'bout me, eh?"

With a quick movement, Margaret stepped in front of Sarah. Her eyes widened as Mitford casually drew his knife from his pocket. "Peter! Do something. The man is mad! Disarm him at once!"

"Disarm him?" Peter croaked. "Oh, right! Quite so!" Taking a deep breath, he stepped forward. "Look here, my man, enough is enough!" He held out his hand. "Give me the knife, like the good fellow you are."

Mitford's jeering smile turned into a snarl of pure rage.

"Give you me knife, you say, you bleedin' swell? Aye, I'll give it ter you!" Lifting the knife, he stabbed viciously at the outstretched hand. "Now you got it, ain't you!"

With Madam Gilbert's scream ringing in his ears, Peter stared dazedly at his bloodied palm. "By Gad!" was all he could find to say, "Oh, by Gad!" The hand awoke from numbness to a throbbing, burning pain. Peter started like one awakening from a nightmare, then, with an agile bound, he was past Mitford and racing for the door. He wrenched open the door. "Clary!" he bellowed. "Clary, get in here! Help. Murder!"

"No, 'e ain't comin'," Mitford's thick voice said from behind him. "I seen 'im go orf down the street." He put a heavy hand on Peter's shoulder and spun him round. The door slammed shut. And Peter, impelled by a well aimed and brutal kick in his posterior, flew across the room and collapsed in a gasping heap at my lady Witherley's feet.

Madam Gilbert stared with dilated eyes at the bloody handmarks on her green carpet. "We will all be murdered!" she screamed hysterically. "Tom! Save me! Where are you, Tom?"

His little eyes narrowed, Mitford strode up to the screaming woman. "Shut up!" he snarled.

Madam Gilbert looked at him with terror-stricken eyes. "Tom! Help me!"

"All right! You asked for it!" Mitford doubled up his fist and smashed it against her screaming mouth. A whimpering sound came from her as she collapsed. Mitford stared at her for a moment. "That's shut you up, ain't it, you old cow!"

Mitford turned away and walked over to the moaning Peter. "As for you," he said, stirring him with his foot, "you jus' let me 'ear one word out o' you, jus' one, an' I'll crop your bleedin' ears so close ter your 'ead that you ain't never goin' ter be able ter keep your 'at on!"

Peter quivered, wondering if the man could possibly mean it. Terrified, he nonetheless said in fainting accents, "Watch your tongue, my man."

Fortunately for him, Margaret spoke at that moment. Darting Peter a look of despair, she sought to command him into action. "Get up, Peter! He is but one man. Surely, between us, we can disarm him?"

This seemed to amuse Mitford, for he gave a snort of laughter. Then, his amusement dying, he turned brooding eyes to Margaret. "What, 'im?" he jeered. "You don' expec' that cove ter 'elp you, do you?"

Margaret flinched before the look in his eyes. Pulling herself together, she said in a voice that only wavered slightly, "Keep away, you mad creature! You shall not touch Sarah."

Sarah saw the dull red of fury flood Mitford's face. There was a dangerous glitter in his eyes, and a prominent vein in his temple began a heavy pulsing. Suddenly she was more terrified than ever she had been before, and in the instant, she found, though she had often prayed for death, that she had no real wish to die. But for all that, it was better that Mitford should claim one victim, rather than that he should go berserk and attempt to kill them all. She darted a quick look at the shop door. If only someone would come in, even the odious Tom Gilbert, anything to distract him for a moment. She took a deep breath. She was not particularly brave, but, she decided, she must take her chance with the man. She could only pray that something would occur to save her. "Lady Margaret," she whispered urgently, "you must not antagonize him further. He is very dangerous, and I do not wish you to be hurt. He has come for me, only for me, and it might be that I can fend him off until you can get help. Perhaps Sir Peter can, in some way, manage to overpower him whilst his attention is distracted."

"Stop that whisp'rin'!" Mitford shouted.

Margaret ignored him. He was like a dangerous animal who might attack at any moment, but she must not let him sense her fear. She looked down at Peter. Peter? Overpower Mitford! Nay, he was but a broken reed of a man. There was much that he could do, but, if she knew anything about him, he would do nothing. It was up to her then. She stiffened with resolve. It might be that she could not save Sarah, but it should not be from want of trying. She flung out both arms in an unconsciously dramatic gesture. "If he wishes to get to you, Sarah, it will have to be through me."

"No, no, please stand aside, Lady Margaret!"

"I will not! He is a madman!"

Mitford's mouth twitched. "I ain't mad!" he screamed. "Don' you say that. I ain't mad, an' not you nor no one is lockin' me away in that place again!" He pointed the knife at Sarah. "It's 'er what I wants. I'm goin' to kill 'er. Once she's dead, the pain in me 'ead'll stop."

Madam Gilbert whimpered. "Let him have the wench, my lady," she pleaded. "If you do not, he will kill us all!"

"Tha's right," Mitford agreed. "I will an' all."

A coldness crept over Peter. The man meant it. The frightful bounder was a raving lunatic! It was up to him to do something. But what? Aye, what could he do? Never before had he been placed in such an appalling position. His eyes round with horror and fear, he looked up into Mitford's distorted face. "Now then, my man," he babbled, "we have had more than enough of this ghastly menace!" He inched painfully forward. "Look here," he said, his hand pawing at Mitford's leg, "think a bit. If you touch one hair on Mistress Barry's head, you will hang for it. I can faithfully promise you that, old lad."

"Shut up!" Mitford aimed an absent kick at him, but his eyes were still on Sarah. "Come 'ere, pretty loonie," he said, advancing on her slowly. "Do like I tell you." He held up the knife. " 'Ere's me knife all ready for you, see. I don' wan' no more pain, so I got ter kill you."

Sarah wrenched free from Margaret's desperate clutching hands. She began to back slowly. "Listen to me," she said, forcing the words from her dry throat, "killing me will not help you. It will not stop the pain."

"It will!" Mitford spat the words at her. "I don' wan' you ter tell me it won'."

"But I must tell you," Sarah persisted, "because it-it is t-true. You think I have power over the pain in your head, and y-you are right. Kill me, and I will send back the pain. Only this t-time it will be much worse, much s-stronger."

"Shut up! Shut up!" Mitford hesitated, staring at the knife in his hand. "I don' believe you. I got ter kill you!"

"I warn you again that I will—" Sarah's words were ended in a despairing scream as Mitford lunged toward her. "No! No!" She twisted frantically, trying to evade him.

"No, you don'!" Mitford's hand grasped her hair. He twisted at it savagely, bringing her to her knees. "I got you now, you bleedin' loonie. Laugh at me, will you! Send back the pain, will you!"

"Peter!" Margaret rushed toward Mitford, almost tripping over Madam Gilbert's sprawled body. She doubled up her fists and began to batter frantically at Mitford's head and shoulders. "Help me, Peter! Stop him, for God's sake stop him!"

Peter saw my lady Witherley thrown aside, and he was filled with a blinding rage that swept aside all considerations of life and limb. With the rage, there came such an exhilarating surge of courage that it went to his head like a draught of strong wine. Feeling that he was invincible, he clambered to his feet and, with a hoarse, purely primeval bellow, he launched himself straight at Mitford.

Mitford, taken by surprise, gasped as a fist caught him a stinging blow on the side of the head. He reeled slightly, but there was not sufficient power behind the blow to fell him.

Snarling, he turned upon his unexpected adversary. "Why, you bleedin' little fancy sod!" he shouted. "I'll slit your bloody gullet for that!"

Some of Peter's newfound courage faltered before the blaze in Mitford's eyes, but he continued to bob and weave and feint with his good hand. "Come on, old lad!" he panted. "Come on, let's have at you, you scaly bounder!"

The knife still clutched in his hand, Mitford stood still, his malignant eyes following the whirlwind antics. Peter, with the disadvantage of his heelless shoe, stumbled, and Mitford seized his chance. His scarred face further contorted in a grimace of rage, he rushed forward, jostling in so close that Peter was taken completely off guard. His heavy body knocked the slighter man off his feet, and Peter, with an anguished cry, fell backward.

Madam Gilbert screamed as Peter fell heavily across her. But any further utterance she might have made died, as Mitford lurched to his knees and held the knife pointed straight at Peter's throat. "Now I got you, ain't I?" Mitford said, laughing with triumph.

Shuddering, Madam Gilbert closed her eyes. Murder was about to be done, and hers was the body that cushioned the victim! She did not hear my lady Witherley's frantic screaming, because, for the first time in her life, she fainted.

Chapter Twenty-two

My lord Witherley strode rapidly along Briar Street. Behind him, his shorter legs flailing, his chest heaving as he sought to keep up, panted Doctor Sanders. And behind the doctor, her ruby-red cloak flying in the wind of her progress, her cheeks vividly and becomingly flushed, Mistress Opal Sunderland.

My lord Witherley paid no attention to the doctor's muffled cries of protest, his urgings for him to slow down. He was impelled by more than his wish to see Sarah, his haste was occasioned by something he felt, and that something had taken the form of a curious nagging anxiety that he could not put a name to. Much time had already been wasted, and, with each moment that passed, the anxiety had grown stronger. First there had been the fruitless visit to Opalhall. Arriving there, he had been informed that Sarah now resided in Briar Street, where she had a position with Madam Gilbert. Which was something that the doctor, to his chagrin, had not known. Then courtesy had forced him to wait for Mistress Sunderland, who had insisted upon being present when he once more came face to face with Sarah. And finally, finding Briar Street blocked by carriages, he had had no other recourse but to leave his own carriage in Elton Mews, and walk the rest of the way. Madam Gilbert's was at the other end of the long street, and the time-consuming walk had but added to his anxiety.

My lord Witherley stopped walking as he saw the curious group of people clustered outside Madam Gilbert's shop. Some were endeavoring, without success, to peer through the draped windows. Others had their faces pressed to the door.

"Look!" a man cried. "The curtain over the door's not too thick. I can see a little. Something's going on in there, I tell you."

"What?" another man said impatiently.

The first man's self-importance was diminished by this blunt question. "I don't know," he said sheepishly. "I can't see that clear."

A stout woman clad in a blush-pink silk gown and a lavishly feather-trimmed cloak, said in a high, indignant voice, "I have asked you several times to let me pass. Stand aside, if you please. I have an appointment with Madam Gilbert."

The gathering ignored her imperious request. "If something is really going on," somebody called, "shouldn't we go into the shop and see for ourselves?"

"Not me," came the answer. "I'm not getting tangled up in other people's troubles. Whatever it is, let them get on with it, I say."

"I 'eard a scream," a woman's shrill voice volunteered. "Made me blood run cold, it did."

"We all heard the scream," the man at the door said impatiently. "Why else do you think we are here?"

As though giving point to the shrill-voiced woman's statement, the screaming began again.

"What the devil—" Doctor Sanders began. Glaring at the people who impeded him, he followed after Jason, who was already thrusting his way through.

Jason threw open the door. For a moment he stood there transfixed, staring at the scene before him. Sarah was huddled against the wall, her green skirts ballooning about her, her hair falling over her white face. In the center of the blood-marked carpet lay a black-clad woman. Sprawled helplessly on top of the woman was Peter, his distended brown eyes staring with the fascination of horror at the knife in the hand of the man who menaced him. Above them stood my lady Witherley, wringing her hands and emitting those piercing screams.

My lady Witherley's screams broke off abruptly. "Jason!" For a moment she could only gape at him, like someone who doubted the evidence of her eyes, then she was stumbling toward him. Her hands touched him, as though even now she feared he might vanish. "Oh, Jason, thank God! Thank God!"

Jason put her gently but firmly to one side, then, with the doctor following on his heels, he was across the room in a bound. His hand grasped Mitford's collar and hauled him roughly to his feet.

Sarah was standing now, supported by Opal's comforting arm. She felt dazed, as though she were watching a scene in a play. "The young lion!" The words leaped into her mind as she watched Jason. "The young, avenging lion!"

"Le' go o' me!" Mitford's snarling voice said loudly. "I'm goin' ter kill the loonie!"

Mitford's eyes found Sarah. With a burst of strength, he tore himself from Jason's grasp, and lurched toward her. "Kill the loonie!" he muttered. His voice began to rise. "Kill 'er! Kill 'er!"

And then Jason was upon him. The knife flew from Mitford's hands as Jason's fists battered him to his knees. A sound came from Mitford's throat, a high, howling sound, then he rolled sideways and regained his feet, and the knife was once more in his hands. He made a rush for his enemy. Jason sidestepped, but he was not quick enough, the knife entered his shoulder.

Sarah saw him sway, the patch of spreading darkness staining the shoulder of his light-brown jacket. "Jason, no, no!" She pulled free from Opal and ran stumblingly toward him. "Jason, my darling!"

He did not look at her, his attention was all on Mitford.

"Keep back, Sarah!" he snapped.

Mitford came on again, the knife, stained at the tip, glittering in his hand. There was a smile on his lips. He would finish the interfering swine once and for all! He found that he had underestimated the strength of his opponent. The tall, hated figure side-stepped again, and Mitford screamed as my lord Witherley's fingers crushed his wrist, forcing him to drop the knife. Cursing, he screamed again in frustration, and he did not see the fist that came up to fell him.

Breathing heavily, Jason stood over the fallen man, waiting for him to rise, but there was no further movement from him.

With a wordless cry, Sarah was at Jason's side. "Darling! Darling!"

Doctor Sanders cleared his throat loudly. "Now, then, Mistress Barry, step away from the lad. There's time for all that crooning later." Then, as she continued to cling, he added testily. "The lad's hurt, he's going to fall. Unless you think you can hold him up, you'd better get back and let me tend to him."

Sarah stepped away hastily as the little doctor's hands, unexpectedly strong, caught Jason's sagging body and lowered him gently to the floor. "Now then, lad, let's look at that shoulder." He snorted fiercely, "Never saw the like in all me born days. There are cursed bodies lying all over the place." He looked up. "You there, young Peter, don't stand around goggling. Go over and close that door. We don't want an audience, eh? Eh?"

"Oh, right." Peter said. "Quite."

Jason pushed the doctor's hands away. "Never mind about me for the moment," he gasped. "Look to that fellow over there. Tie him up, or something. We cannot have him getting away."

The doctor hesitated. "All right." He nodded to Sarah. "I'll not be long. Look to the lad."

Sarah knelt beside Jason. She groped for the kerchief in her sleeve, then began gently to wipe away the small globules of perspiration that had formed on his forehead. "Lie still," she soothed. "All will be well."

"Will it, my Sarah?" Jason's eyes, a faint smile in them, met hers. "You said that to me once before. Do you remember?"

She nodded. "Aye, I remember."

Her busy hands were stilled as he said in a low voice, "You must never leave me again, Sarah. I forbid it."

"We-we will talk of that later, my lord."

Doctor Sanders came back. He stood very still, looking down at Jason. At the expression on his face, the others drew near. Even Madam Gilbert, who, having regained consciousness, was once more on her feet, crept over to the group on legs that trembled beneath her.

"There's nothing I can do for him, lad," the doctor announced in a firm voice. 'He will not need tying up. He is dead."

"Dead?" Jason stared at him in bewilderment. "What the devil are you saying! How can he be dead?"

"He is dead all right," the doctor answered. "He struck his head hard when he fell. It was that blow that killed him." He scowled fiercely. "You are not to be blaming yourself, lad. It was an accident, a freak of fate, no more."

"But—" Jason tried to struggle up. "But I cannot have killed him. 'Tis impossible!"

The doctor knelt beside him and laid a soothing hand on his uninjured shoulder. "Have I not said it was an accident? In any case, the man is better off dead. I have seen some cases of insanity in my time, and he seemed to me to have been pretty far gone along that particular road. We have no way of curing a sick mind, you know that. Take my word for it. Better to be dead than to be sent to Bedlam Asylum."

Jason's head was reeling. He could not quite take in the doctor's words. Had he said the man was dead, or had he just imagined it? He saw Sarah bending over him, and he ceased to struggle with the problem. There was only one thought in his mind now. Sarah must never leave him again. He looked up into the ring of faces. He saw his mother's drawn and anxious. Peter's expression, his round brown eyes opened at their widest, which, oddly, gave him the look of a startled hare. The doctor's scowl, which, he knew from experience, covered anxiety. Opal's face, her mouth tremulous with sympathy, and the haggard face of a woman with hard eyes, and disordered pale-blond hair. He said in a clear voice, "You have all heard Mistress Barry address me as darling. You are all witnesses. Pray do not let her run off. Tie her, if you have to, but do not let her go."

"I will see to it, darling," my lady Witherley said. "We certainly cannot have your bride-to-be running off, can we?"

Jason's faint, rare smile touched his lips. "Those words from you, Mother? Mayhap you believe me to be dying?"

My lady Witherley burst into tears. "Nay, darling," she sobbed, "I do not believe t-that." She looked from Jason to Sarah. "If you could, both of you, find it in your hearts to forgive me, I will be very happy."

Sarah glanced quickly at Jason. "I do forgive you, Lady Margaret."

"And I, my pretty, foolish little mother," Jason said. "I knew that—" His voice trailed away, and his head fell heavily sideways.

"Get back!" the doctor snapped. "Give the lad some air. He has fainted."

With some forethought, the doctor had picked up Mitford's knife. Sarah shuddered as he used it to slit Jason's sleeve. She watched for a while as he examined the wound with gentle fingers. "Is—is it serious?" she ventured at last.